Praise for

A Matter of Honor

"Drawing on five years of historical research and a lifetime of sailing, Hammond vividly recreates an early chapter in American history."

—*Publishers Weekly*

"In the genre of nautical fiction, this new book, a novel based on the American Revolution, is more than just top-notch. In scope and brilliant writing, it's a fitting companion to the maritime tales of Patrick O'Brian."

—*Easton (MD) Star Democrat*

"Hammond . . . provides readers with everything from romance, passion, war, and strife. A powerful maritime tale, *A Matter of Honor* is sure to entertain anyone looking for a dramatic look at the American Revolution through the eyes of a young seaman intensely embroiled in the fight for independence."

—*The Historical Novels Review*

"This is one of the best Revolutionary War novels I have ever read. Deeply researched and exceptionally written. . . . I was hooked from the first pages. . . . [Hammond's] descriptions of life aboard the sailing ships of the era create vivid scenes of life and warfare at sea."

—*Muzzleloader* magazine

A MATTER *of* HONOR

A MATTER
of HONOR

To Bill King —
FAir winds & Blessings —
Bill Hamm

WILLIAM C. HAMMOND

CUMBERLAND HOUSE
NASHVILLE, TENNESSEE

A MATTER OF HONOR
PUBLISHED BY CUMBERLAND HOUSE PUBLISHING INC.
431 Harding Industrial Drive
Nashville, Tennessee 37211

ISBN-13 978-1-58182-660-9 (paperback : alk. paper)
ISBN-10 1-58182-660-5 (paperback : alk. paper)

This is a work of fiction. Names, characters, places, and incidents either are the product of the author's imagination or are used fictitiously. Any resemblance to persons, living or dead, events, or locales is coincidental.

Cover design by Gore Studio Inc., Nashville, Tennessee

The Library of Congress has catalogued the hardcover edition as follows:

Hammond, William C., 1947–
   A Matter of honor / William C. Hammond.
      p. cm.
   ISBN-13: 978-1-58182-609-8 (hardcover : alk. paper)
   ISBN-10: 1-58182-609-5 (hardcover : alk. paper)
   1. United States—History—Revolution, 1775–1783—Fiction. 2. Domestic fiction. I. Title.
PS3608.A69586M37 2007
813'.6—dc22   2007024326

Printed in the United States of America

1 2 3 4 5 6 7 8 9 10—12 11 10 09 08

To my wife
Victoria Karel Hammond

Cattle Die, Kindred Die,
Every man is mortal.
But one thing never dies—
the honor of a good life.

—An old Icelandic verse

PREFACE

*T*HE YEAR WAS 1777. Because the momentum of the American Revolution had become stalled by military setbacks in New York, many people of British descent on both sides of the Atlantic were convinced that this was to be "the year of the hangings." Soon, these people crowed in alehouses from London to Charleston, from the Solent to Narragansett Bay, the upstart Continentals would suffer the full weight of the king's displeasure. No one would be spared who could not confirm a Tory pedigree. Never again would any colony dare challenge the rule of king and Parliament, so total would be the retribution. From the spruce forests of New Hampshire, through the manored plantations of Virginia, to the swamps of Georgia, rebels kicking and gagging from gibbets and yardarms would serve as testimony to history itself that rebellion against England was as futile as it was foolish.

Those of loyalist persuasion had reason to crow. At the time of the battles at Lexington and Concord, scarcely one-third of the colonial population was willing to stand up to be counted as patriots. Another third remained loyal to the Crown. The others wanted nothing more than to be left alone to go about their business. Now, two years later, the number of patriots had dwindled severely, either through attrition in battle or by a pragmatic decision not to be on the losing side. Oratory that had so stirred the soul of the citizenry was being drowned out by the drumbeat and marching boots of British grenadiers. Even the Continental Congress, united in euphoria a year earlier with the signing of the great declaration, was now in disarray, unable to agree on anything, including where the seat of government should flee to next. Philadelphia would no longer serve. A British army under Gen. Sir William Howe was encamped thirty miles due east, in New Jersey, and intelligence had it that he was preparing to march due west.

True, the Continental Army, such as it was, remained in the field. General Washington may have been set back, but he had not been defeated. Last December he had even taken the offensive, crossing the Delaware on Christmas

Eve and attacking Hessian mercenaries first at Trenton, later at Princeton, victories both. As shocking as these defeats may have been to British generals, they were summarily dismissed as anomalies. Of course the Continentals had prevailed at Trenton. The Hessians were abed and recovering from Christmas merrymaking. Christmas, by God! Who could have dreamt the rebels would violate the rules of civilized warfare in such a dastardly way? But no matter. The fact remained that those in the Continental Army able to stand and fight now numbered fewer than five thousand, a shadow of the forces England had stationed throughout the colonies. And many of these colonial soldiers were nothing more than farmers brandishing pitchforks. The British army, it seemed to nearly everyone, including many senior American officials, had only to engage the ragtag Continentals in a pitched battle, and the war would quickly be over.

Then there was the British navy. Steeped in the tradition of duty and discipline, it had since the rousing defeat of the Spanish Armada been the enabler and defender of empires. France and Spain had finely constructed ships and fleets to match the British in numbers, but even the most stalwart of enemy sea captains thought twice before maneuvering his vessel within range of Royal Navy guns. Under the imperial command of the Admiralty in Whitehall were more than three hundred ships of the line, with countless others of lesser but still impressive authority. Such was its reputation that many within Parliament continued to argue that Britain need send only her navy to America and blockade the colonies into submission. Their fragile economy could not be maintained for long without aid from France. The outlaw government would topple, and what was left of rebel resolve would collapse along with it.

Since the outbreak of hostilities in 1775 the Marine Committee of the Continental Congress had debated how best to launch a navy. There already was a de facto navy, sanctioned by General Washington and comprised of merchant vessels fitted out with small guns. But the captains of these ships were basically privateers, men in private practice who would have been labeled pirates were it not for their official letters of marque that legitimized their preying on enemy shipping. Rarely were such men inspired by patriotism; profit was their motive. No, men of honor insisted, the colonies required a navy built along the lines of the Royal Navy, with ships designed for combat, not commerce. The construction of twelve frigates was authorized, along with the creation of the Marine Corps, and by 1777 the ships of the fledgling Continental Navy were being readied for battle.

The famed stiffness of his upper lip notwithstanding, had Adm. Richard Lord Howe, commander in chief of British forces in North America, been made fully aware of the Marine Committee's plans, he would have chortled at the thought of such a puny force being arrayed against him. After all, the broadside of a one-hundred-gun First Rate could spew more firepower than the simultaneous broadsides of all twelve of the new American frigates. If the line-of-battle ships of France and Spain were wary of leaving the safety of Toulon and Cadiz to challenge His Majesty's navy in open water, what threat could this so-called navy pose? For that matter, what serious military threat to English sovereignty existed anywhere on the Atlantic or on the North American continent?

It was a question that stilled the hearts of even the staunchest of patriots in June 1777. But these few men and women had long since crossed the Rubicon. Whether their faith was in the justice of their cause, the benevolence of a divine providence, or a strategic alliance with the fickle French, they had vowed to fight on, and fight on they would, forever in prayer that a miracle would somehow manifest itself and reveal to them a pathway to deliverance.

WRITING A novel is, without question, a formidable undertaking. It has been said that if an aspiring author in today's publishing world were made fully aware of what he was getting into, of how lonely and frustrating was the task before him, and of how deep the abyss into which he would surely tumble, he would choose to read a good book rather than try to write one.

While I sympathize with the sentiment of that statement, I do not accept its premise. For me, and I'm sure for most writers of fiction, the act of creation is an intensely personal one, simply because that is the nature of the beast. If what I create pleases others, that is a wonderful thing, but it's not why I set my alarm for 4:00 each morning. Simply put, there is no abyss to fall into if one is doing what one truly wants to do; the work carries its own rewards, however grueling and, yes, however hard that work can sometimes be.

When a novelist tinkers with history, as I have done, he assumes a special mantle of responsibility. What he is writing about is likely part of a time-honored historical record that does not brook casual or convenient interpretations. Accountability becomes ever more poignant when the author introduces historical figures into the plot and assigns them speaking roles. Did Benjamin Franklin say such a thing? More to the point, from my perspective at least, could he have, under the circumstances?

In humble acknowledgment of this responsibility, I invested three years of research before beginning chapter I, and another two years while developing the manuscript. My research included reading perhaps a hundred books, most of them nonfiction, on the life and times and personal memoirs of John Paul Jones, John Adams, Horatio Nelson, the Marquis de Lafayette, Alexander Hamilton, and other figures of historical note who appear within its pages. Much of this ground I first covered years ago in high school and college history classes and later in my own readings for pleasure. As a self-proclaimed student of history, I have endeavored to the extent possible to be true to my calling.

As to writing being lonely work, I suppose it seems that way, although I have never felt lonely doing it. My characters were there to greet me every morning, and together we set our compass course for the next several hours. And I always knew that when I finished a chapter and had slogged my way through my own rewrites and edits, standing by was a loyal team of readers eager to offer helpful criticism and to remind me that still more polish was required before the text could be presented to that most hallowed of eminences, the editor. These individuals, whose names appear below, were and continue to be my greatest asset and inspiration as a writer. The debt I owe each of them is one I can never repay.

Diana C. O'Neill: my sister and number-one cheerleader and champion of the feminine mystique. Bill Elmquist: friend and part-time accountant for my daytime job as a business consultant. Bill Dorn: friend, founder of Dorn Communications, and now my business partner. Renée Hecker: French teacher extraordinaire at Minnehaha Academy who bravely stepped forward to oil my rusty French. Al Kilborne: friend and esteemed teacher of American history in Washington, D.C.

Special acknowledgment is due my editor and agent, Upton Birnie Brady of Hartland Four Corners, Vermont. The literary skills and cogent judgments of this former naval officer and executive editor of the Atlantic Monthly Press have proven their value over and over again. Upton will continue to serve as my pilot and navigator as long as he is willing to stand beside me on the quarterdeck.

Lastly, and most important, my love and gratitude go to my wife, Victoria, to whom this book is dedicated, and to our three wonderful sons: Churchill, Brooks, and Harrison. They've had to put up with quite a lot from me during these past several years.

William C. Hammond III

A MATTER
of HONOR

Part 1

I

HINGHAM, MASSACHUSETTS

June 1777

RICHARD CUTLER DREW ASIDE the flaps of the oilskin cloak draped around his shoulders and stared down in disbelief at his watch. He used a dry corner of his cotton waistcoat to wipe away tiny droplets collecting on the crystal and stared again. Seventeen minutes to go. Had it been only five minutes since he last checked?

He glanced up at the house that was his destination, a two-story clapboard structure on Otis Hill weathered to a slate gray by decades of fog and sea air. On the roof, a small square picket fence provided protection and height to anyone searching eastward beyond the long, narrow, crooked arm of the Nantasket Peninsula for a glint of rising sail. To the northwest, he could make out through the drizzle the beacon pole at the crest of the square mile bump of pasture land in the heart of Boston. Above it, in the far distance, a long, thin yellow line intruded between the formless gloom of clouds and earth.

"Clearing before sunset," Richard mused, confirming by the sway of tree-tops that the wind was freshening and veering in a westerly direction. He turned his attention to what he had first noticed when he arrived here at the end of Crow Point almost an hour ago.

Rebecca, as the topsail schooner was named, was herself not unusual, though larger and sleeker than most coastal packets plying the waters between Boston and the South Shore. Quays along Hingham harbor were alive with these coastal merchantmen loading and unloading goods for sale or barter. The hull of this particular craft was freshly painted black, and Richard noted that her sails were neatly furled, "in Bristol fashion" as his uncle in England was wont to say. She was not a commissioned naval vessel; nevertheless, what made her stand out amid the din and bustle of dockside commerce was the green-coated marine standing at rigid attention by her gangway, his eyes dead ahead, a sea-service musket at his side. What made it a further object of curiosity to passers-by was the flag fluttering atop her ensign staff. The thirteen red and white stripes remained the same, but in its canton the Union Jack had been replaced by a circle of thirteen white stars set against a backdrop of navy blue.

Another check of his watch. It was time.

Along the way up Broad Cove Lane, Richard returned the friendly greetings of citizens he met, though he avoided eye contact or anything else that might suggest an interest in conversation. Not even the perky hello from Sarah Fearing distracted him. She was a beauty, and he sensed her eyes on him as he strode past. This afternoon he avoided her normally welcomed attentions.

At the front door of the clapboard house, he removed his beaver felt tricorne hat and coaxed unruly strands of blond hair away from his face. After brushing off loose water from the front of his cloak, he breathed in deeply and knocked.

His knock was answered by a stooped, white-haired man who had a smile on his lips and a twinkle in his eyes when he saw Richard. He motioned him inside and drew the cloak from his shoulders, then led him to a room that was small but comfortable, containing shelves of books, a satinwood writing table set against the wall, an oblong table placed between two wingback chairs by the hearth, and a luxuriously thick Persian rug that gathered everything in the room together into a snug fit. A fire had been laid and was now crackling agreeably, a defense against dampness more than chill. The old man held up one finger, smiled again at Richard, and bowed before leaving the room.

"Thank you, Caleb," Richard called after him, with affection. Caleb was a favorite of his and his family and of many people in Hingham. During the recent war with the French, he had served as sergeant in the Massachusetts militia under the command of then Col. Benjamin Lincoln, whose house Richard was standing in now. Richard's father had served as lieutenant in the same company and credited Caleb with saving his life more than once. During a skirmish near Deerfield on the western frontier, Caleb had been taken by Mohawk warriors. Colonel Lincoln and Lieutenant Cutler had rallied the militia to his rescue, but not before Caleb's tongue had been cut out. Since the war, Caleb had served in the personal employ of now Gen. Benjamin Lincoln. Such was the respect of Richard's father for Caleb that he had named the youngest of his three sons after him.

Though normally a voracious reader, Richard scanned the library of books more as something to do than with any real interest. He willed the meeting to start. It seemed an eternity to him, not just days, since he had learned of this opportunity while in the company of his father and the master of one of his father's ships. It was what he had wanted, more than anything, and he could hardly believe his good fortune in being singled out for consideration. But he could not ignore or forget his father's stern warning as he had explained to Richard what would be expected of him, and what he might expect in return, should he be selected.

"As a midshipman," his father had said, "you will have senior officers relying on you to carry out orders and seamen relying on you to give them orders. Your life and theirs will depend on how well you do both."

The memory of those words, inflamed by waves of anxiety nagging at him, caused Richard's stomach muscles to contract and the scar high on his forehead to pulse. Angry at himself for entertaining any element of doubt or fear, he picked up a pamphlet from the desk and began rereading the words that for him and for many patriots in these united colonies were tantamount to readings of Scripture.

"These are times that try men's souls, what?"

Richard was startled by the voice, even more so by the appearance of the man coming toward him. He was shorter than Richard by a good four or five inches, and his frame was slight and wiry, not at all what Richard had expected. Being almost six feet in height, Richard was used to looking down slightly when meeting someone. He often felt awkward and ungainly when doing so, especially if the other person seemed at all self-conscious. This man did not. Nothing about him suggested any sort of human frailty. Resplendent in blue coat and white breeches—not the prescribed blue and red uniform of the Continental Navy—he was a study in poise and self-confidence. In elegance too, exemplified by his long auburn hair combed back neatly in a queue and the gentleman's white silk stock he wore around his neck. These things impressed Richard. What impressed him more was an intangible quality about the man, something he could not describe but that nonetheless served to define the essence of one born to command, at sea or wherever destiny might require him.

"Good afternoon, Captain Jones," Richard said, bowing slightly. "I am Richard Cutler. I am honored to meet you."

"I know who you are," replied Jones, smiling, "and I assure you, the honor is mine." He indicated the pamphlet in Richard's hand. "Tell me, lad: Are you a summer soldier? Or a sunshine patriot?"

"I am neither, sir," Richard replied. He placed the copy of the *American Crisis* back on the desk. Jones offered him his hand, and he shook it firmly. "And you may be assured, Captain, that I shall not shrink from the service of my country."

"Bravely spoken, lad. Bravely, indeed. Tom Paine has it right, eh? Please, sit down."

As if by prearranged signal Caleb entered the room with a silver tray bearing two steins of ale and a plate of bread and cheese and meats. He set the tray on the table between the two wingback chairs and busied himself stoking up the fire. The room had a warm, cozy feel to it when he walked out, quietly closing the twin panel doors behind him.

There was a pause as Jones and Richard contemplated the fire. Though not yet having acquired a taste for ale, Richard gratefully accepted a mug.

Jones said, as if reading his thoughts, "I trust your parents won't scold me for requesting ale served us here. Tea is hard to come by these days, and some consider the mere drinking of it an act of treason. I'm afraid coffee does not suit me. Usually I prefer lemon or lime water."

"Ale is fine, Captain, thank you. And as I am seventeen, there is no reason for anyone to find fault."

"Quite." Jones raised his stein in salutation. "So, Mr. Cutler, time to whet our whistle, eh? Here's to America and victory."

They clinked their mugs together and drank. In the hearth a half-burnt log fell off its perch with a jolting pop, sending a burst of sparks up the chimney. When Jones spoke again, it was with purpose and with a hint of a highland burr.

"My time is limited, Mr. Cutler, so I shall come right to the point. Here's my situation. The Marine Committee, in its infinite mercy, has finally offered me command of a ship. Her name is *Ranger,* out of Portsmouth. I may be her captain, but I have had no say in the selection of my officers. My commissioned officers, that is. The committee, however, is permitting me to select my midshipmen, God be praised. Under the circumstances, the selection of these four individuals becomes a critical matter to me. You have been recommended by what I must say are rather inspiring sources: two ships' masters, including Mr. Winthrop, a man I know and respect, and of course, General Lincoln, whom I also respect. I would not be surprised to hear of you from General Washington himself. I understand your father sent him two brigs last year."

"Yes sir, he did," Richard acknowledged.

"Refitted as privateers?"

"Yes sir. They're based in Beverly, and they've had some success. Their biggest prize was three British merchantmen bound for Cape Ann with munitions for Admiral Graves. General Washington was pleased to accept those munitions in his stead. I suspect the British might still be in Boston had these ships not been captured."

"I couldn't agree more. Which is why I've invested so much time pounding the tables of Congress in Philadelphia. We need a strong navy for the very same reasons we need a strong army. We cannot rely for our defense on state militias or other local groups anymore than we can rely on privateers or state navies. If we are to prevail in this rebellion, our ships must do more than simply disrupt supplies coming from England to America."

"We have more than a hundred privateers at sea, Captain," Richard pointed out. "Have not the supplies they have seized helped our cause?"

"Yes, they have. And they have also done much to line the pockets of the owners of those vessels." Jones took a deep swig of ale. "Privateering is not a calling, Richard. It's a business, pure and simple. A damn profitable business, I might add. So much so that it's become nigh impossible to recruit able seamen for our navy. Everyone wants a share of the riches on the civilian side. But while privateers serve one purpose—and I concede, it's an important one—the navy serves quite another. And the navy's mission will ultimately prove more important to victory."

Richard gave Jones a puzzled look. "If not to disrupt trade, Captain, what would its purpose be? Surely you don't mean to challenge the Royal Navy."

"That's exactly what I intend to do," Jones replied, "though perhaps not in the way you imagine. *Ranger* is a sloop of war. Were she a Royal Navy vessel, she would be captained by a lieutenant and unrated. She's no match for a heavy frigate, much less a ship of the line. Any lubber in a barn knows that. But a well-crewed sloop can reap havoc upon the enemy if her guns are trained on the right targets."

"I see," said Richard, though in fact he did not. "I should think General Washington would agree. He too has called for a strong navy."

"To his credit, he has. One of the few. Pity he no longer commands our navy."

Richard placed his empty stein back on the tray. "I suspect Congress considers General Washington a better soldier than sailor," he remarked somewhat lamely.

"And Congress would be correct," countered Jones, "were it seamanship we're discussing." He took a piece of bread from the pewter plate and carefully arranged a piece of cheese on it, followed by two layers of thinly sliced ham. Satisfied with his creation, he took a bite and chewed gently, in a contemplative manner.

Richard shifted in his chair to look more directly at Jones. "Captain," he said, "thank you for stating your position. If you please, I will now state mine. I very much appreciate the kind words of those who have recommended me. I am honored by them, and I pray you find me worthy of their trust. Your reputation precedes you, and the privilege of serving with you exceeds anything I could have imagined. But Captain, if I may ask, what circumstances were you referring to a moment ago?"

Jones cocked his head in question.

"You said, 'Under the circumstances, selection of my midshipmen becomes a very important decision for me.' With respect, can you share with me the nature of those circumstances?"

Jones looked at Richard as if for the first time. "You are an observant sort," he said, not unkindly. He dabbed at his mouth with a linen napkin, hesitating before answering, as if weighing pros and cons. "Mr. Cutler, what I am about to tell you is strictly confidential. Under normal circumstances it is unbecoming for an officer to discuss subordinates in such a way. In this case, however, I believe it is warranted.

"I was referring to the officers assigned to me. 'Assigned' is the right word, for as I indicated, I have had no say in their appointments. These gentlemen have no naval or combat experience. What experience they do have is limited to coastal trading, as master's mates, not even as ships' masters. You are quite a bit younger than they. But from what your sponsors tell me, you have considerably more experience in ocean sailing. I shall need to call on that experience in ways I shan't often be able to express aboard ship. Under *no* circumstances must I compromise the chain of command. Do you understand what I am saying?"

Richard nodded. "Yes, Captain. I understand that. The question I have, again with respect to all concerned, is why men lacking proper credentials are granted commissions in the first place. Please forgive me if I speak out of line."

"You may ask me anything you wish," Jones chuckled. "That is, until I am your superior officer. I must say, you are a straightforward young man, as well as an observant one." His voice became devoid of humor. "The question you raise has a one-word answer: patronage. Favors granted by cronies in government. Rank bestowed on someone because he happens to have someone's ear who has influence in the right chambers of Congress. In our navy, Mr. Cutler, merit or experience seem to matter not a fig. It's called 'interest' in the Royal Navy, and I thought I was well rid of it. Apparently I am not."

"But you have been appointed captain."

"So I have," Jones laughed bitterly. "A captain ranked seventeenth on the seniority list. Seventeenth! I warrant there is not one ranked above me more qualified than I. Not one! Most don't deserve to even be on such a list. I have but one patron in Congress, a Mr. Hewes, but clearly he is not able to help me."

"Is Captain Saltonstall not qualified?" Richard asked, coming to the defense of a family acquaintance. During the captain's brief tirade he had noticed his Scottish burr becoming more pronounced. "I understand you served as his first lieutenant in the Bahamas. On *Alfred,* during the raid on New Providence."

Jones muttered something about Boston patricians such as Dudley Saltonstall having more sail than ballast, then dismissed both him and the general topic with a wave of his hand. "Enough of this," he said, his poise returning. "I have overstepped my bounds, and for that I apologize. Please, tell me about yourself, Richard."

Richard settled back in his chair. "There's not much to tell, really. You know my parents, my father at least. I have a younger brother, Caleb, and two younger sisters, Anne and Lavinia. My family has lived in Hingham since coming here from England in '55. My Uncle William—he's my father's brother—still lives there, in the town of Fareham, near Portsmouth. He owns a sugar plantation on Barbados, and he and my father work together in the shipping business. What ocean sailing I have done has been on my father's brig *Eagle,* bound for England and the Indies, and I have learned much from Captain Winthrop, her master. I love the sea, Captain. I always have. My dream before the rebellion was to have my own ship someday."

"And what is your dream today?"

"To serve in the Continental Navy."

"Why now? And why the navy? Could you not serve your country just as well in one of your family's privateers?"

"I promised my parents I would not enlist until I was seventeen," Richard replied. "As to being a privateer, we have discussed that. Like you, I choose to fight for something other than profits."

"What is that, pray?"

Richard fell silent. He knew where this line of questioning was leading, and he knew it would go there; still he dreaded having to explain it all again. It was forever this way. The pain, the sadness, would not let him be. During rare moments when he was able to experience joy, even exhilaration, as when on the deck of a brig running free on a broad reach, or at the tiller of a small boat under sail, the memories would return, sooner or later, to remind him of what was compared to what might have been. His father understood. His mother too, of course. But they could not help him. They had their own demons to battle. It was the same for them.

"Might it be revenge?"

The question sliced deeply into that private place. "Excuse me, Captain. What did you say?"

"There are many reasons why men choose to go to war," offered Jones. "I asked if your reason is revenge."

The fire in the hearth was dying. Richard got up to put two fresh birch logs on the diminished heap. He craved another round of ale, any sort of liquid, but he could not bring himself to pull the cord by the window drapes that would summon Caleb from the kitchen.

"You know about Will." It was a statement, not a question.

"A little. I should like to know more, lad. I need to hear this, however difficult it is for you."

Richard nodded. He knew Jones was right. If he were to serve under him, even as a lowly midshipman, a matter of this significance that was common knowledge in Hingham must be broached. When he spoke, his face was deadpan, and he had to struggle to conceal his true emotions.

"Will was my brother, Captain. But he was much more than that to me. He was my best friend. My mentor. My . . . patron, to use your word. Everyone liked him. Ask anyone in Hingham about Will Cutler. People not only liked him, they respected him, even the Tories. You could laugh with him too; he could joke around with the best; but when it came down to it, they listened to what he had to say. He was not a great orator. Will was no Sam Adams. People listened because they knew he cared, he would give everything he had, including his life, to those he loved and the causes he embraced. And he had no greater love than for his family, no greater passion than for the revolution.

"That's what tormented him so. Back then, in '75, many people here considered themselves Tories. My parents did. They're English. They supported the king though not always Parliament. Like everyone else, they had concerns about Admiral Graves and his administration in Boston. And like everyone else, they opposed the quartering of redcoats in our homes. We were spared, no doubt because of father's connections, but most families were not so fortunate. To people like my father, such things had to be endured. We were British citizens, and rebellion against the king was unthinkable. To people like Will, they were abominations, cause enough for rebellion.

"It was not the taxes. That's what some people believe, but Will didn't care much about taxes. It was British arrogance and cruelty he despised. We had friends in Boston forced to eat rats and dogs while Clinton and Howe feasted and paraded about. Others who knew nothing about the Sons of Liberty were brought in for interrogation—if that's what you want to call it. It was torture, Captain, pure and simple.

"Will joined a local Committee of Correspondence and begged father to let him fight. Breed's Hill. Concord. Hearing about these battles drove him nearly insane. He wanted desperately to join General Washington in Dorchester. Father was aghast. He refused to allow Will to join the Continentals. I told father Will would leave anyway, but he was adamant. 'No son of mine will raise arms against the Crown,' he said. I wish he had listened to me. I wish he had listened to Will."

Absorbed in the telling and drained by it, Richard glanced across at Jones. It was only then that he realized that Caleb had come back into the room with a fresh pitcher of ale. Jones was sipping reflectively from his mug, and it was several moments before he asked, "What was your position during all this?"

"My position?" Richard's tone was one of self-loathing. "I am ashamed to tell you, Captain, I had no position. I feared only for Will. And my family. Nothing seemed worth having us torn apart."

Jones uncrossed his legs and stretched out slightly, his hands clasped together at his midsection. "If you and Will were not able to sway your father," he asked, "was he not persuaded by the blockade? The injustice of it?" He was referring to the act of Parliament which, in harsh retribution for the dumping of tea into Boston harbor and other perceived affronts to British authority, had closed the port of Boston to commercial traffic. "Since his ships could not sail, his business must have suffered terribly. I mean no disrespect, but in my experience a need for money has a way of influencing one's moral compass."

"Yes, his business suffered," Richard replied. "And our family suffered as a result. But you don't know my father, Captain. He said it was the price of loyalty. He even refused special exemptions and favors offered by the British."

"Admirable. Your father is a man of principle, Richard, and of that you should be proud. I can assure you, there are precious few of those to be found on either side these days. More ale?" He gestured at the pitcher between them. Richard poured himself a small amount.

"Will did not join the Continentals," he went on, after a drink. "But he did leave. He signed on with a merchantman bound for Falmouth in the Eastern Province. He needed time to think, he told me, and what better place for that than at sea. He loved the sea as much as I. His leaving pained my mother, but father was relieved. He assumed Will would be safe on a merchant vessel."

In the pause that ensued, the cruel irony of that assumption was lost on neither of them.

"The brig sailed to Falmouth. Or what was left of it. The British had sacked the town and burned it to the ground. Why, no one knows. We had no regular army there and the rebellion had hardly begun. Pure spite, it had to be, for detaining a British officer earlier in the year. It cost hundreds of innocent people their lives.

"On the cruise back to Hingham, a British frigate intercepted the brig off Marblehead and forced it to heave to. Royal Marines came on board and selected ten Americans at random for the honor of serving in His Majesty's navy.

Tom Pickett, a close friend of Will's from Scituate, was the first to be picked. Will was second.

"The brig's captain was outraged, but there was nothing he could do. Will and Tom and the others were rowed over to the frigate. You can imagine the reception they got there."

Jones could well imagine.

"How long was Will on that ship?"

"Not long. Less than a fortnight. Anyone who knew Will knew he could not survive long in those conditions." Richard pulled back his shoulder-length hair from his forehead and began massaging a two-inch scar high on the right side. It was the first time Jones had noticed it. "We don't know all the details. We do know that Tom Pickett was accused of doing or taking something. No doubt he was framed. Tom's a good fellow, not the sort to arouse suspicion or pick a fight. No matter. As punishment for whatever it was he was supposed to have done, he was awarded three dozen lashes. The entire crew had to watch, the Americans up front by the capstan. Near the end, when Tom was screaming in agony, Will went berserk. He lunged at a ship's officer and struck him with such force he broke the man's jaw. He took several more down with him before he was finally seized and beaten unconscious."

Jones grimaced, aware of the inevitable outcome of such an assault in the Royal Navy. Article 21 of the 1757 Articles of War was quite specific on the punishment for striking a warrant officer, midshipman, or commissioned officer.

"Will was awarded a hundred lashes," Richard said, in a voice so gravelly Jones had to strain to hear. "What was left of him was strung up on a larboard yardarm. I pray he was dead before they hanged him. "

For some time the only sounds to be heard were the crackling of the fire and the rhythmic ticking of a Gütlin clock on the mantle. From outside the house, on Broad Cove Lane, the silence was broken by the shouts of men on the docks encouraging one another as they warped in a newly arrived coaster. Shadows accentuated by sunlight lengthened in the room. As Richard emerged from the depths, he noted to his surprise that the afternoon had drawn into evening.

"Let me tell you about her," said Jones suddenly.

"Captain?"

"*Ranger.* Our ship. Let me tell you about her."

Richard heard the words "our ship," and for the first time that day his mood eased. "I should like that," he said.

Although Jones was fifteen years older than Richard and a ship's captain, he spoke now in the animated tones of any sailor of any age or rank when describing his intended. "I'm too low on the seniority list to merit one of the new frigates. That's why I was assigned a sloop. She's ship-rigged, three hundred tons burthen, a hundred sixteen feet on the waterline. Twenty ports on the weather deck for six-pounders. We have swivel guns on the quarterdeck, and we'll add more on the tops. She's narrow on the beam and stern, with a steeper deadrise and smaller tumblehome than most vessels her size."

"Built for speed," Richard observed.

"Aye, lad, she is. Not unlike a French corvette. And we shall need her speed, for I intend to take her into harm's way."

Jones laced those last few words with such boyish enthusiasm that Richard could not resist smiling.

"Is she fitted out for sea?"

"Nearly. I sail for Rising Island tonight. I shall be dealing personally with Mr. Langdon in the matter of her ordnance and provisioning. Mr. Langdon, you should know, is the in-law of my first lieutenant, Mr. Simpson. These discussions could prove interesting, what? In any event, we shall have sea trials by August first, no later." He began gathering himself together for departure. "You will report for duty, Mr. Cutler?"

Richard gave Jones a hint of a grin. "Aye, Captain, I will."

"Excellent. My mission here has been a success. Do you have final questions for me?"

"Sir, if I may, what are our sailing orders?"

"I can't tell you that," Jones replied flatly. "Our orders are sealed until closer to our sailing date. But from what I know of these orders, Mr. Cutler, if it is revenge you are seeking, it is revenge you shall have."

Richard did not flinch from the hard stare Jones gave him.

"Your uniform, Captain," he said. "Forgive me, but you look more like a Royal Navy officer than one in the Continental Navy."

Jones smiled broadly. "As I remarked earlier, Mr. Cutler, you are an observant young man. The resemblance to a Royal Navy uniform is intentional. Several captains and I agreed upon this design recently in Boston. It will serve us well in what we are about. If the Marine Committee has a problem with this, I say let them jolly well stuff it. . . . Other questions? I'm afraid I must sail with the evening tide."

There were indeed other questions Richard would like to have asked. Suspicions lingered in both American and European social circles about the character and background of Captain Jones. Slave ships, women betrayed, courts of inquiry, murder: these had by now become the grist of rumor mills and the daily bread of scandalmongers everywhere. But he would not, could not, ask these questions now. General Lincoln and Captain Winthrop thought highly of Jones, as did his father. That was enough.

"No, Captain. I have nothing to add except to thank you for the honor you have bestowed upon me. I shall not disappoint you."

With a single nod of his head, Jones conveyed his grasp of just how deep was Richard's gratitude. He arose and held out his hand, closing the deal as he had opened it, with a firm handshake.

"Godspeed to you then, Midshipman Richard Cutler."

FROM OTIS Hill to where Richard lived near the center of the village was about a mile. But he was in no hurry to get home. He walked slowly along the edge of the harbor, pausing now and again to gaze out at ships at anchor or quayside. He wanted time to reflect on the events of the day and sort out the welter of emotions churning in his mind. Now that his dream had become reality, he had to consider more pragmatically the ramifications. Soon he would have to leave his family and this town he loved. Despite the intense satisfaction he felt, the thought of leaving was not easy to absorb. He was profoundly aware of what this would mean to his mother, a good woman forced too early in this conflict to accept the unacceptable, to bear the unbearable. What would happen to her should he not return? And his father, still in anguish over Will's murder, as he continued to refer to it, would Richard be able to avenge him as well? As he watched an anchor light in the harbor being hoisted on a mainmast halyard, Richard wished he could sit down with Will, as he had in former days, and laugh a little while Will so easily calmed his troubled waters while explaining everything to him.

In the far distance a ship's bell—*Rebecca's* no doubt, since Captain Jones would insist on following naval procedures even on so small a vessel—rang twice in the first watch. Nine o'clock. Richard picked up the pace. Turning right onto North Street, he walked briskly past the rowdy ruckus spilling out from Seth Cushing's tavern and, a little farther on, the more sober dwelling of Ebenezer Gay, minister of the First Parish, the Cutler family church. Then onto South Street, where neatly arranged clapboard shops and homes stood beneath spermaceti street lamps purposely unlit tonight in the ample glow of a full moon. At the intersection with Main Street, he turned left uphill toward the old meetinghouse built a century earlier, the shape of its steeply pitched roof giving the impression of an upside-down ship's hull. Beyond were parade grounds for the local militia, and farther still, west of Hersey Street, vast areas of farmland where, until a few years ago, African slaves had tilled the fields of flax and corn for General Lincoln and other Hingham gentlemen farmers.

Richard's home was two-storied and spacious, its thick clapboard construction holding the cool of night well into the heat of day. Hardly had he opened the front door when he heard Lavinia's cry of delight. Around the corner she came, in bounding leaps from the sitting room, catapulting herself into his arms. She was the youngest of the Cutler children and, from her perspective, Richard's favorite. In rapid order came Anne and Caleb, then their mother from the kitchen. Richard put Lavinia down and gave her backside a playful slap.

"I need to talk to mother," he said to his three siblings. "We won't be long. Caleb, a game of checkers before bed?"

Caleb looked beseechingly at his mother, who shook her head no.

"It's getting late, children," she said. "Your father is coming home tomorrow, and I don't want any of you out of sorts. Off you go. I'll be up shortly."

Anne and Lavinia obeyed grudgingly. Caleb lingered a moment, hoping for a last-minute reprieve. Richard grinned at him and pointed upstairs, to the room they shared next door to their two sisters. Caleb groaned in protest and began trudging up the stairway. When he reached the top, he looked down and sadly waved goodnight. In response, Richard snapped to attention and gave him a mock salute.

In the hush that ensued, mother and son looked intently at one another.

"It went well?"

"Yes, Mother, it did."

Nothing on his mother's face changed. Nor was there any other visible sign to indicate what she was thinking. Only her hesitation in asking the next question provided a clue.

"When must you leave?"

"In a month. I am to report aboard *Ranger* for sea trials off Portsmouth."

"Where will you sail from Portsmouth?"

"I don't know. Captain Jones couldn't tell me."

"I see. . . . Well, perhaps we can discuss more of the details tomorrow with your father. I know he will be proud of you, Richard. As I am. You know that, don't you?"

"Yes, Mother, I do."

Richard blinked, feeling the wash of tender emotion swell within. He loved his mother dearly, and he knew she would not try to dissuade him. What needed to be said had been said many times over the course of many months. How these discussions would ultimately conclude, however, was never in serious doubt. Duty and loyalty were two words that had long held sway in the mists of Cutler ancestry. What had changed as the result of recent events was the cause to which the Cutler family now believed duty and loyalty were owed.

"Would you like some supper? I saved some for you."

"Thank you, no. Caleb took good care of me."

"Of that I am certain."

They both smiled in their mutual affection for the old sergeant. Richard was about to comment further on him when his mother motioned down the hallway, toward the room where the children had been waiting impatiently for their brother.

"There's a package in there for you. It's from your father. He told me he wanted you to have it tonight, after your meeting with Captain Jones."

"Do you know what's in it?"

"I do. Apparently he never doubted the outcome of your meeting."

Despite his curiosity to see what his father had left him, Richard remained where he was, waiting for his mother to leave first. It took several moments, and when she did move, it was to come to him. She took him in her arms and held him not as a child, but as her son, her lifeblood, drawing from him whatever strength and comfort she could.

"Go with God, Richard," she whispered into his ear, pressing him close. "Go with God and with the love of your mother."

Then she was gone.

Richard could still feel the sting of hot tears in his eyes as he sat on a sofa, clutching the package from his father in his lap. It was bulky and wrapped in light sailcloth, and he had to hold it up to the light of twin candles on the table behind to read the inscription. The message was printed in his father's bold hand and read simply: To my son, on this day. With affection, Father.

Richard opened the package and removed its contents. He unfolded the material and laid it out before him. Instinctively he knew what it was. He had seen ones like it before on Royal Navy personnel in Boston. He held it up to his chest. Perfect fit, he thought to himself, before carefully placing the jacket back on his lap. He stared at it, wondering for an instant what lay ahead for him, glory or dishonor, while serving in this uniform. But such thoughts were for tomorrow and the days, months, years to come. Tonight his thoughts would drift back in time to the events that had brought him to the home of Gen. Benjamin Lincoln and the interview with Capt. John Paul Jones. Running his fingers lightly over the cerulean wool and gold buttons of a midshipman's dress coat, he closed his eyes to the flickering light and cast back, remembering . . .

2

The Great Triangular Route

1774

*I*T HAD BEEN A memorable day. His father had arrived home from his shipping office at Barker Yard near Hingham harbor and had casually asked his wife if the post had arrived and—with a knowing wink—would she kindly summon the boys?

It was not necessary for Elizabeth Cutler to summon Will and Richard. They had seen their father making his way home up Main Street and had come running, with Caleb in distant tow. It was highly unusual for Thomas Cutler to leave his office so early; something was in the wind.

"Hello, Father," they said, one after the other as they came trooping into the sitting room. "Hello, Father," Caleb piped in moments later in a voice several octaves higher.

Their father regarded his older sons sternly. "Well, boys," he said, holding up a piece of paper and shaking it. "I see you two were outside playing your little games while your mother and I pay a king's ransom to your tutors—one of whom, by the bye, has informed me that your studies are slipping badly. Your Latin would embarrass a chambermaid, he said, and you seem not able to recall a word of French. As to your arithmetic calculations, Will, I trust you won't be navigating a ship of mine anytime soon. You'd soon have her wrecked and washed up on some African beach."

Will grinned broadly.

"In that case, Father," he said, "consider my opportunities to speak Latin with the natives." He placed a hand on each hip, lowered his chin, and spoke in a deep macho voice. *"Ave, puella pulchra Africanus. Quid tu es tam tristis? Homo albus tibi salûtem dicit."*

He poked Richard in the ribs with an elbow. Despite himself, Richard burst out laughing. Caleb giggled at Richard's reaction. Lavinia wandered in, sucking her thumb, wondering what all the commotion was about.

"Boys!" their father admonished. "I am quite serious. This is not a laughing matter."

Will and Richard snapped to. They were puzzled by this turn of events, Richard especially. The previous week he had overheard a conversation between his mother and one of their tutors. That hoary man's comments regarding Richard's academic progress flew in the face of his father's assessment. Although Will had not received such high praise, the tutor hardly considered him a dullard. He strained, without success, to glimpse what was on the paper his father had held up.

Thomas Cutler dismissed Caleb and Lavinia from the room. With an audible sigh he sat down and picked up the newspaper that had been delivered by a post rider as part of the morning mail. For agonizingly long moments he appeared engrossed in the latest reports from Boston. "Well," he said finally, peering over the top edge of the paper, "if that's the way it's going to be, I am afraid your mother and I are left with no choice. We shall have to engage a tutor to accompany you on your voyage. We had hoped this would not be necessary."

The two boys shot each other a questioning glance. Richard asked, "Um, Father, what voyage? Where are we going?"

"I'm not going anywhere," his father replied nonchalantly. He turned a page and shook the paper to smooth the creases. "You two are going to England."

"England?" they cried at once.

"Yes, England. It's an island off the north coast of Europe. You have heard of it, I trust?"

"Yes, Father," Richard managed.

"Well, that's a relief. Your tutors have taught you something at least." He folded the newspaper and laid it aside. "You will be sailing with Captain Winthrop aboard our brig *Eagle,* carrying ship's stores and rum for delivery to your Uncle William. You will be staying with him and his family for a few weeks while he and our agent transact our business. Mind you, this will not be a pleasure cruise. You will be part of the crew, and you will be expected to earn your keep. Captain Winthrop understands how strongly I feel about this. And you must promise me that you will keep up with your lessons."

Will whooped with joy and began punching the air with his fists. Richard too was smiling when he asked, "What's our cargo coming back?"

His father gave him a deadpan look. "Molasses."

"Molasses?" Richard was confused. This was not standard procedure on trans-Atlantic trade routes. "From England?"

"No. From Barbados."

Will and Richard stared slack-jawed at each other. Until now, the farthest either of them had sailed was to the Piscataqua River to the north and Mystic, Connecticut, to the south. On these coastal voyages they had served as idlers, passengers really, helping out only with the most mundane of shipboard tasks. On occasion they had hauled on the braces and bowlines, and in calm seas, Will had been allowed aloft to the topsail yards to experience the real work of handling a square-rigger. On this passage they would sign on as bona fide members of a crew bound for England. That alone seemed miracle enough until their father had tossed the Indies into the mix. Barbados!

"Holy jumpin' Jesus Christ!" Will rejoiced.

Thomas Cutler let that blasphemy pass. "You'll be gone seven months, eight perhaps, depending on conditions. You'll be home for Christmas, I should think."

☆ ☆ ☆

RIDING A strong ebb tide out between the Hull Peninsula and Peddocks Island, *Eagle* had all plain sail set as she broke free of Hingham Bay and dove into the broad swells of the Atlantic. She was initially on a course east by north that would keep the wind fair on her starboard quarter and her sails at maximum drawing power. It was the brig's fastest point of sail, and Captain Winthrop was determined to reach Portsmouth in less time than the four weeks normally required for an eastbound passage. If the prevailing westerlies held, *Eagle* could run in broad sweeps across the ocean, her flying jib arched like a bow and her long jibboom pointing like an arrow toward Great Britain.

The ship's complement of forty crewmen was divided into two watches. Will and Richard were assigned to the starboard watch as foremast topmen. In a private conversation held at anchor in Hingham harbor in the captain's after cabin, Captain Winthrop had explained their duties to them.

"You are responsible for the t'gallant sail and yard on the foremast, as well as the mainmast stays'ls. You've never done this work before in open water, but you've seen it done and understand what's involved. Will, you are the older and more experienced. Your father is counting on you to keep an eye on Richard, as be assured my mates and I will be doing. You may ask anything of me at any time. My mates and I will teach you as much as we can while at sea. *Eagle* is your family's vessel, so you needn't worry much about protocol. If you are asked to do something you feel you cannot do, tell me, here in my cabin, not in front of the crew. Don't be foolish. Avoid unnecessary risks. Above all, when aloft, never forget these two rules." He held up one finger. "Don't ever let go of one rope until you have another firmly in your grasp." He held up a second finger. "*Always* keep one hand for the ship and one for yourself."

Richard was not inclined to forget either rule as he stepped out for the first time from the larboard chain-wale onto the tar-encrusted standing rigging. He had been aloft before, to the semicircular platform at the maintop, and farther up still to the crosstrees at the juncture of the topmast and topgallant mast. Those times, the vessel he was aboard had been lying at anchor or secured at dockside. Here, with a ship heeling to larboard and pitching and rolling in great ocean swells, the task seemed a great deal more formidable. Halfway up from the deck to the foretop he froze.

"Don't look down, Richard," said Tom Pickett, an experienced seaman climbing alongside. "That's right. Always look up to where you're going, not down to where you've been. And keep your hands on the shrouds. Ratlines are for your feet."

Richard flushed. He knew these things. The cook in the galley knew these things. Furious with himself, he heaved himself to the next ratline. Glancing straight up at the foretop, he saw Will already at the futtock shrouds.

"Hey, Richard! Watch this!"

Richard ignored his own fears as he watched, with mounting anxiety, Will climbing out like a spider onto the rope mesh leading from the foreshrouds in ever steeper angles up and around the sturdy oaken platform that defined the foretop. Able seamen of every nation used this route to the top, viewing with contempt the alternative route, a lubber's hole cut through the base of the platform directly above the final length of shrouds. When Will reached the area where the angle was most acute, he hooked his legs in and around the crisscrossed hemp strands. Locking himself firmly into place, he let go his upper body. With his torso swinging upside down, he began bellowing gleefully and pounding his chest with both fists.

"Will! For Chrissake!" Richard cried up to him.

Tom Pickett shook his head in disbelief. "The captain'll be wanting a word with him," he chuckled.

Captain Winthrop did want a word, and as a result, Will was confined to the deck and the stricter scrutiny of his tutor. True to his word, Thomas Cutler had retained the services of a scholar to tutor his sons aboard his ship in return for free passage to England, to visit family there. He was Harvard-educated and took delight in the rigors of academe, a perspective shared by neither Will nor Richard. Conjugating Latin verbs in the pluperfect tense was not what they had envisioned when they had first swaggered aboard *Eagle* to sign their names in the muster book.

There was other learning more to their liking. *Eagle* was, at her core, a wooden structure propelled along the ocean by two pyramids of canvas. Each section of each pyramid was supported by a carefully balanced framework of masts and yards, and each section was controlled by a complex web of standing rigging that sustained the masts and running rigging that worked the sails.

"When we reach Portsmouth," Captain Winthrop had told them in Hingham, "you'll have grasped the essentials of what it takes to sail a square-rigger. Learning the rest of what's involved will take you a lifetime."

By the time *Eagle* had reached midocean, Richard and Will were testing each other with growing confidence on which sheet belonged to which clew, which brace was attached to which yardarm, what brail gathered in which sail, and what tackle each was rove through to be sent below and coiled around which belaying pin on which pin rail by the bulwarks or fiferail by the masts.

"Well done, lads," first mate Ezrah Harley declared one day after the boys had demonstrated to him what they had learned. When he added, with conviction, "Well done indeed," Richard had never experienced such pride.

To Captain Winthrop, Richard had a natural gift for working the quadrant, a triangular-shaped instrument used to measure the height and angle of heavenly objects. Whether sighting the sun at noon or the Polar Star at night, he quickly grasped the technique of bringing the celestial body down to the horizon, then consulting a list of numbers in published tables to convert the measured angle to an exact line of latitude. Calculating sights into fixes came less easily to Will. He could determine his degree of latitude at night if northern skies were clear and moon glow revealed the horizon, since latitude in the Northern Hemisphere equaled the height of the Pole Star above the horizon. During the day it was more challenging. On one occasion, Richard found Will slumped against the mainmast, cursing his inability to comprehend the mathematical relationship of secants and cosines to a global position. Richard squatted down beside him and put a sympathetic hand on his shoulder.

"Don't fret, mate," he said. "Africa's a big continent. You'll find it."

Will laughed at that, and as always, when Richard succeeded in pulling his brother up from the depths, he felt he had returned a favor.

With Ushant and the western approaches to the Channel two days away by dead reckoning, the weather turned foul. A gentle wind had backed suddenly, and the second mate reported to Captain Winthrop in his cabin that thickening clouds were gathering ominously ahead. *Eagle* was sailing on a close-haul with her yards braced up; cold spray splattered over her foredeck as her bows cut into pewter gray seas becoming roiled by a strengthening wind. Ahead and to the north, white cumulus clouds had deteriorated into menacing billows of charcoal black, an omen to all hands that the worst lay ahead.

Hurrying on deck, Captain Winthrop took the speaking trumpet from its becket. "Stations to shorten sail, Mr. Harley!" he shouted to his first mate, standing in dripping oilskins amidships. "Hands by the t'gallant halyards! Up fore course; in spanker and topgallants! Goose-wing the main course! Set the storm jib! Ease off lee topgallant and topsail sheets!" Lowering the trumpet, he ordered the helmsman to luff her up a half point. As *Eagle's* bow edged into the stiffening breeze, her sails shivered at the leeches, then banged and thundered in protest as the sharp heel came off her.

Eagle's crew leaped to their stations. Waisters on deck grappled with sheets, halyards, lifts, and braces, while topmen scrambled aloft—Richard and Will among them. By now Richard was familiar, if not yet entirely comfortable, with the toil and grit demanded on each yard of each sail, in particular the topgallant to which he had been assigned. Climbing with resolve, he heaved himself up to the crosstrees, looking down only when he felt firmly wedged into position by supporting ropes. Directly below, laid out on both sides of the topmast yard, he could see other topmen with both arms over the yardarm, struggling to attach the second reef points of the topsail to their yard. Below them, bent over the longest yard like twelve yellow half-opened jackknives, the strongest and most experienced of *Eagle's* crew waged war with the fore course. With legs splayed out precariously on quivering footropes, they battled fistful after fistful of flailing canvas up to the yard with the help of buntlines, leech lines, clew garnets, and the sheer force of human will.

Despite its daunting height above deck and the harsh rolling motion at that height in choppy seas, the topgallant was the easiest sail to furl. Its yard was shorter and narrower than the others, and because the sail was intended for use in lighter winds, its flaxen material was more manageable than the heavier canvas on the topsails or courses. Moments before an onslaught of thick, merciless rain began pelting *Eagle,* the topgallant yard was settled on its cap, and the six-man crew had the sail secured with gaskets. What only minutes before had been a gentle, relaxing breeze was now a stiff wind moaning in mournful wails of warning through the rigging.

"Lay in and down!" cried a mate positioned at the topsail bunt. "Everyone on deck!"

No one required extra prompting. With her plain sails furled, or reefed, and the calming effect of the lower staysails taking hold, *Eagle* steadied herself, yielding to the forces of nature. But she pitched and heaved as she rode up each wave and plunged into the depth below, her reefed topsails barely high enough in the trough to catch the wind and maintain her present course.

One by one the topgallant crew lowered themselves from the yard onto the windward shrouds, exploiting the heel of the ship to facilitate the climb down. When it came Richard's turn, a rogue wave threw *Eagle* to leeward, causing the mast to lurch sharply and Richard's foot to slip off a ratline. He grabbed for the mast but was unable to hold onto the slick pine. He grasped at the yard and furled sail just as *Eagle* yawed on a severe downroll, forcing her beam ends over and his hands to lose their grip. With a desperate lunge, he seized hold of the Flemish horse at the yard's extremity. For several terrifying moments, teetering with one arm through the rope stirrup, he glanced down at the wind-whipped churning water rapidly drawing away from him as *Eagle* fought to right herself. Closing his eyes to the horror, he swooned toward the inevitable fall just as someone's arm came under his armpit and around his chest.

"Hang on, Dubber," Will shouted over the shriek of wind. "I've got you."

He was leaning out from the yard, one arm around Richard, the other around the single-rope topgallant mast shroud leading to the truck. With a mighty heave, he tried to haul Richard upward. With his strength failing him, he tried, unsuccessfully, to lug him sideways toward the mast. Straining under the effort, he cried out for help.

"Behind you, Will!" he heard Tom Pickett call out.

Tom had worked his way along the yard and was reaching down to grab Richard under his other armpit. With their combined muscle, he and Will managed to drag Richard back to the relative safety of the mast and shrouds. Richard clung to those shrouds, as if to life itself, while Will kept his arm tight around his brother's waist. At length, both the wind and Richard's hard trembling eased.

"All right?"

Richard nodded, exhaling, unable to speak. With panic ebbing slowly from its high-water mark, he stared blankly at Tom Pickett, then at his brother. Will grinned back at him.

"Fun, ain't it?"

As Captain Winthrop had predicted, the squall quickly blew itself out. Thirty minutes after arriving back on deck, the crew was back at it, setting a full press of canvas that propelled *Eagle* forward, eventually into the English Channel along the south coast of Cornwall. When St. Catherine's Point on the southern tip of the Isle of Wight was slightly abaft her beam, she turned north direct for Southampton Water and the Solent, an arm of the sea that together with Portsmouth harbor and the adjacent coves and inlets formed the littoral heart of England.

His watch off duty, Richard walked forward to the larboard foremast shrouds to survey the scenery ashore. Will joined him, as did most of the ship's crew. It was the first land they had seen in nearly four weeks, and for the older sailors aboard, it was homeland.

"Look, Will," said Richard, pointing abeam. "Those ruins over there on that cliff. Ancient fortresses, I suspect. Wasn't it the Tudor kings, the Henrys, who ordered them built to protect the naval base here?"

Will did not respond. Richard continued to watch with fascination as history passed by him on either side of the brig. "There's another one, Will, to starboard. Take a look," he implored. Again Will did not respond. Richard turned to look at him; when he saw Will staring transfixed ahead, he looked forward to see what his brother had found so engrossing. Confused by what he saw, he decided to go to the prow for a better view. To his surprise he realized there was no room to move forward. What seemed the entire ship's company was standing on or near the forecastle in silent contemplation of what *Eagle* was approaching. Thoroughly bewildered, Richard grasped a backstay and stepped out onto a larboard chain-wale. Leaning out, he searched ahead to where the Solent met Southampton Water between Portsmouth harbor and the Isle of Wight. There, stretched before him as far and wide as sight would permit, was a display of naval power beyond imagining, each ship looming ever more imperiously into view as *Eagle* glided serenely through the protected water.

"Spithead," remarked a seaman, as if explanation at this point was necessary.

It was a virtual forest of masts and spars, a basin covering a vast area filled with ships of every description and size, some bigger than Richard had ever envisioned. Bustling about among these leviathans was subservient water traffic: longboats and bumboats and lighters powered by sail or oars shuttling back and forth between the great ships and Portsmouth Town, bearing the officers, crew, cargo, provisions, water barrels, ordnance, and dispatches to sustain an empire. Up until now, Richard had considered a brig such as *Eagle* a large vessel. He had seen larger ones of course. A Royal Navy frigate had once sailed into Hingham Bay, and a year ago in Boston his father had pointed out three ships of the line anchored in the harbor. But those vessels he had viewed from a distance, and from that distance they appeared more like the toy models he and Will used to build as children. Certainly they had seemed far less formidable than the ship they were now closing on, so close that *Eagle* seemed in comparison a mere water bug cruising by. Ezrah Harley identified her as the flagship of a vice admiral of the Blue, pointing up at the long blue pennant fluttering self-importantly from the foremast truck. Three tiers of gun ports were closed shut on her starboard side, and a Jacob's ladder hanging down from the waist to the waterline seemed to lead up to the Almighty himself, in command on the quarterdeck.

"How many warships do you think, Will?"

"I dunno. A hundred, maybe?"

"More than that, mate," a seaman corrected him. "And them's just the ones happen t' be in port. The Royal Navy's been called the wooden wall of England. Now ye knows why."

It was with a keen sense of humility that *Eagle's* crew took her on a final tack through the narrow and crooked entrance of Portsmouth harbor and dropped anchor near the commercial wharves at Gosport, at the opposite end of the harbor from the Round Tower and the long stone buildings of Portsmouth Dockyard, a Royal Navy facility that by 1774 had become the largest industrial enterprise the world had ever known.

THE HOME of William Cutler was in an inland town called Fareham, about an hour's ride north. Although close to Portsmouth, it was a world apart from the noise, stench, and confusion of that old walled city. Here, amid the rolling fields and forest glens of Hampshire, was a land ruled by serenity and gentility. The estates they passed were all worthy of note, the least imposing among them, to Richard's mind, a considerable step up from the mansion John Hancock had recently built on Beacon Hill, trumpeted as perhaps the finest in Boston. Manors here were constructed mostly in Georgian style: red brick with white colonnades in front, whiter trim around the windows, and statues of Greek or Roman origin placed strategically for the best view from within the house and for those passing by on the road. Each estate bespoke wealth—whether inherited or earned wealth a subject of endless speculation over pots of tea and decanters of sherry—but wealth nonetheless.

"Look, Will and Richard, see that house? My best friend Katherine lives there. She's coming for supper tomorrow with her family. You'll enjoy them ever so."

Richard smiled at Elizabeth Cutler. He had met her for the first time earlier in the day when she had accompanied her father to his shipping office to welcome her cousins to England. Richard was immediately drawn to her. She was about his age and looked a lot like him: not as tall, but the same Saxon hair and blue eyes, the same strong cleft chin and thin nose. Her unaffected enthusiasm was infectious; whenever she laughed, which was often, her carefully coifed blond curls jiggled around her head.

"I shall look forward to that, Lizzy," Richard replied affectionately.

"The Hardcastles are Royal Navy," William Cutler remarked. He was sitting straight up on the cushioned bench inside the post chaise, his arms crossed and his right leg stretched out to brace himself against a sudden jolt from the deeply rutted road. "Katherine's father is a post captain, retired. He has three sons in the service. Jeremy is based in Gibraltar, Hugh in the Indies. James will be shipping out later this summer or fall. You'll meet him tomorrow. He's a year younger than you, Richard, a midshipman at the age of thirteen. Capital young fellow."

Another half mile and the carriage veered down a long pebbled drive with a view of a pond to the left and, to the right, a dazzle of flowers and hedgerows of shrubs lining the entire length of road. Beyond lay a perfectly manicured lawn, a swash of emerald green extending from the hedgerows to a sharp demarcation of forest a cable length in the distance. Turning in a wide arc, the carriage shivered to a halt in front of a six-columned portico at the entryway to the Georgian manor. A footman appeared beside the door of the carriage. He opened it and placed a footstool beneath the three-rung debarkation ladder. As he was sitting closest to the door, Richard stepped out first and stretched his legs, feeling in them the motion of the sea.

"Well, what do you think?" Lizzy asked her cousins, moments later when they were standing on the portico. They could hear shouts from inside the house. Other family members were coming out to greet them.

Richard did not know what to think, but it took Will a mere glance or two around to make up his mind. "We're getting into the sugar business, Richard," he said with such conviction he made Lizzy giggle.

Their first day ashore was consumed with family matters. William Cutler had not seen his brother Thomas in five years. Until this day he had never met any of his children. There was a lot of ground to cover: so persistently did he press for information that for much of the day it took considerable effort for his wife, Emma, or son Robin to get a word in edgewise. Robin too was keen to learn about his cousins and life in America. Emma absorbed what she could while directing staff hither and yon to provide for her nephews' comforts and ravenous appetites. The cascade of questions and answers, opinions and comments, continued well into the summer night, until the glow of family communion was inevitably dimmed by fatigue. With a final round of hugs from Aunt Emma and Lizzy—a firm handshake from their Uncle William and Robin—Will and Richard trudged up the grand stairway to their room on the second floor, where they collapsed into the bliss of goose-down bedding. Tonight, there would be no hammocks swaying in the forecastle, no mate to rouse them out for the graveyard watch.

The next morning, they picked up where they left off, for much of the day outdoors. It was a beautiful July day in Hampshire, a tinge of cool air combining with the warmth of the sun to bring everything into distinct and pleasant focus. Refreshed by a twelve-hour sleep, Will and Richard spent the day exploring the Cutler estate, at one time in a romp with Lizzy and Robin, at another in a slower, more contemplative walk with their uncle across the lawn and along a well-trampled path deep within a forest of silver birch, beech, and pine.

"We'll be going often to Portsmouth these next few weeks," William informed them. "Your father wants you to learn as much as possible about the family business from this end, and my offices are a good place to start. He hopes, as I do, that someday you and Caleb and Robin and John will take over the business from us and manage it much as we have done. Your cousin John, if you recall what I told you last night, is in Barbados. You shall be visiting with him there. He's learning from the overseer on our sugar plantation."

This was news to Richard.

"You bought a plantation, Uncle? Why? I thought you—ah, I mean, we—were in the shipping business."

"We are. And I didn't buy the plantation. I inherited it, in a manner of speaking. English shippers often lend money to planters who are their clients. This one planter defaulted on his loan, so I assumed his mortgage as payment. I had intended to sell the property but decided instead to hold it for a time to see what developed. I'm glad I did."

"Do you grow just sugar on the plantation? Is it really that profitable?"

William Cutler chuckled.

"There is a reason, Richard,why sugar is called 'white gold.' Demand for it just about everywhere is as insatiable as your appetite yesterday, and it grows by leaps and bounds every year. And it's not just the sugar. The real value of cane lies in molasses, which as you may know is a by-product of sugar. From molasses comes rum, and if you want to start feeling a bit giddy, consider how many barrels of rum it takes each year to quench the thirst of the Royal Navy. Quenching that thirst alone could maintain us for some time in quite comfortable circumstances, I can assure you. As I trust you will learn during your visit with us, the economics of sugar production are quite agreeable."

Richard whistled softly. "Father never put it that way."

"He wouldn't. He keeps that sort of thing close to his vest. Which is a good lesson for us all. It is never wise to flaunt a good thing. Since you two are coming of age, we feel it is time to allow you a peek under the covers, so to speak."

"Let me see if I understand," said Will. "You produce sugar in Barbados. Some of that sugar is made into molasses. Sugar and molasses are shipped to America and sold as is or made into rum which is then shipped to England or another of her colonies. However sugar is sold, in whatever form in whatever market, the seller makes a tidy profit, everyone involved along the way coming out well in the end."

"That's the gist, certainly. It would be the same for any product enjoying such high demand. Some sugar is shipped directly to England of course, and there are planters who distill rum right on the island. Mount Gay is an example. They've been making rum on Barbados for a hundred years. But for reasons I cannot fully explain, rum ages best in barrels made of American white pine. Which explains your cargo and why you'll be carrying molasses with you to Boston. Still, I understand why a few families have decided to build their own distilleries. Taxes are one of our biggest expenses, and following the Mount Gay example would reduce them considerably. Planters pay a pretty purse to the Crown each year. Four million pounds last year alone, more than three times what the East India Company paid in. The investment necessary to build a distillery, however, is quite prohibitive. And there's always the risk of it being demolished by a hurricane. So I seriously doubt this is something we would ever consider doing."

"Taxes I understand, Uncle," said Will, a sullen tone entering his voice. "What we pay in taxes enables the British army to remain in America."

"Quite so. And elsewhere throughout the empire."

William Cutler had noted the shift in Will's tone of voice. "The afternoon is slipping by, boys," he said. "What say we wear ship and head home for a spot of tea?"

Inside the manor all was astir as servants and cooks scurried about preparing for the visit of the Hardcastle family. By late afternoon, when Will and Richard went upstairs to change for the evening, aromas of roast lamb and other delectables were wafting up from the kitchen. Will's stomach was growling in fierce anticipation as he and Richard came downstairs to join the rest of the family.

A butler announced the arrival of a carriage. He clicked open the large front door from the inside and bowed deferentially as the guests came up the steps of the portico and into the front hall. The adults greeted each other genially but formally, as people of consequence who are acquainted with each other are wont to do. The men were attired in gaily colored breeches with silk stockings to the knee, lavishly embroidered waistcoats opening in a V beneath the stomach, white linen cravats edged in lace, and the high-heeled buckled shoes that had become the rage in both Paris and London. Over his ensemble, Henry Hardcastle wore the full-skirted coat of an earlier age, while William Cutler preferred the newer style frock coat. The women too were fashionably done up, the understated elegance of their gowns and accoutrements a testament to class and good breeding. Will and Richard greeted the post captain and his wife with as much social grace as they could muster, feeling clumsily self-conscious in the latest European fashions borrowed for the occasion from their uncle and cousin.

"Will, Richard," said Lizzy eagerly, "meet Katherine and James. Katherine and James, may I introduce you to my dear cousins from America."

Will shook Jamie's hand and gallantly showed a leg in response to Katherine's deep curtsy, inclining his upper body slightly forward with his right hand over his heart. After an awkward pause, he cleared his throat, adding, "And this is my brother Richard."

"Hello, Richard," said Katherine. She swept him a graceful curtsy as well. "Welcome to England. I hope you enjoy your stay here."

He was gawking at her. He realized he looked ridiculous standing there like that, but common sense and propriety seemed to have abandoned him. She was an inch or two shorter than he, though taller than most young women, and he had gathered from Lizzy that she was nearly a year older, closer in age to Will. She was wearing a fetching gown of purple velvet brocade with a belt to match, the delicate white of a cotton fichu covering the gap at her chest. On her left wrist was a thin round bracelet of gold, the sole adornment she wore that evening. Her hair was an appealing chestnut brown in color and was drawn back tastefully in a chignon, from which a lock had escaped to fall down over her right shoulder. She was smiling at Richard, her hazel eyes sparkling with mirth over his predicament.

Her brother cut through the impasse.

"Hello, Richard," he said, coming over and holding out his hand. "I am James Hardcastle. But please call me Jamie. All my friends do."

Richard gratefully shook the young midshipman's hand. "Jamie, then," he said, relieved to have the introductions over. Relieved even more, moments later, when the butler announced dinner.

"You're drooling, Dubber," Will whispered to him as hosts and guests began filing two by two into the dining area. Grinning, he held out a handkerchief to him. "Here, you might need this."

Richard gave his brother a piqued look, irked more by his own recent behavior than by the mention of his childhood nickname. "Don't call me that," he whispered back.

The dining area was a long rectangular room adorned on one side by six windows of identical proportions, each one richly draped in purple satin. On the opposite wall was an open fireplace and oil paintings of prominent Cutler ancestors hung in gilded frames, three on either side of the dormant hearth. The dining table was twelve feet of mahogany covered with a white damask tablecloth and supported by two three-legged pedestals. A pair of silver candelabra had been placed upon it, their candles freshly lit to reveal ten place-settings of blue-on-white Wedgwood china: the same china, Richard noted, that his mother in Hingham brought out whenever important company was coming for supper. Two footmen wearing the peruke and attire of young English gentlemen stood stoically against the outer wall, ready to serve or resupply whatever might be desired.

Seating was arbitrary, in the custom of the day, though deference was afforded the hosts who sat one on each end of the table. Henry Hardcastle sat at a corner by the hearth next to Emma Cutler. His wife, Jane, sat kitty-corner from him, next to William Cutler, with Richard next to her followed by Robin and Will. On the opposite side sat Jamie, across from his mother, followed by Lizzy and Katherine. Once everyone was properly situated and a first course of smoked eel and white wine served, Henry Hardcastle cleared his throat.

"It is a custom in the Royal Navy," he said with authority, "that the youngest officer dining at the captain's table should toast the king. At this table that honor should rightly fall to James. But tonight, Richard, as your uncle agrees, we would be obliged if you would do the honors."

All eyes swung to Richard. He grinned back uncertainly, groping for the words he knew he had to find—and quickly. He glanced at Will, who was staring down at his plate on the table. He glanced across at Jamie and Lizzy. They were nodding at him, urging him on.

Richard gripped the stem of his wine glass and rose uncertainly to his feet. "To King George," he said to the room at large, raising the glass, his voice gaining confidence when he noted Katherine smiling at him from down the table. "May his reign be long; may his enemies be confounded; and may his empire endure forever."

"Here, here!" the room responded as one, except for one. Richard sat down, pleased with himself. As the others downed their wine, he chanced a glance at Katherine. She was staring in Will's direction, a questioning look on her face.

"By Jove, well done, my boy!" boomed Henry Hardcastle. "Nailed your colors to the mast with that one, eh? These days, a loyal Jonathan is as hard to find as an honest bogman."

He meant it as a joke, an amusing piece of wit. He was beaming in anticipation of the table's reaction when Will said, unexpectedly, "Jonathans would be loyal, Captain, if king and Parliament would give us cause for such loyalty."

Henry's smile vanished as a hush swept over the room. Richard looked to his left, around Robin, at his brother. Will was staring straight across the table at Captain Hardcastle, his right hand gripping the stem of a glass not touched during Richard's toast.

"Explain yourself, sir," Henry Hardcastle harrumphed.

"Please, Will," Emma agreed. "You do owe us an explanation, if not an apology."

Will's blue eyes remained firm on the retired naval officer. "I mean no disrespect to you, Captain," he said, "or to anyone at this table. If I have offended you, I do most sincerely apologize. I merely wish to point out that loyalty to a king or country is something that must be earned, not decreed. Unfortunately, most members of Parliament do not seem to understand this. Nor do the king's ministers, except for William Pitt and perhaps one or two others. King George has called us 'ungrateful children.' Lord Sandwich promises us 'a jolly good spanking.' Is that all we Americans are to you? Children to be whipped into submission?"

"Poppycock!" Henry bellowed. "Has not your family fared well in the colonies? Should that alone not inspire loyalty in you? And what's all this bosh about children?"

"You're right, Captain," Will agreed. "We have fared well. We are fortunate to have family in England with means and influence. Most people in Massachusetts do not have such advantages. They are not treated as kindly, I can assure you."

Henry Hardcastle threw up his arms in frustration. His daughter said, "Are you suggesting, Will, that my father is somehow responsible for how people are treated in America?"

"No, not directly, Katherine. But every Englishman in a position of influence must bear some responsibility."

"I say!" Henry fumed, his dander up.

Jamie asked, in steadier tones, "Is Parliament's position so unreasonable, Will? Surely you must realize that the cost of maintaining an army in the colonies is quite staggering, and that England must pay exorbitant annual tributes to the Barbary States to protect American shipping in the Mediterranean. Should the colonies not contribute to these costs? Your so-called Sons of Liberty resist paying taxes but ignore the simple truth that these taxes are raised primarily for your own defense and safety."

"And bear in mind," added Robin, "the taxes we pay in England are much higher than what you are asked to pay in America. Twenty-five times higher, in fact. Had you the representation in Parliament you seem to desire, you'd find no sympathy for your position there. Your own Dr. Franklin was booed off the floor last session when he tried to present your grievances."

"Understand," Will immediately countered, "it's not just about taxes. If that's what Parliament believes, Parliament is wrong. What we in the colonies want— what we have sought in every petition we have sent King George—is simply to be granted the same rights as all free Englishmen. Our grievances have been ignored. Why? Do we not deserve the courtesy of a reply? Are we so unworthy?"

Richard had heard Will speak often on this topic, but not to this extent and never with such eloquence. Still, he resented Will for broaching the subject. It was one that lay in waiting like a Pandora's box behind every discussion in Britain gravitating toward "the American situation." Once it was opened, the ills of empire were released, consuming in their fiery wake all possibilities for civil conversation. William Cutler was determined this evening to keep that box firmly shut. He rose to his feet and gently rapped a glass with the edge of a spoon.

"My friends," he said, when he had everyone's attention. "I agree these are difficult times calling for complex solutions. To answer your question, Will, yes, we are indeed all Englishmen, a large family if you will, separated by an ocean; but a family nonetheless that can and will resolve its differences as we have for centuries. Tonight we are gathered as a smaller family, one of blood and special friends, the best kind. We are here to welcome my nephews to our homes and to the special relationships we here at this table enjoy. May they find their own joy in these relationships, and may they take home with them a trove of memories that shall remain with them a lifetime." He raised his glass to each nephew in turn. "A toast, I say, to Will and Richard Cutler!"

"Here, here!" the room responded as one chorus, the gruff voice of Henry Hardcastle included.

Servants bustled into action, clearing away one course, introducing the next. Platters of poached salmon and minted lamb made the rounds, along with plates of diced turnips and creamed asparagus, breads and cheeses, pastries and nuts. Outside, dusk was yielding to nightfall. Additional candles were lit throughout a room where, for a contented interlude, the only sounds were those of clinking silverware, the sighs of gastronomic pleasure, small talk, and the cracking of walnuts.

After a second helping of lamb had made the rounds, Jamie raised a different, more welcomed subject of national interest. "Captain Cook should be returning to Portsmouth soon," he said, "possibly in a month or less. I wonder if he has found the Southern Continent on this voyage."

"I wager he has," his father replied, "given the measure of the man." He was studying a platter of salmon held before him, debating his ability to consume yet another helping of the delicious pink flesh. Reluctantly he shook his head no. "James Cook is not a man to quit, whatever the odds against him. If the Southern Continent exists, he'll find it, mark my words. I must say, I envy the man. With all my years in the navy, Bombay was my limit to the east, Brazil to the west. The Great South Sea. Imagine."

"People in Boston have heard of Captain Cook," Richard said, "but we don't know much about him. Can you tell us more, Jamie?"

Jamie was eager to oblige. To his attentive audience he recounted the facts of James Cook's first voyage, to Tahiti to study the transit of Venus. From there he had sailed south to New Holland to claim Botany Bay and other lands in the name of the king, then farther south where no European had sailed before him, in his primary quest to find the Southern Continent that scientists of the Royal Society were convinced must exist on the bottom of the world as a counterweight to the arctic mass on top. Faced with hurricane-force winds and bitter cold in the high latitudes, *Endeavor* was forced to retreat north to New Zealand. A year later, Cook again departed Portsmouth, this time as captain of *Resolution,* bound once more for the Great South Sea. On this voyage, he intended to sail far beyond the realm of the Royal Navy, thus no word from him had been received for almost a year. But word was expected soon, based on the dead reckoning of how long such a journey should take. A swift dispatch vessel was expected any day now from Bombay or Capetown or Kingston with news to electrify the civilized world. In the meantime, London newspapers continued to print accounts of the spectacular lands and peoples Cook had encountered on his first voyage.

"They almost didn't make it off the island," Jamie concluded, referring to Cook's first voyage and his retreat to New Zealand. "The natives there are cannibals. Captain Cook had to fight them off on the beach. He and his crew barely made it back to *Endeavor.* His log has much to say about those savages with their pierced noses and lips and tattoos all over their naked bodies, head to foot."

Richard had a follow-up question in mind when something Lizzy whispered into Katherine's ear caused Katherine to suddenly blush scarlet, clap a hand over her mouth, and erupt in a sea of stifled giggles. William Cutler looked down, smiling, and swirled his wine glass. His wife was not so bemused.

"Elizabeth Cutler!" she scolded. "You will behave like a lady or you shall be excused from the table. Do I make myself clear?"

She did, perfectly. In proper style, Lizzy and Katherine managed to calm the sea to an intermittent giggle or two. Richard and Jamie stared blankly across the table, each looking to the other to make sense out of what had just happened.

The dinner reached its fitting crescendo when a silver bowl of trifle rich with sponge cake, syllabub, dry sherry, and berries was placed before Emma Cutler, who took great delight in serving oversized portions to her protesting guests. As beakers of French brandy were placed before the adults, Richard picked at his helping of pudding, brooding over how the evening might end. He liked Jamie. A lot. That much, at least, was simple. His feelings for Katherine were more complex. He was drawn to her, irresistibly. Why? What was it about her? Her physical appearance, certainly, but he enjoyed the acquaintances and, according to Will at least, the fantasies of many attractive girls back home in Hingham. Rarely had he felt self-conscious or ill at ease in their presence. Which was how he felt tonight in the company of Katherine Hardcastle. She possessed a unique quality, one that fascinated him as much as it unnerved him. Perhaps, he thought, it was her poise and self-confidence, though such characteristics were expected of one raised in the shadow of wealth and privilege. Perhaps it was the utter lack of foppery and patrician airs so often assumed by those of high social standing. Or perhaps it was the joie de vivre she seemed to share so openly with Lizzy. Whatever it was, he knew he had to see her again, despite a creeping dread that, in her eyes, he could never measure up against what had to be legions of local male admirers.

Seated next to him, Jane Hardcastle placed her spoon on her plate and her napkin on the table. "Richard," she said pleasantly, "you and Will must come to our home for a visit. Katherine loves to ride a horse, and I must say, she does it quite well. Jamie does too. Is this something you'd like to do?"

"I should say," Richard blurted out. "Riding is a passion of mine, Mrs. Hardcastle." He dared not glance in his brother's direction.

"Oh, do come!" Katherine exclaimed, looking right at him, and his heart leaped.

☆ ☆ ☆

THEIR VISIT to the Hardcastle residence, arranged for the following Monday, had to be postponed. Bad weather had skulked in from the Atlantic, bringing with it a dank gloom unwilling to budge for several frustrating days. William Cutler made certain his nephews made good use of their time in the Gosport shipping office or aboard *Eagle* or another ship loading or unloading the goods that were the trade of empire. Yet even he found himself consulting the auguries of weather in the hope that such dreary conditions would soon end.

Finally the sun broke through. The next morning, Will and Richard were delivered by coach to the Hardcastle estate.

Jamie met them outside by the semicircular entryway. "My, don't you two look every bit the equestrians," he remarked impishly, grinning at their obvious discomfort. Will and Richard were not amused. Consequences be damned, at that moment either one of them would have gladly surrendered the confining breeches, coat, and leather boots they had on for the infinitely more comfortable garb of a sailor.

Jamie offered them a brief tour of the grounds. The Hardcastle residence was similar in design and construction to the Cutler estate, though not as large or imposing, with an emphasis more on landscaping than architecture.

On both sides of the house, as well as in front, well-maintained gardens of foxgloves and primroses thrived. Behind the house an appealing semicircle of blue and yellow pansies embraced a small domed marble gazebo with a fine view of a pond. Reeds growing around the pond swayed back and forth in the summer breeze, as if waving in greeting at a pair of swans swimming languidly by.

They met Katherine at the stables. She was dressed in a dark green riding jacket, white linen shirt, brown leather boots, and a pair of light tan culottes designed to resemble a skirt but which in fact were trousers.

"Welcome," she greeted them happily. She held by the reins a handsome roan hunter. She had been speaking to it as if to a friend while gently massaging its neck. "This is Tucker, Richard," she said, handing over the reins. "He's a good horse and minds well. Be careful for sudden jolts or jerks, else you'll startle him. Will, your horse is over there, by Jamie's. Shall we?"

Richard took the reins. He put his left foot in a stirrup and tried, unsuccessfully, to hoist himself up. A second attempt failed. Tucker snorted and shook his head disgustedly as Jamie came over to lend a hand. "Heave ho," he said, clasping both hands together under Richard's foot and giving him a leg up. Once aboard, Richard concentrated on the finer points of horsemanship he knew well enough in theory but rarely practiced. As they made their way from the stables and paddock area into the gently rolling Hampshire countryside, he sat up straight while keeping his shoulders square and the heels of his boots down at a slant from the stirrups.

Will nudged his steed over beside Katherine's. "I thought all proper English girls rode sidesaddle," he said, grinning.

"Really?" she replied, as she signaled a command to her horse with two swift pats on its neck. "Well, I should think all proper English girls do."

She picked up speed on a course following close beside a long stone hedge recently erected as a boundary marker to keep animals in and unwanted trespassers out. Will and Jamie followed her into the distant fields. Richard drew in his reins, content to sit and watch.

She was a joy to behold as she moved effortlessly from a walk into a posting trot, pushing up with one beat of the motion, sitting down with the next. It was as though the horse were an extension of her own body, so together were they in rhythm, energy, and precision timing. She was in a canter now, riding effortlessly as if on a rocking horse, along the quarter-mile length of hedge. When she reached the limits of private ownership, a speck in the far distance, she led her horse around without breaking stride and cantered back to where Tucker was stamping the ground impatiently. Will was a good ways behind, at a walk, and Jamie had turned back to ride beside him.

"Join me?" Katherine asked. There was a pleasant scent of leather and hot horse about her as she commanded her steed forward with a gentle nudge. Richard did likewise.

"You don't enjoy riding much, do you?"

Richard glanced at her. She was sitting straight, but her head was cocked sideways at him, wisps of chestnut hair blowing across her face. Seeing her that way made it impossible for him to lie. "I confess, I confess," he said in mock tones, holding up one arm in surrender. "I didn't quite tell the truth the other night. I'm no equestrian, Katherine. I ride a horse, but only when a boat won't get me where I need go. I'm guilty as charged."

She rode on, pondering his words before replying, in equally mock tones: "After careful consideration of the facts at hand, the court finds you not guilty on the grounds that no crime has been committed."

They smiled at each other, her eyes locking on his in silent inquiry. His heart was thumping when she asked, in a more serious tone, "Why did you say that to Mum at dinner the other night?"

He stared down at his hands holding the reins, carefully considering his response. Above all, he wanted to avoid saying anything that might expose his feelings for her to mockery or rejection. Ultimately he decided to tell the truth, realizing she would not have asked that question unless she already knew the answer.

"I had to do something to see you again."

Her eyes probed his. "Thank you, Richard" she said, thrilling him by the way she pronounced his name. "And by the way, thank you for the kind note you sent my parents. That was sweet of you. Mummy hopes to see a lot of you in the weeks ahead. She thinks you'll make a fine catch some day."

She said it without irony or humor, simply as a matter of record.

"Thank her for me, please," he said, adding, "I'm sure she meant to include Will in that."

"Perhaps. She likes Will too, though Father finds him a bit brash. We all worry about him. He's like you in many ways, Richard, yet so different in others. He's wrong about King George, and I fear his views will be his undoing.

Watch over him, will you? Trouble is coming. I sense it. Jamie does too. Whatever happens, Richard, you *must* promise me that you'll watch over yourself, above all else."

Richard swallowed hard, her last three words lingering in the air like the echo of beautiful music. He did not know what to say in response, his entire body of knowledge and experience up to this point providing him with, "Are your other brothers as nice as you and Jamie?"

Katherine laughed. "Oh, well, I suppose. I haven't seen them in a while. You'd take to Hugh. Like you, he prefers a boat to a horse. Perhaps you'll see him when you're in Barbados. He's assigned to the Windward Squadron in Bridgetown, a midshipman on *Alarm*. He's chasing pirates. Not much else to do without a war going on. Do you think you might visit with him?"

"If he's there, yes," Richard promised. "He's your brother: that's reason enough."

They rode on in silence, Richard deeply resenting the stone hedge coming up at them fifty yards ahead. Reaching it would mean reining the horses around and heading back to the stables and the company of others. Being with her alone, talking with her about anything, these were truly wondrous things. It was incredible. He hardly knew her. But oh how strongly he felt about her. Abruptly his thoughts were interrupted by the sound of pounding hooves coming up hard from behind. He and Katherine turned in their saddles to see Will and Jamie galloping together side by side as if in a race, aiming for the hedge. As they swept past, Will waved his arm at them in a raw display of bravado.

"They mean to jump it!" Katherine exclaimed. Caught up in the excitement, she drove her horse forward in pursuit. Richard hung back. Then, with jaw set, he jabbed the heels of his boots hard into Tucker's side, setting off a sudden and violent release of energy.

Up ahead, Jamie had cleared the three-foot-high stone barrier. Will was airborne, crouched down too low, his weight dangerously forward of his horse's shoulders. Miraculously he managed to stay aboard as he cleared the hedge to land safely on the other side. Katherine followed in a perfectly executed jump.

It was Richard's turn, and he would not fare as well. He had lost control of Tucker the instant he had lunged into a gallop. Richard had let go the reins and was holding on desperately to the horse's mane, his feet dangling free of the stirrups, the hedge looming up fast. He could not survive a jump. That he knew. He also knew the horse would jump regardless, or, worse, rear up, throwing him off, trampling him. His only hope, he reasoned in those last desperate moments, was to fall off, now, before reaching the hedge, and take his chances on the ground. With a silent prayer to Jesus and all that was holy, he let go, his last vision being of the ground rising up to slam him. By the time the others were aware of what had happened, he was sprawled out on the grass, unconscious, and he did not know until sometime later that it was Katherine who reached him first, cradling his head in her lap and ripping off the silk stock from around her neck to stem the flow of blood seeping from an ugly gash high on his forehead. She stayed with him that way until later in the afternoon, when Will and Jamie finally returned with help.

☆ ☆ ☆

> Now farewell to you, ye fine English ladies,
> Now farewell to you, ye ladies of the Main.
> For we've received orders to sail to the Indies,
> And perhaps we may never more see you again.

A SEAMAN in *Eagle's* waist was singing this ditty to himself as he flemished a rope flat onto the deck in a perfect spiral. It was a takeoff of a popular tune among sailors, Spain the country in the original script. Will had long since deduced that on any particular day, aboard any particular ship, the rhyme and name of the country changed with whatever port a sailor happened to be leaving.

"You *will* see her again, Richard," he said, reading his brother's thoughts. Astern, directly in line with the wash of *Eagle's* wake, they could make out the twin white peaks of the Lizard hovering low above the fading Cornish coast.

"I know," Richard replied, feeling more the man than the boy he still was.

He could hear Katherine saying similar words to him, two days earlier, as they had walked alone together in the cool of a late September evening toward the gazebo by the pond. She had said it with such faith and endearing conviction that on impulse he had taken her in his arms and kissed her, awkwardly, for they were young and inexperienced. They had clung tenderly to each other as he moved from her lips to her cheeks and nose and forehead, lingering at her eyes to kiss away the salty evidence of tears until they heard Katherine's mother calling for them in the distance, breaking the spell. From that moment on, he vowed, he would not, could not, betray her. He would forever hold her to him in that secret place one maintains in the far reaches of the heart to safe-harbor both blissful memories and grievous losses.

"And," he added, with a smile not entirely forced, "it is good to be back at sea with you, Will. We have the Indies ahead to look forward to."

"That we do, squire," Will agreed. He put his hand on Richard's shoulder. "So let's get to it. It's our watch."

They left Portsmouth on the first of October, anticipating a six- to seven-week passage to Bridgetown, with a four- or five-day stopover there to load on a cargo of sugar and molasses for the homeward passage. They were to sail south by the Bay of Biscay and the Iberian Peninsula along the Canary Current off the Azores, then westward on the North Equatorial Current via the northeast trade winds to the Indies. It was a sea-lane first charted centuries ago by Portuguese and Spanish explorers and had long since become the preferred route of mariners sailing from the Old World to the New.

☆ ☆ ☆

BY THE time lookouts had been posted in the crosstrees for the first sighting of land, Richard found himself actually looking forward to going aloft. Work on the topgallant yard had become routine, safety always a concern though no longer an obsession; when off duty, he often skylarked in *Eagle's* top-hamper with Will, Tom Pickett, and other members of the crew. On one memorable occasion, he had scampered up the lower shrouds without once looking down, then on to the maintop and around on the futtock shrouds, up without pause on the narrower topsail shrouds until he had reached the topgallant yard. From there he had shimmied up the topgallant mast all the way to the main truck, slapping his hand on top the round knob as proof of his accomplishment. He had lingered there a moment, admiring a view of forty miles horizon to horizon, not a sail up anywhere on the lazy blue tropical sea. On the way down, he had wrapped his legs over a backstay leading down from the topmast trestle-trees and had descended rapidly, hand under hand, to the starboard chain-wale, jumping onto the weather deck from there. With tar-smudged hands and breeches, and with the smug grin of a rite-of-passage completed, he had gratefully accepted a tankard of grog from Will to celebrate the occasion "by splicing the main-brace," as Ezrah Harley put it.

"On deck, there! Land ho! Two points off the larboard bow!"

The lookout's cry brought everyone's attention ahead until, some time later, a small mound began rising from the sea, the low peak in the center of Barbados becoming increasingly visible beneath puffy white clouds. *Eagle* kept the island to starboard, rounding up from the Atlantic Ocean into the Caribbean Sea and the port of Bridgetown on the island's southwest corner.

Bridgetown was the naval headquarters of the Windward Squadron and a key outpost of the Royal Navy. Not as large as the Caribbean bases on Antigua or Jamaica, it nonetheless controlled the eastern reaches of the Spanish Main and provided a critical base from which to monitor commercial and military activities on the French and Spanish islands nearby. When necessary, it could combine forces with warships from the Leeward Station at English Harbor or the main naval base at Kingston to squeeze in a lethal vise any enemy with designs on St. Lucia, Grenada, Dominica, or other British possessions in the Caribbean. Theirs was critical work. Guadeloupe might not be much larger than tiny Anticosti Island in the mouth of the St. Lawrence River, but what it contributed to the exchequer in London was worth twenty times what all of Canada provided.

In appearance it was a miniature version of Portsmouth. Anchored in the crescent-shaped Carlisle Bay was a squadron of naval vessels ranging in size from a seventy-four-gun ship of the line to small cutters of four guns, their shallow drafts and fore-'n-aft rigs ideal for exercising British authority where other vessels dared not go. Richard's eyes scanned the harbor, his gaze taking in the fully laden quays and the buildings of cream-white stucco with red tiled roofs arranged in a semicircle around the bay. On the parapets of Fort Charles on the eastern slope of the harbor, flecks of red beside black extensions of cannon indicated that the British army had been advised of their arrival. By the time *Eagle* had reached the commercial docks and had come into the wind to drop anchor, they had ghosted past every frigate of the Windward Squadron. Richard had not seen HMS *Alarm* among them.

There was work to be done, and expeditiously, if they were to depart Barbados on schedule. William Cutler's agent in Bridgetown came aboard that very afternoon accompanied by the overseer of the Cutler plantation. John Cutler came aboard as well. He was a young man approaching twenty years of age, whose upright carriage and expressionless face conveyed little of the effervescence of his sister Lizzy or the inquisitiveness of his brother Robin. He was cordial enough to his cousins, but all business—"fussy" was Will's word—as he checked and rechecked the coopers' barrels and staves to be unloaded and stowed in warehouses at dockside. He found little humor in Will's antics and grimaced whenever his cousin whistled at a doxy ashore, a gesture as often as not returned with an expression suggesting a different kind of commerce.

"I suggest," John said in exasperated tones, following a day of constant interruptions and catcalls, "that you two go ashore and busy yourselves exploring the town. There is serious work to be done, and you seem more intent on what's happening there than here. I will join you when I am able."

Captain Winthrop and the Cutler agent approved on two conditions: Will and Richard must at all times remain within sight of *Eagle's* maintop, and they must take with them two able-bodied seamen.

These conditions readily accepted, Will and Richard, in the company of Tom Pickett and another able seaman named Zeke Morse, set out to explore the quays and byways along Front Street, the cobblestone thoroughfare of Bridgetown running from the western outskirts of the town along the curve of the bay to the fort and government buildings perched high on the eastern side of the harbor amid glades of palm trees and clusters of rich undergrowth. It proved an enlightening experience for two Bostonians constrained from birth by Puritan dogma.

Bridgetown was an exotic seaport rife with sudden danger and illicit pleasure, a hotbed of seduction that could turn a parson into a roué and where the unsuspecting could end the day devoid of coin and stricken with wretched ailments. Sailors of three continents swarmed along its streets, swaggering into any alehouse that caught their fancy, many of them half-seas over when they emerged, their arms draped around each other for mutual support. Street hawkers on corners or by open storefronts plied their wares as vociferously as veteran whores plied theirs, standing in seedy contrast to the carriages of aristocracy rattling along the cobblestones and bearing merchants and planters and wives decked out in the latest European fashions. They were in from the sugar plantations on official or family business, handkerchiefs held daintily to their noses to blot out the reek of rotting fish and human refuse rendered putrid by a baking tropical sun.

"Heavenly Father, would you look at that," Will exclaimed, watching as a British tar with a silly grin on his face handed over a pouch of coins to a dour-faced wench dressed in tight-fitting, far-too-revealing garb. Shuffling in front of them was a line of shackled Negro slaves being led to market. They kept their heads down, paying no mind to the different sort of transaction in human flesh taking place nearby. "Who in Your creation would want to rut with that beast?"

"For a month's pay," Zeke Morse commented.

"Barbados is not all like this," Tom Pickett remarked. "What you see here is the worst of it. Parts of Bridgetown are actually quite nice. See that low-lying building up there, by the fort? That's Government House. And if you fancy that area, you should see the plantations in the interior. As fine as anything we have in America."

"How many times have you been here?" asked Richard, envious of one so young who had covered so many sea miles in his father's employ.

"Three. I've never stayed long, though long enough on one occasion to visit your uncle's plantation. Pity you won't have that opportunity."

"Not on this trip," said Will. "Captain Winthrop insists we leave tomorrow. Richard, where are you going?"

"To speak to that fellow over there," Richard replied, pointing to a young British naval officer standing with his back to him across Front Street at the docks. "I'll be back in a moment."

The officer was observing a crew of five ordinary seamen applying a fresh coat of white paint along the gun-port strake of a sloop of war. He had his hands clasped behind him in Royal Navy quarterdeck fashion, and even from behind Richard could sense the finery of his attire: a full dress uniform in defiance of the noontime heat.

"Excuse me," Richard said in a friendly sort of way, as he came up beside him. "I am wondering if you can help me. Are you by chance acquainted with the frigate *Alarm*?"

"I am," replied the youth. He remained exactly as he was before, as though unaware that a question had been put to him.

"I'd appreciate any information you might have about that ship," Richard went on. He was standing squarely beside the officer and could not help admiring the single-breasted indigo jacket he wore, so clean and creaseless it looked as though it had just been perfected by one of London's finest tailors.

Gold buttons with a fouled anchor design flashed in the sun with his slightest movements.

"I am hoping to meet with a midshipman serving aboard her," he explained further, when the officer chose to ignore him. "His name is Hugh Hardcastle. Are you acquainted with him?"

"I am."

For the first time the officer deigned a glance at Richard, the thin cut of his lower aristocratic jaw half-hidden by the jacket's stand-up blue and white collar. "He's a close friend of mine, actually. What business might you have with him?"

Richard smiled encouragingly. "I've never met him, but I know his family. I have come from England and am sailing home tomorrow to Boston. I had hoped to see Hugh before leaving."

"*Alarm* has just put to sea, I'm afraid."

"I see . . . Is *Seahorse* your ship?" he asked, indicating the vessel in front of them.

"She is."

"If I were to write a note, and have it delivered to your attention, would you see that Hugh receives it?"

"I might." The officer removed his oversized, semicircular hat and wiped his brow with a kerchief. He replaced the hat just so on his head. "What, sir, is your name?"

"Richard Cutler." He offered his right hand.

The officer contemplated the proffered hand before shaking it lightly. "Horatio Nelson, midshipman, at your service. I have heard of you, Mr. Cutler."

"You have?" Richard was stunned. "From Hugh?"

"From Mr. Hardcastle, yes. Apparently you made quite the impression on his family." He said it as though not having a clue as to how such an impression could have been achieved. "At least that is my understanding from the letter he received before sailing."

"A letter? Who from?" Richard's heart was pumping fast.

Nelson narrowed his eyes in closer scrutiny. "I say," he remarked, in a voice conveying sincere concern. "That's a nasty bump you have there on your forehead. Are you quite all right?"

"Yes, thank you. Mr. Nelson. May I ask again please: who sent the letter to Mr. Hardcastle?"

"I believe it was from his sister, Katherine."

The joy of hearing her name was short-lived. Will and his two companions had crept up behind him and had listened in on the conversation. The moment Nelson mentioned Katherine's name, they pounced on him. Will tousled his hair, and Tom Pickett jostled him about. Zeke Morse formed wings with his arms and flapped them rapidly up and down while uttering a harsh screeching sound meant to emulate some sort of lovesick bird. Horatio Nelson gazed down at the goings-on, shaking his head in disgust. "Colonials," he sniffed, as he turned away to resume his walk down the length of the quay.

"What's with him?" asked Pickett, panting from exertion.

"Another Miss Molly in the service of the king," Will said, a remark that ignited howls of laughter from his mates.

"Prefers the windward passage, I'd wager!" cried Zeke, setting off another round. The three were laughing uproariously as they wheeled around to head back to their brig.

Richard hung back. "Thank you, Mr. Nelson," he called after the retreating midshipman. "I'll have the message delivered to you later this afternoon."

Nelson briefly raised his right arm in acknowledgment without interrupting his close inspection of the seamen's progress. He was offering some comment or criticism when Richard took his leave to catch up to his shipmates.

At dawn the next morning, *Eagle* was again at sea, in the Antilles Current that would take them northwest across the Caribbean to the Bahamas, onward to the east coast of Florida and the swiftly flowing Gulf Stream, the aorta in the great clockwise arteries of Atlantic Ocean currents that Postmaster Benjamin Franklin has first depicted on a chart a decade earlier. North of the Outer Banks they would exit the eastbound Gulf Stream and steer north by east for Nantucket Island, then north around the tip of Cape Cod and, finally, west by north into Hingham Bay. Barring the unforeseen, they would be home for Christmas.

3

North Atlantic

November 1777

VIEWED FROM A GULL'S wing, Rising Castle Island would appear like a stepping-stone plopped down in the brackish waters of the Piscataqua River meandering between the township of Portsmouth, New Hampshire, on its southern shore and the pine forests of the Eastern Province of Massachusetts to the north. Although unpretentious in size, the island had long served as a center of shipbuilding in America, the skills of her Yankee shipwrights as much in demand by the British Admiralty as the quality of the White Mountain timber so near and abundant. During the preceding two centuries, the Royal Navy had all but stripped England bare of her prized oak, the construction of one double-planked, three-hundred-ton-burthen line-of-battle ship requiring one hundred thirty tons of the hard wood to complete. With the ships' stores of America denied her by the outbreak of war, England was forced to look elsewhere for sources of supply to maintain her battle fleets.

John Paul Jones was convinced that ships' stores in Portsmouth were being denied him with as much determination.

Arriving aboard *Rebecca* from Hingham, he had immediately set about procuring provisions and guns from John Langdon, proprietor of the Rising Castle shipyard. Jones had taken a room at the home of widow Sarah Purcell, a relative of the powerful Wentworth family that had long ruled the colony in a succession of royal governorships. Mrs. Purcell had been quite accommodating to Jones, as had many Portsmouth society ladies. During the July Fourth celebration they had presented him with the new national flag for *Ranger's* ensign staff hastily sewn, they claimed, from the linen of their petticoats. Despite the Wentworth family's influence now being decidedly with the patriots, Captain Jones made little headway in preparing *Ranger* for her shakedown cruise. As one frustrating day blended into another, it became clear to him that Langdon's attentions were focused instead on *Raleigh,* one of thirteen new frigates authorized by the Second Continental Congress. Jones was forced to secure his own provisions, voyaging on one occasion to Boston to purchase, among other items, three silver bosun's whistles.

"What would you have me do?" he had raged at Langdon. "Yell at my crew, as in the merchant service? Damn you, sir, you do me an injustice. The Marine Committee shall hear of this!"

Langdon's curt reply, "I shall be pleased to inform them myself, Captain, the next time that I, as a member, meet with the committee," had thrown Jones into a fit of rage.

Circumstances had not improved much by the time his officers reported for duty. Since there was little for the junior officers to do aboard ship, and since *Ranger* was seriously short of manpower, Jones ordered his four midshipmen out to the seaside communities of New Hampshire and Massachusetts in search of additional crew. Richard Cutler and Agreen Crabtree scoured the coastal villages of Kittery and York to the north, while Charles Charrier and David Wentworth Wendell combed the Essex County ports of Ipswich, Salem, Gloucester, and Manchester. Dangling the lure of sea adventure and prize money before prospective recruits, along with a signing bonus of twenty dollars, the midshipmen returned to Portsmouth with barely enough Jacks to fill the ship's complement, after crossing out from the muster roll those opportunists who pocketed the bonus and ran.

With a ship's crew at the ready, Jones still had before him the challenge of outfitting *Ranger* as quickly as possible without alienating those few dockside workers and shipwrights assigned to the task. His mission was of critical importance and could not suffer further delays. Or so he assumed. In mid-October, as the few remaining splashes of autumn color were yielding to uniform gray, reports from the battlefields of New York tempered the immediacy of that mission. Post riders galloping breathlessly into town squares along the eastern seaboard carried the news that stunned every citizen and threw the patriots among them into paroxysms of joy.

The British had surrendered at Saratoga! Under the nominal command of Gen. Horatio Gates, and the more able leadership of Brig. Gen. Benedict Arnold and Col. Daniel Morgan, an American army had come to terms at last with a British army commanded by Gen. John Burgoyne, a peer of the realm of such exquisite pedigree that he had carried in his baggage train from Québec, along with munitions of war, his officers' wives and mistresses, silver cutlery and linen tablecloths, and the finest of French champagne. They had followed a torturous route, snaking south through the Canadian and northern New England woods from Montréal past Lake Champlain to the Hudson River, their objective being to join forces with Gen. William Howe's army advancing north from New York City. Together they would mop up any resistance they met along the way, seize the rebel strongholds at West Point and Fort Mifflin, and establish British authority at key outposts along the Hudson that would effectively cut off New England from the rest of the colonies. At the last minute, however, General Howe had decided to march south toward the social graces of Philadelphia, leaving General Burgoyne and his entourage to wage war alone against swarms of mosquitoes and black flies and the frontier-style tactics of rebel fighters. When the two armies finally met face to face at Saratoga, the body of the British army was so debilitated, it could fight for little beyond honor.

Such monumental news had to be communicated to Paris—and quickly. Since the outbreak of hostilities between England and her American colonies, France's role on the world stage had made for artful theater. Stung by the loss of valuable possessions overseas in an earlier conflict with England, and eager for restitution of these possessions, her ministers had become skilled in diplomatic subterfuge, covertly supplying the American rebels with *matériel de guerre* while expressing shock and dismay to diplomatic audiences in Europe over British accusations of collusion and violations of international law. As to the revolution itself, King Louis would not publicly applaud the Americans twisting the British lion's tail until he had reason to believe the Continentals could actually win the war, or at least prevent so lopsided a victory for the British that any nation allied with America would be earmarked for retribution.

The rebel victory at Saratoga had seemingly provided what the government of King Louis required. In a rare act of unity and purpose, the Marine

Committee of the Continental Congress designated two ships to carry an identical stack of dispatches addressed to Benjamin Franklin, head of the American delegation in Paris. *Penet,* a French ship, would sail from Annapolis; *Ranger,* an American sloop of war, would sail at the same time from Portsmouth.

The committee's decision finally drove John Langdon's shipwrights into action aboard *Ranger.* The effort, however, proved to be too little too late, as the best materials and supplies were already affixed aboard *Raleigh.* Jones seethed with anger over what he perceived as Langdon's insufferable behavior, and he bristled with impatience over a storm-brewed east wind that for days locked his ship to her moorings in the Piscataqua as surely as a jailer with keys.

On All Saints' Eve, a torrential rainfall followed by a shift in wind to the northwest summoned in cool, cleansing air from Canada. Early the next morning, *Ranger's* entire complement of one hundred forty men was on deck to make ready for departure. Ashore, a crowd of well-wishers was assembling to see them off as the crew attended to braces, halyards, tacks, and sheets.

"Anchor's hove short, Captain," Jones was informed by the sailing master, who had been informed by the bosun of the watch. "And the tide's slack."

"Very well, Mr. Callum. Take her to sea."

"Aye, aye, sir."

As the ship's master, Callum was the senior warrant officer aboard ship and, along with Captain Jones, her most experienced sailor. He had the look of repeating a well-rehearsed routine as he raised a speaking trumpet to his lips. "Hands aloft to make sail! Lay out and let loose! Sheet home and hoist topsails! Stand by the foresail halyards! Look lively there, you men!"

Shrieks from the bosun's whistles relayed the orders to the crew. Topmen scampered aloft on the standing rigging, up to the topsail spars and out on the footropes, removing the plaited cords that secured the furled sails to the yard. Once the two captains of the tops had confirmed gaskets away, Callum directed his considerable voice at the waisters and marines on the weather decks.

"Man the tops'l halyards and sheets! Stand by the weather braces! Lively, step lively, you lubbers!"

Another salvo of bosun's whistles was reinforced by curses, cuffs, or verbal threats to anyone reacting in a confused or leisurely manner. Above, topsails on both masts bellied out, caved in, then bellied out again from their raised yards. When sailors had halyards chock up and clews sheeted home, other sailors within the bowels of the ship heaved on seven-foot capstan bars, singing out in cadence to unify their strength as they marched around in a circle, their painstakingly slow progress in hauling up the anchor marked by the sound of pawls clanking slowly into grooves set in the rack at the capstan's base. With a set of topsail, the great iron weight finally released its grip on the riverbed. As the anchor emerged from the depths, sailors in the bows hooked it on to the anchor ring and slung a second tackle from the foretop onto the anchor's arm, lifting it sternward and lashing it to the cathead on the starboard side of the ship. Two decks below, waisters guided the wet, slimy cable coming in through the hawser hole down to its storage area in the cable-tier on the lowest deck on the ship. Five men stationed in that rancid hold coiled the thick hemp as best they could, to prevent snarling when the hook was eventually dropped again and the cable run out.

With her helm hard to starboard, *Ranger* veered to leeward on the slack of the tide and gained headway, paying off on a larboard tack down the Piscataqua toward the open sea. As she passed by Portsmouth proper, a small band of fifes and drums launched into a spirited tune. The crowd was considerable; excitement filled the air. Men waved hats in a frenzy of final farewells, and women shouted words of encouragement or endearment, the more sentimental among them weeping for the loss of loved ones real or imagined.

"Aloft there! Eyes forward!" Jones yelled up to the tops and crosstrees, at lookouts blithely watching the spectacle ashore, oblivious to the threat of a British cruiser prowling the waters ahead, off the entrance to Portsmouth harbor. None was spotted there or farther offshore by the Isles of Shoals, but the danger persisted until *Ranger* had twenty sea miles in her wake and was beyond the normal patrolling grounds of the North American Station. Only then did the tension on the quarterdeck ease.

"Clear decks and up spirits, starboard watch first," Jones said to Thomas Simpson, who repeated the order to Joshua Loring, third lieutenant and officer of the watch. Loring repeated the order to a bosun's mate who set off a shrill of whistles that informed the starboard watch it was free to go below to dinner and a splash of rum.

"The officers shall confer in my cabin," said Jones to Simpson. "Mr. Callum, I request your presence as well. The quartermaster has the conn."

"Aye, Captain," Callum replied. After carefully noting the approximate wind speed and direction, together with the time and the ship's bearing on a gray slate attached to the side of the binnacle, he descended a short ladder leading from the quarterdeck to the weather deck. From there he took his turn on a longer ladder leading down to the semi-enclosed gun deck, where a green-coated marine sentry stood guard outside the captain's cabin.

That cabin may have been a modest affair compared to what might be found aboard a Royal Navy vessel, but it was large enough to accommodate the nine men present. Extending athwartship from starboard to larboard quarter, it was essentially one large space with a cubby sternward on the larboard side where the captain slept on a low wooden bunk suspended from the deckhead by ropes. Forward of the cubby, a small desk with inkwell and quill was positioned to catch the light coming in through the glass of the quarter gallery. A few feet forward of the desk, a black gun of twenty-six hundred weight rested on a freshly painted red truck, its muzzle drawn up tight against the bulwark and lashed to two eyebolts above the closed gun port. A second gun similarly secured for heavy weather lay directly across on the starboard side. Toward the back of the cabin, abaft the mizzenmast piercing through from the quarterdeck above, stood a long wooden table and eight heavyset chairs. A settee running along in front of the stern windows provided a degree of domesticity to the cabin, its bright forest green padding of some comfort to the four young men seated upon it. Sunlight streaming in from a deadlight cut into the quarterdeck directly above the table danced around the cabin with the motion of the ship.

"Well, gentlemen," Jones said, when everyone was settled in, "we are underway at last. We have come to know each other by now, but as this is our first time at sea together, I am curious to know your first impressions of our ship . . . Mr. Simpson? May I ask you to lead off, sir."

Thomas Simpson, a long-legged, jut-jawed man with a flinty New England disposition, shrugged his broad shoulders. A decade older than Jones and six inches taller, in dress and demeanor he bore himself like one accustomed to the rigors of life at sea, though the smooth, pale skin on his face and hands suggested a career less exposed to the elements. As first lieutenant, he was responsible for the day-to-day running of the ship and the dispositions of crews. He also selected the petty officers and assumed command of the vessel should the captain step ashore or be incapacitated.

"It's too soon to tell for certain," he said, "but she seems fit enough to me. Her sails aren't what we'd prefer, certainly. How unfortunate Mr. Langdon was unable to come by a new set before we sailed, though Lord knows he tried his best. We shall attend to that once we are in France, I assume?"

He was referring to the inferior hemp-and-jute blend of *Ranger's* plain sails, all that was available, according to John Langdon, on such short notice after the victory at Saratoga. It was material more often used for bagging.

"That is my intention, Mr. Simpson. Mr. Hall? What is your opinion?"

Elijah Hall nodded his head approvingly. As second lieutenant he was the senior duty officer, next in line to assume command, and senior officer on the gun deck.

"I agree with Mr. Simpson, sir. Like he said, *Ranger* appears sound enough. She has a clean run. Secure proper canvas on her, and we could play cat and mouse with any vessel our size."

"An excellent metaphor, Mr. Hall, assuming we have prepared ourselves to play the part of the cat and not the mouse." After some polite laughter, he asked, to the room at large, "Is there anything else?"

"Aye, there is," commented David Callum. He personified both seamanship and authority as he sat resting his elbow on the table, gently stroking his grayish-white beard. "Her ballast is off, Captain. And she's too heavy in the bows. Move twenty-five, maybe thirty pigs aft from the forepeak to midships and she'd sail better."

"I agree. Make it so, Mr. Simpson . . . Other observations? You midshipmen there: have you anything to add?"

He glared at the four midshipmen lined up on the settee. David Wendell, at twelve years of age the youngest and most recent aboard ship, recoiled from the thrust of the question. He squirmed in retreat, wiggling backward until he was leaning against the stern glass. Being in so sacred a space as the captain's cabin was humbling enough; being directly addressed by the captain left him staring wide-eyed and mute.

"Sir," said Richard Cutler, "I agree with Mr. Callum that *Ranger's* bows are heavy and that moving lead aft will help balance her. But with respect, I believe the problem is more with her spars. They seem too big for a ship this size. And I believe her main and fore masts are stepped too far forward. I agree with Mr. Hall, her hull does have a clean run, but she's overburdened aloft. The way she's rigged is pushing her stem down, slowing her."

Jones nodded his approval. "Thank you, Mr. Cutler. You have stated my own observations, exactly."

Jones allowed his gaze to relax a moment on Richard Cutler, who noticed instead the look of astonishment mixed with disapproval contorting the face of Thomas Simpson. Jones turned back to his more senior officers.

"Gentlemen, let us review our orders. We are bound for France to deliver a dispatch of utmost importance to our commissioners in Paris. Nothing must interfere with our purpose or delay us unnecessarily. Therefore we shall not be taking prizes on this leg of the cruise. *But,*" he said in louder tones, above a burst of grumbling at the table, "delivering dispatches has never been our primary mission. Once *Ranger* has the repairs she requires, we shall take her across the Channel into English waters. This I have already told you. What I have not told you is what I intend to do once we get there."

He unrolled a chart on the table and continued talking as he placed weights on the four corners to hold them down. "While I am in Paris, you officers will see to the repairs. Mr. Simpson, you will be in charge. Before I leave, I will make arrangements for payment to be made to the Nantes shipyard which, I am told, is one of the finest in France. Which is saying something. The French make damn fine ships. When I return, I expect to find *Ranger* ready for sea.

"We shall then sail from Nantes for England, to this area here." He indicated a general area north of Wales, between Britain and Ireland. "I know these waters. I was born and raised there, in Arbigland. I can think of no better place to carry out our orders."

"Which are to hamper enemy shipping and capture prizes?" queried the second lieutenant hopefully.

"No, Mr. Hall. That is not what we are about, though prizes may come our way as a result of what we do." Jones placed his hands flat on the chart and leaned forward, a thin smile on his lips and a gleam of fire in his eyes. "Gentlemen, hear me out. What I intend to do, no man has done since William the Conqueror. I intend to attack England herself, where she is most vulnerable. Here." His finger stabbed at a wide-mouthed firth cutting deep into the land, a strip of water that marked the border between England and Scotland. "Whitehaven is a large shipping port in the Irish Sea. I can assure you, there will be boats aplenty lying at anchor in the harbor. Merchantmen mostly, some fishermen perhaps. The havoc we wreak there will turn our enemy on his ear."

Thomas Simpson laughed out loud. "A one-ship invasion force?" he scoffed. "Surely, Captain, you jest."

Jones gave Simpson a look that no one in that cabin would soon forget.

"I do not jest, Mr. Simpson. I . . . do . . . not . . . jest. My orders from Congress are to proceed in the manner I deem most appropriate for destroying the enemies of the United States, *by sea or otherwise*. I intend to comply with those orders."

"If I may, sir," said the captain of marines. The shock in his voice betrayed the steady outward appearance of the professional soldier. "What do we attack with? I have but thirty marines under my command. And your sailors, if I may, are not trained for a mission of this sort. It seems a plan of extremely high risk unless we are able to strike and run, with the element of surprise entirely on our side."

"Quite so, Mr. Wallingford."

There was no one in that cabin Jones respected more than Lt. Samuel Wallingford. Tall, broad-shouldered, and dignified in his green dress coat, he was every man's image of a seasoned military officer. More than once Jones had wondered what act of God had brought this stylish and competent officer to his quarterdeck.

"I assure you, sir," Jones went on, "that we shall have ample time to review our campaign to the last detail, and that I shall not proceed with any plan before seeking your counsel. As to the risks, I remind you that we are at war. War necessitates taking risks, even when those risks seem insurmountable. Given what I am convinced will be the result of our efforts, I believe the risks are worth taking.

"As to our present cruise, *Ranger* is a naval vessel, and as such, we must demand naval discipline of ourselves and our crew. Beginning today at three bells in the afternoon watch, and every day to follow with the exception of Sundays, we will clear for action and drill with guns, small arms, swords, and pikes. We have powder enough but limited round shot. For that reason we must delay live drills with the guns until their crews have mastered the basics. In addition, I want those crews at their stations every morning at dawn, prepared to fire. The odds are small, I grant you, but the cloak of night, once lifted, could reveal our enemy close by.

"That is not all," he said, his voice rising with pique aimed at his first and second lieutenants who were staring at each other and not at him. "Each day at four bells in the forenoon watch, we will conduct a different sort of drill. Let's see how long it takes to send the topsail yard down to a gantline and haul it back up with the capstan. In a storm, gentlemen, we won't have time to consider what should be done. We must react to what *must* be done, which is to get those spars off her as rapidly as possible. The same holds true in battle. Should we lose a mast or piece of rigging, or be holed by the enemy, every man on this ship must know what to do *at that moment.* Improper training breeds doubt, and I needn't tell you gentlemen that hesitation in battle could mean the loss of our ship and our lives.

"You have your orders," he said, concluding the meeting in more normal tones. "They are not open to discussion. Unless you have specific questions of me, you are excused to your duties until three bells."

Officers scraped back their chairs and began filing out of the cabin in order of rank, the four midshipmen last.

"Mr. Cutler, a word, if you please," said Jones unexpectedly. Richard stood at attention in front of the settee until the others had gone and they were alone.

"I shan't keep you long," Jones said, sitting down by the table and beckoning Richard over. "I haven't had much opportunity to speak to you privately since you arrived in Portsmouth. All is well, I trust?"

"Yes, Captain, thank you."

"You're finding your way about the ship?"

"I am, sir. Mr. Hall is right. She's a fine ship. With a few repairs, she'll make us all proud."

"It seems that's the one point we can all agree on," Jones said wearily. He rubbed his eyes with his fingers. "Changing the subject, I note with interest your friendship with Mr. Crabtree. I understand why. He may be a bit odd in his ways, but in my opinion he has the makings of a fine naval officer. It's why I selected him. He is well regarded in Portsmouth shipping circles. . . . As for you, Mr. Cutler, I must say, you have established a rapport with the crew that in my experience is really quite remarkable. Chain of command involves respect going down as well as up. It's a difficult concept for many officers to grasp. You seem to have mastered it rather quickly."

"Perhaps, Captain, that's because I have served before the mast in my father's ships. I have lived their life and know how demanding such a life can be."

"Worse even than that of a midshipmen?" smiled Jones.

"Hardly that bad, sir," Richard replied, returning the smile.

"Yes, well, whatever it is, the men do what you ask and they appear to do it willingly. That, I assure you, is a rarity at sea."

There was a knock on the door. Jacob Walden, surgeon's mate doubling as captain's steward, entered the cabin holding a tray.

"Yer dinner, Captain. Would ye be havin' it now?"

"Leave it on the table, Walden," Jones replied, adding, when the door was shut, without so much as a glance at what was in store for him, "I'd wish my steward's talents on Admiral Howe himself. That would end this war soon enough. Black Dick would choke just looking at what my steward sets before me." He heaved a heartfelt sigh of regret before changing the subject again.

"What do you make of my plan to use *Ranger* as a one-ship invasion force, as Mr. Simpson describes it?"

"It's bold, Captain," replied Richard, having given the matter some thought during the previous few minutes.

"Bold?"

"Yes sir. It's bold because it doesn't rely on success. American marines landing on British soil will have its effect, no matter the outcome."

Jones banged his fist on the table. "Thank you, Mr. Cutler. I see my confidence in you is not misplaced. Have no doubts: you shall land with the marines at Whitehaven. I promised you revenge, and by God you shall have it."

Richard nodded, his steadfast gaze communicating the gratitude he felt.

"Now I must ask another question of you," Jones said, holding that gaze. "A rather delicate one, I realize. What are the men saying about me? I am asking you because a midshipman is the captain's link to the fo'c'sle and because I trust your judgment. You may speak frankly. I need to hear the truth."

Richard hesitated. It was indeed a delicate question given the vast difference in rank and experience between them. As he often did when faced with a dilemma of this sort, he resorted to giving what was requested: the truth.

"Yankee seamen are not accustomed to naval discipline," he said. "Therefore they don't always take kindly to it."

"That, or any other sort of discipline," Jones scoffed. "We're not in a bloody town meeting aboard this ship, though that's what my senior officers seem to think. . . . Sorry," he said, remembering himself. "That was uncalled for. Please advise me, Mr. Cutler: given the crew's lack of naval discipline, how do I best deal with them? They're your people, not mine, and their perspectives are quite outside my experience. Remember, you have my permission to speak frankly."

Again Richard weighed the question carefully before answering.

"When circumstances permit, Captain, I would advise you to act more like a Yankee sea captain and less like a Royal Navy officer."

"Yes? And what exactly does that mean?"

"A Yankee captain is viewed by his mates and crew as a first among equals. He has earned his position, and he must continue to earn it. Therefore he would not isolate himself in his cabin or on the quarterdeck. If invited, he would dine with his officers in the wardroom, and he would be visible to the crew on deck. He would also invite his officers to his cabin, not as a group, perhaps two at a time. That way, he would come to know them as individuals and they would come to know him as their captain."

"Sea captains throughout history have isolated themselves. It's a requirement of the service."

"In the Royal Navy, yes, Captain. But here in the Continental Navy we have no history or traditions of our own. These men are silversmiths and shopkeepers, untested in battle, and they do not know you. And begging your pardon, sir, Yankees are not prone to like Scots. You have not lived long in America, and perhaps they are wondering why you're fighting on our side. I believe it's possible for you to gain their confidence and trust without losing their respect. But it will take time."

Jones gave that perspective some thought. "Good advice, Mr. Cutler. Difficult advice for me to follow, I daresay, but good advice nonetheless. And I thank you for being so open. Not many junior officers would have spoken to their captain the way you just did." He cleared his throat, an act that simultaneously cleared the thoughtful expression from his face. "One final item. As soon as we anchor in Nantes, and I have seen to *Ranger*'s repairs, I shall be leaving for Paris. On my journey I shall require the assistance of an aide-de-camp. I have selected you, Mr. Cutler. You will accompany me and Mr. Wallingford. I have informed Lieutenant Simpson of my decision. That is all."

"Aye, aye, Captain."

Richard gathered up his cocked hat and overcoat from the table. He saluted Jones and walked through the door of the cabin, past the marine sentry, out onto the sun-washed gun deck where he noted Joshua Loring amidships examining one of the sixteen guns. He touched his hat to the youthful officer, grateful he was on board. Normally a ship the size of *Ranger* would not require a third lieutenant, but in the Continental Navy there were more officer candidates than there were slots to fill. Loring came from a good Salem family and was, to Richard's mind, a thoroughly decent individual and competent sailor. Jones agreed with that assessment and had, on his own authority, signed him on.

Blowing on his hands and rubbing them for warmth, Richard made his way through a hatchway and down a ladder to the main deck. Toward the stern, from the wardroom located directly beneath the captain's cabin, he could hear the muffled voices of commissioned officers and those warrant officers of wardroom rank discussing something. They were speaking softly, but it would have been difficult under any circumstances to overhear their conversation since the canvas bulkheads of the modest officers' cabins served as an effective buffer zone between them and those of lower rank housed forward.

Bending over in the confined space and giving his eyes a moment to adjust to the dim light of whale-oil lamps, Richard walked forward to where the four midshipmen shared space with the lesser warrant officers: the purser, gunner, carpenter, and bosuns. Immediately forward of that was where the marines were quartered, strategically positioned, as in all warships, between the officers in the stern and ordinary seamen in the bows.

"Ahoy there," Agreen Crabtree called out when he saw Richard squeezing his tall frame into the cramped, dank space of the midshipmen's mess. He was sitting on his sea chest by a low table, a plate of food scraps before him, studiously rubbing a bow of yew with a ragged cloth steeped in a foul-smelling substance. Despite the lanterns on the deckhead and the cloudless conditions two decks above him, to do his work he had set two candles waxed onto squares of tin in front of him on the table.

"Ahoy, Agreen," Richard greeted him back. He slumped onto a sea chest and scanned the table for anything that seemed remotely edible. "Where is everybody? Finished already?"

"What's there t' finish?" Crabtree asked, spreading out his hands as a barrister would to a jury. "A musical score makes for nasty eatin'." He grinned at Richard's puzzled look. "Our cook's a composer o' fine music, didn't you know, matey? For our eatin' pleasure this noon, he's served us up his last movement."

Richard chuckled along with his friend. Besides Will, Agreen Crabtree was the one person in Richard's life who could so easily make him laugh. He gazed fondly at the young midshipman whose boyish good looks and towheaded bowl of hair and freckled cheeks and nose had no doubt melted many a pretty girl's heart. Agreen returned his gaze with a sheepish look.

"If you've a mind, Richard," he said, "I'd be much obliged if you'd do me a favor."

"Ask it."

"Call me A.G. Spelled A-g-e-e. It's what my pa called me as a lad. He made it up from the first two letters of my name. All my friends call me that now."

Richard's broad smile concealed a warm rush of sentiment. "Thank you, Agee," he replied. "I'm proud you include me among those friends." He allowed the bond between them to strengthen for a moment, then said, in a more lighthearted tone: "Just what is that god-awful stench you're rubbing on your bow?"

"Slush from the cook's pot. Figure if it's good for the riggin', it's good for the bow." He was referring to a common practice in the galley. The cook would skim off a buildup of scum from the galley pot where salted meat was simmering and set it aside in a kid kept near the stove for that purpose. When the container was full, sailors hauled the stinking brine aloft and rubbed it over the running rigging to preserve its hemp fibers and to prevent abrasion when lines passed through the blocks.

Richard picked up the unstrung bow. It was a simple piece of smooth, curved yew four feet in length with a notch on each end to clinch on a bowstring. A handle fashioned from a spare bowstring wrapped tightly and thickly around its middle served as a brace for the hand and a support for the arrow.

"What Indian squaw taught you how to use that thing?"

Crabtree chuckled. "Well, now, I'm not exactly sure what 'thing' you're referrin' to, but I'll assume it's the bow. It's true I learned it from Indian friends of mine in Maine—or the Eastern Province as you high-brows from Boston prefer t' call it."

"I've never used a bow. How accurate is it?"

"Accurate? Well, it's a mite better'n that half-cocked pistol of yours. And for every shot you get off, I get off three, maybe four. And an arrow is . . . *quiet.*" He lowered his voice to a mysterious hush with that last word and thrust his head close to Richard's. "Who might the arrow strike next? A mutineer? A sodomite? A first lieutenant on the quarterdeck?"

"Have a care, Agee," Richard cautioned, instinctively peering back over his shoulder.

"Aye t' that," in a normal tone of voice. "So what did the good captain have t' say?"

"It seems I am to accompany him to Paris."

"Are you now? Well blow me down an' stomp on my face. Ain't *that* a trick!" Agreen's voice was laced with humorous sarcasm. "Just think, Richard. There I'll be in Nantes, sittin' around pluckin' my bow so to speak, and there you'll be in Paris, with *les jeunes filles* of the French court, with any lick of luck doin' exactly what my mother warned me not t' be doin.' What justice is there in that?"

"It's official business, Agee," Richard said, in an official sort of tone that belied the excitement he felt. "We're to deliver the dispatches to Dr. Franklin, that's all. Captain Jones picked me because I speak French. We won't be gone long, I shouldn't think."

"Aye, but long enough," said Crabtree with a wink, adding, "Seriously, Richard, I have joy for you in this. Captain Jones has picked the right man. I will miss your company, though. I want you t' know that."

From the hatchway above, the junior duty officer announced to the main deck below that the hourglass had turned at two bells on the afternoon watch. It was time for officers to man their stations on the quarterdeck or gun deck. Crabtree picked up a mug holding the last of his ration of rum. "To King George the Turd," he said, before downing the contents. Together the two midshipmen hurried to the ladder leading topsides.

There they were met by Lieutenant Simpson, emerging from the wardroom.

"A word, Mr. Cutler, if you please," he said, mimicking the words and, to some extent, the accent used by Captain Jones at the conclusion of the meeting in his cabin.

"This does not concern you, Mr. Crabtree," he told Agreen, jerking his head toward the ladder when the young midshipman held his ground. Reluctantly, Agreen stepped up the ladder to the gun deck, leaving them alone on the main deck.

Simpson studied Richard with narrowed eyes, his left wrist supporting his right elbow as he repeatedly tapped a finger on his chin. All Richard could do was stand at attention with eyes forward. From the deck above, they could hear the voices of petty officers ordering men to stations.

"I am watching you, Cutler," Simpson said, his tone menacing.

Richard's eyes met his.

"Sir?"

"Don't play the innocent with me, boy. You may get away with that kind of nonsense with the captain, but you shall not get away with it with me."

Richard remained at rigid attention.

"I know all about your pretty-boy ways," Simpson went on in the same menacing tone. "I've experienced your kind of shit in my life. You think you're better than the rest of us, don't you? You think that because you have an in with the captain, you can bypass Mr. Hall and me, quick as you please, and cozy up to him behind our backs. Well, Mr. Cutler, I am here to tell you, you cannot. And if you continue doing it, I promise you, I shall make your petty little life even more miserable. I have that power, and by God I shall use it. I'll make you wish you had never signed on with this ship. I'll make you wish you had never left your mother's skirts. Do I make myself clear?"

"You do, sir."

"Anything to say in response?"

Richard felt his right hand inadvertently clench into a fist.

"No sir."

"That is wise of you, Mr. Cutler. Very wise indeed. Now attend to your duties. And remember, I am watching you."

At precisely the third strike of the ship's bell, a young marine drummer on the weather deck launched into a staccato tattoo. Immediately the drumbeat was taken up by a second drummer on the gun deck. "Beat to quarters! Clear for action!" cried Lieutenant Simpson through a speaking trumpet. He was standing at the rail of the quarterdeck, in front of David Callum at the helm. Captain Jones stood on the weather side of the helm, holding his waistcoat watch before him in his right hand. On either side of him stood the two younger midshipmen, David Wentworth and Charles Charrier, ready at their captain's command to deliver a message from the quarterdeck to any part of the ship.

The second and third lieutenants were on the gun deck, Elijah Hall having overall command of the larboard side, Joshua Loring the starboard. The other two midshipmen and two quarter-gunners had command of individual gun crews. Gunner Seth Bingham, a petty officer with Royal Navy experience, supervised the dispersal of round shot and powder stored in the bowels of the ship and lugged up from the magazine by young lads signed on to the crew as powder monkeys. Agreen Crabtree and Richard Cutler were stationed amidships, each in command of four cannon, two on each side of the ship.

Theirs were designated number-two and number-three batteries, respectively. One quarter-gunner, Jim Sitterson, supervised the four forwardmost cannon, number-one battery, and the other, Jonah Roy, the six sternmost cannon, number-four battery.

A crew of five men served each gun. Before they could do that, however, the ship needed to be cleared for action. Galley fires had to be extinguished; pumps made ready; sand strewn around the gun deck; and fire buckets filled with water as topmen scampered aloft to reduce canvas to fighting sail—jib, topsails, and spanker—to permit better vision and to reduce the risk of a sail catching fire from a stray ember floating up from the guns. Waisters on the weather decks let fly the halyards and sheets of the topgallants and royals, while others stationed below unshipped the light partitions of the officers' cabins, including those at the entrance to the captain's cabin, and stowed them in the sternmost hold along with any other movable objects, such as sea chests, chairs, and wall paintings. In a duel between ships at sea, a sailor was more likely to be struck down by a flying splinter of wood than by a flying shard of metal.

It was a seriously flawed process. During these initial drills, no amount of verbal threats by the commissioned officers or painful cuffs from the petty officers succeeded in whipping the crew into shape. Confusion reigned amok.

"We're fish in a barrel," David Callum lamented as he observed a nine-pound ball being dropped on a sailor's foot, an accident that sent him howling below to the surgeon. "God help us if we come up against a Royal Navy vessel anytime soon."

Captain Jones walked to the railing and whispered something in Simpson's ear.

"Ship's crew to the guns!" Simpson shouted. A high-pitched screech of bosun's whistles and a sharp roll of drums instantly reinforced the order.

It was pantomime, but serious enough. *Ranger's* crew sprang to battle stations on the gun deck as the four battery captains took charge of the crews assigned them. Although they had never fired live guns, the lieutenants knew well enough what was required. They had been drilled in a hard school in Portsmouth presided over by Captain Jones himself.

"Level your guns!"

The lieutenants' first order to the battery captains was repeated to the gun crews, who freed the guns from their lashings and hauled them inboard by their tackle. As deftly as they were able, they removed a round wooden tampion from the muzzle of each gun and shoved a four-pound flannel cartridge of black powder inside, ramming it home with a wad of rope yarn to keep the cartridge in position within the barrel.

"Shot your guns!"

The next order quickly set up a short chain gang of three men. The first man selected a nine-pound ball of cast iron from a long, rectangular box set amidships and held it up for the battery captain to quickly inspect for nicks or indents that might cause erratic flight. He then handed it off to a second man standing by the gun, who relayed it on to the sponger positioned at the muzzle. The sponger rolled it down the barrel and rammed it down tight.

"Run out your guns!"

Men clapped onto side tackle and heaved the gun outboard until its carriage hit the bulwark with a loud thud and the black muzzle stuck out through the gun port.

Other steps were involved before the cannon could actually be fired, but that last command marked the limit of the sequence for today's drill. Today's exercise, however, was far from over. In fact, it had just begun. Each step was repeated again and again and again and again, in the exact sequence as before, once the ball and powder had been removed from the guns at the end of each sequence and the guns were lashed anew to the bulwarks. It was not until the middle of the first dogwatch, with men bent over and panting from their exertions, that Jones mercifully called a halt to the drills.

"Summon the crew aft, Mr. Simpson," Jones said. His voice was somber, and the joyless wail of the silver whistles seemed to reflect his mood as *Ranger*'s crew shuffled aft toward the foot of the quarterdeck. The topmen among them formed three separate divisions, one for each mast, and the gun crews arranged themselves behind their captains. Powder monkeys came forward as a group and knelt in the shadow of the quarterdeck, the round black faces of Cato and Scipio Africanus peering up reverentially at the railing and the austere figure of Captain Jones, the brother of their former slave owner. Once the two young Negroes had signed their X in the muster book in Portsmouth, they were enthusiastically adopted by the ship's crew, Cato's antics and the perpetual grin on Scipio's face forever brightening the mood in the fo'c'sle. Jones had been reluctant to allow them aboard, at the tender age of ten, but they had pleaded on their knees to join him aboard *Ranger* after his brother William Paul had died without issue and bequeathed his Virginia property to Jones.

Whistling ceased abruptly. From the quarterdeck, Captain Jones drew his arms from beneath his cloak and gripped the railing, staring down intently at the bedraggled faces of the men and boys staring up at him, the dirt and grime on their duck shirts and wide-bottomed trousers a testament to their efforts if not their results.

"Men," he said in a deep, commanding voice, "we have serious work ahead of us. For most of you, this was your first drill at sea. I understand that. And I understand that accommodations must be made for crews in training aboard a ship denied the opportunity for a shakedown cruise. But mark well, each and every one of you: we have precious little time to spend learning basics. At any moment we could find ourselves in the sights of a Royal Navy frigate. I ask you today, on this quarterdeck, what chance would *Ranger* have in a fight with such a vessel?"

He let the answer linger in the air as he consulted his watch.

"This afternoon it took us twenty-two minutes to clear for action. Twenty-two minutes may not seem like much, but it is seventeen minutes longer than a well-trained British crew requires. And lads, *all* British crews are well trained. We are not. Not yet, at least. In seventeen minutes a British frigate could fire ten broadsides into us. Ten broadsides, lads, think on it. Ten broadsides means a ton of iron fired by our enemy before we could answer, assuming we had a gun left to answer with. Does anyone among you have trouble understanding my calculations? Or their significance?"

The crew's silence suggested they did not.

"Therefore," Jones concluded, "starting tomorrow, here is the rule we shall follow: what is acceptable one day shall not be acceptable the next. What this means is simple: every day we must show improvement. Until we have this ship cleared for action within seven minutes of the drums, we shall drill and we shall drill and we shall drill—until you're so sick of it you can't stand another round, and then we'll drill some more. Starting tomorrow, and every day after that with the exception of Sundays, rum rations will be issued at supper, not at noon. Each day we improve our timing by a minimum of one minute compared to the previous day, an extra tot of rum will be issued to the entire crew. Do we show improvement by less than one minute, but improvement nonetheless, you will receive your normal ration. Do we show no improvement at all, compared to the previous day, there will be no rum issued that day to any of the ship's complement, including her officers."

"Captain, that is hardly fair," Tom Simpson interrupted. He was standing directly to Jones's right, his right arm outstretched as if in supplication to the crew below. "I respectfully and most earnestly protest that decision. These are good men under your command, and they have sacrificed much to serve on this ship. They are trying their best, and they are as much a patriot as you or I or anyone else. Under no circumstances should their rum ration be cut off—a ration, need I remind you, that is already in jeopardy because you failed to load on enough barrels in Portsmouth. It is their one diversion from drudgery. You must not deny it to them."

Positioned as he was in front of his gun crew, Richard could clearly observe the color darkening on Jones's face. Around him, murmurs of agreement rumbled across the weather deck. "Steady, men, steady," he said, his voice low and meant for those in his division. "Let the captain respond."

It took a while for that response to come. When it did, it was delivered to the crew, not to the first lieutenant, in a voice that was ominously measured. "Mr. Simpson," he hissed, "I do not question the resolve of these men, nor their motives in joining this ship. I question only their ability to survive in a fight with the enemy. My duty, as their captain, is to do everything within my power to ensure they *do* survive, in a battle only a fool would believe is not just over the horizon. By God, sir, I *will* do my duty! Company is dismissed."

"Ship's company! Dismissed!" shouted the bosun of the watch. His mates began moving among the divisions, directing sailors aloft to their stations or below to supper.

On the quarterdeck, Captain Jones turned to his lieutenants. "Conference in my cabin, five minutes, all officers."

As the officers entered the stern cabin, they found their captain standing with his back to them by the stern windows, seemingly basking in the warmth of a setting sun filtering in through the quarter-windows. One stern window was hinged open, despite the cool November air outside, and through the opening Richard could see *Ranger's* wake shooting out like a giant white arrow, marking her eastbound destiny.

When the door clicked shut with everyone inside, Jones turned slowly around to face his audience. For what seemed an eternity, he stood there glowering at them, with his arms folded tightly across his chest. When he spoke, his voice held the fury of a father berating a rebellious child.

"I will say this one time to you gentlemen, and one time only. If ever any of you does what Mr. Simpson just did on the quarterdeck, I shall have you taken below and clapped in irons, your rank be damned. That is all."

As Captain Jones had promised, a daily shipboard routine was quickly established. Up at 4:00 a.m., all hands struggled awake by the guns or at stations to trim sail as lookouts on deck climbed aloft once it was light enough to see two hundred yards around the ship. Once a clear horizon was confirmed, one watch went below for a snatch of sleep while the duty watch wetted down the weather decks and sprinkled sand on them, scrubbing the oak planks with holystones until they gleamed. With the cry "All hands up hammocks!" at 7:30, the entire crew came topsides to stow their bedding in netting racks secured fast to the gunwale at the top of the bulwarks. At 8:00 the hands were piped to breakfast. At 8:30 the lower decks were holystoned and scrubbed and sprayed clean by pumps, sending loose residue out to the scuppers, and from there into the sea. Sail drills consumed the balance of the morning watch and continued until the noon sun sighting and the official start of another naval day. Dinner hour afforded a limited opportunity for men to relax or attend to personal needs. At 1:30 they were back at it, sweating over the gun drills until supper and the much-anticipated rum ration at 5:00—a ration which, to the captain's satisfaction, was so far earned every day but one, and that had been after twenty-four hours of heavy weather. Under the circumstances, he had ordered the rum served anyway, to the relief and cheers of the crew.

After supper, depending on the weather, entertainment was provided in or on the fo'c'sle by a shipmate gifted with the fiddle or hornpipe while duty officers on deck supervised the reduction of canvas aloft for nighttime sailing and the proper placement of six lookouts, two each in the bows, midships, and stern. At 8:00 the hammocks topside were taken below and slung, and all unnecessary lights extinguished. Those sailors off duty settled in for a four-hour sleep, until the start of the second watch at midnight, their hammocks swaying in rhythm with a mate's hammock slung sixteen inches away on either side.

Sunday provided the one breather in the weekly grind. Men were at their stations at dawn and throughout the day as needed to sail the ship, but otherwise time was theirs to fill or waste.

On the third Sunday in November, the wind blew chilly from the northwest, covering the sky with low-lying leaden clouds. Because *Ranger* was making good time and was now but a few days shy of Brittany, Captain Jones kept a full set of plain sail on her, ever mindful of the strain even so moderate a wind placed on her sails of patchworked jute. Her four midshipmen were on the quarterdeck, in a row with Samuel Wallingford and Joshua Loring and facing seaward on the starboard side. On the weather deck, the ship's purser held thirty dollars in a pouch, a pool of money wagered among the officers on who could most directly hit a target about to be thrown outboard from the ship's waist by Bosun Sam Crocker. Thirty dollars was an amount sufficiently high to draw the attention of sailors gathered on the weather deck and in the rigging, many of whom placed bets of their own, carefully recorded by the purser, on who would take the prize.

Sword and small arms drill was part of the daily routine on the quarterdeck. Each officer had improved his performance with the pistol, some more than others, but this was the first time the crew would see Agreen's bow in action. Joshua Loring had objected to its use, but Jones had allowed it, arguing that when the rules of the contest were agreed to, no one had specified by what projectile the target must be struck.

At a signal from Jones, each man bit off the tip of a paper cartridge and poured a measure of fine black powder into the muzzle of his gun. A ball and wad followed, firmly tamped down the twelve-inch barrel with a ramrod attached to the underside of the pistol, the entire process a replication in miniature of preparing a cannon to fire.

As his fellow officers primed their pistols, Agreen Crabtree stepped back with bow in hand toward the mizzenmast. Tying one end of a string to a nock in the lower end of the bow, he braced that end with his foot until the bow was bent sufficiently to tie the upper end of the string to its nock. He flicked a fingernail against the string, testing for tension. Satisfied, he stepped back into line and drew an arrow from a rawhide quiver slung across his back. He awaited his turn by smoothing down the three white feathers on the end of the shaft.

Jones pointed at Crocker, and the bosun heaved out a small keg forward of the ship. Attached to the barrel was a light line fastened to the ship's stern, the rules stipulating that the officers must fire in rapid succession, one after another, as the keg floated by the lee side of the quarterdeck. The contest would last less than a minute and would end when the forward motion of the ship snapped the line taut.

The keg was abeam of the mainmast when Charles Charrier, first in line, raised his pistol. He pulled back the hammer to full cock, took aim, and squeezed the trigger. The hammer slashed forward and down, the flint clenched in its jaws igniting a flame in the frizzen that carried through the touchhole and set off the powder charge in the barrel. His aim was wide, the recoil of the pistol kicking him back two steps.

David Wentworth, next in line, grasped the butt of his pistol with both hands, took aim, turned his face to the side, and squeezed the trigger. The pistol roared; a plume of water shot up five feet to the right of the keg.

Joshua Loring's aim was better but still off the mark.

Samuel Wallingford stepped to the bulwark. He looked dignified in a knee-length blue watchcoat and tricornered felt hat, the red-on-white cockade pinned to its front side indicating a lieutenant's rank. He held out his pistol and took aim. The gun cracked and a plume shot up just behind the keg. Groans of disappointment erupted from those among the crew who had placed their bets on him and whose weekly pay was about to be docked as a result. "Damme," he said softly, in disbelief.

The keg was now parallel to *Ranger*'s stern. There were perhaps twenty, no more than twenty-five seconds before the keg was jerked forward on its towrope. When Wallingford took aim and fired, Agreen Crabtree notched an arrow onto the bowstring and held it there with the index and middle finger of his right hand. The instant Wallingford's miss was confirmed, he brought the bow up from a horizontal to a vertical position, extending it with his left hand and drawing back the string and arrow with his right hand to full stretch, until the stave was bent in a quarter-circle. Pausing to adjust his sighting to the up and down motion of the ship, he released the arrow with a sharp twang. The arrow hit the keg dead-center with a dull thump heard on the quarterdeck.

Cheers breaking out from the crew quickly subsided as Richard Cutler brought his pistol straight up over his head. The keg was on its last length of line when he lowered it stiff-armed in a slow arch. He took aim and fired. His shot hit the very top of the keg, sending a spray of tiny woodchips up into the air just as it was swallowed by a swirl of white water.

Cheers broke out again when Captain Jones announced Agreen Crabtree the winner of the contest. Richard grinned and shook his friend's hand in congratulations. Others were coming forward to do the same when a lookout's cry from the foretop pierced through the jollity.

"Deck, there! Ships to leeward!"

"Where away?" Jones demanded at once, looking up.

"Broad on the starboard bow, sir. I can't make them out yet. . . . I see four, five . . . no, make that six vessels. No, more than that. Many more."

"Mr. Cutler!"

"Sir!"

Jones thrust his own long glass into Richard's hand. "Lay aloft and tell me what you see."

"Aye, aye, Captain."

Richard slung the glass by its lanyard over his shoulder and walked briskly down the steps from the quarterdeck. Jumping up on the bulwark and hammock nettings and onto the weather shrouds, he climbed past the maintop through the lubber's hole to save time. When he reached the trestletrees, he crouched down on the narrow perch and brought the glass around, training it southeastward. *Ranger* came off the wind to allow him better vision straight ahead between the spread of topgallant shrouds.

"What do you see, Mr. Cutler?" Thomas Simpson shouted impatiently from below.

"It's a convoy, sir," Richard called down a moment later. "Indiamen, I believe. Eleven of them, plus two others that appear to be escorts." A pause. "One looks like a frigate, the other a seventy-four. They're heading northeast, about fifteen miles from us."

"Have they seen us?"

"I believe they have, Captain. The frigate is hauling her wind."

"Very well, Mr. Cutler. You may come down."

"Shall we alter course, Captain?" asked the sailing master.

"No, Mr. Callum. Steady as she goes."

"Steady as she goes, aye, aye, sir."

Jones paced the weather side of the quarterdeck alone, deep in thought. The convoy was sailing northeast on a beam reach. *Ranger* was sailing due east on a broad reach, making seven, perhaps eight knots, faster than a beamy, heavily laden Indiaman. A quick calculation suggested that if *Ranger* maintained her present course, she would be in with the convoy in three, maybe two and a half hours. Of more immediate concern was the frigate. She had hauled her wind and was sailing due north on a course that would bring her guns within range in less than an hour.

"She'll be thinking we're an American privateer," Simpson remarked, "soon as she spots our flag."

"Yes, Mr. Simpson, thank you." Jones squinted at the frigate through a glass, a diminutive pyramid of white in the far distance. "And on the quarter-deck you will kindly address me as 'captain' or 'sir.'" He collapsed the glass with a snap and laid it aside.

"Mr. Wendell!"

"Sir?"

"Light along to the signal locker and haul out the British ensign. And the yellow jack."

"The yellow jack, sir?" asked the young midshipman, confused.

"Yes, Mr. Wendell," replied Jones impatiently. "Don't stand there as though paralyzed. You understood my order. Now pray carry it out. Mr. Charrier, haul down the Stars and Stripes."

"Aye, aye, Captain."

Richard Cutler guessed what the captain was about and made a different sort of mental calculation. The yellow jack was an international signal flag warning all other vessels that a ship was under quarantine from some horrible sickness. A Royal Navy vessel under quarantine on the course *Ranger* was following would almost certainly be returning home from the Indies or the Spanish Main, notorious breeding grounds for a deadly disease. It would take four to five weeks for a cruiser to sail from there to where they were now. A ship under quarantine normally flew the yellow jack for three to four weeks. Like the frigate bearing down on them, Richard thought, this *ruse de guerre* was sailing as close to the wind as she could lie. For certain the frigate captain would be making similar calculations once he spotted the all-yellow flag fluttering beneath the Royal Navy ensign abaft *Ranger's* spanker.

"Mr. Cutler," Jones said to him, a gleam of excitement in his eyes, "you once asked me why I changed the uniforms of the Continental Navy to resemble those of the Royal Navy. I believe you are about to have your answer.

"Mr. Simpson," he addressed his lieutenant, "I want all duty officers and crew on deck. Marines are to doff their dress coats. We are to look like any other British ship returning home to base. Everyone not on deck duty I want stationed by the guns. Do not—I repeat, do *not*—open the ports. Keep them closed and do nothing without my direct order. Understood?"

"Aye, Captain."

"Mr. Hall, stow the glass. We're the ship in doubt here. If the frigate sees us watching her, it could rouse suspicion."

The frigate was hull up now, three miles away. To Richard, she seemed a longer, more seasoned sister ship to *Ranger.* Her hull was similarly painted black and had a broad yellow stripe running along the entire length of her gun-port strake. Her bow had the same fine sweep, her stern the same jaunty undercut, and her masts too were stepped with a stylish rake. In contrast to *Ranger,* she was a bigger ship and her sails were a dazzling white, their weather leeches held taut by bowlines as she sailed on the wind on a course of interception, her lower yards braced sharp up and her sheets hauled aft as far as possible. White water spewed out from her bows as she dove into white-capped swells, a vision of terrifying beauty summoned forth by strengthening westerly breezes.

"At least we look like a ship in quarantine," Crabtree smirked, the strain in his voice only partially concealed. He motioned upward at *Ranger's* patched sails.

"Aye, Agee, there is that," Richard commented, his mind roiling with the same strain Agee was feeling and with an idea that suddenly had come to him. He took two sidesteps to his left, close by the third lieutenant.

"Sir," he said in a confidential voice. "We can't outrun the frigate and we can't fight her. Might we shorten sail and prepare a burial at sea?"

Loring gave him a quizzical look. "*What?*" he asked, as though he feared the midshipman had taken total leave of his senses.

"A burial at sea, sir. That frigate may need some convincing."

"Ah. I believe I catch your drift, Mr. Cutler."

Loring walked over to where Jones and Simpson were standing and conferred quietly with them. Jones nodded his head in apparent agreement with what Loring was suggesting.

"Mr. Charrier," Simpson called out, motioning the midshipman over. "Inform the bosun and surgeon that we shall take in the main course and make ready a burial amidships on the starboard side. Use whatever is handy for the body."

Charrier blinked. "The body, sir?"

"Yes, Mr. Charrier. A body. Move it, boy! And lower the ensign to half mast."

Charrier touched his hand to his hat and took off in a run across the quarterdeck.

"Walk, Mr. Charrier!" Jones admonished him.

"Aye, aye, sir," replied Charrier, slowing his pace. "Sorry, sir."

At midships a grating was set up and what looked like a body wrapped in sailcloth was placed upon it, resting on a plank. A Union Jack was draped over the plank, and members of the ship's company were gathered around in a semicircle. Thomas Simpson presided over the mock service of the dead, next to Ezra Green, the ship's surgeon.

When *Ranger* passed due north of the frigate, the two ships were less than a mile apart, close enough for those aboard *Ranger* to make out individual ropes on the frigate's rigging and for those aboard the frigate to witness the shrouded "body" sliding out from under the flag and splashing into the sea, weighted down by two cannon balls sewn into the canvas shroud. As *Ranger* passed by, the frigate veered off the wind and set a new course that brought her swiftly alongside the sloop of war, twenty-five yards off to starboard. Her crew spilled her wind to maintain the same distance from *Ranger,* now under her lee.

"What ship is that?" an officer demanded from her quarterdeck through a speaking trumpet.

Jones raised his own trumpet. "His Majesty's Ship *Ranger,*" he replied in a crisp British accent. "Out of Antigua. We are under quarantine, as you can see."

There was no immediate response. Officers on *Ranger's* deck understood why and what printed sources the British officers were consulting. Finally the response came. "We have no knowledge or record of such a ship."

"You wouldn't, sir. She's American. Taken by HMS *Rose* off Narragansett Bay, Captain James Wallace in command. I was commissioned to take her to English Harbor for refit, but the bloody flux intervened. My new orders are to take her to Portsmouth during the period of quarantine."

"Whom do I have the honor of addressing?"

"Lieutenant Paul Jones. My commission is from Admiral Sir Samuel Barrington, Jamaica Station, at the time of his promotion."

The names of the British commanders and the cruising grounds of HMS *Rose* could be quickly confirmed by those aboard the frigate. Jones knew it would be impossible under the circumstances to confirm his own commission in the rank of a mere lieutenant, especially if it came at the discretion of one promoted to admiral rather than through more traditional channels. He also knew that a promotion by Admiral Barrington would signify to the frigate's captain that Jones had sufficient interest in Whitehall to warrant the personal attention of a commodore, now widely publicized as a rear admiral of the White.

There was another pause, shorter this time.

"Very well, Captain Jones. Carry on. Is there a service we might render on your behalf?"

"If it pleases you, Captain, there is," Jones shouted through the trumpet. A broad smile on his lips belied the stoic tone he conveyed in his voice. "I request permission to join up with your convoy to England."

Richard glanced askance at Agreen. Their eyes locked until the answer came back from the frigate.

"Your request is denied, Captain. Under the circumstances, I am sure you can understand my decision. God speed to you, sir."

"And to you, sir," Jones shouted back, taking in the name emblazoned in gold on the frigate's stern as she veered off to rejoin the convoy. "May *Ranger* cross tacks with *Invincible* again."

4

Paris, France

Winter 1778

*T*HEY WERE WALKING ABREAST by Pine Hill, their muskets casually balanced across their shoulders, heading north toward World's End, an almost-island in Hingham Bay linked to the mainland by a thin sandy bar. The deer they were stalking had crossed that bar and was trapped. Richard could almost taste the venison pie his mother would be making for supper.

"Will, look," Tom Pickett suddenly warned. He pointed back toward Martin's Well, a small cove indenting the eastern shore of Hingham harbor, at a patrol of British redcoats.

"Rebels!" their leader shouted, spotting them. "After them," he ordered, and the red line advanced.

"Quick, across the bar," Will urged.

They ran across the bar and set up a defensive perimeter behind a grove of white birch trees, facing south on a small rise. The redcoats began jogging across the bar in single file. Three shots rang out; two enemy soldiers fell.

"We can't hold them off for long," said Richard, swapping his empty musket for one freshly loaded by Katherine.

"The hell we can't," said Will. He thumbed back the hammer on his weapon, took aim, and fired. A redcoat staggered, fell to his knees as though in prayer, then collapsed face forward, dead.

"Richard's right, Will," said Tom Pickett. "There are too many of them and we're almost out of shot."

"We can't retreat. There's nowhere to go."

"Yes, there is," said Katherine. "We can swim to Nantasket. It's not far across, and the redcoats wouldn't dare follow us."

Will thought for a moment. "Right. You and Richard go. Tom and I will cover you."

"No," Richard said emphatically. "I won't go without you."

"All right," Will agreed. "One more volley and we run."

The British made another attempt at the bar. Will, Richard, and Tom fired in unison. Three redcoats fell. The others hesitated despite exhortations from the rear, from an officer bearing an uncanny resemblance to Thomas Simpson.

"Now!" said Will.

They dropped their muskets and ran across an open field dotted with shrubs and low-lying trees to the northern edge of the peninsula. Fifty yards across Hingham Bay lay the long and narrow peninsula of Nantasket and the town of Hull—safety.

"Can you swim, Katherine?" asked Richard.

"Yes, Richard, I can swim," said Katherine, impatience in her voice, as though she had been asked that sort of question too often in her life.

"Then stay close by me. The water will be cold."

Her eyes were level, her voice calm, her hand warm and tender on the side of his face. "I promised I would always stay close by you."

They began wading into the water. They could hear the shouts of their pursuers behind them and, to their horror, the sudden commands and creak of oars aboard a British gunboat emerging into view from around the north side of the peninsula. Mounted in the bow was a mammoth cannon; crewmen were backing oars to level the barrel at them.

"We're trapped!" yelled Tom.

"I love you, Katherine," Richard said, pulling her close to shield her body with his own.

Orange fire belched from the mouth of the beast. Richard heard the whine of a ball that crashed onto the rocky shore with such violence it caused the ground beneath to tremble and Will to cry out in pain . . .

☆ ☆ ☆

DAMME!" SAMUEL Wallingford cried out as a wheel on the post chaise jounced into a sinkhole. His head went forward then snapped back against the front side of the interior, causing his black tricorne felt hat to fall off. "Can't that blasted cropper take in some rein?"

"He has orders to the contrary," said Jones, seated across from him and facing forward. He grinned as Wallingford retrieved his hat with a huff and smoothed his tawny-colored hair back to the silk ribbon holding it in place.

Richard had awakened with the lurch and was listening to the conversation as though from a faraway place. Loath to leave that place, it took him several moments to get his bearings.

"Ah, I see my young aide-de-camp is awake at last," said Jones. "You are feeling refreshed, I trust?"

"Yes, Captain," Richard replied. He blinked his eyes. "Where are we?"

"Near Crécy, I believe. As you are a student of history, Mr. Cutler, I believe that name should mean something to you."

It did, and it brought Richard fully awake. He leaned closer to the glassed window and looked out on the open fields and rolling hills flashing by. It was here, in 1346, where one of history's most decisive battles was fought. An army of ten thousand English troops led by the Plantagenet king Edward III and his son the Black Prince had landed on the beaches of Normandy, intent on reclaiming lost possessions in France. Opposing the invasion was Philip VI, the flower of French knighthood following behind him on horseback. The French charged the enemy at full tilt and were swept down not by English knights charging at them, under the traditional rules of war, but by English longbowmen deployed on a side of a hill in a wide M formation, their skills tested in battle against the Scots, their weapons able to pierce steel plate at a distance of one hundred yards. It was an unmerciful slaughter. French knights were either killed instantly by arrows or thrown to the ground and done in by trampling hooves and Welshmen brandishing daggers.

"May the French serve us better than they did themselves in that battle, eh, Mr. Cutler?"

"Let's hope so, Captain," Richard agreed. He was trying to imagine the shock to medieval society when it realized the age of chivalry was over.

Samuel Wallingford changed the subject.

"Are we on schedule to reach our destination tomorrow, Captain?"

"Yes. We'll stop tonight in Abbéville. We should arrive in Passy by late afternoon tomorrow."

"Are you certain Dr. Franklin will be there?"

"As certain as I can be. Passy is Dr. Franklin's headquarters. He would not leave except for an emergency."

"He has a grandson with him, does he not?"

"Two, actually. Young Ben and Temple both sailed with him on *Reprisal* from Philadelphia. He is very close to his grandchildren."

"Less so his son William, I hear tell."

"Quite. William Franklin still considers himself the royal governor of New Jersey. Apparently he has never seen the light. Strange, for the son of so ardent a patriot as Benjamin Franklin."

"He's an illegitimate son," Wallingford pointed out. "Perhaps that explains it."

The coach-and-six took another lurch. Instinctively the three Americans braced themselves with both hands on the plush velvet cushioning. It seemed to Richard that the carriage was actually increasing in speed, and he marveled at the endurance of the horses. He was grateful they were riding in relative comfort aboard a royal post chaise, not in one furnished by a local livery stable. The fleur de lis insignia boldly emblazoned in white and blue on each side of the carriage confirmed that this vehicle was on king's business and had *priorité absolue* everywhere it went along the route from Nantes to Paris. At two-hour intervals the carriage thundered into a *relais* where government officials supervised the replacement of sweat-lathered horses with a fresh team of six. The passengers hardly had time to relieve themselves and purchase some food and drink before they were back aboard and under way with a snap of a whip.

They spent that night at *une auberge* in Abbéville, a town noted for its woolen textiles and comprised of modest gray stucco houses clinging close together and paying homage to the more splendid residences clustered around a large octagonal town square built during the Renaissance and positioned at the heart of *le centre ville*. Here the houses were of white sculptured stone capped with red tiled roofs and embraced with tiers of wrought-iron balconies. Trees and shrubs planted about the square were as barren and bleak in this season of winter as were the flowerless plots of sod dotting the landscape. Nonetheless, with its well-lit streets and *les grandes résidences,* and with the charmed manner of living of its privileged few, *le centre ville* emanated a sense of warmth and elegance that was denied, both by design and decree, to those citizens of lesser means. The farther one's dwelling was from the center of town, the lesser those means appeared to be.

Their inn was several blocks from the square. It was a modest but comfortable affair, essentially *une salle à manger* on the first level with rooms upstairs for overnight lodging. It faced the square at an angle, as though the building had been rotated during construction to welcome in its more favored clientele. Clearly it was a popular spot for the rich and powerful to meet and socialize. When the three Americans came downstairs to sit at a table near a huge stone fireplace, its five-foot logs ablaze, the room was crowded with *haute bourgeoisie* sipping wine, smoking from long-stemmed clay pipes, and discussing the issues of the day. Not a few glanced with interest at the foreigners, dressed as they were in simple off-white breeches, heavy cotton shirts, and pure white vests. Only one, the oldest, wore the blue uniform coat of a naval officer.

None of the clientele acknowledged them formally, and the Americans kept to themselves. They lulled the evening away saying little, preferring to feast on cuisine that was hardly shipboard fare and to sample a local red wine that Samuel Wallingford declared was among the finest he had ever tasted, as he poured himself yet another round from a crystal carafe and settled in to sample a good deal more. Jones accepted a glass of wine, but as was his custom, he sipped at it sparingly.

The room was clearing. Jones had paid *l'addition* and Wallingford was beginning to nod off when their waiter approached their table. His torso was wide at the shoulders and tapered to his waist, and the muscles in his arms and shoulders flexed under his tight-fitting shirt as he rubbed his hands on his white apron. He spoke to Richard, apparently selecting him as the one most accessible, and his voice was quiet, almost conspiratorial in tone.

"*Vous êtes américains?*" he asked, though the answer was obvious.

Richard glanced questioningly at Jones, who gave him a brief nod in reply.

"*Oui, américains. Parlez-vous anglais?*"

"*Un peu.* Yes. A leetle. *Messsieurs, je veux dire seulement* . . . I wish you *bonne chance,* good luck, *avec . . . avec* . . ."

"With."

"*Oui.* With. *Merci.* I wish you good luck with *votre révolution. Mes amis, je vous dis,* France watches."

Those last two words confused Richard. "France?" he queried the man. "Do you mean the people just in here?" He gestured before him at the vacant room. "*Ces gens-ci?*" he translated when the waiter seemed not to understand.

"*Non, monsieur.*" The waiter jerked his thumb back in a general direction opposite the town square, to an area where the lower classes of Abbéville resided. "*Ces gens-là. La France!*"

He bowed and walked away. At the doorway he raised a hand in salutation. "*Bonsoir et bon voyage, messieurs. Vive le docteur!*"

"What in blazes was he talking about?" Wallingford demanded to know when they were alone. "And who is this *docteur?*"

"Dr. Franklin, I believe," mused Jones, impressed with the extent of the commissioner's reach into the French countryside. He was watching the open doorway through which the waiter had disappeared. "But I have no idea who or what he was pointing at. Any thoughts on that, Mr. Cutler?"

"None whatsoever, sir," said Richard, as baffled as the others.

The village of Passy was small but of considerable consequence, situated as it was between the urban sprawl of Paris three miles to the east and, fourteen miles to the west, the palace of Versailles, the seat of the royal court in which ten thousand individuals lived or worked, from lowly kitchen staff to highborn courtiers who could trace a noble ancestry reaching back to the year 1400. It was a peaceful and orderly village of residences only, no shops or hawkers allowed in to disturb the sensitivities of the very rich living within its villas and chateaus. Each residence had been carefully planned, the architects and craftsmen responsible paid handsome fees to guarantee the owner the widest possible vista of Paris and the river Seine on the one side and, on the other, the heavily wooded forests of the Bois de Boulogne. So thick, dark, and compact was this forest, it seemed as though it had been planted centuries ago as an impregnable wall to protect the village in the future from unwanted intrusions.

As grand as each chateau must have seemed to any new arrival in Passy, the chateau de Chaumont was, by any standards, the grandest of them all. It was an enormous affair of smooth limestone, four stories of fastidious taste constructed in rococo style from the majestic entryway on the first level, up past the rows of windows flanked with light blue shutters, to the gentle roll of red tile on the roof. Surrounding this enormous structure were formal garden plots where myriad dazzling colors would bloom come April. Leading down from both sides of the chateau were layered marble terraces. At the bottom of each terrace perched a guest house on a grassy bluff overlooking the river, its structure identical in miniature to the chateau above, giving each guest house the appearance of a little child hovering in the shadow of its stately parent. Over one of these guest houses, the one on the south side where officious-looking men and women in splendid attire seemed to have it under siege, flew the newly minted flag of the United States of America.

It was to the chateau that the three Americans were delivered first, late the following day as Captain Jones had predicted. Footmen saw them properly out of the carriage and into the front hallway. There they were requested to wait while one servant, a young man wearing a white-hair peruke and smooth silk clothes with tiny silver tassels on his vest, hurried down the enormous marble corridor in search of *le maître de chateau.*

"You wish to see *le docteur?" le maître* called up to them, moments later, from down that corridor. The hard soles of his gold-buckled satin shoes echoed off the gleaming black and white diamond-patterned floor as he strode up to the front entryway. When he stopped before them, the echoes died off upstairs, and the air became heavy with the scent of a pungent perfume.

"*Messieurs,*" he sighed with regret, shaking his head and smiling conde-scendingly at the presumption of the request he had been told they had made. "*Je le regrette, mais tout le monde veut voir le docteur.* Eet ees not *possible.* Tomor-row, *peut-être.* I weel see what I can do. But first, you make ze appointment with me in ze morning. *Bonsoir, messieurs.*"

He turned to go.

"*Monsieur!*" Jones barked out angrily, with such vehemence it caused the official to whirl around. "I am Captain John Paul Jones of the United States Navy, and I have traveled three thousand miles to see Dr. Franklin. I am on of-ficial business of my government, and I demand to see him. Now! *Maintenant! Comprenez-vous, monsieur?*" He spat that last word.

The official's mouth opened and closed once, twice, like a dying fish in the bottom of a boat. Unsure what to do next, he sighed with relief when the twin doors of a nearby antechamber opened, and a short, stout man emerged wear-ing a simple blue suit offset by a pale yellow vest and a pure white linen neck-stock. His hair was thin on top and lined with streaks of white, though it was thicker along the sides, curling in grayish brown waves down to his shoulders. He was wearing spectacles and was stooped forward, to better focus on what he was seeing or as the result of old age, Richard was not certain.

"Did I hear the name 'John Paul Jones'?" he inquired. As he approached them with the aid of a bamboo cane, a slight limp became noticeable in his right leg. "My God, sir, this is an honor," he said to Jones, identifying him by his dress uniform coat and the harsh glare he continued to give *le maître*. "I have read with great interest your exploits on *Alfred* and *Providence*. You are an accomplished sea captain, by all accounts."

"Thank you, Dr. Franklin; the honor is strictly mine," Jones said, calming down and giving Franklin his full attention. "May I introduce my two companions: my captain of marines, Lieutenant Samuel Wallingford, and my aide-de-camp, Midshipman Richard Cutler."

"I am honored, gentlemen." Franklin shook each man's hand enthusiastically, a broad smile of welcome accentuating his kindly features. What drew Richard instantly to the man were the firmness of his grip despite an advanced age and a youthful twinkle in his pale green eyes.

"Please, gentlemen, will you join me?" Franklin said when the introductions were over. He flipped up his cane and pointed it at the antechamber. "I was just being serenaded by a young friend. We can talk in there. Your visit is timely, to say the least."

His "young friend" turned out to be a young woman seated behind a gilded harpsichord. Her hair was a silken sheen of black swept up and held in place by jeweled hairpins. Her lips were full, her cheekbones high, and her liquid eyes were as deep a blue as Richard's. When the men entered the room, she stood and came around to greet them, sweeping a low curtsy to them as a group. Her dress was of dark violet satin, and a double string of off-white pearls on bare skin complimented the handsome contours of her face and a neckline that dipped from her shoulders to reveal the delicate swell of her breasts. Richard was not the only one to notice her fresh beauty and sensuous allure.

"Anne-Marie, meet my new friends from America," Franklin said, adding, as the round of introductions was made, "Anne-Marie is the daughter of a dear friend of mine, Madame Helvétian. I have been granted the distinct honor of taking Anne-Marie under my wing, so to speak. Not only is she lovely to look at, her music is lovely to the ear."

Anne-Marie blushed prettily. "Dr. Franklin flatters me," she said, in a way that suggested she was not unaccustomed to flattery. "What skills I have are because of him. He encourages me in my music. I call him '*cher papa.*' He is so kind. And generous. You will see. Men of all ages respect him, and women of all ages adore him."

Franklin beamed. "Now who is the flatterer!" he said, before turning to Jones. "Sir, what brings you to Passy in such haste?" Before the captain could answer, Franklin added impishly, "Let me guess. We have won a great victory at Saratoga."

Jones's expression fell. *Penet* had beaten them to France! But they had not seen her in the harbor at Nantes.

"A Mr. Austin delivered his dispatches to me just yesterday, from Brest," Franklin explained, causing Jones to bitterly recall the east wind that had kept *Ranger* tied to her Portsmouth moorings for five wasted days. "No matter. I am delighted you are here. You can help us celebrate this wonderful turn of events and perhaps assist us in what follows. As you can imagine, we are now at a most sensitive stage of diplomatic negotiations. But first, is there other news from the battlefields?"

He addressed the question to Richard, an amused glint in his eye as he observed the young midshipman struggling to extricate himself from the coy glances being cast by Anne-Marie Helvétian.

"There is other news, Doctor," Richard replied, "though I fear not as favorable. As you've no doubt read in the dispatches, General Howe has taken Philadelphia."

Richard had expected that piece of news to dampen the celebrations, especially since Franklin must also have read in the dispatches that a British major named John André had taken up residence in his own home on Market Street. To his surprise, Franklin appeared jubilant.

"I know. I read about that last night. Young sir, this may surprise you, but I am actually relieved by this turn of events. General Howe has not taken Philadelphia. Philadelphia has taken General Howe. His is a pyrrhic victory. He cannot remain there. The British will soon be forced to leave Philadelphia, as they were forced to leave Boston. Which is where you are from, if I am not mistaken."

"I am," said Richard, taken aback. "How did you know that, sir, may I ask?"

Franklin chuckled. "I have my ways, young sir. I have my ways. Boston proper?"

"Hingham. On the South Shore."

"Yes, I know it. A lovely town. I was born and raised in Boston, did you know?"

"No sir, I did not."

"It's true. I am Philadelphian by trade, so that's where most people think I am from. But Boston is where I was born and raised. And I must say, there are times I sorely miss that fair city." Franklin's gaze became wistful, his thoughts apparently lost for the moment somewhere along the shores of the Charles River. Then he said, "Gentlemen, my apologies. Pray forgive the wanderings of an old man. You must be exhausted from your journey. You will take quarters in my residence, the pavilion you may have noticed on your way in flying our flag. While you are here, you will be guests of state. The day after tomorrow, my delegation is to meet with Monsieur le comte de Vergennes. He is the French foreign minister. You are welcome to join our discussions. In fact, I must insist on it. Having just arrived from America, you may have something to contribute to our conversations. That evening, in the comte's honor, we are hosting a ball here in the chateau, in *la Salle de Fêtes*." With a mischievous lilt to his voice he asked, "You are up to the minuet, Mr. Cutler? In Paris, handsome young men from America are much in demand as *danseurs*. Is that not so, Anne-Marie?"

Her smile was radiant. "*Je ne sais pas, cher papa.* The only handsome young man I know from America is you."

THE MEETING with the French foreign minister took place two days later in the lantern room of the chateau. It was a spacious area of mirrors and windows, a floor above the grand ballroom on the first level where *l'affaire d'État* would be held that evening. A long shiny mahogany table rested on a plush Persian carpet, commanding the attention of those who would be seated comfortably upon identical chairs of a pink and gold fabric, the tips of their armrests curling under themselves in ornate concentric circles. Paintings of Rembrandt and Rubens adorned the walls, their subjects often a French magistrate of an earlier age. One subject, a thin man in an ebony black suit with a goatee to match and a wheel of crenulated white fluff circled around his neck appeared as though he had just been briefed on the outcome at Crécy, so incredulous was the expression on his face.

Before the foreign minister and his entourage arrived, Ben Franklin introduced the three newly arrived Americans to the other two commissioners. Silas Deane they had met briefly the night before, over a glass of wine. Arthur

Lee had arrived from his quarters in Paris earlier that morning and had paced about the hallway brushing imaginary dust off his clothing and readjusting his white linen cravat. The man either was simply not likable, Richard thought, or he was excessively nervous. Either way, he questioned the wisdom of Congress in sending such a man to France on so vital a mission. No wonder Lee was about to be recalled and replaced by John Adams. Perhaps public knowledge of that decision was at the root of his impolitic behavior.

"Our discussions will be entirely in French," Franklin explained. "My secretary, Edward Bancroft, will keep the notes of the meeting. Mr. Deane and Mr. Lee have a working knowledge of French, as do I, and we shall rely on our dear friend Monsieur de Chaumont"—he indicated the owner of the chateau, a fashionably dressed man who inclined his head at the acknowledgment—"to interpret anything we may have missed. Remember, gentlemen, this meeting with the foreign minister was previously scheduled, but the agenda has changed in light of the dispatches from Congress. The comte has been advised of Saratoga and met yesterday with King Louis at Versailles."

Franklin went on to clarify roles. The three American naval officers would sit behind the commissioners in full dress uniforms in chairs placed against the wall. They would thus be removed from the front lines of negotiations but close enough to lend support if and when such support was needed. As an American naval captain of British heritage who was already gaining notoriety in France, Jones could speak convincingly on military matters. Samuel Wallingford would sit on Jones's right and assume the role of precisely what he was: a man of accomplishment and military bearing who would personify America's resolve to see the war through to its rightful conclusion. Richard would sit on Jones's left, his fluency in French viewed by Franklin as a check on what the interpreters were interpreting and as an aid to Jones.

As for Jacques-Donatien Leary de Chaumont, their host, he would assume his customary role as the intermediary preferred by both sides of the negotiations to ensure that discussions remained on course. He was a government official attached to the Ministry of Marine who was openly sympathetic to the American cause, covertly supplying arms and munitions to the Continental Army in ships that had once conveyed the riches of the East Indies to France. He was, he claimed, motivated by the enlightened thinking of men such as Voltaire, Rousseau, Hume, and Locke. The American commissioners suspected he was equally motivated by the vast sums of money he received for the contraband goods he sold, but they were willing to overlook that so long as Chaumont remained an American ally of eloquence and substance.

At the glass-panel door to the lantern room, a liveried servant announced the arrival of Monsieur Charles Gravier, the count of Vergennes and French foreign minister.

At the entryway a man of considerable girth rolled into the proceedings. He was dressed in a glaring combination of ochre pants and white stockings, his sky blue vest and green coat straining to properly cover a torso enveloped in a loose-fitting white cotton shirt. Across his chest and over a sizable paunch ran a red sash of office on a diagonal. A white-laced stock edged in tiny jewels hid his stout neck; on his head he wore a riot of brown curly sheen that cascaded over his shoulders, an accoutrement now deemed *passé* by trend-setters in Parisian society. Once inside, the minister stopped to size up the room, swiveling his head this way and that, causing the ample flesh on his cheeks to jiggle like the wattles on some plump bird.

"Now *there's* a pompous ass for you," Jones whispered in Richard's ear.

The remark was so unexpected and so utterly sincere, Richard caught himself in a near laugh. His face colored when Arthur Lee shot him a look of keen disapproval.

Vergennes and his staff of three were met by Franklin and the other two commissioners. The American naval officers were introduced, the count paying particular attention to Captain Jones.

"I have heard of your exploits at sea, Captain," he said in French, "and I am honored to make your acquaintance. May I add that I am pleased you are on the American side in this war. My philosophy is, 'The enemy of my enemy is my friend.' Your enemy is England. So you are my friend. You are welcome to stay in my country for as long as you wish."

Jones bowed in consular fashion. Although he had a working knowledge of French, he replied in English, his words translated by an interpreter. "You are most kind, Monsieur le Comte. Nothing could please me more than to remain in your beautiful country for an extended visit. But I must return to my ship once we have concluded our business here. My duty is in battle against our common enemy. America will defeat that enemy, sir, have no doubts. We cannot fail, not with *La Belle France* fighting alongside us."

Powerful words, Richard thought, and the right ones to say. The count's aversion for everything British was well documented in European embassies, as was his thirst for revenge for the humiliations his nation had suffered during the previous war. He bowed in turn to Jones, as low as protocol and the constraints of close-fitting apparel would allow, before inviting everyone to take a seat.

Richard crossed one leg over another and settled back, listening carefully to the proceedings. He was fascinated by the way both sides jockeyed for position by using the subtle inferences and cautious niceties of diplomats, infusing humor when appropriate, resorting to obstructive tactics when necessary, defusing perceived affronts whenever the mood of the discussion darkened or a valued position was threatened. It was clear enough to everyone that the victory at Saratoga had provided a critical and powerful bargaining chip. But there was the fall of Philadelphia to consider as well as the doubts being cast by French military officers serving in America. Saratoga notwithstanding, questions remained about how long General Washington could continue to field an army and remain a viable military threat to British land forces. Saratoga had marked the end of the fall campaign; freezing weather had since swept in; in the coming months, how many Continentals would desert the harsh conditions of Valley Forge for the warmth and embrace of sweethearts and home? What would be the costs to France in a military alliance with America? What would be the benefits?

These questions were addressed primarily by Silas Deane and Arthur Lee or by Jacques-Donatien de Chaumont. During the early stages of negotiations Benjamin Franklin kept his cards close to his vest, speaking only when spoken to or when he had something of consequence to say. That was Richard's impression, and his respect for Franklin grew as the diplomatic back-and-forth continued. With each positive point Franklin built up, and with each negative one he broke down, Richard began to sense why the aging American had become so popular in France. Counting Edward Bancroft, there were nine men seated at the table, four on each side and Chaumont at the head, all dressed in the fashions of diplomats accustomed to public scrutiny and the importance of being seen in the trappings of state. All, that is, except for Franklin. He was dressed in his usual simple attire more suggestive of the American frontier than the French court. Before him on the table, no doubt to promote his image as a backwoods sage, he had placed the marten fur cap he had acquired in Montréal two years earlier when, at the age of seventy, he was implored by Congress to travel to Canada to convince Québec to join the American cause. That hat by now had become a symbol of American homespun virtues throughout France. Facsimiles had sprouted up in shops everywhere and were worn with pride by men on every social tier.

Richard was convinced that behind that affable smile and benign informality lurked a mind finely tuned in the skills of diplomatic nuance and subterfuge.

"Then we are in agreement," Silas Deane concluded the central point of discussion. "France will immediately recognize the independence of the United States and make public this decision."

Vergennes understood what Deane had said but waited for the interpreters to finish.

"We are in agreement."

Franklin responded, "Sir, does this recognition include a military alliance between France and the United States?"

Vergennes held out his hands palms up in the classic French expression, "What is a man to do?"

"That, alas, will require more time, Doctor. Certainly you can appreciate France's position. Such an alliance would be viewed by England as an act of war. Holland has a treaty with England, and the situation in Spain is uncertain. Our aim, yours and mine, is to isolate England and bring her to her knees. She cannot fight America and the maritime powers of Europe at the same time. France is seeking alliances with these powers, be assured, but alliances of this nature take time to forge. Until that time, France will continue to supply weapons to America through the auspices of Monsieur de Chaumont and others in our service."

Franklin peered at Vergennes over the top of his spectacles. "I do acknowledge your position, sir," he said, not unkindly. "Now I please ask you to acknowledge ours." He cleared his throat and requested a fresh cup of tea. As a servant made haste to satisfy his request, Franklin huddled with Deane and Lee. He then motioned to Jones to come over. "Ask your officers, Captain," he said to him, "to watch the reactions of our French friends during the next few minutes. We are about to have some fun here."

Franklin resumed his seat and took a sip of tea.

"My friends," he said across the table to Vergennes and his three assistants, "you may be assured that the United States government appreciates all that France has done and continues to do on its behalf. Your supplies and support have maintained our army in the field. Without them, all might have been lost. As to France recognizing our independence, it is an unparalleled blessing to be applauded by free men everywhere who believe and put their trust in the ideals and principles espoused by our revolution. Even if she were to do nothing further, France has earned the eternal respect and gratitude of a young nation."

As one, the four French officials inclined their heads forward.

"But, gentlemen," Franklin continued, "I must explain the realities of our situation. America can win this war against Great Britain. But to achieve victory we need armies, not just arms; ships of the line, not just frigates and dispatch vessels; field cannon, not just muskets. In short, what America requires is a nation in open alliance with her, a great nation seeking to fulfill her own destiny and claim her rightful place on the world stage."

Vergennes nodded sympathetically.

"Well spoken, Dr. Franklin. Your words are heartfelt and inspirational. You have my promise and the promise of my king that France will continue to do everything in her power to support your revolution. Your cause is our cause. But as I have said, forging a military alliance between our two countries will take time."

"We may not have that time," Franklin responded. He gave Vergennes a hard look, his tone taking on a sudden sense of urgency blended with a hint of rebuke. "Are you aware, sir, that my fellow commissioners and I were approached yesterday by Lord Stormont?" He was referring to the British ambassador to France.

"No sir, I am not," said Vergennes, caution entering his voice. "Might I ask the reason for this approach?"

Franklin shrugged. "From what I understand, the British are now prepared to concede to us everything we sought before the revolution began: home rule, our own parliament making our own laws and taxes, our own prime minister. A separate country from England, in effect, bound together with her by a common heritage and love of liberty, not to mention mercantile and military interests. A very intriguing proposal, I must say. Totally unexpected."

Vergennes shifted uneasily in his chair. "Why do you think the British are offering this?"

Franklin held up his hands exactly as Vergennes had done.

"The British want peace, it seems. More to the point, they no longer want war with America. We are speaking today of national interests, are we not? Apparently, Great Britain has come to a better realization of where her national interests might lie."

"You would accept such an offer?" Vergennes demanded, aghast.

Franklin shrugged a second time.

"It is not for me to accept or decline any offer, sir. I am but a humble printer asked to speak on behalf of my country. Congress must decide. And Congress will act, I suspect, based on what it perceives our national interests to be. In the same way France must now act."

Vergennes pursed his lips, his mind apparently absorbed in a chessboard on which the might of the British Empire was combined with the resources and latent power of the United States in a military and mercantile alliance that would checkmate Britain's ancient enemy, France.

"Thank you for sharing this information with me, Doctor," Vergennes said, unable to conceal an edge to his voice. "Be assured, I will use it to our mutual advantage. In the meantime, may I beg your indulgence in keeping this overture confidential?"

"I shall try, sir. But I cannot guarantee results. As I have said many times, three men may keep a secret, if two of them are dead."

Vergennes seemed confused by the statement, its humor apparently lost in translation. Wallingford, however, was having a jolly time with it.

The meeting concluded, Vergennes and his entourage left the room and were in the process of boarding their carriage outside when Richard Cutler approached the negotiation table.

"Dr. Franklin," he said with deference, "if I may, that was a brilliant maneuver. I believe your ruse produced the result you wanted."

Franklin finished stacking his papers and thrust them into a brown leather satchel.

"Thank you for the compliment, Mr. Cutler, but that was no ruse. And it will not take long for French spies in the British embassy to confirm that it wasn't. London has indeed extended a peace offer to us on the terms I described. How we respond depends on what France does now."

The ball that evening was a formal affair of state. Hundreds of people were invited, *la crème de la crème* of Parisian society traveling to Passy to celebrate both the occasion and each other. Men were dressed in their most fashionable attire, but to Richard's eye, it was *les dames aristocratiques* who commanded center stage. They wore huge multilayered dresses expanding out from a wasp waist in grand panniers, and their hair was coifed in outlandish styles and wrapped in brightly colored silk turbans, a spray of exotic bird feathers pinned to them with precious gems. Jewels sparkled in candlelight like so many tiny prisms as ladies and their escorts, ever *en garde* for the socially correct, vied for position around the comte de Vergennes, Monsieur de Chaumont, and Benjamin Franklin.

Captain Jones was visible in the crowd for the same reason Richard stood out in contrast to everyone else: his naval uniform of white breeches and blue coat, its simplicity emulated only by the plain brown suit worn by Doctor Franklin. Richard had scrupulously scrubbed his spare dress breeches for the occasion, and he had on his best dress midshipman's coat, the one his father had given him that day six months ago. Captain Jones had on the same uniform but with gold lace edged on his waistcoat and dress coat, gold also on the buttons and button holes of his coat and on the fringed epaulet he wore on his right shoulder embroidered with a rattlesnake and the words DON'T TREAD ON ME.

He made a dashing figure, and Richard noted it was a figure greatly admired by the ladies. To his surprise, because he had never seen his captain in so glittering a setting, Jones seemed as comfortable in this sanctuary of *le beau monde* as he did on *Ranger's* quarterdeck. His winsome ways had women of high social standing blushing and giggling like pubescent girls; even their male escorts found themselves taken in by his chivalrous behavior and cultured wit. Few of the *mesdames* or *demoiselles* managed to get too close to him, however. Madame de Chaumont made certain of that. She was the wife of Jacques-Donatien de Chaumont and the official hostess of the evening. She was also a woman of striking beauty. To Richard's mind, she was exploiting her official position to stake her personal claim on the captain's company this evening.

The center of the ballroom began to clear in preparation for a formal dance. Richard retreated back toward a wall, searching for Samuel Wallingford or Silas Deane or someone else in search of company. He spotted the green-coated marine lieutenant not far away, engaged in conversation with a noble lady of grand stature and enormous bosom who clearly did not wish to have their *tête-a-tête* intruded upon. Seeing no one else he knew nearby, Richard yielded to the inevitable. He leaned against a Doric pillar and folded his arms across his chest, content to while away the evening watching a spectacle he had never in his wildest imagination thought he'd ever be privy to. From across the room he heard a harpsichordist signaling all present to take their desired places.

"*Alors, le bel aspirant de marine n'a pas de partenaire ce soir?*"

Richard turned, recognizing the voice. Anne-Marie Helvétian was beside him, a demure smile on her lips. She was dressed similarly to the older women though her *accroutrements* were far less pronounced and her neckline plunged farther down a dress of blue and white taffeta, the advantage of youth and an alluringly sculpted body. Her hair was simply but attractively done up in a fashion similar to when he had first met her, and it carried the pleasing fragrance of jasmine.

"Anne-Marie," Richard exclaimed happily. "I didn't expect to see you here. I was told you were going to *la Comédie Française* tonight."

"That was my intent," she acknowledged. "*Le barbier de Séville* is being performed at the Tuileries, and I am still hoping to see it."

"What is being performed?"

"The Barber of Seville. A play by Beaumarchais. You have not heard of him?" she asked when Richard gave her a blank look. "*Vraiment? C'est dommage.*" She stepped closer. "You should know that in addition to being a revered playwright, Monsieur de Beaumarchais is a keen supporter of your revolution. He has set up a false company to send guns and munitions to America. He works with Monsieur de Chaumont in this regard."

"Then I am twice in his debt," Richard smiled. "For service to my country, and for allowing leave of so ardent and lovely a *devotée* from his audience tonight."

"My time will come," Anne-Marie said. She scanned the ballroom floor with an indifferent eye. "Normally I do not care for these kinds of affairs. They are too formal and stuffy, with too many older people trying to impress and act young. Then I said to myself: think of poor Richard Cutler. He is under strict orders to attend, like it or not, and he too is young and will need someone to talk to, perhaps even dance with. Was I wrong to think this way?"

"Quite the contrary, I assure you," Richard said. "I am delighted to see you, Anne-Marie. Thank you for coming. And I would be honored to be your dance partner this evening, if you can suffer the company of a bumpkin from Boston who has never danced the minuet."

She put her right hand through the crook of his left elbow and gave his lower arm a slight squeeze. "I will suffer the bumpkin's company under one condition."

"What is that?"

"Some day soon, on a date of my choosing, he will accompany this poor, forlorn maiden to la *Comédie Française.*"

Richard put his right hand on her arm. "The bumpkin accepts the lady's kind invitation," he grinned, "though not her premise. Subject, of course, to the approval of his captain."

"His captain will approve," she said, as a matter of fact.

Together they watched a dance of symmetry and elegance unfold. Couples in the first round took to the open floor, among them Captain Jones and Madame de Chaumont. They bowed first to the audience, then to each other, honoring those watching and those participating. To the light and soothing tunes of Loeillet, the couples began a fixed sequence of dance movements, one couple at a time across the wide parquet floor: a lead-in, right-hand turn, left-hand turn, and two-hand turn closing, all the while gliding in a broad Z-figure diagonal. Richard studied the movements, taking his cue from Captain Jones who, he observed, was as gracious and fluid in his movements as any courtier on the floor. The couples were dancing sideways in close accord from one corner of the ballroom to another, opening out to the spectators at the end of the sequence and honoring them with a bow from the gentleman, a curtsy from his dancing partner.

Polite applause scattered about the room, increasing in volume when the comte de Vergennes bowed deeply to his *danseuse distinguée,* his right hand over his heart, his left leg forward, and his left arm held out rigidly from his side.

"No one knows how to show a leg like the French," Richard observed.

"They have had centuries of practice."

"They? I assumed you were French."

She shook her head. "I am Swiss. My father was a diplomat to the French court. He died a year ago. Dr. Franklin was an acquaintance of his and a friend to my mother. *Cher papa* adopted me, as it were, when my father died. He felt sorry for me at the time, I suppose. We have grown very close to each other since."

"So I have noticed. And I am sorry to learn about your father."

111

Her mouth twisted. "I rarely saw him. My mother and I lived in Passy, he in Paris. Doing his duty, he said, neglecting his duty to his wife and daughter. Dr. Franklin has been a better father to me."

"Where did you learn to speak English so well?"

"In school, here and in Switzerland. I have studied English for seven years." She smiled at him. "*Et toi, mon ami? Tu parles français très bien, je crois.*"

"*Merci, mademoiselle. J'ai étudié le français en école, aussi pendant sept ans.*"

"*Vraiment?*" she mocked him. "I hadn't realized you have schools in the colonies."

"We call them states now. And yes, of course we have schools. What do you think we are, bumpkins? We learn useful things such as how to skin a rabbit or dig up a turnip or sew a mobcap."

They laughed together. Then something caught Anne-Marie's eye that caused her expression to plunge from one of relaxed merriment to one of despair and resignation.

"Alas. It is Monsieur Villiers. He may be of noble blood, but he is a dog who will not take no for an answer. For reasons I cannot explain, he is an intimate of Marie Antoinette, the queen. He has considerable influence in court and uses that influence to get what he wants, especially from the women he desires."

Richard saw the not unattractive, middle-aged courtier of finely chiseled Gallic features making his way toward them. People on the dance floor obsequiously made way for him to pass, then filled in his wake as he strode by, watching him, speculating on which *demoiselle* he fancied for his pleasure this evening. Villiers acknowledged those who greeted him but kept the conversations brief. When talking politely to whomever, his eyes repeatedly went ahead to Anne-Marie, as if to reassure her that it was she, not any of these others, on whom he was about to bestow the ultimate blessing of his company.

He reached her at length and bowed low in a courtly fashion. His Lyonnais suit of blue coat and breeches was expertly tailored to conceal the effects of advancing age, and his neckstock and knee-high stockings were of the purest Asian silks. On a diagonal across his chest, under his jacket, he wore the crimson sash of the Order of Saint Louis, and on his head, a powdered wig of white hair that curled at the ears and ran straight down in the back, a crimson silk ribbon tied at the base. The skin on his face was unblemished, and the scent he gave off was musky and cloyingly sweet.

"May I have this dance, mademoiselle?" he said in French. It was more a statement than a question.

Anne-Marie bobbed a quick curtsy. "I do regret, monsieur, but I am already spoken for in this dance." She looked at Richard.

Villiers arched his eyebrows. "So? Well," he soothed, jutting out his jaw at Richard as he gave him a cursory once-over. "I am certain this nice young man will concede his enviable position and grant me my request. Am I correct, sir?"

"No sir, you are not," Richard answered in French.

The shock inflaming the nobleman's face was visible to everyone in the vicinity. Muted conversations on the dance floor around them died as though cut off by a sword.

"Who *are* you?" Villiers demanded in English, assuming that anyone acting in such a vulgar manner could not possibly be of his native land.

"I am Richard Cutler, sir, midshipman aboard *Ranger,* a United States ship of war. I am also this lady's escort this evening, and she has granted me the honor of this dance."

"An American rebel," Villiers sniffed.

"An American, yes."

Villiers drew himself to his full imposing height and scrutinized Richard up and down. "Do you know whom you are addressing, my young rebel friend?" He curled his lips with disdain and flared his nostrils.

"Yes sir, I do. I am addressing a man who considers himself a gentleman." He let whatever conclusion Villiers wished to draw from that statement be expressed through his hard stare.

There were sharp intakes of breath nearby.

Villiers advanced one step and thrust his face forward. "And what would you know about being a gentleman?" he hissed at Richard, who stood his ground. Villiers swung his eyes to Anne-Marie; he saw no sense of outrage or indignation there. Quite the opposite, judging by the way she was ogling this upstart American boy. "I have never heard of such a thing!" he fumed.

"You have now, sir. If you will excuse us, the lady and I have a minuet to dance."

Richard offered his arm to Anne-Marie, who took it, squeezing hard this time. They walked purposely through a crowd of spectators that had come alive with a frenzy of hushed conversations and tight-lipped giggles as the details of what had just happened fanned out across the ballroom.

"You showed the old cock," Wallingford chuckled softly as Richard passed by.

"*Bien fait,*" his matronly partner sighed.

Captain Jones approached them, the makings of a grin bracketing the sides of his mouth. "Well, Mr. Cutler," he said confidentially, "now that you have created an international incident and have jeopardized our pending alliance with France, thereby ensuring America shall lose this war, I hope you enjoy your evening.

"*Enchanté,*" he said to Anne-Marie, bowing low. "Tonight it appears my midshipman has bested every man in Passy, his captain included."

Anne-Marie gave him a smile and a graceful curtsy as the next round of dancing was announced.

Whether from a surge of adrenaline courtesy of Monsieur Villiers, or the beguiling movements of Anne-Marie on the dance floor, or the sudden attentions of high-bred noble men and women applauding them for what appeared to be acceptable approximations of the minuet, at that moment Richard Cutler felt happier and more alive than he had for a very long time. Together he and Anne-Marie glided effortlessly in a sideways pattern, his inside hand holding hers, the complexity of the four steps to six beats of music no longer a mystery but a pleasure to engage. At the two-hand turn closing near the end of the dance, he whirled her around in a three-quarter turn and their eyes met, remaining transfixed in that state of grace until the dance was over, the applause welled up, and it was time to honor the spectators. And, importantly, each other.

Christmas came and went without much fanfare. There was a break in the diplomatic give and take between Passy and Versailles, and a holiday feast of suitable proportions was served to the Americans in Passy. Richard passed the day in memories of his family in Hingham, speculating on how Anne, Caleb, and Lavinia were getting on and wondering if the Christmas traditions his parents held so dear were being observed during this year of war.

Temple Franklin was in Passy for Christmas, home from a boarding school east of Paris. Richard spent time with him when he was able and found Temple to be a thoroughly likable young man. He enjoyed his company, though not nearly as much as he enjoyed the company of the ever more likable Anne-Marie Helvétian. Temple quickly became a fast friend to both Richard and Anne-Marie; together they saw in the New Year, an evening of snow and wine and seasonal tunes played on the harpsichord, inevitably off-set with more sober reflections on the war in America. No one needed to remind Richard Cutler that Continental soldiers wintering in Valley Forge did not have this fire, this wine, this beautiful young woman to warm their hearts and souls. And not one of them would pass an evening dancing the minuet.

☆ ☆ ☆

It took a minimum five to six weeks for news from America to reach Paris. Each day, Christmas included, the commissioners waited with anticipation for a post carriage to arrive from the Breton coast with any intelligence from Congress that might influence their diplomatic strategy or the tactics with which to implement that strategy. Although it was a clumsy process for all concerned, the delays in communication did give Benjamin Franklin an opportunity to use the great span of ocean to America's advantage. "I cannot act without the approval of my government," he would inform a polite but increasingly frustrated Lord Stormont in the morning; in the afternoon. he would say to his hosts. "*Merci, Monsieur le Comte,* we will send your proposals to Congress in Baltimore once we have secured the services of a ship to deliver them."

"We can send *Ranger,* if need be," Captain Jones confided to Franklin on a cold, overcast day in early January. The count of Vergennes had just departed from Passy after stressing in no uncertain terms the extreme importance of a communiqué he desired sent forthwith to Congress. "I have received word from my first lieutenant that her repairs will soon be completed. He could sail with the dispatches and I could remain here until his return, or until I am awarded another ship."

Franklin shook his head.

"That is most generous of you, Captain, but there is no other ship for you to command. We thought there might be—the frigate *L'Indien* recently completed in Rotterdam—but the Dutch government won't release her even to France. Its treaty with England, remember? No, we need *Ranger* here. Your plan to attack England may be just the medicine our patient requires."

"It's unfortunate the other commissioners don't see it that way, especially our friend Mr. Lee."

"Perhaps not," Franklin agreed. "I value my esteemed colleagues, but they rely too much on hope and circumstance and not enough on audacity. As I have always said, he who lives upon hope shall die fasting. It is men like you, Captain, men of vision, who will see this war to its rightful conclusion."

"We will, with the help of God and as many Dr. Franklins as He can summon to our cause."

The men bowed to each other in mutual respect.

A mischievous smile flickered across Franklin's face.

"You are enjoying the company of Madame de Chaumont?"

"I am, Doctor. She is a charming lady. And her husband too has become a good friend."

"I should hope so. Were that woman my wife, I would entrust such time with another gentleman only to my dearest and most trusted friend."

Jones detected a note of irony in Franklin's voice and offered nothing in reply. Franklin changed the subject.

"That midshipman or yours, Mr. Cutler, has made quite an impression here in Passy. I like him. He's quiet, like me, but he observes everything with a keen mind. There's a lot of old-fashioned common sense in that young man and, I suspect, an excellent naval officer. He knows his trade, and he can stand up for himself, as we noted at the ball. By the bye, we have seen neither hide nor hair of our friend Villiers since that incident. No loss to us, I might add."

"Cutler is an excellent officer," Jones agreed. "One of the best I have seen. For his sake, I hope we see action soon. He is quiet and that is his nature, but it's a brooding and tormented quiet. Inside him I fear there's a powder keg smoldering."

"Oh? Why, pray?"

"His brother was impressed into the Royal Navy and thrashed to death after striking a ship's officer. His name was Will. He and Richard were very close."

"I see," said Franklin sympathetically. "I had not heard that."

"You wouldn't, from him. It's not his way."

"Even Mademoiselle Helvétian cannot lift his spirits?"

"If anyone can, she can. I must say, there seems something a bit odd when it comes to Mr. Cutler and young women. They are attracted to him for reasons that I'm sure are quite obvious. He doesn't spurn them, nor does he exploit his looks and charm to light a flame under the relationship, so to speak. Most men would revel in the sort of female attention he gets, myself included."

"I hadn't noticed you lacking that sort of attention," Franklin commented dryly. "As to Mr. Cutler, is there someone else? A sweetheart in Hingham, perhaps?"

"If there is, he has said nothing to me about her."

"I'm glad for that. As you have no doubt noticed, Captain, my dearest Anne-Marie has become quite fond of your midshipman. I would hate to see such devotion come to naught."

ANNE-MARIE CHOSE January 19 as the date to visit the Tuileries Palace and view a performance of *Le barbier de Séville,* which had débuted in Paris two years before. It was Richard's eighteenth birthday, and this was her gift to him. She retained the services of a comfortable carriage, and they set out for Paris immediately after the two o'clock meal.

The morning had started out overcast and damp, the temperature on the cusp between snow and cold rain or sleet. As the day progressed, clouds began slowly dispersing, and the sun broke through here and there, picking out parts of the city with shafts of yellow light that contrasted whatever they enshrined with everything else in a city still in the somber throes of a bleak mid-January afternoon. On the sidewalks and quays, patches of dirty snow and human refuse clung to the shadows of majestic architecture, classical domes, and Gothic spires, their juxtaposition so symbolic, Richard thought, in this sprawling city of glaring contrasts.

Paris was by far the largest city he had ever visited. Boston and Portsmouth, England, were his two bases of comparison; either one in its entirety would be counted as nothing more than an urban adjunct of Paris, and certainly not one in its more fashionable districts. Everywhere was history on a grand scale, but the citizens Richard observed seemed oblivious to their glorious past, intent instead on pursuing the haggling and hawking and whoring of the less fortunate, or the socializing and theater-going and coffee sipping of the more educated and refined. As it had on his two previous visits, Paris seemed to Richard a variegated stew encompassing the best and worst of the human condition.

"What do you think?" Anne-Marie asked him, trying to read his thoughts.

Richard was staring ahead, across the Seine at the twin rectangular Gothic towers of the cathedral of Notre Dame, rising like the masts of a flagship within a vast armada of stately vessels. The towers were so awash in golden sunlight, along with the stained-glass windows and the great bells they housed, that it seemed as though this winter scene had been painted by the hand of a celestial being. In the stark blue waters of the Seine, bargemen were bundled up in layered clothing and were working their long wooden boats with or against the current, as oblivious as everyone else to the majesty all about them on either bank and on the small island at midriver.

"It's beautiful," Richard said simply.

"No, Paris I mean."

Richard continued to look ahead toward the Louvre and the Tuileries Palace now looming into view. "It's a far cry from Boston," he remarked, settling back beside Anne-Marie. He took her hand and smiled at her.

"*C'est vrai?*" she laughed.

Richard felt her warmth through her thick animal-skin pelisse. "What a wonderful birthday gift, Anne-Marie," he said, moving his arm up and around her shoulders. "I will always remember it."

"You're welcome, Richard," she replied, cuddling closer. "I hope you enjoy the play."

"I will. But the gift I was referring to is the gift of your company."

She lifted her eyes to his. On an impulse he leaned over and kissed her lightly on the cheek.

"What's so funny?" he grinned, when she giggled a little.

She cocked her head at him. "It's a custom in France, *cher Richard,* that when a gentlemen wishes to kiss a lady out of respect or friendship, he should kiss her on the neck, so to not disturb the rouge on her cheeks."

"I see," he said with mock gravity. "Thank you for that counsel, madam. I shall lock it away for safekeeping." They looked at each other, unsmiling despite his levity. On a second impulse, one that was no longer within his ability or desire to control, he took her hand in both of his and brought it to his lips. He kissed her there, letting his lips linger on the smooth silken flesh. "And what, *chère Anne-Marie,* is the custom in France when a gentleman wishes to kiss a lady with respect and with something far beyond mere friendship?"

Her eyes rested on Richard's face. Her free hand came up and smoothed back a loose strand of blond hair to behind his ear, her touch so soft and tender it made him shudder.

"I think," she said, her voice a throaty whisper as he pulled her slowly to him, "that the custom in France is the same as in your country."

He took her in his arms and brought her tightly against him, kissing her on the mouth. Their lips parted, each seeking the inside of the other, gently at first, tentatively exploring, then with more urgency and hunger, until her breath came in short audible gasps, his lips went to her cheeks and nose and lashes and forehead, her hand pressed down suggestively on his upper thigh, and the driver announced from above that they had crossed over the Pont Neuf and *L'Île de la Cité* and had arrived at the Tuileries Palace.

5

THE CELTIC SEA

April 1778

CAPTAIN JONES PACED THE quarterdeck impatiently. Again he brought the long glass to his eye and surveyed the French naval squadron riding at anchor to starboard before the great granite cliffs of Quiberon Bay. His gaze settled on *Bretagne,* the one-hundred-gun French flagship, and he held the glass steady on the commodore's quarterdeck. He noted nothing unusual there, certainly nothing to suggest a decision had been reached in the ship's grand cabin. Cursing under his breath, Jones collapsed the glass and peered ahead. *Ranger* was ghosting along under topsails, jib, and spanker into the hollow of the bay, as close in to a lee shore as he dared go.

"Bring her about," he snapped at his first lieutenant. "Lay her on a reciprocal course."

Simpson repeated the order to the duty officer, the duty officer to the bosun, whose mates called sailors into action with a shriek of whistles. Quartermaster Higgins put the helm down. Sailors heaved on the braces and swung the yards over; slowly the sloop of war turned into the southwesterly breeze. Timing the maneuver with his watch, Jones lingered by the helm until he was certain Higgins would not miss stays as *Ranger* moved through the wind in a wide arc and paid off on a course to the south-southeast, out of the bay. Twelve and a half minutes, without incident. Nodding to himself, he sucked in his stomach and tucked the watch away.

"I'm going below," he informed Simpson. "Summon me the instant you even suspect something."

"Aye, Captain," Simpson assured him. Officers on the quarterdeck could hear the captain's footsteps descending to his cabin and the marine sentry at the cabin door stamping the butt of his musket on the deck in recognition.

"Why the delay, d'y' think, Richard?" Agreen Crabtree asked. He was standing to larboard of the mizzenmast with the other three midshipmen.

"I don't know, Agee," Richard replied. He studied the shoreline of Quiberon Bay, a huge horseshoe-shaped body of water thrusting northeastward into the southern coast of Brittany. Here, twenty years earlier, during the dying days of the war between England and France for North America, a British squadron under the command of Adm. Sir Edward Hawke had sailed hell-bent through the shoals in pursuit of a considerably larger enemy force. French line-of-battle ships were trapped in the bay and put out of action either by going aground or by being pounded by British guns, or both—a fleet destroyed that was to have conveyed twenty thousand French soldiers to Scotland for an invasion of England. The staggering victory was immortalized in the song *Hearts of Oak*. At the time that song had been sung aboard colonial merchant vessels with as much gusto as it was today aboard Royal Navy ships stationed throughout the world.

"What I still don't get is *why* we're here," commented Midshipman Charrier. He had his arms akimbo as he surveyed the line of powerful French warships. "Why is it so hell-fire important we're saluted at all?"

"*Try* to understand," David Wendell said, his frustration apparent. "We've been through this before, Charlie. It's not the act itself. It's what it symbolizes." His astute observations and mature tone of voice caused Richard to reflect again on how much this youngest midshipman had seemed to mature over the winter in Nantes. "Our captain simply wants to know, does France recognize our flag."

"Wouldn't know about that," Charrier huffed. "What I *do* know is that this delay has given the men a much needed rest from the guns. There's grumbling belowdecks, have you noticed? Our captain has been drilling them hard these past two weeks."

Agreen Crabtree folded his arms and leaned in confidentially toward the clutch of midshipmen. "You ask my opinion, David's right. It'll happen, an' it don't matter a hound's bark how many rounds we get. Seven, eleven, thirteen: it's all the same so long as it gets done. Captain wants t' be first t' have our flag saluted."

Ranger was sailing past the Passage de Beniquet, a narrow inlet marked with brightly painted buoys and stone pillars to guide vessels in or out of the bay between sandy flats exposed at low tide. It was where they had last worn ship at this end of the bay, and it was where they would wear now, to keep the French squadron in plain view between them and the long narrow sandy beach etched at the base of the cave-hollowed granite cliffs.

The squadron was bearing up on the starboard bow when a lookout shouted from *Ranger's* foremast top.

"Deck, there! Flagship's lowering a boat."

"Are officers boarding?" Jones called up from two decks below. He had stepped out onto the gun deck the instant he heard the cry.

"One moment, sir . . . Yes, two officers, it appears."

"Very well."

Jones ascended to the weather deck, then to the quarterdeck with as purposeful a step as Richard had ever witnessed. He was attired in full dress uniform, as were his officers, and he had his hair pulled back taut in a neatly tied queue under a black tricorne hat with the red and white ribbon insignia of a captain pinned to its front. The air temperature was biting cold; a man could clearly see his breath in the feeble warmth of an early April sun; not one officer wore a cloak.

"Heave to, Mr. Callum," he ordered the sailing master. "Mr. Wallingford, assemble the marines."

"Aye, aye, sir," the two officers replied.

David Callum brought the helm down, edging *Ranger* into the light breeze. He kept the wind purposely to larboard as crews swung her fore and mizzen yards in opposite directions. The two counterbracing forces boxed *Ranger* in, the forward thrust of the fore topsail precisely offset by the aft-pushing tendency of the other held aback. She was hove to, drifting to leeward, her main topsail to the mast.

The ship's complement of thirty marines took position along the starboard gangway on the weather deck, their gleaming weapons held out before them in exact formation, their uniforms of white breeches, pipe-clayed crossbelts, and green coats with red cuffs and facings spotless in the hard scrutiny of a mid-afternoon sun. Lieutenant Wallingford was at the quarterdeck railing dressed in a similar uniform with a gold torque around his neck in place of the stiff leather neckstocks worn by his men. He faced the larboard entry port amidships holding a gold-hilted sword straight out before him, the tip pointing down at the freshly holystoned deck.

"Is the side party properly assembled, Mr. Crocker?" Jones demanded, though he clearly saw those involved standing at attention by the entry port.

"Assembled, sir," the bosun assured him.

The gig from *Bretagne* sidled up against *Ranger.* At the order of her coxswain, her crew handsomely tossed oars to the vertical. French sailors in thick cotton sea jackets hooked on to the fore chain-wale and held the small craft steady against *Ranger's* hull where steps built into the hull led up from the waterline. Two officers superbly attired in white uniforms, each with a knee-length scarlet cloak draped around his shoulders and fastened at the neck with a silver clasp, waited their turn to grab onto the twin manila ropes serving as handholds, one on each side of the steps.

Protocol required that the highest-ranking officer board first. The instant Wallingford confirmed his large black fore-'n-aft bicorne hat rising up from the tumblehome, he raised the tip of his sword. As one, his marines stamped the butt of their muskets on the deck and raised their weapons to the same forty-five-degree angle.

"Marines . . . Make ready . . . *Fire!*"

Ranger's starboard side erupted in an explosive *feu de joie,* an honor identical to what French marines had bestowed on Captain Jones when he had been welcomed aboard *Bretagne* earlier that day. One volley and the marines stood down at attention, passing on welcoming honors to the side party. Amid a roll of drums and shrill calls from bosun's whistles, the French commodore faced aft and doffed his hat to the quarterdeck and the colors, holding it stationary over his head. Jones returned the salute in the same manner, then stepped down to the weather deck. He bowed to the commodore and his lieutenant and invited them to the privacy of his cabin. As the three naval commanders proceeded below, American officers and crew on deck were left to speculate on what would be agreed to in the captain's cabin.

"A week's pay he doesn't get thirteen," Charrier wagered on the quarterdeck.

"You're on, Charlie," said Wendell. "I have it on good authority that the captain has already told the commodore he won't give the French thirteen unless he gets thirteen in return. And the captain gets what he wants, doesn't he, Richard?"

"Usually, David, but not always," Richard answered, recalling a conversation he had overheard in Passy in which a rather indignant Madame Chaumont had complained to Dr. Franklin about certain improper advances made upon her by Captain Jones.

Whatever conversation there was below, it did not last long. In short order the French officers were back on the weather deck preparing to return to their ship.

"Get her under way, Mr. Callum," Jones said crisply once all honors had been dutifully performed and the gig was clear. "Same set of sail, same course: northwest by north. Pass the word for the gunner," he said to the duty officer, a slight smile beginning to twitch the corner of his mouth.

Word was quickly passed forward. Moments later Seth Bingham emerged from a forward hatchway and came scurrying aft.

"Captain!" he panted. He saluted, then sheltered his eyes from the sun as he gazed up to the quarterdeck.

"We shall fire thirteen rounds, Mr. Bingham," Jones called out, in a voice loud enough for the crew to hear, "once we wear ship in the bay and *Bretagne* has dipped her flag. The French shall respond with nine rounds. Nine rounds, let it be known, is the honor the French Navy grants to all republics."

Within one turn of the hourglass Quiberon Bay erupted with thunderous claps of guns, their ear-piercing reports ricocheting off the stone cliffs and continuing out in prolonged, rolling peals until finally dying off in a far distant echo. *Bretagne* may have fired fewer rounds than *Ranger,* but to a landsman's ear, the roar and reverberations of her massive thirty-two-pound guns made a far bolder statement to the environs and to the world than the earnest but less persuasive reports of the nine-pounders preceding them.

☆ ☆ ☆

FROM QUIBERON Bay *Ranger* sailed west by north until the last remnants of Belle Isle had dipped astern into the gathering night to eastward. She then veered northwest by west, keeping the treacherous approaches to Brest to her lee, steering on a larboard tack until she had two hundred sea miles behind her and her lookouts had reported the hundred-island archipelago of Scilly well off to starboard. *Ranger* then eased her sheets to settle into a more northerly course that would bring her into the Celtic Sea, a body of water bounded by Wales, southeastern Ireland, and southwestern England. Once the rich hunting grounds of Viking, Norman, and Celtic pirates, today these waters were patrolled by the Royal Navy, giving chase and no quarter to what few smugglers and brigands remained.

On the graveyard watch during the second night out from Brittany, Richard Cutler walked the decks as officer of the watch. Because *Ranger* was now sailing in enemy waters, the entire larboard watch was on duty on the weather deck or below on the gun deck. There was little for the men to do. The wind continued to blow cold but fair from the west southwest, filling the top sails, spanker, and single jib, propelling *Ranger* on during the night at a sustained and easily manageable pace; nothing in the star-spangled sky suggested a change in conditions anytime soon.

At two bells into the watch, Richard ordered Ben Farley, the master's mate, to determine the ship's speed. Farley yielded the helm to Richard and summoned a second petty officer on watch duty nearby. At the stern taffrail he picked up a sizable chip log in the shape of an equilateral triangle attached by line to a reel. After checking for possible kinks in the line knotted at forty-seven foot intervals with white strips of cloth, he tossed it overboard at the same time his mate turned over a twenty-eight-second hourglass. Together they carefully recorded how many strips of cloth passed through Farley's fingers before the sand in the hourglass ran out.

"Five and a half knots, sir," was reported to Richard.

"Thank you, Mr. Farley. Steady as she goes."

"Steady as she goes, aye, sir," said Farley, resuming his position at the wheel.

Richard recorded the ship's speed, wind direction, and course on the chalk slate hanging by the binnacle and did some dead reckoning of his own. At this speed, with a clear horizon, they should sight the southeastern coast of Ireland by midmorning, absent any unanticipated quirks in ocean currents, tidal flows, or wind shifts. From what he could see and sense tonight, Richard discounted the possibility of any such contrary force during the next twenty-four hours. They would sight the Irish coast midway through the morning watch, he would bet on it. The captain would bring her in close to that rocky shore where deep water was confirmed by reliable charts, then jibe her over on a run to the northeast into St. George's Channel, which connected the Celtic Sea with the Irish Sea.

The prospect of imminent battle weighed heavily on Richard's mind, as he knew it did on the mind of every man aboard *Ranger*. It was a subject that lingered just below the surface of shipboard conversations like raw meat set in a trap, yet it remained one unspoken, taboo, the trap mechanism rarely engaged. Richard fought hard to keep such thoughts at bay by focusing on the tasks at hand and by reminding himself whence he had come and why. He refused to broach the forbidden subject, though he knew his messmates wished that he, as senior midshipman, would. He did not know, could not yet know, why he refused so adamantly—his messmates were, after all, his closest friends aboard ship, and Agreen one of his closest friends ever—but he sensed his reticence was born not so much from a fear of dying as a fear of something he believed was worse than dying: becoming maimed, crippled for life, a deformed creature cast out, no longer of use to anyone. As he walked the deck and inspected the guns, he saw in the eyes of those who greeted him that they too had crossed mental swords in the timeless self-examination of men about to engage in battle.

"Mistah Cutlah. Mistah Cutlah, suh!"

Richard was on one knee beside a gun when Scipio Africanus came bounding up to him. His teeth and the whites of his eyes shone brilliantly in the glow of a three-quarter moon.

Richard stood up. He put his hands on his hips and looked squarely down at the young boy. "What are you doing on deck, Scipio? You should be below, asleep."

"It's my watch, suh," Scipio replied, grinning.

"Your watch? What are you talking about? Powder monkeys are exempt from night duty. You know that."

"I do, suh. I knows it well. But I got t' thinkin' my place be here on deck with you, suh. I been 'signed to number-three bat'rey," he said, his skinny chest puffing out with pride when he added, "That's your battery, Mistah Cutlah."

"I'm aware of that," Richard said with mock resignation. During the previous day he had been informed by Joshua Loring who had been informed by Captain Jones that Scipio Africanus was to be transferred to number-three battery. It was not an official transfer, since powder monkeys served all guns. But it was the battery that the boy had requested. "You, Scipio, are the only person aboard this ship who can get whatever he wants from the captain, whenever he wants it."

"Thankee, suh. I knows that too!" The grin on Scipio's face expanded if such a thing were possible. "Think we'll see action tomorree, suh? I do."

"I doubt tomorrow," Richard said, "but soon enough." He laid his hand on the boy's shoulder. "Get below and get some sleep, Scipio. I need you rested in case we do see action tomorrow. Can't have you nodding off on duty, now can we? Not with a job as important as yours."

"No suh. I mean, yessuh. I mean, aye, aye, suh." Scipio giggled at his confusion. "But Mistah Cutlah, it smells somethin' *awful* down there."

Scipio was right. It did smell something awful down there. The bracing scents of freshly hewn oak and cedar had long since yielded to the rancid odors of one hundred forty men sleeping, smoking, eating, and, when rain thrummed on the crew's latrines outside on the beakhead, urinating in a confined space shared with rats and other denizens thriving in an environment of filth and stench. Such rank odors resisted the efforts of sailors' scrubbing the decks with a mixture of sulfur and vinegar, as they had done since the days of Magellan, and burning stale tobacco in metal pots. Where Scipio and the other ship's boys were berthed, in the forwardmost part of the forecastle by the manger, lurked the most fetid odors of all. It was here that the pigs, ducks, sheep, and chickens herded aboard at Nantes were tethered in pens seldom cleaned out. "A fish stinks from the head," was an expression Richard had once heard in Boston. To his mind, it was an expression equally applicable to a ship long at sea.

"Below with you, lad," he commanded.

"Aye, aye, suh." Scipio saluted and raced off to the fore hatchway leading below. "Good night, Mistah Cutlah," he called out, his grin as infectious as ever.

Good night? Six bells had struck at the forecastle and at the small bell mounted at the break of the quarterdeck railing. In less than one hour, at four o'clock in the morning, bosun's mates would be weaving among the hammocks, rousting out the starboard watch. This morning, Richard reminded himself, the crew must take extra care in cramming their hammocks tightly within the bulwark nettings. In the event of battle, they would provide much needed cover to those on the weather decks.

Richard resumed his methodical walk, touching his hat to David Wendell, the junior watch officer, walking slowly toward him.

"All is well, David?"

"Aye, Richard. You?"

"Yes."

Richard moved on but something made him stop and turn around. David Wendell was standing a few feet away from him, watching him, his features faint in the glow of moon and lanterns.

"What is it, David?"

Wendell stepped closer and spoke softly lest anyone overhear them. "Nothing, really . . . It's . . . eerie, that's all . . . I mean, here we are, one small ship. And there's England out there, our enemy, with the most powerful navy in the world. And we're about to attack it." He held his hands out with palms up, as a priest would during communion. "Lieutenant Simpson's not right, is he, Richard? This cruise isn't just lunacy, is it? We will survive, won't we?"

"That's certainly the captain's intent," Richard assured him, his measured tone meant to convince himself as much as the younger midshipman. They were edging toward that forbidden zone of conversation; Richard proceeded carefully. "This is no suicide mission, David. Remember that. We have surprise on our side. The British don't know we're here. The last thing they would expect is what we're about to do."

Wendell laughed nervously. "For what our enemy is about to receive may the Lord make us truly grateful," he said, with impressive bravado.

At eight bells the watch changed. Richard and David Wendell met Agreen Crabtree and Charles Charrier on the quarterdeck. They returned their salutes and handed over the reins of responsibility to them. Joshua Loring emerged from a hatchway amidships, followed by Elijah Hall as the commands and shouts of bosun's mates bellowed up from below amid groans and curses of men roused from dreams into drudgery. Dull shards of daybreak were brightening the eastern sky as lookouts scampered aloft to scan 360 degrees around the ship for any nick of sail or, worse, the hull of an enemy ship.

"All clear!" the lookouts shouted down from all three masts, and the morning routine began anew.

Despite a serious lack of sleep in recent days, Richard was not tired. He was off duty and could have opted to go below to coax what rest he could. Instead he remained on the weather deck amidships, out of the way of sailors going about their predawn duty of scrubbing, polishing, and coiling. Pulling the warmth of his woolen boat cloak tightly around him, he gazed out upon a scene changing color like a slow-moving chameleon from black to dark gray, from slate to white gray, ultimately to a startling deep blue in the frost of an April dawn. Everywhere the morning sun danced serenely off the waves, casting a panorama of glittering jewels before him. *Ranger* had held true to her northwesterly course, and Richard felt her bow lift as sailors aloft lowered the fore course from its fixed yards and hauled up the flying jib. Topgallants and royals remained furled, however, to make *Ranger* less visible to a passing ship.

"Blessin's of the morning to ye, sir," a gunner's mate greeted Richard. A veteran of the Royal Navy in the late 1760s, he was wearing the short blue jacket and round woolen cap of a petty officer, and he had his hair tied back in a queue with a piece of codline. He knuckled his forehead in salute and gave Richard a smile that verified which front teeth had been punched out in Nantes during a drunken tavern brawl. Only the quick and hard-lined intervention of Lieutenant Simpson with the local magistrates had kept much of *Ranger*'s complement of petty officers out of a French prison.

"And to you, Covey," Richard replied. "It's a fine morning we're blessed with." As he spoke, he couldn't avoid noticing the right side of Covey's face, swollen as it was with an ugly discoloration from the lower jaw up to where a silver ring hung from the man's ear lobe. "Have you seen the surgeon recently?" he asked.

"Have not, sir," Covey confessed, instinctively massaging the area with his fingertips. "I did see 'im after it 'appened though. The fight, I mean. Broken, 'e told me, and it'll take weeks, mebbe months to 'eal proper, 'ssumin' it ever does. Which it won't. But no matter. 'Taint nuthin' anyone can do."

"I'm sorry. It looks mighty painful."

"'Tis, sir, 'tis. But it's me own bloody fault. I 'preciate yer concern, though, sir, sincerely I do." Covey knuckled his forehead a second time and ambled aft.

Richard leaned against the bulwark and folded his arms in front of him above the hammock nettings, at chin level. The wind had freshened a knot or two and felt inviting against his face, the chill it carried more soothing than anything else. Amid the beauty and serenity of an open sea at dawn, always his favorite time of day, it did not seem possible that *Ranger* was sailing on an irrevocable course of death and destruction. Feeling instead a sense of contentment rare for him these days, he stared out at the white-tipped waves and summoned to mind images of life, not death, and what life signified to him while in the arms of Anne-Marie Helvétian.

☆ ☆ ☆

THEY HAD made it through the first act of *The Barber of Seville*. Earlier that after-noon, during *un déjeuner très agréeable* at Passy, Richard had listened with amusement as Anne-Marie described with girlish enthusiasm the play they were to see that evening at the Tuileries. Richard found himself caring little about Don Bartolo and Count Almaviva and their love triangle with Rosina, but Anne-Marie would see nothing suggesting disinterest on his face as she rambled on excitedly. After they arrived at the palace and were seated in the sky blue theater within a private alcove reserved for them by Anne-Marie, her manner bore no resemblance to what he had witnessed earlier in Passy. Well into the act, during a scene in which Figaro was plotting with the disguised count on how to win the heart of the popular Rosina, she rested her head on Richard's shoulder and began rubbing her hand up and down the upper arm of his blue midshipman's coat, her thoughts seemingly far removed from the farcical doings on stage. When Richard, questioning, gently lifted her chin, in the same motion she brought her lips to his, her left arm curling around his neck, her lips parting, her tongue an indicator of her fierce desire. When the act was over and the audience preoccupied with applause and shouts of ap-preciation, they arose together, drawn up by the same conclusion, and walked from the alcove to the grand hallway, with its massive Doric columns and magnificent stairway, and out the front doors of the palace to where their car-riage waited at curbside.

"Please, hear me out, Anne-Marie," Richard had managed as their carriage approached her residence in Passy, her mother away for the evening, never one to interfere with her daughter's *affaire de coeur.* The world was swirling around him: he had no foothold, no anchor, nothing to stem the heady tide of passion save for fleeting vestiges of his rigid Puritan upbringing and fast-evaporating, misguided notions of female sexuality drummed into him by overzealous, Bible-thumping preachers of God. "Is this really what you want? I'm leaving soon for my ship. I may never come back here. I may never see you again."

She nuzzled into the hollow of his neck, kissing him there. *"Je sais bien,"* she whispered, her breath sensually warm on his ear, her husky voice reinforcing his own arousal. "Our days may be numbered, *mon chéri,* but even so, I shall al-ways have the memory of you."

Always have the memory of you. Richard had savored those words then as he savored them now, their mere recollection stirring his loins. Only one other person had ever said anything like that to him, and that had been years ago, in another, more innocent age when he was young and free and uninitiated and her country was not at war with his. He was older now, a young man who had been swept deeply and willingly into the blissful abyss of physical rapture with a young woman of beauty and substance and sexual appetite who could have had any man she desired—and she had chosen him. He cared for her deeply, and he knew she cared for him that way. But was there more he could feel? Should feel? He may have been young in those days of innocence, but what he had felt then, and what he had held close to his heart ever since, was something quite unlike what he now felt for Anne-Marie.

On the morning of his departure from Passy she had smiled brightly at him and had chatted in casual tones as he and Captain Jones and Lieutenant Wallingford said their goodbyes to the assembled hosts. It was as though he was embarking on a routine call to duty and would be returning to her before the week was out. Only her brief, hard cling at their last embrace confirmed what feelings were being restrained. His last view from the carriage was of Anne-Marie standing before the magnificence of the chateau de Chaumont beside Dr. Franklin, the old man's arm draped consolingly around her shoulders as she raised her hand in final farewell.

THE SOUND of seamen piped to breakfast brought him back with a start. A quick glance of the sun off the horizon confirmed how long he had been daydreaming. He looked to his right. Agreen was leaning against the bulwarks exactly as he was, with his hands folded before him.

"How long have you been there?" Richard asked him.

"A spell. Figured you might want t' talk. If I figured wrong, just tell me t' shove off."

"I'd prefer you stay," Richard said a little sheepishly. He knew Agreen would not open the subject of Anne-Marie. Upon Richard's return from Paris, Agreen had sensed that something profoundly personal had happened to his friend there. Whoever she was, Richard made it clear more from what he didn't say that she would not be subjected to typical shipboard swagger and crude jokes. "Any change in our course or speed?"

"No change. Callum claims we'll be sightin' Ireland anytime now. We're makin' near ten knots last time I checked."

Richard glanced aloft at the yards braced half-over and the snowy white courses and topsails bellying out taut from them. "Those French shipwrights sure know their trade, don't they, Agee? Have you noticed how much better *Ranger* sails now? Whatever the cost, it was worth it."

Crabtree chuckled. "I agree. But you should have been there when those shipwrights started cuttin' down her masts an' yards. Hall was fit t' be tied, a mad cock peckin' on frickin' hens in the coop, with them Frenchmen cursin' and hollerin' Lord only knows what. If the Frogs had said the hell with it, an' the captain had come back with *Ranger* not ready for sea, I'd've jumped ship."

"Why was Hall so mad?"

"Waste of time 'n money, he kept sayin.' If *Ranger* had been out takin' prizes, he claimed, we'd all be gettin' rich 'stead of doin' all this work ashore an' the captain dallyin' about fancylike in Paris. A lot of men agreed with him, I'm sorry t' say. Hall met with the crew an' reads out the pamphlet he and Simpson drew up. Asks for a show of hands like we're in some sort o' frickin' Congress. Some sailors took his side. No marines did, though. Probably figured if they had, Wallingford would see 'em choked with their own neckstocks when he returned."

Richard whistled softly. "So that's what was behind the petition."

He was referring to a formal petition presented to the captain by Lt. Elijah Hall after Jones's return to Nantes. It had been signed by certain members of the ship's crew, and it sought approval on a policy for taking prizes as *Ranger's* primary objective in European waters. The petition went on to request that representatives of the crew be informed of the captain's intentions, with power to override his orders if they were deemed contrary to the agreement. Jones had calmly read the petition out loud at the quarterdeck railing, with his officers beside him and the entire ship's complement assembled below on the weather deck. He had then taken his time tearing the document into tiny shreds, letting the pieces fall as litter onto the deck below. Further discussion of this petition was forbidden, he informed the crew. Henceforth, any man heard so much as whispering this sort of mutiny would receive two dozen lashes at the grate. Any man openly espousing it would be hanged on the spot. Was he understood?

He was. The matter was dropped—but forgotten?

"Haven't had much time t' talk with you, Richard, since Simpson put us on different watches."

"I understand, Agee. But tell me, Where was Simpson in all this?"

"I'm surprised you have to ask that, Mr. Cutler."

They turned, startled, to face the gangly first officer, the curl of his lip conveying his opinion of them both. They had not heard him approaching, nor were they aware that their voices had risen in volume to tones of normal conversation.

"Who's on duty here?" Simpson demanded, his narrowed eyes flickering from one to the other. Seamen on that section of the weather deck promptly found chores to do elsewhere.

"I am, sir," said Agreen, at attention.

"So it's my *other* nemesis, Mr. Crabtree," Simpson said, with a tinge of disappointment. "If you are on duty, what are you doing here lollygagging with Mr. Cutler?

"Answer me, Mr. Crabtree!" he barked when Agreen did not respond.

"Mr. Crabtree and I were not lollygagging, sir," Richard said tightly. "He was asking my opinion about—"

"Shut your gob, Cutler," Simpson sneered, his face darkening. "I wasn't addressing you. When I want your opinion about something, I'll ask for it, though I'd advise you not to hold your breath waiting." His eyes swung back to Agreen. When he spoke, it was in an odd, sing-song kind of voice. "Well, Mr. Crabtree, here you are, my duty officer, clearly acting as though you're off duty. That alone is cause for punishment, wouldn't you say? What's more, I have caught you leaning against a bulwark while on duty. You do realize that is forbidden a midshipman?" It was a rhetorical question and technically he was correct, but it was a Royal Navy regulation that Jones had never enforced.

"What to do, what to do," Simpson pondered, stroking his chin as he balanced the scales of justice in his mind. "Aha, I think I have it. As punishment, you, Mr. Crabtree, shall spend twelve hours in the foremast crosstrees . . . No . . . No . . . Let's make that twenty-four hours. That would serve better. Give you more time to think about your dereliction. Go to sleep up there and you might even learn some humility, should you survive the fall. Mr. Cutler will bring your vittles up to you. Trust me, Cutler, you so much as whisper to

Crabtree while you're up there, you shall receive the same punishment. In fact, I—"

"Land ho!" The shout from the lookout above drew everyone's attention forward. There was nothing to see, of course. The lookout's perch gave him a good fifteen-mile advantage in range over those on deck.

"As I was saying," Simpson resumed, and again he was interrupted.

"Sail ho!" another lookout cried with a great deal more urgency.

Simpson glanced up, annoyed. He cupped his hands around his mouth. "Where away?"

"Two points off the starboard bow, sir."

"What is she?"

"Can't see her hull yet, sir. She's ship-rigged, showing plain sail to royals. She's coming straight at us."

"Very well," Simpson harrumphed. He looked back at the two midshipmen, the lurid gleam gone from his eyes. "Trust me, gentlemen, this conversation is not over. Mr. Cutler, go below and inform the captain of this ship, a merchantman most likely."

"Aye, aye, sir."

The marine sentry stiffened as Richard approached the captain's cabin. Without uttering a word he knocked three times on the door and announced that Midshipman Cutler was outside and wished to see the captain.

"Show him in," Jones called out.

Richard ducked under the door beam and entered a cabin awash in morning sunlight. Captain Jones was seated at his desk in plain white shirt and breeches, holding a mug of steaming coffee at his lips. Across the table from him sat Israel Baker, the ship's purser, a weasel-looking man with a long neck and thin head, with only a trace of eyebrows and long bushy sideburns. Judging by the way he kept wringing his gnarled hands, his accounting of the ship's stores was, as usual, not going well.

"Good morning, Mr. Cutler," Jones said. "What news?"

Richard saluted. "Good morning, Captain. Lieutenant Simpson's duty and there is a ship fine on our starboard bow."

"What sort of ship?"

"I don't know for certain, sir. She's hull-down. But she's ship-rigged and showing all plain sail. Including royals," he added significantly.

"Bearing?"

"To the north, sir. Her heading is due south, and her topsails are rising."

"Pennants? Flags?"

"None reported by the lookout, sir."

"Damn it, man, you should have asked him!" Jones snarled, causing the purser to wince. Then, in a more contrite tone: "Very well, Mr. Cutler, thank you. I shall come up presently." He went back to studying the books.

"Aye, aye, sir."

Richard made to leave but turned back, hesitating.

Jones glanced up. "Is there something else, Mr. Cutler?"

"Sir, the lookout reported all plain sail to royals. In that case, she's not likely a merchantman."

"Very perceptive of you, Mr. Cutler. The thought had occurred to me. As I said, I'll be up presently."

Moments later the captain was on deck in his shirt and breeches despite the cold, his long auburn hair fluttering lose about his face and shoulders as he directed a glass northward. He lowered the glass, scoured the horizon with his bare eyes, then raised the glass again, extending its length, contracting it, searching for the point of sharpest focus. Not satisfied, he slung the instrument over his shoulder and hauled himself up onto the mizzen shrouds, climbing rapidly up the ratlines to the mizzentop. There he remained, his glass trained on the other ship, studying the tiny pyramid of white growing larger by the minute. By the time he descended to the deck, the other ship was nearly hull up, a few miles away, not quite high enough off the horizon for the other officers to see what Jones had seen: a thin white line running from stem to stern along a strake halfway up from the waterline. A British warship typically had her gunport strake painted white or yellow, to identify her in the smoke of battle.

"She's a Royal Navy corvette," Jones confirmed, "a light frigate about our size. Her captain has seen us and obviously has an interest in us."

"Shall we run up the Union Jack, sir?" Agreen asked, assuming the captain would again seek to pass *Ranger* off as a British ship.

Jones mentally calculated distance, time, and relative positions of the two ships. They were six, maybe seven miles apart, the Britisher sailing south close-hauled, *Ranger* sailing northwest with the wind abeam. Given the course each was following, they should converge in approximately thirty minutes. Ireland lay to the northwest, her coastline still not visible. So there was ample sea room ahead.

"No, Mr. Crabtree. Stand by the Stars and Stripes, and pass word for the drummers." To the helmsman: "Keep her steady, northwest by north, a quarter north."

"Northwest by north, a quarter north, aye, sir."

Jones also passed word for his lieutenants and midshipmen. When they were assembled on the quarterdeck, Jones addressed them with the same controlled exhilaration Richard had noticed before whenever serious danger beckoned.

"Mr. Simpson, Mr. Hall," he said to his two most senior officers, "ever since we set out from Portsmouth, you have been hounding me about taking a prize. Am I correct?"

Simpson and Hall remained stone silent.

"I shall take that to mean yes. *Yes sir,*" Jones added wryly. "Gentlemen," he said to everyone present, "here is our situation. We are about to engage the Royal Navy. We're evenly matched as far as I can tell. I'm betting they'll think we too are British and engaged in gun drills, so we'll try to lure her in with a blank shot from number-two gun in"—he consulted his watch—"ten minutes. Run out the other guns and load them with chain shot and grape. Aim high for her rigging, quoins out all the way. I'm wagering she'll bear up to windward of us, so stand by the larboard guns. Now gentlemen, let us beat to quarters."

"Beat to quarters!" Simpson shouted out. "Clear for action!"

The call was taken up by marine drummers striking out a sustained rapid tattoo on both the gun and weather decks.

From long and insistent drilling the crew moved like automatons through the evolutions for preparing the ship for battle: extinguishing galley fires, dismantling cabin bulkheads, sprinkling sand around the guns for better footing, rigging the head pumps, stowing anything portable and wooden in the lazaret in the stern. Forward of the midshipmen's mess, at the magazine, heavy canvas curtains soaked in water were hung around the approaches to deny life to any stray spark that might find its way below. Scipio and Cato and the other powder monkeys, in their youth oblivious to danger, waited excitedly to receive canisters of powder and shot from Gunner Bingham. Above, on the weather deck, axes were placed beside each mast in the event it went by the boards and its standing rigging had to be hacked away. Marines armed with Brown Bess muskets crouched low at the bulwarks, out of sight behind tightly padded hammock nettings. Others scrambled up the shrouds to the swivel guns positioned at the tops, muzzle-loading each infant cannon with flannel bags of half-pound balls.

On the gun deck, crews unfastened the lashings securing each cannon and hauled the weapon inboard on train tackle until the breeching rope was taut and the muzzle was inside the opened port. Men thrust handspikes under the breech, and using a step on the side of the truck as a fulcrum, levered up its back end just enough to allow the gun captain to remove the thick wedge-shaped quoin beneath the base. Each gun was thus positioned at the maximum twelve degrees of elevation.

Preparing the guns for battle had by now become standard drill with one exception: it was not round shot the gun crews rammed down the barrels, rather chain shot—two round balls connected by a two-foot piece of chain, designed to play havoc with a ship's top-hamper—or tin canisters of grapeshot, a mass of eight-ounce balls mixed together with scraps of chain, lead bolts, bits of broken glass, anything small and metal and sharp that would explode, when fired at close range, like a mammoth blunderbuss, sweeping enemy decks and rigging clear of anyone in its path.

One by one, the loaded guns were run outboard.

One deck below, in the midshipmen's berth, Ezra Green and his mate Jacob Walden smoothed a sheath of white canvas over a wooden plank secured over four sea chests. Laid out beside this makeshift operating table were a row of tourniquets and an evil-looking array of saws.

The British frigate was closing in. Richard could see her hull clearly through an open port. She had a black hull with a sweeping sheer accentuated by the sharp white strake where ten square black cavities marked where her gun ports had been opened. Once she crossed *Ranger's* wake she would, he suspected, round up to take position on a parallel course. That maneuver would give her the weather gauge, a relative position in battle favored by the Royal Navy. In any combat at sea, so ruled the lords of the Admiralty, a ship to windward of another ipso facto held the advantage for a number of reasons relating to superior maneuverability and control of the engagement. There was no cause, yet, for the British captain to suspect that *Ranger* might be an enemy vessel, but if only to protect his reputation, he would haul to windward and open his ports.

Ranger had spilled her wind and had her fore and main courses brailed up, hanging in their gear, her speed slowing as if to acknowledge the British captain's intent and allow him to catch up more quickly. Richard knew that what Jones really was doing was altering *Ranger's* sail plan for battle.

On the gun deck, standing at attention by each hatchway, marines stood ready to prevent anyone from going below who was not on official business.

From the weather deck above, David Wendell called down to Joshua Loring, the officer of the starboard battery, in a voice carrying the cocky authority of one serving the captain.

"Captain's compliments, Mr. Loring, and please fire number-two gun."

"Firing number-two gun," Loring confirmed. He blew gently on a glowing slow match, brought it to life, then brought the linstock down to the touch-hole. There was a sharp hiss, and the gun breathed fire, jerking back in a harsh recoil until restrained by its thick breeching ropes. Men stationed by the muzzle rammed a pole down the barrel with a wet sponge at the end, twisting it, extinguishing any stubborn sparks or smoldering shreds of cartridge. With the pole removed, others reloaded the gun with powder cartridge and wad, and this time, with a thrust of chain shot.

The crew had functioned as a team, doing what had to be done as efficiently as possible, relying on every man to execute his assigned task. The captain would be pleased, Richard thought.

"Action's acomin', suh! I told yah! I told yah so!"

Scipio, grinning as ever, was sitting on a cylindrical wooden cartridge box in the middle of the deck. He had his hands clapped over his ears, and his eyes clearly were smarting from acrid smoke lingering about. Richard drew a kerchief from a pocket in his midshipman's coat and handed it to him.

"Wrap this around your ears, Scipio. It doesn't fit me anyway."

"Aye, aye, suh. Thankee, suh! I told yah we'd see action t'day, didn't I, suh?"

"You did, Scipio. Now stay low."

Those aboard *Ranger* waited to see how the close-hauled British ship would respond. Firing a blank round to leeward was an international signal of good will between vessels at sea. Trouble was, it had become an overly used *ruse de guerre,* a trick to lure an enemy to within close range. A wise sea captain received such a message with caution. Which was why, Richard suspected as he peered out to starboard, this Royal Navy captain had ordered his guns run out.

Suddenly, inexplicably, the British ship tacked through the southwesterly breeze and assumed a new course to leeward of *Ranger.* She had slackened sail but was nonetheless gaining on the American. Richard estimated the two ships would be parallel within ten minutes.

Midshipman Wendell relayed the captain's urgent order below. Gun crews sprang from the larboard side of the ship to guns directly opposite on the starboard side. Men shoved handspikes under the horns of the truck and hauled on side tackle to lever the back end of each gun to the left, foot by foot, inch by inch, until every gun forward of the ship's beam was trained aft as far as possible.

When the tip of the British ship's jibboom was parallel to *Ranger*'s stern, Richard heard Jones's voice on the quarterdeck.

"What ship is that?" he demanded through a speaking trumpet.

"His Majesty's frigate *Drake*," the bold answer came back. "I am Captain Burden. Who are you, sir, and what is your ship?"

Jones lowered the trumpet and signaled to Charles Charrier to send up the American colors. To his sailing master: "Nudge her into the wind and slack the mizzen. At my command, have the mizzen sheets hauled in and the fore course set. I'll need that done smartly, Mr. Callum."

To the British captain, he called out, "I am Captain Jones sir, and this vessel is the Continental ship *Ranger*."

There was a pause. "Say again, sir?"

"You heard me correctly, Captain Burden. This is a ship of the United States Navy."

Drake's bows were parallel to *Ranger*'s stern, fifty, perhaps sixty yards to starboard. Though *Drake* was in *Ranger*'s lee, she had more sail set and was sailing a little faster. The breeze picked up. As *Ranger* eased into the wind, Callum ordered the sheets loosened on the driver, causing the great mizzen sail to jounce and slatter. Her way quickly came off her, as did her heel, thus elevating her starboard guns.

"I do not take kindly to your jest, sir," the call came back in the impeccably modulated tones of English aristocracy. "And why that flag? I say, are you a privateer?"

"I am not, sir," Jones replied. "A privateer would run from you. I intend to fight you."

Richard could only imagine the difficulty Burden was having comprehending the situation. Here was a ship flying a traitor's flag in the heart of

British home waters, a flag none aboard his ship had ever seen. What's more, her rogue captain had just threatened a Royal Navy vessel.

Drake was inching ahead in relative position to *Ranger*. She had shadowed *Ranger's* slight turn into the wind, and her bow was parallel to *Ranger's* main-mast. The guns of each ship were now trained on the other. Burden, exasper-ated, ventured one last stab at credulity.

"Why do you jest, sir? There *is* no United States Navy."

"No? Well, perhaps this will convince you."

Jones calmly put the speaking trumpet down and picked up a glass, di-recting the lens toward *Drake's* quarterdeck. "Fire as they bear," he said to Lieutenant Simpson.

Simpson hesitated giving the order. Jones glowered at him, rage embed-ded in his eyes and voice.

"Do it, Simpson, damn your soul!"

"Fire as they bear!" Simpson shouted below. An instant later *Ranger's* star-board side erupted as nine thunderous blasts hurled spears of orange flame at the enemy, a vomit of bright yellow sparks trailing in their wake. Projectiles shrieked through the air, cutting a savage swath through rigging and sails, slashing canvas and rope and the flesh of screaming men. So simultaneous was the broadside that the three-hundred-ton *Ranger* was shoved sideways against the Atlantic, flinging her crew off balance into gray, stinging clouds of spent gunpowder.

Richard stumbled, wrapped his arm around the mainmast for support. "Worm and sponge out!" he shouted blindly to his men. "Reload!"

Men coughed and sputtered and waved their arms furiously to clear the air. Staggering back to the guns, they somehow managed to reload the guns and heave on the side tackle, hauling them outboard with their wheels squeal-ing in protest.

Drake veered to starboard. Coming off the wind a point to allow her after guns to bear, she answered *Ranger's* onslaught with a broadside of her own. In a perfectly timed sequence, one report immediately following the other, her ten larboard guns belched fire and round shot. Two six-pound iron balls crashed against *Ranger's* thick wooden strakes, bouncing off harmlessly. Several others sent spumes of water high into the air nearby. An-other found a less resilient target. At the helm, a quartermaster's mate screamed in horror when a shot hit the top of the wheel, sending up fragments of wood, flesh, and bone. Shipmates helping him below tried to stem the flow of blood squirting like some gruesome water hose from the stump of his forearm.

"Let fall the fore course! Trim the mizzen sheets!" Jones cried on the quarterdeck. *Ranger* surged forward with the added press of sail. "Up helm! Brace the yards! Stand by, starboard guns!"

Ranger fell off the wind, her yards square, on a course that would take her across *Drake's* bow at a distance of twenty yards.

At number-seven gun, Agreen beckoned Richard over to an open gun port, pointing to the mayhem visible on *Drake's* weather deck. With *Ranger's* opening salvo, both ships had been sailing with the wind on their beam, their yards braced half-around. The lowest yard on *Drake's* mainmast had been struck by chain shot streaking end over end through the air, nearly severing its larboard end. The broken piece hung down like a lower leg with its shinbone broken, still attached to the knee by thin strands of tendon.

The two ships were sailing close on opposite tacks; the two midshipmen could see *Drake's* crew frantically struggling to toss fallen rigging and rent canvas overboard as American sharpshooters high on the tops and low behind the hammock nettings had at them without mercy. British sailors and marines were falling onto the deck or into the sea with every sharp crack of musket fire and the louder, more caustic pomp of swivel guns.

"What madness is this, Agee?" Richard exclaimed. He was aghast, watching in morbid fascination, as though he were some sort of idle spectator detached from the mayhem. "What is her captain thinking? We're about to rake her and he doesn't seem to give a damn."

Sailors on both ships, British and American, understood that there was only one position worse in a sea battle than where *Drake* found herself now, with an enemy crossing her bow, preparing to rake her. She had no bow chasers and could not train her cannon directly forward; thus she was naked, exposed, her entire body open to the blood lust of her enemy. There were only two reasons why a naval captain would stomach such punishment to his ship: either he could no longer effectively maneuver his vessel, or by taking the punishment, he would have his enemy in the *worst* tactical position, exposed to a rake from the stern. Captain Burden had apparently made a conscious decision to suffer hell and remain on course.

"Stand by the starboard guns!" Joshua Loring cried out, his voice high-pitched with fear and defiance.

Richard squeezed Agreen's arm and returned to his station. It was time. *Drake* was near enough for *Ranger*'s crew to make out the carved figurehead slanting out from the stem, her serene, almost saintlike expression ludicrously out of place in this scene of carnage.

Agreen fired the four guns under his command. Richard's battery was next. He bent low to windward over number-nine gun, holding the linstock in his right hand with the glowing end up. He didn't bother to take aim; it was point-blank range. "Stand clear," he warned his gun crew, then "*Fire!*"

He jabbed the slow match down, igniting the powder. The cannon thundered and recoiled sharply, lurching against its ropes.

He whirled to his right, to the next cannon, number eleven, jabbing fire at the touchhole. The gun roared and recoiled, the cacophonous sequence continuing until all nine starboard guns had shot and an eerie quiet had settled over the deck, broken by men coughing and wheezing, staring out numbly, gazing up past the weather deck to the fore and mainmast tops where the battle raged on with small-arms fire. A marine in the main top was hit. He reeled backward with the impact, hesitating a moment as if unsure whether to stem the flow of blood from his stomach or grab onto something to stop the fall. He whirled once in a full circle, then toppled from the platform, careening off the inside railing on the weather deck, hitting the gun deck on his back with a dull thud. He lay still, his blank eyes gazing upward, blood oozing from his mouth and nose.

His throat raw from smoke and his eyes burning, Richard stepped up beside a hot muzzle and peered astern through its port. The broadside had taken a savage toll. *Drake* was on her original course, making little headway. Her fore-topsail was all but useless, a mass of riddled canvas no longer able to belly out and power the ship forward. Spars and yards lay gashed and splintered; sails flapped impotently back and forth in the steady breeze. The battle was over; as a fighting platform, HMS *Drake* looked as though it had been reduced to a drifting mash of rubble heaped onto her weather deck.

That was Richard's impression, which was why, a moment later, he stared in disbelief as *Drake*'s crew suddenly came to life on the fore course footropes and worked the great sail loose, letting it fall from a miraculously undamaged yard. The white spread of canvas caught the wind, propelling the ravaged warship forward to one last act of retribution.

"Down helm! Down helm! Brace up! Clap on t'gallants! Move you men, smartly now, damn your sorry hides!"

The demands from the quarterdeck brought Richard quickly to his station by the guns, their crews pared by the captain's frantic call to sailing duty. Never before had he heard panic in the voice of John Paul Jones.

Dazed men, their ears ringing, reacted slowly, grudgingly, to the commands all but screamed at them by bosun's mates. *Ranger* was in mortal danger. Jones had gambled that two withering broadsides, one a rake from the bow, would effectively put his foe out of action. He had guessed wrong. Her body may have been ravished, but *Drake* still had fight in her soul. As her fore mainsail dropped down and was sheeted home, she lunged forward with every remaining shred of canvas to train her starboard guns on her enemy's vulnerable stern. *Ranger* had to haul her wind—and quickly. She began her jibe to the southeast, her jib boom sprouting more sail to kick her bow into the wind and her stern away from the enemy's guns. With his lips pursed, Richard stood staring at the stern windows until he heard the report of a distant gun.

"Down! On deck! Everyone down!" Joshua Loring cried.

The ball fell short, ten feet from the stern, throwing up a plume of water. A second ball whined overhead, punching through the main-topsail, then the fore-topsail, hitting nothing of substance before splashing into the sea ahead. *Ranger* was turning faster now. Another thirty seconds, forty-five at most, and she'd have turned enough to have her hull facing the enemy, her own guns primed to fire. Some men, assuming the immediate danger had passed, began to rise to their feet, prompting Richard to do the same.

He was balanced on one knee when one shot, then two exploded through the starboard quarter-gallery. Glass shattered and flew about, lacerating the skin of men stationed at number-four battery. The balls careened on, striking a gun with an infernal clang, ricocheting this way and that, pulverizing planks, mast, and bone, launching shards of jagged wood into flesh and muscle, seeking vengeance like iron demons gone mad until finally exhausting themselves in one last dreadful spasm of demolition. It had lasted but a few seconds; in the gruesome aftermath, even badly injured men watched spellbound as the two black balls streaked with blood and sand rolled harmlessly about the deck.

Richard lay flat on his stomach with his forearms crossed over his head. In a cruel void filled by the soft moans and shrill cries of wounded men, he listened for blasts of gunfire, a command from the quarterdeck, any sign of continuing action. He heard none. Tentatively, he hauled himself up. A sailor was before him on all fours, writhing in pain from a ragged splinter of wood harpooned deep into his lower thigh, the rhythmic spurting of blood proof positive that that his femoral artery had been severed. He would make it, Richard speculated; his leg would not.

"Get that man below," he managed to croak at two seamen nearby. Men were stirring anew, assessing damage to the ship, to themselves, and to shipmates unable to rise. Richard limped to a port, his leg painfully cramped, and confirmed that *Ranger's* course was now dead away from *Drake*. Across the deck in a larboard battery he dimly noted that one gun was atilt, the side of its truck in smithereens and a wheel blown off.

"Report that to the captain," said Elijah Hall, coming up. He was walking unsteadily as though intoxicated, his skin pale, his voice seemingly an echo.

Richard did not respond or salute. He made for a ladder and was about to climb up when he felt a hand grip his shoulder.

"Agee!" he gasped, grateful beyond measure to see his friend alive. "Praise God you're all right. I'm off to report to the captain."

Crabtree's lips were pursed tight; the hair on his forehead was matted straight down above slits of eyes riveted on Richard. His uniform, face, and hands were flecked with blood not his own, and his arms hung down listlessly at his side. "Jesus," was all he could mutter.

The air on the quarterdeck was cold, cleansing. Richard found Jones by the helm, inspecting the damage to the wheel. Given what *Ranger* had just endured, Richard thought, not without a stab of bitterness, the captain was in surprisingly good spirits.

"Well, Mr. Cutler," Jones said when he saw Richard approach, "a little excitement below, what? Glad to see you up and about. I trust that limp is nothing serious. What of the other officers?"

"Near as I can tell, sir, they all made it through." His voice was as depleted as his expression.

"Splendid. Splendid indeed. And the crew?"

"We've taken casualties, sir. We don't know the number yet. I came to report number-fourteen gun out of action."

"Aha. Well, that shouldn't hamper us much." Satisfied the helm remained fully functional, Jones faced forward with his hands thrust behind his back.

"In a moment, Mr. Cutler, we shall come about, and we shall once again engage the enemy. She's ours for the taking, tell the men that. Tell them that today we take a Royal Navy vessel as a prize, and they shall all share in the glory and share in the reward. By God, if that doesn't cheer them up, I don't know what will."

"I'll tell them sir." Richard made to go.

"Mr. Cutler."

"Sir?"

"See to the men," Jones said, empathy entering his voice at last. "And send me the butcher's bill once the battle is over."

"Aye, aye, sir."

Richard's spirits had revived in the bracing sea air. He stepped down to the gun deck where men were hard at work clearing away debris and restoring some sense of order to what a few minutes ago had been a scene of utter chaos. Men injured but able to walk were making their way below to the surgeon or assisting those more seriously wounded.

"We're coming about!" Richard called out to the men. "Stand by the larboard guns. We're going to take her, lads. We're going to take her!"

A sailor leaning against the scarred mainmast let out a cheer that was echoed by others, one by one at first, then quickly increasing in momentum and volume as crews resumed positions by their guns. Up on deck, sailors hauled in *Ranger's* yards until she was sailing on the wind on a south by southeast starboard tack.

"Ready about! Stations for stays!" Jones commanded from the quarterdeck.

"Ship's a good full for stays, sir," David Callum advised him a moment later, meaning that *Ranger* was in position to be turned about with maximum efficiency.

"Ready! Ready! Ease down the helm!" Jones shouted.

Ranger began her tack. Jib sheets forward were eased off, and her spanker boom was hauled in amidships, its great leveraging power helping to draw her stern around like a giant weather vane. Commands and evolutions continued until the order "Main topsail haul!" brought the main and crossjack yards on the mizzen swinging around together, followed by the fore topsail yard. Under a full press of canvas *Ranger* surged forward. Ahead, *Drake* was making desperately for the coast of Ireland and the twin circular turrets of an ancient

Anglo-Norman fortification barely visible on a cliff. It was as though her captain believed the ghost of King John, who had built that fortress, would rise up in biblical fashion to smite the rebel infidels closing fast from astern and thereby redeem his place in history.

It was not to be. *Drake's* guns were intact, but her crew was unable to maneuver her properly. Captain Burden must have realized the battle was over—tactics and relative positions were no longer his to control—still he remained defiant as *Ranger* swept past her stern to pound her aft windows and quarterdeck with nine-pound shot, taking scant punishment in reply.

When *Ranger* tacked around to offer up another withering volley, *Drake* was sagging off the wind. Her rudder post was a shambles, and her driver gaff was severed between the throat and peak halyards, causing her ensign to be dragged behind her in the sea. She had become a shadow of her former self.

A man on *Drake's* quarterdeck desperately waved an arm back and forth as *Ranger* drew near. "Quarter!" he shouted through a trumpet. "In God's name, I ask for quarter, sir!"

"Are you Captain Burden?" Jones shouted back through the speaking trumpet. He had not recognized the less-than-patrician voice.

"Captain Burden is dead," the man affirmed, "as are Lieutenant Dobbs and the other officers. I am the ship's master, I am now in command, and I ask for quarter!"

"Very well, sir, you shall have it," Jones assured him. "And please accept my condolences for the loss of your captain. He was a brave man." After a pause, he called out, "Heave to under my lee as best you can. I am sending over a boat."

Jones stepped forward to the railing amidships and called below to the gun deck.

"Mr. Hall, to the quarterdeck."

When the second lieutenant was standing before him, Jones said: "Mr. Hall, select a crew of fifteen men, plus four marines. Take a boat across to *Drake*. Inform the master that he and two others of his choosing shall be released in the morning to row to Ireland. I want our victory announced in Whitehall, but not for several days. Lock up the rest of her crew, except for any who seem willing to work. We shall send over the carpenter and sailmaker and the more seriously wounded, assuming *Drake's* surgeon is able to care for them. We'll then take *Drake* in tow for twenty-four hours. That should allow enough time to make repairs before you sail her to Brest. When you get there, please inform the American agent of our prize and the French officials of our victory."

Hall's jaw fell. "I am to leave *Ranger,* sir? Would not Lieutenant Loring be a better—"

"You have my orders, Mr. Hall," Jones interrupted him. He turned away.

Richard went below. By a forward hatchway on the gun deck leading to the lower deck, he met Samuel Wallingford coming up. The two shared a look of silent anguish over what the marine lieutenant had himself witnessed. At Richard's questioning look, Wallingford held up six fingers: six marines dead. That left twenty-four alive or clinging to life.

The scene greeting Richard on the main deck was beyond hellish. Where he stood was dark, stygian, reeking of spilled blood and vomit. On the deck lay shadows moaning and whimpering, many begging for someone or something to put them out of their misery, not caring if that meant life or death. Farther aft, in the marines' quarters now serving as an impromptu sickbay, men waited their turn to be examined by the surgeon, dreading more than death itself the one remedy he had in his arsenal for most afflictions. Like Richard, they could see the current patient on the plank beneath the light of two swaying lanterns, and they could too easily hear his muffled screams as two men held him by the shoulders, two others by the legs. Ezra Green, his white apron soaked in blood, picked up a semicircular saw and pressed down hard on the victim's arm halfway between the shoulder and elbow. Moving the saw back and forth in even, rapid motions, he severed the arm and tossed it aside as his mate sealed the raw, bloodied stump with the same hot pitch used to caulk seams. A gag had been stuffed into the wretch's mouth, but there was nothing else to relieve the pain or fear of Green's merciless weapons of amputation. At least, Richard thought, as if such thoughts could make such horror more bearable, Green was a kindly and sober man, Harvard-educated, not the stereotype of a naval surgeon.

Jacob Walden picked up the severed arm and threw it into a large wooden tub accommodating the day's harvest. Green dipped his saw in a smaller basin and swished the serrated edge around in the bloody water. Wiping it off on his apron, he looked around for his next victim. As the poor wretch was carried in, Richard recognized for the first time the man whose arm had just been cut off and whose body was now limp in a dead faint. It was Jim Covey, the gunner's mate who had greeted Richard on the weather deck that very morning.

Richard felt nausea heaving in his guts, waves of dizziness in his head. To hell with compiling the butcher's bill, he had to flee from this godforsaken torture chamber. Seizing a rung of a ladder, he paused, breathing in gulps of air, looking up to the gun deck, steadying himself. It was then that he heard the miserable weeping of a young boy. Forcing himself to look around, he searched for the sound among the wreckage and spied Cato amidships by the larboard bulwarks. He was on his knees, bent over a small body laid out on a pallet. Richard could not see who it was, but he knew well enough. Weaving his way through the wounded, he came up to Cato and dropped to one knee beside the still body. He took a limp wrist in his hands, searching for a pulse he was certain he would not find. Cato's wretched sobbing was confirmation enough that the grin on the face of Scipio Africanus was gone forever.

6

WHITEHAVEN, ENGLAND

April 1778

SNOW BEGAN FALLING SOMETIME during the night of April 22, gently at first in the slack wind, the tiny flakes of mushy liquid hardly noticeable to men stationed about the upper deck. It was difficult for them to distinguish flecks of snow within the chilling fog that had enveloped the Irish Sea the day before, creeping over *Ranger* like an eerie shroud and rendering her foresails nearly invisible from the quarterdeck. Although lookouts could not see far into the sloppy murk, their finely tuned sea senses could still detect sounds of approaching danger: a shout from a nearby ship or the suck of water swirling around a partially exposed reef.

Closer to dawn, the snowfall intensified. When all hands were piped below to a breakfast of warmed-over burgoo and Scotch coffee, white flakes were powdering the upper decks and drifting below onto the partially exposed gun deck. Wet snow clinging to rigging, spars, and railings transformed *Ranger* into a sort of specter ghosting eastward toward the Firth of Solway.

Wintry weather conveyed certain benefits. Cold, bracing sea air served as a cleansing agent for men mourning the loss of shipmates sewn up in spare sailcloth and dropped overboard into the cold green water to be forever entombed upon the ocean floor amid the many more of *Drake's* fallen. Too, they sheltered *Ranger* from dangers as much as they exposed her to them. Although such heavy snowfall in the Irish Sea at this time of year was unusual,

151

the fog and mist were not, and they concealed *Ranger* from her enemies. Should these conditions persist, Jones boasted cheerfully to his officers over a breakfast of shirred eggs and toast, he could lay her bow to on St. Bee's Head without need of the coarse red canvas hanging over her sides that concealed her yellow strakes and disguised her as a merchantman. His officers remained skeptical.

Ranger sailed on alone under foresails, topsails, and spanker. *Drake* was gone. The evening before, with her rigging rerove and jury-rigged repairs completed on her rudder and rigging, her skeleton crew had cast off the single cable-laid hawser linking her to *Ranger*. Bound for France, she disappeared into the gathering gloom, the Union Jack fluttering despondently abaft her mizzen sail directly beneath the Stars and Stripes.

By four bells of the morning watch, snowfall had slacked to occasional flurries. Visibility improved, though not enough to take a noon sun sight. It was not until midafternoon, when a brisk northwesterly breeze sprang up and the thick cloud cover broke apart, that remaining wisps of fog disappeared. When it did, there on the horizon directly ahead to eastward, as though a magician's cape had been snapped aside to reveal the miracle within, stretched the British shoreline, the wide gap of the Solway Firth at once identifiable between the low hills and open fields of Dumfries and Galloway to the north and the more heavily wooded plains and hill farms of Cumbria to the south. In the far distance, snowcapped peaks glistened brightly beneath a late-day, surprisingly warm April sun.

"How in hell-fire did he do *that?*" Agreen Crabtree wondered aloud. He had his right arm looped around a topsail backstay amidships and was holding a glass to his eye.

"He was born and raised here," Richard reminded him. He had his own glass up, scouring the horizon for a square sail or anything else to indicate they were sharing close quarters with the Royal Navy. "He knows these waters. It's why he chose this spot."

"I realize that, Richard. But t' end up here, right *here,* through all the gunk we've sailed through? How is that possible?"

At the quarterdeck railing, Acting Second Lieutenant Loring raised a speaking trumpet to his mouth. "Officers to convene immediately in the Captain's cabin!" he shouted out. The two midshipmen hastened aft to the gundeck ladder.

In the cabin, Jones's expression conveyed no glint of pride in having just achieved an extraordinary feat of seamanship. He waited patiently by the bulwark until his commissioned officers were seated in chairs arranged in a semicircle abaft the heavyset wooden table. The midshipmen, as usual, sat behind them, on the cushioned settee beneath the stern windows. When the marine sentry shut the door from the outside, Jones walked to the after side of the table. He leaned against it, folding his arms across his chest as he gave each officer in turn an appraising eye.

"Gentlemen," he said at length, "we are about to embark on what we set out to do six months ago. By now I'd wager that each of you could recite our mission in your sleep. Nevertheless, I need remind you that this mission is of critical importance. Congress and the Marine Committee are depending on us. As are the commissioners in Paris, as are our families back home. We must not fail them.

"You may ask, how is success defined in this mission? It's a fair question. One I'd wager you've given some thought to. One more time, for the record, here is my answer: success tonight means we create such havoc, such destruction, such utter chaos in Whitehaven that we cause widespread panic not just here but throughout the British nation. Whitehall will have to respond, preferably by sending the entire Channel Fleet after us. God willing, this will not be our only strike on British soil. But it will be our first, and therefore it is the most critical. I say to you that what we do tonight will have a profound effect on our revolution. Are you with me so far?"

They answered him with silence.

"Excellent."

Jones unrolled a large sheet of plain white paper he had earlier placed on the table and summoned his officers over. They watched in silence as he penciled in two slanting lines starting wide apart on the left side of the paper and gradually converging to a point on the right side. Above the upper line tending downward he drew a large S for Scotland. Under the lower line tending upward he inscribed an equally large E for England. Between the two lines he printed the word *Firth.*

The lower line contained a large indent bulging southward, about a third of the way in from where the line began. In the middle of this indent, he printed the letter H. On the western side of the indent, at the upper corner, he drew a stubby protuberance jutting out into the firth. Opposite it, near the northeastern edge, he drew a small square. Below that square and set back from the indent, he framed a series of horizontal and vertical lines in a grid pattern. In the center of the grid, he inscribed the letter T.

"This is the harbor of Whitehaven," he explained, indicating the H. "The promontory up here on the northwest side is St. Bee's Head. It forms a natural breakwater for the harbor. For that reason, most vessels anchored in White-haven will be in its lee, here, on the west side of the harbor. The water there is not deep; as I recall, not more than two fathoms at low tide. There could be as many as two hundred vessels in this area, all the way from St. Bee's down to the quays here"—he indicated the southern end of the harbor where he drew three pudgy lines running northward from the land. "They'll be small vessels: brigs, smacks, herring busses, you know the sort. Because there will be so many vessels anchored in so confined a space, they'll be rafted up close together, side by side." He smiled as he considered the possibilities.

"What about the Royal Navy, sir," Joshua Loring asked. "Are they likely to be in this area?"

Jones shook his head. "Not in Whitehaven, Mr. Loring. It may be one of England's busiest ports, but I have never seen or heard of a British warship entering the firth. No doubt the Royal Navy believes the fort provides adequate protection." He jabbed a finger at the square he had drawn at the northeastern entrance to the harbor, where it began bulging south from the firth on the eastern side of the harbor. "And what enemy of England would have the gall to sail up the Solway, blithe as you please, and attack it?"

There was a scattering of laughter.

"The fort is newly built," Jones continued. "I have never seen it. But I do know how the British construct such a fort. They employ a simple design, really. Barracks and whatnot for the garrison inside; ramparts, a terreplein; a blockhouse for a sentry post. The guns are most likely thirty-six pounders. Big guns, but no threat to us once they're spiked."

"The garrison, sir," David Wendell asked, his brow knit in heavy concentration. "How many men do you estimate?"

"That is the unknown, Mr. Wendell. As I have discussed with Mr. Wallingford, a fort of this size in this sort of location normally maintains a modest garrison. What need would there be for a larger one? But I must confess I am not certain. Which is why I intend to direct the bulk of our force initially against the fort and why the element of surprise is so critical . . . Are there other questions?"

Richard pointed at the T on the map. "I assume that is the town of Whitehaven, Captain. Anything of note there?"

"Just that it's a very unusual town, Mr. Cutler. Note the grid on the paper. That's actually how the town is laid out. Its streets and alleys are in a precise mathematical relationship to each other. Perfectly logical, perfectly symmetrical. I've never seen anything like it anywhere else." There was an amused lilt to his voice when he added, "Except, of course, in Boston."

There was richer laughter. These men were well acquainted with Boston's infamous reputation for street construction.

"The town is set back from the beach by, oh, half a cable length," Jones explained. "There's open ground in between, a grassy field . . .

"Right. Now, gentlemen, let us review our plan. For the time being we shall continue standing off and on at the entrance to the firth. At midnight we shall sail in a short ways. The Solway is deep in most places, especially between the Mull and Whitehaven—a firth has many of the qualities of a Norwegian fjord, you understand—but currents can be strong and fluky, and they can stir up the bottom and shift navigational aids. I recall as a boy seeing more than one vessel aground where deep water was indicated on the charts. That's more likely to happen farther up the firth, past Whitehaven, but why take unnecessary risks when we have a windward tide in our favor.

"At six bells in the second watch we shall take to the boats. We'll take forty volunteers with us. I will command the ship's cutter. Mr. Wallingford, Mr. Cutler, Mr. Crabtree, you will come with me with twenty-five volunteers. Our responsibility is the fort. Mr. Simpson, you will command the jolly boat. Mr. Loring will accompany you with fifteen volunteers."

"What about me, sir?" David Wendell immediately put in. "What is my role in this?"

"You have a very important role," Jones assured him, not unkindly. "Whilst we others are ashore, you and Mr. Charrier shall assist Mr. Callum with the running of the ship. Of greater importance, you are also responsible for ensuring we are picked up at the proper time."

Unconvinced, Wendell shoved his hands into the pockets of his breeches and stared down at the deck. His peevish attitude did not sit well with Jones, and he was about to upbraid the young midshipman when Simpson said, "He can have my place, Captain."

Stunned silence pervaded the cabin. Officers hardened to years of discipline stared in disbelief at the first lieutenant sitting in the middle of the group. His right leg was crossed casually over his left, and his nonchalant expression did not flicker when the others in the cabin met his eyes. Nor did he flinch when, raw moments later, Jones approached him.

"Excuse me, Mr. Simpson?" he asked. His voice was soft, measured, threatening. "I could not have heard you correctly."

Simpson stood up, faced Jones.

"You asked for volunteers," he replied easily. "I do not intend to be one."

Jones glared up at him.

"When I used the word 'volunteer,' Mr. Simpson, I was referring to my crew. I never dreamed it would need apply to one of my officers."

Simpson shrugged. "Perhaps. But it matters naught. I have no intention of taking part in this little expedition of yours, Captain. I believe it to be both foolhardy and reckless. Further, I believe there is but one reason why you intend to put this ship and her crew in such jeopardy."

"What is that, pray?"

"To extract personal revenge against people in this part of England you believe have insulted you in earlier days. That is what I believe, and that is what I intend to include in my report to the Marine Committee."

Jones was appalled and unable to immediately respond. His lips trembled and curled, the left side parting to reveal clenched teeth. Instinctively his right hand went to the haft of his sword.

"So it has come to this, has it, Mr. Simpson?" he said, his voice deadly calm, his eyes inflamed with menace. He stepped closer, his chest nearly touching the stomach of his lanky lieutenant. "Let me remind you, sir, that I am captain of this ship. As captain, I have the power of God over you and everyone else aboard. And never forget, sir, that I am captain because I am a better man than you, a statement I am prepared to back up at any time, at any place, with any weapon of your choosing . . . Eh? What say you to that?"

Simpson had nothing to say.

"I thought as much," Jones spat. He withdrew a step. "You, sir, have no honor. You, sir, have no guts. You, sir . . . Sentry!"

The door opened. "Captain?"

"Summon the master-at-arms."

In short order the ruddy-faced marine sergeant stamped into their presence. He had been off duty when summoned and was wheezing and perspiring slightly as he finished adjusting his green dress coat to military regulations. His demeanor became all business, however, as his gaze took in the situation and the livid features on the captain's face.

"Reporting as requested, sir," he said, saluting.

"Thank you, Sergeant," Jones replied. He spoke to the master-at-arms with his eyes piercing the very soul of his first officer. "Mr. Simpson is confined to quarters until I say otherwise. I want two marines guarding him at all times. If he attempts to leave his cabin, you have my permission to shoot him."

The sergeant arched his eyebrows.

"Aye, aye, Captain," he said grimly. He hesitated, then walked over to Simpson and clasped him lightly by the elbow. "This way, Lieutenant, if you please."

Simpson picked up his cocked hat and placed it under his left arm. With a rueful but resolved expression he scanned the environs of the cabin a final time. Then, as though accepting the fate of a lonely martyr, he departed, bending low through the door as he went out, the marine sergeant following close behind.

Jones walked back to the drawing on the table. Rage so evident moments before had evaporated as quickly as had the fog earlier that afternoon.

"Well, Mr. Wendell," he said almost cheerfully, "it appears fate has smiled on you this day. Are you ready, sir?"

"I am, Captain," Wendell replied evenly.

"Good lad. Mr. Loring, you will command the jolly boat. Mr. Wendell will assist you. Everything else remains exactly as we discussed. Understood?"

It was.

"Gentlemen, time is getting on. We must conclude our business. Now where were we? Ah yes . . . We shall take the boats to the quays and tie up there. Those in my command will proceed to the fort. When we have secured it and disabled the guns, we will fire off a blue rocket. Mr. Loring, that rocket is intended as a signal to Mr. Callum to bring *Ranger* in. It is also intended as a signal to you to get back to the quays, no matter what you are about. Understood?"

Loring nodded, then said, "With respect, Captain, what if you are unable to overcome the garrison and thus fire off the rocket? What are my orders in that case?"

Jones was definite.

"Under all circumstances, Mr. Loring, your orders are to proceed with your objective and get back to the boats. If we are unable to meet you at the quays, if we are delayed for any reason, do not attempt to come to our aid. You are to get back to *Ranger* as best you can. In the drawer there"—he pointed his finger at the writing desk pushed up against the larboard bulwarks—"you'll find your orders. I had prepared them for Mr. Simpson. Now they are meant for you, a fact I shall record in the log before we depart. You are to bring *Ranger* back to France with all possible speed and report to Dr. Franklin in Passy.

"Now then, gentlemen, it is time. Good luck and Godspeed to us all."

JONES HAD no difficulty raising forty volunteers. To a man, under the watchful eye of Samuel Wallingford, nineteen marines stepped forward. The remaining five marines had been ordered to remain aboard *Ranger,* two of them not sufficiently recovered from the battle with *Drake;* the others would serve as security on board. They were three of Wallingford's most reliable men, and he would have much preferred to have them with him ashore. But he and Jones agreed that, under the circumstances, with pockets of sympathy for Simpson lingering in the forecastle, it was a necessary precaution.

Who else would join the raiding party was determined by drawing straws among those seamen willing to cast their lot with their captain. Once ashore, the bulk of these men would go with Joshua Loring, the marines with Jones.

At two bells in the first dog watch, the crew was piped to supper. Sailors eager to get below to what had caused unusually compelling aromas to waft up from the galley would not be disappointed. Set before them on tables lowered with ropes from the bulwarks were large pewter pots of mutton stew thick with peas and carrots and potatoes and the stringy meat of a freshly slaughtered sheep. It was a relative feast; even the hardtack had been warmed over to enhance its flavor. Sailors ate appreciatively but in silence, whether savoring the meal, or contemplating the night ahead, or brooding over what rumors claimed had transpired in the captain's cabin, it was impossible for Richard to tell.

"I've never seen it like this," he confessed to his mates in the midshipmen's mess. He had made his usual rounds in the forecastle as the men were eating.

"It's odd, considering the food and extra ration of rum. Sprague, Williamson, Freeman with that brogue wit of his. We can always rely on them to brighten the mood belowdecks. Tonight they're as sullen as the rest."

"It's the captain's fault," Charrier said somewhat churlishly. His upper body was leaning in over the table, and he kept his voice low. "Simpson can be an insufferable bore, we know that. And we know he has it in for us mids, especially you, Richard. But why make a bad situation worse? Why not let the man stay aboard and deal with him later, after we're gone from here?"

"He had no choice, Charlie," was David Wendell's opinion. He was contemplating the contents of his deep-cut wooden spoon, deciding whether or not to force food down into a digestive system that had no appetite for it. With a sigh he placed the spoon back in the bowl. "You were there."

"We were all there," Crabtree agreed. "My opinion? Come a fight, I'd rather have Simpson here in his cabin than ashore with us. I don't trust the man. Never have." He pushed his bowl away and stood to button up his white vest coat. The other midshipmen followed suit.

From his sea chest Richard took up a leather belt that had attached to it a silver-hilted twenty-four-inch naval dirk, sheathed. He drew the belt around his waist and buckled it. From a mahogany weapon's case lined with flannel he selected a powder horn, a small leather bullet pouch, and a Parker sea-service pistol. The horn and pouch he slung over his left shoulder rifle-style, adjusting the straps until they rested comfortably on his right hip just below the hem of his blue midshipman's coat. He double-checked the workings of the pistol, then hooked it onto his belt with a long thin metal prong running halfway down along the barrel from the wooden stock.

Wendell did himself up in similar array. Charrier as well, though he would remain on board *Ranger* during the attack. With the captain's permission—rather, at the captain's insistence—Crabtree would go tonight without a pistol. Slung across his back from left to right was a leather quiver crammed tight with white-feathered, bronze-tipped arrows.

"Nervous, Richard?" he asked softly, as he tested the tension of the bowstring.

Richard threw a dark blue boat cloak over his shoulders and hooked together the silver metal clasp at the neck. All officers must wear dress uniforms, Jones had decreed, with commission papers on their person in the event they were captured. Each officer was also ordered to wear a dark-colored, knee-length boat cloak to conceal the white breeches and shirt of his uniform.

"Yes, Agee, very," he confessed. "But I keep thinking of Will and that helps. Somehow I know he'll be with me tonight, no matter what happens, and he'll see me through. Probably sounds daft to you."

"Daft? I hardly think so. My Indian friends believe that between them an' the Great Spirit are their kindred spirits watchin' over them, same as they did when they were alive. My ancestors? Ones I knew, I'm not sure I want 'em watchin' over me. So if you've a mind, Richard, I'd be obliged if you'd ask your brother t' look in on me every now an' again."

"He'd be honored, Agee," Richard said.

At midnight, with the Mull of Galloway far astern and St. Bee's Head not yet visible but approaching to starboard, Jones ordered the main topsail backed. With her fore and mizzen topsails remaining full, and her courses hanging loosely in their brails, ready to be dropped at a moment's notice if need be, *Ranger* slewed partially broadside to the tide and current and drifted slowly up the narrowing tideway toward Whitehaven. David Callum at the helm was ever alert to the rate and direction of drift, mentally debating whether to maintain her sail plan as it was, or to back the mizzen topsail in addition to the main-topsail to slow her pace, or to back all three topsails to bring her headway close to a dead halt.

His master's instincts were prompted by the calls of Seth Gardiner being relayed aft from the starboard fore chains. Gardiner was secured within the deadeyes and shroud ends there and was heaving forward a lead weight attached to a twenty-fathom line marked at half-fathom intervals with scraps of rag, white at one-fathom intervals, red at the half-fathom. Though Callum was quite familiar with the charts of the Atlantic coasts, he had never sailed in these waters, and he took scant comfort from the fact that the captain had years ago as an apprenticed seaman. The captain, after all, was not even on deck. Which was why with the cry of "By the mark, twelve!" or "And a quarter less fourteen!" Callum allowed himself ever so brief an exhale of relief. No shoaling. Yet.

At three bells in the second watch the raiding party began assembling on the weather deck amidships. Though a few men had to be roused from their hammocks, most of them had marked time below wide awake. Up on deck, they formed two divisions, each according to his assigned boat. They stood at quasi-attention, rubbing sleep from their eyes or their hands for warmth.

At the bosun's order, sailors hoisted the cutter and jolly boat off their tiers at midships and onto tackles attached to stays and yardarms acting as cranes.

As the boats were lowered into the water on *Ranger's* lee side, the senior officers finished their inspection of their men and gear. Jones's force, the larger of the two, consisted mostly of cloaked marines armed with Brown Bess muskets. Under the cloak, each man carried a powder horn and calfskin cartridge pouch crisscrossed over his chest.

Mingled within their ranks were four burly seamen wearing dark loose-fitting, slop-chest clothes. Two of them carried coiled manila ropes with grapples on the end that resembled giant fish hooks coupled together back-to-back. The other two gripped long thin spikes, each capped with a sky blue cylinder with a six-inch length of fast-match curling down from its base.

Joshua Loring stood at attention before the smaller rectangle of men, a step in front of David Wendell. The officers saluted as Jones approached.

"You have the incendiaries, Mr. Loring?" He was referring to the fire bombs they had fashioned out of canvas and pinecones soaked in brimstone, in addition to the grenades they would bring along: hollow balls of lead stuffed with gunpowder and a short fuse.

"We do, sir," Loring confirmed.

"Flints? Steels?"

"Accounted for, sir."

"Very well, Mr. Loring. You may proceed to the boats."

"Aye, aye, Captain."

Jones stepped up to the quarterdeck.

"You have command, Mr. Callum. Be close in at dawn. Watch for the rocket. That will be your signal to come in for us."

"We'll be there, Captain. Good luck, sir."

When Jones returned, the twenty-two-foot jolly boat was filled with men and Loring had given the order to bear off and ship oars. The thirty-foot cutter had taken its place below the entry port, and marines were now scrambling over the side. When everyone was at his place on the thwarts, Agreen stepped down, followed by Richard, Samuel Wallingford, and finally, Captain Jones. Wrapped in a navy blue cloak and wearing a black tricorne hat with a red and white cockade, Jones took position in the sternsheets next to Richard, who served as coxswain tonight at the captain's request.

"Give way, all!" Richard ordered, once the cutter was free of *Ranger* and oars had been properly shipped in their thole pins. As the men heaved on the oars, Richard jogged the bow toward the southern shore.

As they were loading the boats, the wind had inauspiciously backed to the southeast and now began to freshen, its contrary effects offsetting the benefits of an incoming tide and rendering useless the lug sail furled on a portable mast beneath the thwarts. There was nothing to do but to row, and row hard.

Despite what he recalled as fluky currents nearer the southern shore, and the numerous strake nets set out there by local salmon fishermen, Jones ordered the two boats close in toward the calmer waters in the lee of the land. From his recollection, the rocky coastline was wild, uninhabited, so there was little risk of being spotted by an overly curious landsman, especially at this hour. Indeed, the only locals that seemed startled by their presence were occasional redshanks or oystercatchers seen poking about in the grassy salt marshes and sea lavender in search of food.

Jones ordered a shift at the oars every twenty minutes; nonetheless, it took them more than an hour and a half to row around St. Bee's Head, considerably more time than Jones had estimated.

The faintest glints of dawn were edging the eastern sky as they rounded the head, bringing into slightly better focus what lay before them in Whitehaven harbor. Dawn came grudgingly this time of year, especially when the sky was overcast. Could they stretch the mantle of night for another hour?

Once the two boats were around the head and in the harbor, the turbulence they had experienced in the firth ceased abruptly, replaced by a chill calm. Only the rhythmic creaking of oars in their wooden pins and the patter of water dripping from the blades disturbed the serenity of the harbor at rest.

Richard glanced about, his gaze taking in the vast flotilla of small craft anchored to starboard: schooners, ketches, brigs, single-masted fishing smacks, and one he could not identify: a French lugger perhaps, judging by the enormous bowsprit jutting out horizontally from the forepeak and a short but sharply raked mizzenmast stepped far astern close to the taffrail. As Jones had predicted, these vessels were nested up close against one another, with as many as ten or twelve berthed at a single mooring. He saw no sign of life stirring anywhere and few anchor or cabin lights.

Ahead, the town of Whitehaven slept.

To larboard, all the way up the eastern edge of the harbor almost to the firth, stood a high smooth stone square that Richard recognized from Jones's drawing as the fort. It was a dark and foreboding structure emitting no light except for two tiny specks flickering low on the western wall, an entryway perhaps, and another light, brighter and higher, inside what Jones had explained was a wooden blockhouse. The fort was perhaps a fifth of a mile from the quays at the southern end of the harbor: too far away in the lingering darkness to pick out anything of consequence along its stone ramparts. Sentries posted there either had not spotted the two boats in the harbor, or if they had, had dismissed them as nothing out of the ordinary.

Extending out from the stone quays to the right and left along the U-shaped harbor stretched a gently sloping beach. Splotches of sand there intermingled with small rocks and pebbles worn smooth by centuries of wave action. Here, at midtide, the beach was about twenty feet in width, and the tide was going out. At the upper edge of the beach, starting near the quays and running along the eastern edge of the harbor to a wide expanse of grass lawn stopping short of the fort, was a rocky, waist-high seawall that protected the town from seaborne assaults of nature. It was man-made, and Richard noted its solid, waist-high length that would provide ideal cover for what they were about. He wondered if it was simply blind luck it was there, or had Captain Jones considered this fine a detail in selecting Whitehaven as his first target? He suspected the latter.

"Up oars!" he ordered softly. The command was instantly obeyed, and the cutter skimmed toward a stone quay where clusters of small boats were tied up from their bows, their oars removed to prevent theft. Just before the cutter hit the quay, a bowman leaped ashore, fended off, then threw a line over a bollard, securing the boat with a clove hitch. The jolly boat bumped alongside and was similarly secured. Its crew, with cloaks off and stowed in the boat, joined the others in front of a warehouse built on a giant slab of granite, which served as a loading area. Stacked inside and against the walls were wooden hogsheads of rum, hemp sacks stuffed with raw sugar, and an assortment of barrels and staves.

"Roundly now, lads, we haven't much time," Jones urged those who were slow to gather around him. Though a candle would still be required to read fine print, dawn was coming fast.

The captain checked his watch.

"It's now four minutes after five. Whitehaven comes alive in an hour, so an hour is all we have. We meet back here, at the boats, no later than six-fifteen. Six-fifteen, got it? Earlier, Mr. Loring, if you see the rocket. Good luck, gentlemen."

The raiders split up. Joshua Loring led his men off to the left, toward the small craft huddled close along the harbor's western edge. Jones took his command to the north along the eastern stretch of beach. Two marines remained on guard by the boats.

Jones led the way along the beach, jogging at a steady clip, slowed only a little by the two sailors lugging grappling hooks and lines. Instinctively they bent forward as they ran, exposing as little of themselves as possible above the rocky seawall. Going was smooth. The sand was hard-packed beneath their feet, and the numerous rocks and pebbles were of no consequence. In short order they were fifty yards from the fort, crouching low where the wall ended and the grassy expanse began. Kneeling in a knot together, the officers studied the parapets and embrasures with miniature spyglasses, searching for a clue as to what step to take next.

"We'll scale the walls," Wallingford announced after several minutes had elapsed and no alternative had presented itself. "Exactly *where* we scale them seems not to matter. I can't make out anyone up there." He continued scrutinizing the parapets, as though he couldn't believe what his own eyes were confirming. "I'll send up four of my best men: two on the south wall, two on the north. Once inside, they'll find their way down to that door there." He pointed at a small, heavy iron door at the base of the west wall. On each side of it a torch blazed in a socket, the two flickers of light Richard had noticed earlier from the cutter. The main entryway was on the opposite, eastern side, from where they could see a well-maintained road running into the countryside. But this door provided an alternate way into the fort, and it was unguarded from the outside.

Jones nodded his agreement. He was as suspicious as his marine lieutenant of the lack of sentries on the ramparts. This fortress may have little to fear from an enemy, but there was military discipline to enforce, even during times of peace. And this was a time of war. He was about to voice his concern when Richard suddenly pointed.

"Captain, over there."

He was pointing at two British soldiers emerging from around the northwestern corner of the fort. They were walking in what appeared to be an odd, unsteady manner; each had his arm around the other's shoulder for support. One held a lantern out in front of him, needlessly in the spreading light of dawn, while the other jangled a set of keys at his side as though the big brass circle were some sort of musical instrument. They were dressed sloppily. By the look of their crumpled scarlet regimental coats, their shirts unbuttoned at the collar, and the white-trimmed cocked hats askew on their heads, they had dressed in a hurry and without much care. And they were . . . giggling, their silly antics just now becoming audible.

"Capital!" Jones exclaimed in gleeful wonder. "Just capital! The buggers are drunk! The lying, thieving, buttock-loving whoresons are *drunk!*" His voice assumed the tone of a crotchety old schoolmaster having nabbed a youthful prankster red-handed. "Sneaking in the back door, are we, me lads? Slipped from your post to sample the local talent, hmm? Hope you enjoyed that quim. It was your last.

"Mr. Crabtree!" he hissed.

Agreen crawled up beside him. "Sir."

"The one with the keys. Him first. Await my signal."

Agreen drew an arrow from the quiver and inserted the string into the grooved end. Kneeling, he held the bow out horizontally in front of him.

Jones held up his hand: get ready. The soldier was fumbling with a key, giggling at his inability to insert it correctly into the keyhole. His mate slurred something indistinguishable to him that sent them both into a fit of stifled laughter. Finally the soldier got the key in and turned it properly. He pushed open the door, but instead of going in, he stepped aside and bowed low with a flourish, sweeping his right arm to the left in a grand gesture as if to say, 'After you, I insist, my dear fellow.' When he straightened, a stupid grin illuminating his face, Jones said, "Now!"

Rising to full height, Agreen flipped the bow to a vertical position, took aim, and fired. The arrow sang through the air and struck the soldier square in the stomach. For a moment he stood slack-jawed, staring down at the projectile with both his hands clasped around the shaft. Then slowly, silently, he slid down to a sitting position, his legs straight out, his head slumped forward.

His mate gawked stupidly at him, then toward the beach. A second arrow struck him just below the rib cage, killing him instantly.

Jones held up his hand: don't move. He paused, senses primed, listening intently for any reaction from inside the fort. He heard nothing from there, but the distant shouts he and the others heard coming from Whitehaven town made them all freeze.

"Pirates! Everybody up! Pirates, I say! Pirates are attacking us!"

"Bloody hell!" Jones swore.

"Who's the fucking Paul Revere?" Wallingford demanded. He jerked his head around at the clutch of men bunched up behind him. "Who's missing?"

There was a quick nose count.

"It's Freeman, sir," a marine corporal told him. "Seaman, Irish."

"Figures," Wallingford spat.

Jones jumped up. "Let's go, lads!"

They charged the fort at full tilt, expecting at any moment the clang of an alarm bell or the whine of bullets fired at them from the parapets. But . . . no. Whitehaven might be astir, but the fort itself was deathly silent.

Jones and Wallingford were first to reach the opened door. They seized the two torches from their sockets and went inside, swinging the light this way and that, sizing up the musty interior dimly lit by lanterns hanging from metal holdings along the walls. To the right was an unbroken corridor leading to the south wall. At the far end was a flight of stairs leading up. To the left was a corridor of equal length, with another flight of steps leading up against the north wall. Halfway down that corridor was another corridor intersecting the west wall in the shape of a T. That corridor led eastward.

Wallingford was as familiar as Jones with how such a fort was constructed. He looked at Jones and pointed to himself, then pointed to the right and up. Jones nodded, pointing to himself and to the left. He held up five fingers: give me five marines.

They split up. Following Jones were the two midshipmen, the five marines, and the two sailors who had dropped their grappling gear on the beach. The rest of the marines and the sailor carrying the rockets followed Wallingford down the west corridor toward the steps leading up to the ramparts.

On the left side of the eastward corridor was a double oaken door meeting in the middle of a wide arched entryway. On the right side were three single doors set wide apart. Officer's quarters, Richard assumed. Jones pointed to the double doors and silently mouthed the word "barracks" to Richard and Agreen. He then went toward the first door on the right, paused there, and held up his hand for silence. He pressed on the handle.

The door was unlocked. Jones gently pushed it ajar and peered in. It was the room of an officer, or two officers, for there were two single beds in it, some scenes of horses and rural England on the wall, two bureaus, and what appeared to be an expensive desk of some girth that added a gentlemanly feel to an otherwise Spartan room. Draped over the back of the brass-nailed, red-leather chair adjacent to the desk was a British Army dress coat with the epaulettes of a major.

Jones backed out of the room. He pointed to Richard and Agreen and to the door on the left, then to himself and the second door on the right.

Richard nodded and motioned to three marines and the two sailors. He led them to the double doors and drew back the hammer on his pistol to half-cock. He put his shoulder against one of the doors and pushed. The door creaked open, revealing wooden bunks in the room stacked three-a-top in typical army fashion. There were numerous sets of cots within the large rectangular space and not all were empty.

"Good morning," Richard greeted those abed as he stepped inside the room. Beside him, the marines and sailors fanned out, their weapons drawn. There were perhaps fifteen or twenty British soldiers in the room early in the process of awakening. They were sitting up in bed or at the side of their bunks, staring wide-eyed at the Americans. To Richard's relief he saw no muskets or pistols in the room, nor any other weapon save for a foot-long dagger lying flat on a table nearby, covetously being ogled by a balding soldier in half-dress sporting a black patch over his left eye.

"'Oo the 'ell 'r you?" a groggy giant of a man with a thick cockney accent demanded.

"I am Richard Cutler, midshipman aboard the Continental ship *Ranger,* at your service." He walked over to the soldier. "Where are the others?"

The hairy mammoth rubbed his eyes, blinked again at Richard as if to confirm the apparition, then folded his fleshy arms across his chest. "Go fuck yerself, little boy," he spat at him, the yellow of his teeth showing through a forest of red beard and mustache. "Go 'ome to yer mother."

At that moment the one-eyed man made a lunge for the dagger. Richard whirled to his right. The cockney redcoat, seizing on the distraction, hurled himself at Richard, tackling him around the waist and bringing him down hard, his hands going for Richard's throat. A shot rang out, and a man cursed in agony. Richard shoved his right hand under the cockney's chin and pushed up with all his might, his left hand groping for his dirk. But the man was heavier and stronger and able to grasp Richard's left elbow, pinning his arm while maintaining a death grip on his throat. Richard gasped wildly for air, felt his strength begin to ebb.

"Damn you, mates, 'elp me!" the redcoat yelled in desperation, but no one was brave or foolish enough to follow his example. Desperately, blindly, Richard searched to his right for the pistol he had dropped when he fell. He found it and was fumbling for a firm grip when a foot shot out above him and slammed into the cockney's gut. The cockney wheezed, faltered, eased his grip around Richard's throat.

"Take that, ya bastard!"

Agreen landed another crushing blow against the cockney's enormous frame. As he did so, Richard heaved his arm up with all his strength and bashed the cockney on the side of the head. The redcoat grunted, exhaled sharply, wavered. Richard bashed him again and again and again; finally the man lay unconscious, slumped over. Two sailors dragged him off while marines covered them with their pistols.

"Right," Richard muttered, back on his feet. "So much for pleasantries." He took a pistol from one of the marines, sidestepped around the splayed body of the one-eyed man, and walked over to a soldier sitting on the edge of his bunk. He thumbed the hammer back from half-cock to full, and nudged the barrel against the man's skull, just above his right ear.

"Where are the others?" he demanded to know.

Whether from the shock of cold steel against his skin or the persuasive tone in Richard's voice, the soldier answered, "On night maneuvers."

"On *what?*"

"Night maneuvers. This 'ere's a trainin' barracks."

"Where are they?"

"Out there." He pointed vaguely eastward.

"When will they be back?"

Despite the weapon trained point-blank at his brains, the soldier smiled thinly as he glanced up at Richard. "Oh, I'd say just 'bout anytime now."

Suddenly, from overhead, they heard a muffled whine followed by the resounding pop of a rocket bursting. The signal to Callum! Moments later, from across the harbor where the fishing boats were anchored, came the sounds of loud explosions going off one after another.

"Round up these men, Agee," Richard said. "I'll find the captain."

He found Captain Jones and the two other marines across the hall in the last room on the right. They were standing beside two British officers sitting at a table. One of the officers was drumming his fingers on the top of the table while the other calmly sipped tea from an elegant china cup.

"Sir . . ." Richard began.

"I know. I just found out," Jones preempted him. "How many soldiers in the barracks?"

"Fifteen or so."

"Nineteen, to be precise," the British major offered. He delicately placed his cup back on its matching saucer and dabbed at the corners of his mouth with a linen napkin.

"Sixteen, to be more precise, Major," Richard said evenly. The officer glowered up at him.

"Get those men in here," ordered Jones, with some urgency. "I've got the key."

When the British soldiers had been herded across the corridor into the cramped officer's quarters, Jones shut the door from the outside and locked it, testing the latch to ensure it was bolted securely.

From down the corridor on the western wall near the rear entry door they heard the sound of men running. Jones led his party out into that corridor and met up with Wallingford and the main body of marines.

"We've got company," Wallingford announced with a look of anxiety. "A whole battalion, it seems."

"Have you spiked the guns?"

Wallingford nodded. "We have, sir," meaning his men had jammed a long iron nail into the touchhole of each cannon, temporarily disabling it.

"Good. Now let's get the bloody hell out of here!"

They ran outside into spreading daylight and made a dash across the grassy sward for the seawall. Immediately a hail of small-arms fire erupted from behind and to their left. One marine dropped his musket and ran five steps, carried forward by sheer momentum and a fierce desire to live. He then fell face down on the grass. A second marine fell. A third. By the time they reached the beach, five men were down in their wake.

On the beach, they were forced to slow their pace to help along the wounded. They crouched low against the rocky wall, their heads level with their waists, searching ahead toward the quays and to what should have been their deliverance.

Richard saw it along with the others. Only the jolly boat was tied up there. The cutter was well away from the beach and was heading out into the harbor, with six men pulling hard at the oars. Richard recognized the sailors on the afterthwart: Hutchison and Peterson: two of the first to sign the petition. No doubt where their loyalties lay, Richard thought bitterly.

Of more immediate concern was the whereabouts of Loring and Wendell. There they were, out ahead of the pack of Americans running toward the quays from the other side of the harbor. At their back was a billowing conflagration fast consuming the flotilla of vessels at anchor, the burning rigging and spars of one vessel collapsing onto another, setting it aflame domino fashion in a wind-whipped, ghastly inferno.

Jones made it to the quays through a shower of ricocheting bullets without losing another man. The tide was still on the ebb; there was now a good forty feet of beach between the water line and the protective seawall. Marines were lined up behind the wall, returning fire.

"What happened?" Jones demanded of Loring, when the two officers met at the loading dock. "Where's the cutter going?"

"Sorry, sir," Loring managed, leaning forward, panting. "Six men left us there." He pointed at the conflagration. "We didn't know until it was too late. They came back here. Surprised the guards. Overpowered them."

"Sorry, sir," David Wendell repeated. He was bent over, hands on his knees, gasping for air.

There was no time for recriminations. Jones did a quick calculation. They had landed with forty-eight men. Five marines were dead. That left forty-three. Six sailors had deserted and one had turned coat. That left thirty-six. The jolly boat was built to hold no more than twenty-five men. Even if they could all get in, it would be so weighed down it would make a fat target for anyone firing from shore.

Wallingford had made the same calculation. "You must go, Captain," he declared definitively. "You must get back to *Ranger*. My marines will cover you."

"I'll stay, sir," Richard said.

"And I, sir," said Crabtree and Wendell.

Jones knew Wallingford was right. He had to go. *Ranger* was his ship. And an act of mutiny had been committed.

"There, sir!" Wendell cried excitedly.

Their eyes swung to where Wendell was pointing, at the western entrance to the harbor. *Ranger* was there, her jib and foresail emerging from behind the spreading bonfire of boats, making her way against an ebb tide. David Callum had seen the rocket and was coming for them!

"Mr. Loring, you will come with me," said Jones, his decision made. "We'll take the wounded and what men we need to man the oars. Quickly now!"

As his men hurried to carry out his orders, Jones faced Samuel Wallingford, his eyes flickering to Richard and Agreen and Wendell. "I implore you, gentlemen, hold this position," he said, his voice cracking with emotion. "I'll send the boat back for you. Hold this position!"

"We'll hold it, sir," Wallingford assured him.

With the jolly boat off, Wallingford and the three midshipmen ran up to the seawall to join the fight.

"How long d'you think, Richard," Agee shouted as they ran, "till they make it back?"

"Thirty minutes," Richard shouted in reply. "Maybe less. She's light. She'll make good time." Though he sounded optimistic, both midshipmen understood the reality. It was highly doubtful they could hold this position for anything close to half an hour.

At the seawall, Wallingford assumed command of operations. He arranged his marines in two rows, one in back of the other. As the rear row rose to fire, those in front ducked down to reload. Then the process was repeated, in reverse, as the front line rose and the rear line reloaded. The red line of British soldiers hesitated before a hail of continuous fire.

Richard and Agreen crawled on their knees to the edge of the rocks and peered over the top. Dead and wounded redcoats littered the field between them and the town of Whitehaven. Yet, for every redcoat down, there appeared to be twenty to take his place. A line of regimental red and white was getting organized and was making ready to advance toward them with muskets held out horizontally in front and bayonets fixed. Soon, very soon, Richard thought, that line would shift into a giant, inverted V, outflanking the Americans and closing in on them from both sides like a giant nutcracker.

The townspeople seemed to understand this. Throngs of them, many still in their nightclothes, had gathered on the edge of town at the rear of the British line. Armed with everything from garden tools to family heirloom swords to old-fashioned, brass-barreled musketoons, they made threatening gestures and screamed indistinguishable epithets at the American rebels.

Richard glanced back at the harbor. The jolly boat was within fifty feet of *Ranger*. No, by God! It was the cutter! Captain Jones in the jolly boat had not yet reached *Ranger*, and the cutter was already coming for them!

"Jesus Christ!" Agreen exclaimed, ducking low from the whine and zing of ricocheting bullets. "Get the fuckin' guns goin', would'ja?" he implored his captain. "Open fire on the bastards."

"He won't," Richard yelled over the din, crouching down beside him. "He won't fire on the town. He'd kill us or innocent people, as likely. It's too risky."

"Not from where I'm sittin' it aint," Agreen shouted back.

The flanks of the British line had reached the beach on both sides of the Americans. The main body ahead was preparing to charge the seawall. The vise was starting to close. Six marines lay dead on the sand. The loading area and quays had fallen to the British.

"Marines, stand down!" Wallingford cried out. "Retreat to the beach! Assume formation there!"

The men dropped back to the beach and formed ranks in a broad U-shaped configuration. Wallingford, Richard, and Agreen held command at the apex, with the marines flanked out on both sides to near the water's edge. What sailors remained were clustered in the middle, to reinforce a breach in the formation or fight where a shipmate had fallen. A hundred yards behind them, the cutter was approaching with every ounce of speed possible.

"Fire at will!" Wallingford commanded. His sword was in his left hand, his pistol in his right. He raised the pistol, took aim, then suddenly dropped it, along with the sword, his left hand at his abdomen. His knees sank down. He reached out with his right hand on the sand to break his fall.

"Mr. Wallingford, are you hit, sir?" Richard cried, bending over him. The marine lieutenant gritted his teeth and nodded, wincing in pain. His right arm gave way, his strength no longer able to sustain him. He slid from a kneeling position to lying prone on the beach, a pool of blood forming beneath his left side.

The cutter was seventy-five yards away.

"The lieutenant is wounded!" Richard shouted out. "Advance forward! Cover him!"

The marines were taking their toll, but the enemy was taking a heavier toll. The situation was becoming desperate. With a blast of fife and drums the main body of the British line charged. The knot of defenders tightened.

Fifty yards out, the oars of the cutter churned the water furiously.

At the front line, Agreen Crabtree shrugged off the quiver from around his chest. He dumped out the remaining arrows, stabbed them tip-down in the sand before him. He came up on one knee and began firing the arrows in rapid succession. At such close quarters, every one found its mark. Behind him, marines and sailors lobbed their remaining grenades at the charging British. The line hesitated, its losses heavy, awed by frontier tactics, stunned by the exploding balls of gunpowder. Redcoats lay on their backs or side, some mutilated, others unmarked save for a white-feathered arrow protruding from them.

The cutter was twenty-five yards away.

"I'm out!" Crabtree yelled at Richard. He was searching wildly for a weapon of some kind when a bullet caught him in the leg. He fell clutching the wound, blood oozing from between his fingers.

The cutter's bow hissed onto the sand and pebbles. "To the cutter!" Richard shouted. "Everybody to the cutter!"

Those closest to the boat readily complied. Others, a ways up the beach, dared not turn their backs to run. Nor could they walk backward over dead comrades while engaged in close-quarter combat.

"Can you walk at all, Agee?" Richard shouted. He put an arm around his waist, helped him to his feet. Agreen slumped back down, shook his head no.

Richard's eyes swept the beach. The cutter had to shove off, else every American on that beach would die. Between him and the cutter he spotted David Wendell. He was curled up like a baby, his arms over his head, whimpering.

Richard squeezed Agee's arm and ran to Wendell. He picked him up and carried him to the cutter, lowering him hastily into the bow.

"Are those loaded?" he demanded of a sailor, pointing at a collection of pistols lying flat in an open cartridge box.

The sailor nodded, handed over two of them. More marines scrambled into the boat.

With a pistol in each hand Richard put his shoulder hard against the bow of the cutter, straining with all his might until he felt it give way and drift free. "My respects to Captain Jones," he shouted to the coxswain. Sailors splashed their oars into the water, pulling on them on the starboard side, backing them on the larboard. The cutter swept around, its bow pointing northward, toward the mother ship.

On the beach, only a few Americans were left standing. Two redcoats were charging Samuel Wallingford. Somehow he had managed to turn himself over onto his back. He held up his sword defiantly in the air.

Richard raised a pistol and fired. One redcoat fell. He fired again, missed his mark, hurled the pistol with a primordial scream at the redcoat skewering his bayonet deep into the lifeblood of the marine lieutenant.

Ahead, the death vice of the British line was tearing asunder the remnants of the U formation. Redcoats had breached the position and were swarming over Americans dead and dying. Agreen had struggled to his feet, was holding a musket. A British officer hacked down on him with a sword. Agreen brought his weapon up, deflected the blow, swung the musket at the officer ineffectively, his strength sapped. He doubled over and collapsed when the officer swung up his boot and kicked him in the groin. A redcoat was there to finish him off. He held his musket high, higher, coiling his muscles for the final strike down on the cringing midshipman just as Richard threw his body at the soldier, knocking him over. Richard unsheathed his dirk. Whipping it across the soldier's chest, he slashed open the jugular at the neck, then rolled over onto his back, defensively, lunging up, stabbing another in the gut so deep he was unable to pull the weapon out. Others came at him. Richard had nothing to fight with now save his fists and feet, and these he brought to bear, flailing, kicking, punching, the fury of ancient warriors unleashed within, inflaming him, consuming him, until the butt of a musket slammed into his solar plexus and something hard crashed against his head.

Then, nothing.

Part 2

7

OLD MILL PRISON

May–September 1778

"Y‍OUR NAME, PLEASE?"

It was the second time the rotund British magistrate with a triple chin and ridiculously large handlebar mustache had asked that question. As his stern expression made clear, he was not about to brook insolence from any prisoner, especially one so young.

"May I remind you that under the North Act you may be accused of"—he glanced down to consult his notes, a movement that caused his pince-nez to fall from his nose. He caught it and replaced it, glowering up at Richard as if the midshipman were somehow responsible for the mishap—'piracy, treason and rebellion against His Majesty on the high seas.' The penalty is death by hanging. I suggest you cooperate, young man."

Richard looked aft beyond the magistrate, doing nothing to conceal his contempt. His head throbbed. He felt dizzy, disoriented. His eyes fluttered open and closed as he struggled to recall the circumstances that had brought him from the beach at Whitehaven to the after cabin of this Royal Navy frigate anchored in Plymouth harbor.

He remembered coming by land, trussed up like the common prisoner he was and lying on his side on the bottom of a juddering wagon, drifting in and out of consciousness during an ordeal that seemed interminable. And he remembered there were others beside him, and another wagon following behind, but throughout the wretched ordeal he could not determine where he was or who was with him. The three days he had been confined in the dark musty hold down on the orlop deck had done little to sharpen his mental faculties.

He glanced about the great cabin. Despite his wretched condition he could appreciate that it was palatial in comparison to the equivalent space aboard *Ranger.* On a squat, cherry-wood sideboard to his right he saw cut-glass crystal decanters topped off with what he assumed were the captain's personal selections of wine, sherry, and port. Before him, the large Queen Anne desk he could have touched had he wanted to, served as a depository for the magistrate and his copious sets of notes. Nautical prints and paintings graced the walls, and he could see shelves of books in the captain's sleeping cuddy at the stern of the ship, on the larboard side. Between that cuddy and the dining alcove on the starboard side aft was a rectangular mirror that caught Richard's eye. He grimaced at the unshaven, hollow-eyed apparition staring back at him.

"For the last time . . . ," the magistrate warned.

"A moment, if you please, Mr. Morath."

The pleasant, patrician voice belonged to a man seated by the larboard bulwark who had been quietly observing the interrogation while sipping tea from a china cup. He was dressed in the full regalia of a sea officer, from the pure white of his kerseymere breeches to the gold-fringed epaulet he wore on each shoulder of his navy blue dress jacket that identified him as a senior post captain. When Richard had come stumbling into the cabin between two armed guards, he leaned forward with intense interest. Something about this young man with an evil bruise on the left side of his head had caught his fancy three days earlier when he had watched him being hauled across the weather deck of HMS *Yarmouth.*

"My name is Captain Fitzhugh," he announced cordially as he walked over to the Queen Anne desk. He settled his rump comfortably against the ornate table, facing Richard. "I am the provost marshal of Plymouth Dockyard." He set his cup down directly before Richard. The rich fragrance of Ceylon tea leaves wafted up, mixing with the faint, lingering aroma of fried eggs and bacon. Richard's stomach grumbled in agony.

Fitzhugh withdrew a six-inch cheroot from an inside pocket of his dress coat. He turned it over between thumb and forefinger, examining it, then ran it under his nose, breathing in the rich, pungent aroma of Jamaican tobacco.

"I'd offer you one of these, old boy," he said, as he searched the desk for lighting materials, "but alas it seems"—he made a point of staring at Richard's bound hands, then looked up at him, smiling—"you'd have somewhat of a logistical problem smoking it, what?"

His ingratiating smile failed. Striking steel on flint, he got the lint going on his first try. He lit the thin, open-ended cigar and took several puffs. Then, after a sip of tea, he asked, "Your name is Richard Cutler, is it not?"

Richard's eyes met his, answering the question.

"I say," Fitzhugh chuckled, "speaking of names, you certainly made one for yourself on that beach at Whitehaven. Quite a show you chaps put on. You and that pirate captain of yours. What's his name again?" He tapped his forehead, as if to jog his memory. "Ah yes. John Paul. Good seaman, I'll give him that. Shame to see such a talented fellow hanged for treason." He peered at Richard over the rim of his cup. "That *will* be his fate, old boy. Frigates have been dispatched."

Richard ran his tongue over parched lips, said nothing in reply.

Fitzhugh tried a different tack.

"You have an acquaintance, a certain Agreen Crabtree. Rather odd name, that. He's the freckled fellow with the Indian bow." He chuckled to himself. "By Jove, an Indian bow! In an attack on Mother England! What a twist *that* put in Major Barnes's knickers!" He chuckled again, shaking his head in wonder.

His use of the present tense proved irresistible.

"Agee's here?" Richard rasped. "Alive?"

"Oh yes, quite alive I'd say. A bit peaky, perhaps. He's lost a lot of blood. But he'll pull through. A bullet went clean through his leg. He's ashore in the prison hospital. The surgeon tells me there's no gangrene, so his leg can be saved. Rather a mystery why you and a few others were spared on that beach."

"Who else?" Richard beseeched him.

"You mean, who else survived your little act of piracy? No one of consequence, I daresay. Most of them have already been transferred to the prison." He turned to the civilian magistrate, who was stroking his handlebar mustache with a bored expression. "Mr. Morath, be a good fellow and order up a glass of lime water for this young man."

The look Morath gave him suggested that the post captain was just as capable, and certainly a great deal more qualified aboard a navy ship, to order up anything from anybody at anytime from anywhere. Nonetheless, he nodded at a nicely dressed cabin boy standing at stiff attention by the sideboard. The lad bowed, then poured out a glass from a crystal beaker. As he brought it over on a silver tray, Fitzhugh untied Richard's hands and tossed the hempen cord onto the table.

"Drink it," he encouraged when Richard hesitated.

Richard seized the glass. He drank deeply, feeling the cool, sweet, syrupy liquid course down his parched throat into his empty stomach. It was ambrosia compared to the rancid water he was given in the ship's hold. "Thank you," he croaked, as he set the empty glass on the table. Instantly it was picked up by the cabin boy who officiously wiped off a ring of moisture on the desk with a small cotton towel. He placed the glass back on the tray and retreated back to his station by the sideboard.

"You're entirely welcome. Another glass?"

Richard shook his head no.

"Right, then."

Fitzhugh resumed his former stance against the table in front of Richard. He took a deep pull from the cheroot and slowly exhaled the smoke from his mouth and nostrils, careful to turn his head to the side. When he spoke, his voice was low, confidential.

"Mr. Cutler, I shall come straight to the point. Your cause is finished. The so-called revolution is nearly over. British armies have been victorious everywhere if you ignore the consequences of inept leadership at Saratoga. You cannot win this war. General Washington *will* be defeated and his army annihilated. There is no other plausible outcome to this nonsense.

"In a few months, General Cornwallis will be returning to the colonies. His destination? Charleston, which our spies tell us is ripe for capture. After the city falls and he has settled in a bit—give the poor man his due, he recently lost his wife—British forces in America will launch what American Secretary Germaine refers to as our 'southern strategy.' Here is the essence of that strategy: Cornwallis will march north from South Carolina with a significant force while General Clinton marches south from New York with an even larger one. The Royal Navy, meanwhile, will be blockading all major ports along the coast and conveying our soldiers to wherever they be required. Am I making myself clear?"

Richard answered him with silence. Fitzhugh continued, "So where might hope hang for you colonials—pun intended, of course. In your patriotic zeal?

In a passion for independence? I should hardly think so, when you consider that only one in a hundred of you so-called patriots has had the courage to stand up and fight. One in a hundred! I'd scarcely call *that* a groundswell of patriotism, would you? And what an army! Farmers in rags, armed with pitchforks, scouring the countryside, stealing food from your own people. No wonder they don't support you. Me, I'd sooner put my faith in the Dons. At least *they* have proper weapons and uniforms. So that leaves the French. The *French!* My dear boy, the one certainty I have learned in my long and, if I may say so, rather illustrious career in the Royal Navy is never—and I mean *never*—trust the Frogs with *anything* that hasn't to do with cooking."

He pulled on his cigar and exhaled, watching the smoke curl upward. As he picked loose bits of tobacco from the tip of his tongue, Richard gave him a quizzical look.

"Why are you telling me this?"

Fitzhugh ignored the question.

"For you, alas, the revolution is already over. You are aboard this ship, as you have no doubt gleaned, for processing. From here you will be taken ashore to Old Mill Prison, down the road a ways from Plymouth Town. Were we to open that port there"—he indicated a closed gun port near where the muzzle of a glistening black cannon lay bowsed up to the ship's side with breeching ropes—"you could see it from where you're standing. Not a bad place, really, compared to some prisons. You've heard of the hulks in New York? Nasty business, those: rotting ships, rotting men, hundreds of them wasting away in their own filth. An unpleasant fate, to be sure, but one richly deserved by traitors."

Richard knew what Fitzhugh was talking about. He had heard the black rumors of atrocities and suffering being perpetrated on American seamen imprisoned aboard *Jersey,* a decrepit Sixty-Four stripped of all her fittings and embedded in the mud at Wallabout Bay in New York harbor. He also had learned the fate of another prison ship, the *Whitby.* That ship had been set ablaze by desperate prisoners preferring a quick death by fire to a slow, agonizing death by starvation and disease.

"Old Mill may be a tad more humane," Fitzhugh observed, "but it's a prison nonetheless. And you shall remain there locked up until the war is over, at which time, I am truly sorry to inform you, you and your mates will be tried for treason. And found guilty and hanged. Unless, of course, you implore the king's mercy. Which I'm afraid he'll be somewhat indisposed to grant. He's rather put out by all this, you understand."

He drew a heavy sigh at the seeming futility of it all and took one final pull on the cheroot. After stubbing it out in an ash-filled tin bowl on the table, he folded his arms across his chest and looked Richard straight in the eye, speaking to him in the measured, matter-of-fact tones of an officer to a subordinate.

"There is an alternative, Mr. Cutler, one that I believe may be of interest to you. I am prepared to make you an offer, one I assure you I am empowered to make. You may go to Old Mill if you wish. Or you may do the prudent thing, be forgiven your treason, and have a glorious career awaiting you.

"How is that possible, you ask? Simple. You enlist in the Royal Navy. You would be rated able seaman to start, but you have my word that I will make certain the powers-that-be appreciate your potential as a future British naval officer. Many privateers have chosen this path and are now serving their country with honor. To sweeten the bargain, I would guarantee equal treatment, if he is willing, for your friend, Mr. Crabtree. We wouldn't assign you to the same ship—can't have you two barbarians berthed together now, can we—but on a frigate if I have anything to say about it, and I do. Furthermore, neither of you would be assigned to the North America Station. You would see duty either here in home waters or, more likely, a faraway place such as India or the Moluccas. Damn intriguing places, those . . . So. What do you say?"

Richard stared mutely, as though pondering the proposition.

"That is my offer," Fitzhugh said, his mood expansive despite the ensuing silence. "A boat is alongside to take you ashore. You can proceed from here either to naval headquarters at Plymouth Hoe or directly to Mill Prison. Which is it to be, old boy? Salt pork and stale beer for dinner this noon? Or roast beef and plum duff, with a spot or two of claret to wash it down."

Richard ran his tongue along his lower lip. His eyes remained half-closed, giving the impression of serious thought. In reality, he was battling a sudden wave of dizziness and nausea. He longed to sit in a chair, anywhere, alone.

"It seems you have left me little choice," he rasped, after a time. From the corner of his eye, Fitzhugh shot Morath a knowing glance. "I will not speak for Mr. Crabtree. For myself, I choose prison."

"Say again?" Fitzhugh cried out, aghast. "I don't believe I heard you correctly."

"With respect, Captain, I believe you did. First, I am not a privateer. Nor am I a pirate. I am a midshipman in the Continental Navy and a prisoner of war. Second, I am already engaged in the service of my country, I hope honorably so. And third, the Royal Navy murdered my brother. I would sooner die than betray his memory."

"Oh you would, would you?" Fitzhugh mocked him. "Well, Mr. Cutler, I daresay you shall have your wish. Mr. Morath, please accept my sincere apology. It appears I have made a colossal error in judgment, and I have wasted your time." He threw up his hands in disgust and turned his back on the midshipman. "Take him away," he snapped.

Guards seized Richard by the elbows. They yanked him around and began hauling him out.

"Thank you for the water, Captain," Richard called back over his shoulder.

"Next!" Morath bellowed.

☆ ☆ ☆

OLD MILL Prison was built on the site of a tidal mill a half mile east of Plymouth. Not far, but it took the better part of the day for Richard and seven other prisoners—only one of whom he knew, Seth Gardiner—to be transferred from HMS *Yarmouth* in a ship's boat across the harbor to a deep-water quay at Plymouth Dock: the same quay, the coxswain informed them, from where the *Mayflower* had set sail for America a hundred fifty years earlier. There they waited in a pitiful group for the military wagon used to shuttle men and supplies back and forth between city and prison. Aboard and away at last, they were forced to pull over to the side of Exeter Road and wait there until a richly decorated carriage powered by eight frothing horses had thundered past. As it sped by, officious-looking passengers inside deigned hardly a glance at the wagon or its cargo, their sentiments perhaps best expressed by the billows of dust the galloping hooves kicked up to shower down unmercifully upon the scraggly knot of prisoners.

Richard started coughing. He tried spitting out tiny particles of dust, but gave up, no saliva. Like deaf mutes, he and the other prisoners watched numbly as first the driver, then the guard beside him, brought a large metal canteen to his mouth and held it there, gulping down the liquid inside and letting it flow freely over their chin and chest. When they had drunk their fill, they grinned at the prisoners and held up their canteens, sloshing about the water that remained inside and making pantomimes as if to share the contents with them. Finally, with a harsh laugh, the driver flicked the reins, and the wagon resumed its doleful plod.

Farther on, the wagon veered off Exeter Road and followed a separate path leading south directly to Old Mill Prison. Richard sat up straight on the wooden plank running parallel to the side of the wagon and twisted his body to face as far forward as possible. Bringing the advantage of his height to bear, he gazed over the heads of his fellow prisoners and strained to see what he could, aware that this was his one opportunity to study the prison environs from the outside. What he saw were stout walls constructed in smooth gray stone between ten and twelve feet in height, or twice the height of the two guards at the main entrance now preparing to open a double iron gate. Other guards, by their casual dress not British Army regulars, patrolled the outer walls. He could see few trees anywhere near the prison, mostly low-lying shrubs interspersed with rolling fields of purple heath and boulders of pink granite clustered nearer the shoreline. Beyond the prison, at the entrance to the Channel, he spied three warships close-hauled and heeled against a stiff, westerly breeze. White water frothed at their bows as they pounded their way toward some distant station. Richard and Seth Gardiner marked the ships' progress wistfully until the prison walls loomed up, blocking their view.

The driver reined in the horses just outside the gate. Guards armed with muskets took up position in a semicircle behind the wagon as its tail gate was unhooked and eased down on its rusty hinges. One by one the prisoners wiggled as best they could off the end of the wagon. They stepped down tentatively, testing for balance with their hands bound behind their backs. Moving their hips back and forth, left and right, they glanced about, searching for anything or anyone that might provide some rationale for hope.

"Roight!" a grizzled old sergeant imperiously barked. "This way, mates!"

In single file the eight prisoners trudged through the portal into the main prison yard. Richard was third in line. Once he was inside the prison proper, past the gate, a sentry removed the rope binding his hands. Richard paused to massage his wrists and survey the area.

The prison was more massive than he had first imagined. Within the huge rectangular stone structure was another, smaller rectangle of identical construction and proportions, except that at its entrance was a wide-open wooden gate. Between the double walls was a grassy area encircling the entire inner yard. This yard was perhaps twenty feet in width to the east and west, thirty or thirty-five feet to the north and south. Near where Richard stood, between the two north walls, were two substantial stone buildings. One, Richard assumed by the guards posted at the entryway, was most likely the prison offices. The other looked to be a military barracks. Idling about in both the outer and inner yards was a large number of scruffy-looking men walking solo or in small groups.

"New prisoners!" one of them shouted, causing others to come streaming out from the inner compound. They mingled among the new arrivals, murmuring a quick hello here, a question there, each in search of something or someone that might provide a link to home. One aging inmate, his breath foul, slouched up close to Richard and peered up at him, nodding his bald head as though possibly recognizing him. Convinced at last of his error, he dismissed Richard with a sharp exhale of breath to his face and shuffled off, muttering angrily. Richard, stunned, watched him go.

"Pay no mind to Zeb," someone said behind him. "He's a bit daft in the head, but perfectly harmless. Been here too long is the problem."

The friendly voice belonged to a man somewhat older than Richard. He was dressed in soiled, loose-fitting trousers and a faded blue pullover shirt, open at the neck to reveal a black shrub of hair on his chest. He had a wide face but a thin nose, hooked at the tip. His mouth was slightly crooked, in a sort of perpetual wry smile, and his bright blue gray eyes appeared to Richard like beacons of safe harbor amid the turbulence of a breaking sea.

"What's he looking for?" Richard asked, watching as the wretch squinted up at Seth Gardiner. Gardiner recoiled from the rancid breath and set off at a rapid clip. The old man hobbled after him, cursing and waving a fist in the air.

"Same as everyone else. Kinsfolk. Friends. Zeb's from Massachusetts. A town called Essex. Most prisoners here are from Cape Ann, so odds are he'll find someone someday who knows someone he knows. My name is Silas Talbot, by the way."

"Richard Cutler."

They shook hands.

"What's home port, Richard?"

"Hingham."

"Hingham, eh? I was born nearby, in Carver. Lived in Providence most of my life, though. Well, welcome to your new home, Richard. Let's get you settled and cleaned up a bit." He pointed ahead toward the inner yard. "I take it you're an officer," he said, as they walked toward the open wooden gate. "Unless I'm mistaken, that's a navy coat you're wearing."

"It is. I am—I mean, I was—a midshipman on the Continental sloop *Ranger.*"

"*Ranger*? Of Whitehaven fame?" Talbot was impressed. "Is that where you got that bruise on your face?"

Richard nodded.

"Well I'll be damned. A naval hero in our midst. Well, Admiral," he grinned, "you won't find many of your lofty status here. We're a sorry lot of privateers, mostly. But there's one or two others from *Ranger* we've piped aboard, including a midshipman. He's in there." He indicated a low stone building at the far end of the inner yard with the words ROYAL HOSPITAL carved in stone above the front door. Richard stopped short.

"That midshipman's name is Agreen Crabtree, Mr. Talbot. He's a close friend of mine. Is it possible I might see him?"

Talbot smiled. He put a comforting hand on the small of Richard's back, urging him on through the wooden gate.

"I'm not your commanding officer, Richard. So please drop the 'Mister.' My name is Silas. As to your visiting the hospital, yes, that can be arranged. I know the surgeon in charge, a fellow named Ball. I'll have a chat with him tomorrow. He's not a bad sort. No one here's a bad sort, really, except for the prison keeper, a chap named Cowdry. See him scudding toward you, my advice is to wear ship and run. He's nothing but trouble. As to the wardens and guards, they're actually quite accommodating. The three wardens are permanent, but the guards and militia officers get rotated out every so often. Probably what keeps them in such good spirits."

They walked through the gate past a small wooden guardhouse and into the inner yard. To their left, in the eastern half, was a two-story windowless structure, a hundred feet long and twenty feet wide, constructed in blocks of somber gray stone leading up to an overhanging slate roof. On the western side was a smaller building of similar architecture, but with windows built in to the stone every ten feet or so. Directly ahead, against the south wall, stood the two-story hospital and, adjacent to it, a box-shaped building with a chimney on each side. The galley, Talbot informed him. Next to the guardhouse was a water pump and a lamppost. That was the sum total of what Richard could make out as he followed Silas Talbot toward the windowless building.

"Here we are, Richard, your new home," Talbot said when they had reached the entrance. "It's officially known as Long Prison, though we have less official names for it. This here is the American side. Over there"—he indicated the corresponding building across the inner compound, the one with windows—"is the European side. It's for non-American prisoners, French mostly, and not many of them so far. But we can expect more to show up, with the treaty signed."

Richard gave Talbot a quizzical look. "What treaty?"

"You haven't heard? Last week the French announced a formal military alliance with the United States."

So it was done. Not just an alliance of friendship and common ideals that had been signed some time ago, but a full-fledged military alliance between France and the United States. Benjamin Franklin and Passy came immediately to mind. "How do you know this?" Richard asked excitedly.

Talbot grinned at his reaction. "You'd be surprised how much we know here. The guards are local militia. They're happy to pass along whatever they hear. And on Sundays the people of Plymouth—Janners, they're known as—come around to buy whatever we can make and sell whatever we can afford."

"What do they sell?"

"Food, clothing. Shoes and trinkets. Wine and spirits are popular items. A newspaper, an offer to post a letter home, that sort of thing. Listen to some of them, and you'd think they're our allies. I'm amazed how many people around here seem sympathetic to our cause. Not all of them by any stretch, but a good many."

"Sympathetic enough to help us escape?"

Talbot eyed him cautiously.

"There have been many escape attempts from Old Mill, Richard. Some have succeeded, most have failed. So if you've a mind to go, I'd advise you to plan carefully. See that grating over there, the one next to the lamppost?" He pointed to it. "That's what we call 'the black hole.' It's four feet long, three feet wide, and four feet high. Just enough room to sit up in, not enough to lie down in. Any prisoner caught trying to escape has his turn in there for forty days, summer or winter, it don't matter. Food rations are bad enough up here as it is; down there you get half rations. Men have near starved in that hole. Tonight at muster—two bells in the second dog watch by the way, don't miss it—Cowdry will give his standard speech to new arrivals: 'We'll treat you decently as long as you obey the rules. Disobey them and you'll suffer the consequences.'"

"Prisoners still try to escape, though."

"Of course. In some damn ingenious ways, I might add."

"What about you, Silas? Have you tried?"

Talbot nodded. "Aye, twice. I've lost a lot of weight in that hellhole," adding, as he glanced down at his waist, "so much so I still have a hard time keeping my pants up. Now Richard, standard issue in Long Prison is a blanket, pillow, and basin for washing yourself and your clothes. You'll berth with us officers on the top floor. The British don't distinguish Americans by rank— to them, we're all civil prisoners, not prisoners of war—but we insist on observing those distinctions nonetheless. Follow me."

Long Prison had a dank feel to it, and it took Richard several moments to adapt to the darkness inside. Sunlight streaming in through the west-facing front door provided the sole source of light for the entire first floor of the building. What Richard could distinguish looked surprisingly shipshape. Infirmary-type cots were arranged in groups of six, each group containing similar furnishings and housekeeping paraphernalia: a low wooden table, six sea chests serving as both storage areas and seats, six bowls for washing, six plates and utensils for eating, and a broom. A few men were idling about, sweeping or chatting, but otherwise the enormous chamber was empty.

Talbot led the way up a flight of stone stairs.

"Just like on a ship," he explained, "and that's no coincidence. The guards may be local militia, but Old Mill is a Royal Navy institution. So we observe the customs of the sea here to the extent we are able. Guards come in every now and then and poke around. Aside from that, we're pretty much left alone. . . . Mind your step. It won't be so dark upstairs."

Richard climbed behind Talbot up the steep flight of steps to the second floor. It did grow lighter as they ascended, and the air smelled less fusty, due in part to six-inch open spaces set in regular patterns around the building between the top of the wall and the overhanging slate roof. Richard wondered how cold it must get up here in the winter. He could see no fireplaces or other sources of heat.

"What are they looking for?"

"The guards? Tunnels, I suspect . . . ah, here we are. Welcome to the quarterdeck of the good ship *Joyous*. And here's my friend and chief steward, Richard Dale, preparing our evening meal. Richard, I have the honor of introducing you to Richard Cutler, lately of the Continental ship *Ranger*."

"Welcome aboard, Richard," the tall, barrel-chested man exclaimed. He was younger than Talbot, not much older than Richard himself. Few would describe him as handsome. Long hairy sideburns framed a large oval face dominated by a ruddy bulbous nose and heavy jowls, yet there was something in the easy, friendly manner of this brute of a man that caused Richard to instantly like him.

"Thank you, Mr. Dale . . . um, Richard."

"He's learning," Talbot chuckled good-naturedly at Dale. "Well-bred Boston-type, I'm afraid. Navy-type, to boot. Suppose we'll just have to live with it. Now then, *Mister* Cutler, *Mister* Dale here is a Virginian. One of the few Southerners in Old Mill. He served in the navy too. The Virginia State Navy, that is. He was captured, turned loyalist on us, was captured again, this time by Captain John Barry, on our side. Barry convinced him to rejoin our cause as first officer aboard *Lexington*."

"Didn't take much convincin'," Dale grunted, as though reminded of his flip-flop allegiances once too often. He winked at Richard, and his eyes flickered with mirth.

Richard grinned back at him. "What's that you're cooking?" he asked, trying to sound casual. Dale made a show of stirring the steaming metal pot. The aromas it emitted were hardly what one could call savory, but it was food, and Richard was very, very hungry.

"Why, the house specialty," Dale said with a flourish. "This evening, and every evening to come, we will be serving—how do the French say?—*un grand potage d'escargots*. Pull up a chair and I'll have Jacques the servant boy ladle you out a bowl."

"Snails?" Richard queried, amazed. "How do you get snails here?"

Talbot laughed. "They're hardly the kind you'd find in a French café. They're land snails, and you can find them all over the yard. Toss in some cabbage stumps, perhaps some old bones and dried peas and other delicacies from the rubbish, and you have a concoction that is at least edible. You'll get used to it," he added, noting Richard's grimace. "You'd better. We're served only one

189

meal a day here, at noon, and there's not much to that. At least this stuff fills your stomach."

"Or empties it," Richard said, not convinced.

Footsteps echoed on the stairway. Other officers appeared, each dressed in well-worn civilian clothes without any indication of rank. Introductions were made and hands clasped in the way men do when they are sharing a fate. To Richard's relief, there was no one reminiscent of Thomas Simpson among the group. Each man immediately accepted Richard as an equal. The fact that he was here, in this prison, after what he was reputed to have done at Whitehaven, spoke volumes.

After supper and the muster of all prisoners in the inner yard at seven o'clock, the officers reassembled on the second floor of the prison. During the next several hours, Richard learned much about his fellow inmates, especially Silas Talbot, who, by his very stature, had assumed the role of American senior officer. It was an appropriate role. Not only was he a privateer captain, he was also a major in the Continental Army, promoted after he sailed an aging brig topped with tar and turpentine and gunpowder down the Hudson River straight into HMS *Asia,* a Sixty-Four anchored in New York harbor. He ordered his own ship set ablaze and all hands to abandon ship; he was the last to go overboard, moments before the fiery hulk struck the man of war. So intense was the resulting explosion, Richard Dale bantered, recounting the story for Richard's benefit, that General Howe and his American mistress were forced to suffer coitus interruptus as they disported themselves ashore in a Loyalist's bedroom.

"And that's not all," commented a man who had earlier introduced himself as Joshua Barney. In contrast to both Talbot and Dale, he had a long, thin face with an aquiline nose and chin, more the appearance of a scholar than a privateer captain. "Another time, Silas was being chased by a British cruiser. He had no stern chasers, and the cruiser was catching up. During the night he had two gun ports cut out of the transom, with six-pounders standing by, loaded with grapeshot and crowbars. Next morning, with the cruiser close astern and a boarding party set to go in her bows, Silas ran out the guns and let 'em have it. The cruiser's headsails and forerigging were carried away, along with most of the boarding party. She veered to windward—to ease the strain on her foremast, you understand—and wham! Silas gave 'er what-for, a full broadside. That did 'er! She sank right then and there. Best damn fight ever you can imagine!"

Some men guffawed even though they had heard the story rehashed many times before.

"That," Talbot countered, "coming from a man who has been imprisoned three times and who has had the damnable luck to escape twice."

Barney pounded his chest with a fist. "He's right, lads. There's not a cage built that can hold me. I'll be out soon. We all will."

"Less'n they start bringing in wenches on a daily basis," quipped a bearded man named Offin Boardman. "Knowing you, Joshua, that'd be the one thing that'd keep you aboard here."

Men chuckled as Barney twisted his facial features to mimic a man over-indulged with drink.

"Offin, you promise to bring those wenches in on an *hourly* basis, and by Jesus, I'd seriously consider stayin'!"

After the laughter died away, Richard asked, quite soberly, "How soon, Joshua?"

"What's that, lad?"

"When will we escape? And how?"

Barney looked serious again.

"I don't know when, lad, and that's the truth. But I do know how. It will be through a tunnel, a different sort of tunnel this time. And when we go, we go together. All of us. Agreed?"

The officers mumbled their agreement.

☆ ☆ ☆

THE NEXT morning, true to his word, Silas Talbot made arrangements for Richard to visit the prison hospital. Richard was there at the appointed hour and was granted admittance by a single nod of the sentry's head once he stated his name and purpose.

Richard walked inside. It turned out to be a single-story building, not two as he had imagined, though with a ceiling high enough to accommodate a second story should the demands of war require it. Placed around the single large room were white cloth screens that separated the space into thirteen separate wards. One person was about, an orderly or surgeon's mate, who came up to Richard when he noticed him waiting by the doorway.

"May I help you?" he asked, not unkindly.

"Yes, thank you," Richard replied. "My name is Richard Cutler. I have leave from Dr. Ball to visit a shipmate here. His name is Agreen Crabtree."

"Mr. Crabtree? Yes. He's in the last ward down there on the left. You have ten minutes, Mr. Cutler. I'm afraid that's all I can allow. I shall come for you then."

"I understand. Thank you."

The ward indicated by the orderly contained four beds. It was impeccably clean, Richard noted. Crisp white sheets and wool blankets tucked properly under the mattresses confirmed that, in this hospital, the staff took its work seriously. One bed was in use, the patient asleep on his back. Richard walked over and gazed down fondly at his friend. A lump formed in his throat as he took in the matted strawberry hair, the gentle rise and fall of his chest, the army of freckles marching across his nose from ear to ear, the source of so much good-natured heckling in the midshipmen's mess. His skin color was ashen, in startling contrast to what was normally a ruddy, hale complexion, and his right hand twitched slightly this way and that, as though searching in sleep for the weapon that so marked his identity.

Richard was loath to wake him, but the ten minutes he was granted were ticking away.

"Agee," he whispered, gently shaking his friend's shoulder. "Agee."

Crabtree's body stirred. His head moved from side to side.

"Agee," Richard said again, louder.

Agreen's eyes fluttered open. He looked at Richard, shut his eyes tight, opened them again.

"Richard!" he gasped, straining to rise. "Richard, is that you?"

"Yes, Agee, it's me. Now lie back." He eased Agreen's upper body back onto the bed and sat down on the mattress beside him.

"Richard! Sweet Jesus! I thought you were dead."

"And I, you. I didn't know you were here until yesterday. I came as soon as I could. Agee, I . . ." He swallowed hard, willing the lump in his throat away. "Are they treating you well?"

Agreen gave him a flicker of a grin. "You kiddin' me? I aim t' finish out the war right here, it's so frickin' nice. Food's a wonder, and the nurses, man, they're pretty as angels an' as horny as church mice." A sudden stab of pain seized him; he looked down the bed at its source.

"How's your leg?"

"Comin' along smartly. Every now and then it kicks up a fuss like this. Surgeon says I'll keep it, though. That's the good news."

"For you. Not such good news for England."

They smiled at that together. So much to say, no time to say it. The surgeon's mate had already materialized behind Richard.

"Sorry, sir. Time's up."

Richard rose to his feet.

"I'll check back tomorrow, Agee. In the meantime, as your mother would say, have a care and do what the surgeon tells you. You'll be back on your feet soon. And when you are, we'll celebrate, like never before." He gave Agreen's arm a gentle squeeze and turned to go.

Agreen called him back.

"Richard?"

"Yes?"

Agreen's lower lip was trembling slightly when Richard looked back at him. "Thank you."

"For what?"

Agreen reached out his left hand. "For savin' my life. I saw what you did."

Richard clasped Agreen's hand in both of his. "Whatever it is I did, Agee, think nothing of it. We're a team. You know that. Besides, you'd do the same for me, in that situation."

Agreen nodded. "You're damn right I would. An' I pray t' God I have the occasion soon t' prove it."

☆ ☆ ☆

AGREEN MADE remarkable progress, his recovery expedited, the surgeon claimed, by Richard's daily visits. Two weeks after that first visit, he was able to hobble out the front door of the hospital with the aid of a crutch. A week after that, he discarded the crutch and joined the other officers on the second floor of Long Prison.

The season had changed from the cool drizzle and fog of spring to the warmth and humidity of summer. July 4 dawned bright and sunny, perfect conditions for the celebrations and makeshift parades planned to mark the occasion. The next day, however, prison life returned to normal. Diversions from soul-dulling drudgery were created by bored men and mandated by their morose conditions. Whittling had become a popular pastime, an activity encouraged by wardens who ensured that ample supplies of wood were made available around the inner yard. They even gave prisoners, upon request, small knives with blunted tips to use for whittling. Such curios as model ships, ladles, and makeshift mallets were sculpted from wood and sold to local citizens visiting Old Mill on Sunday afternoons. Whatever coins the prisoners received were more often than not snapped up by other locals hawking their wares in every corner of the compound. Barter was also a mainstay of commerce. In exchange for a toy pistol Richard had whittled from a slab of oak, an elderly woman agreed to post a letter he had written to his family in Hingham, telling them simply where he was and that he was in good health. She was a kind and caring woman, for she had paid good money for an object that any discerning eye would agree was a poor replica of a pistol. Richard felt certain she would actually post the letter; whether it would ever reach Hingham was far less certain.

For the officers as well as the common seamen, the highlight of any day was the gathering and sharing of information on the war. From guards and Janners the prisoners learned that, in early June, Gen. William Howe had abandoned Philadelphia, along with a substantial number of American Loyalists living there. On the march north to New York through New Jersey, Howe's army had been attacked by rebel forces near a town called Monmouth. The battle was reported in the British press as a victory, an assertion that was challenged by certain members of Parliament. The Continentals had apparently inflicted heavy losses on the British, and they had held their ground against multiple assaults by elite British Army regulars. One newspaper predicted that the Continentals would have won the battle had not one field commander refused to obey a direct order from General Washington to attack a weakened British position at a critical juncture. "Another victory like this," the editorial quipped, "and England will lose the war."

Other sources held that *Ranger* had defeated a second Royal Navy vessel in a battle with a light frigate off Belfast Lough and had brazenly captured within sight of shore a number of merchant vessels heavily laden with the foods, spices, and fineries sought by England's nobility and expanding mercantile class. This turned out to be fact, not rumor. The engagements had been recorded in the *London Chronicle,* a copy of which found its way into Richard's hands compliments of a sympathetic Janner. Together with the other officers, he pored over the article to ensure he had not missed any tidbit of information. According to the news report, these events had enkindled considerable fury in Westminster and Buckingham Palace and had prompted cries for swift retaliation from both chambers of Parliament. Whitehall responded by dispatching one naval squadron of frigates northeast around the north coast of Ireland and another squadron northwest around the north coast of Scotland. A third squadron of heavy frigates was now patrolling the southern reaches of the Celtic Sea. The Admiralty urged calm, assuring the British nation it was only a matter of time until these fiery embers of piracy were permanently extinguished. Some believed. Some did not. Among the latter, Lloyd's of London. Fed up with the capture or sinking of more than seven hundred British merchant vessels by American privateers since the start of the war, and anticipating further raids by the Continental Navy on English seaports, the venerable company drastically raised the fees it charged to insure British cargoes. From Kingston to Halifax to Bombay, British merchants and shipping agents expressed shock and outrage over this decision and clamored for redress.

In mid-August, Old Mill received an unusual visitor. He was John Thornton, an American envoy sent by the American commissioners in Paris to survey Old Mill Prison in Plymouth and Forton Prison in Portsmouth, the two prisons in England detaining American seamen. His visit had been arranged with the help of several members of Parliament in opposition, as well as the British ambassador to France, Lord Stormont, a personal acquaintance of Benjamin Franklin. Thornton's mission was to determine the number of Americans being held, who they were, their rank, and their general state of health.

"This information will be used to arrange for prisoner exchanges," Thornton explained to the gathering of officers at the close of the two hours he was permitted in Old Mill. "You gentlemen, of course, will be at the top of our list. God grant that we can free all three hundred prisoners held here."

"Three hundred?" Richard Dale challenged. "That number includes our French allies, does it not, and more of them are arriving every day. Who gets exchanged first, us or them?"

Thornton coughed delicately into a fist.

"That is a fair question, Mr. Dale," he replied "and a sensitive one. I'm afraid I don't have a final answer for you just yet. You understand there are certain . . . *niceties* that must be observed in diplomatic affairs such as these. You may be assured, however, that our commissioners are doing everything within their power to secure your release."

"Mr. Thornton," said William Russell, his deep, respectful voice drawing everyone's attention to him. A teacher by trade before the war, Russell had started a school in the prison compound for ships' boys and anyone else interested in learning Greek or arithmetic. "Some of us have been in this prison for two years. I doubt any Frenchman has been held here for more than two months. May we depend on your promise to consider this a prime factor when you negotiate with the British?"

"You may, sir."

"In that case, when, in your judgment, may we expect such negotiations to begin? And when may we expect to be released?"

"As soon as humanly possible, on both counts," Thornton assured him. "At the moment we are holding a fair number of British prisoners in France, courtesy, in no small measure, of Captain Jones. Some high-ranking officers are among them, and the Admiralty wants them back. So you see, we already have the basis for an exchange."

"Aye, so we do," sighed Joshua Barney. He shook his head wearily. "Mr. Thornton, I mean no disrespect. I'm sure you believe what you are telling us. Unfortunately, I have had some firsthand experience with your so-called diplomatic niceties, and damn me to hell if the highest-ranking American in this prison is released before the lowest-ranking Frenchmen are long gone from here."

Thornton gathered up his coat and hat.

"Gentlemen, I must be going. I thank you for giving me this list of prisoners and I bid you *au revoir*. You shall hear from me again, that I promise you."

He bowed low to the Americans and hurried outside, where a carriage and a team of horses were waiting by the front entrance to convey him to Portsmouth. Richard followed him out and strode up beside him.

"Mr. Thornton, a word, if you please. My name is Richard Cutler. I would very much appreciate your remembering me to Dr. Franklin upon your return to Paris."

Thornton stopped short and eyed Richard curiously.

"You know him, Mr. Cutler?"

"Yes, I do. I had the privilege of being in Passy last winter. I accompanied Captain Jones there. During that time I came to know Dr. Franklin quite well."

"I see . . . Richard Cutler . . . Richard Cutler . . . Yes, now that I think on it, I do recall Dr. Franklin mentioning your name, more than once in fact. Along with Captain Jones, whom the doctor greatly admires."

"Captain Jones holds Dr. Franklin in equal esteem, I assure you, Mr. Thornton. You will send Dr. Franklin my respects?"

"I will, sir. Immediately upon my return. You have my word on it." They shook hands.

That night, Richard lay on his back on his cot, his mind and body too keyed up to permit sleep. He put his hands under his head and stared up into the darkness, reflecting on the events of the day. Thornton's visit had inspired hope. In him and in every American prisoner, whatever his rank. Still, Richard understood that release would not come quickly. Richard Dale and Joshua Barney were right. French prisoners, certainly French officers, would be exchanged before any American. It would, after all, be the French who would be doing the negotiating, given that the British did not recognize the United States as a sovereign country. What's more, most of the other American officers held the rank of privateer captain or lieutenant. As midshipmen, he and Agee would remain on the lowest rung of any officer exchange list. And he knew Thornton was also right. However much the American commissioners were committed to their release, they could move no faster than the cogs of diplomacy and negotiations would permit. But the wheels were now in motion. That was the critical point. And as a result, Richard had a fighting chance of returning soon to France. Perhaps even to Passy.

The possibility stirred him, but it also came as a startling revelation that lately he had given little thought to either Passy or Anne-Marie. During the early weeks of his captivity that had not been the case. Then, in the dead of night, when all else was quiet and the need greatest to mentally transport himself away from the miseries of Long Prison, she had come to him, or he to her, and she had soothed him, released him, in a way he had experienced only once before. Not with Sarah Fearing in Hingham, though from time to time his memories dwelled on her as well. Like Anne-Marie, she was an endearing young woman who would have given him anything he desired, anything at all.

He well remembered the night she had told him that in those exact words. But however much he was attracted physically to them both, there was something . . . lacking . . . that was entirely beyond the ability of either of them to control or remedy. What was it? His heart knew. But long ago his brain had erected impossible barriers to that knowledge.

THE FOLLOWING evening, after supper and the 7:00 muster, the American officers met on the second floor. It had become a daily assembly, there being much to discuss, but this night assumed a special significance. Silas Talbot presided while Seth Gardiner kept watch at the top of the steps, alert for any signal of warning relayed to him from below.

"Well, lads," Talbot opened the meeting, "you heard what Thornton told us yesterday, and you've had twenty-four hours to consider it. What say you?"

He acknowledged Richard Dale.

"I say we keep on with the tunnel," Dale asserted. "We're beyond the first wall already. We've only thirty feet to go to the outer wall. Then fifty feet beyond that. We should have it done in two months. Three, tops."

He was referring to a tunnel begun in mid-July not long after the July Fourth celebrations. Every American prisoner was aware of this tunnel, and it had been agreed among them that henceforth there would be no other escape attempts. During the day, every man followed his normal routine. At nightfall they began work in one-hour shifts, ten men to a shift. Two men did the actual digging while four others hauled dirt to the surface, where the remaining four dispersed it either into their sea chests, covered over with spare clothes and other personal belongings, or down into the crew's latrines adjacent to Long Prison. What wood they could discreetly gather during the day from wood piles stacked outside for whittling went down the hole at night, along with wooden slats from beneath the mattresses, to shore up the walls and ceiling of the tunnel and prevent collapse. At first light in the morning, all work ceased. The last shift emerged from the hole and replaced the wooden floorboards that had originally been cut away with a contraband knife. A metal cot was dragged over the area and everything tidied up.

It was painstakingly slow and dangerous work. The tools they used were rudimentary; much of the hard-packed dirt had to be clawed away by hand in the skimpy light of lanterns. Logistics of constructing the tunnel, and the strategy underlying it, however, were quite simple. All five previous escape attempts by tunnel had been to the east, a logical choice. Long Prison lay on the eastern half of the inner yard, so the distance out was much shorter to the east. There were also large boulders and thick shrubbery out there to help conceal any escape attempt.

Prison officials realized this, which is why they concentrated their surveillance efforts on the eastern side of Old Mill.

The tunnel currently under construction was directed northward. It was a considerably longer route, and a more challenging one, since between the two walls to the north lay the administrative offices of Old Mill. Such was the logic of tunneling to the north. The last thing prison officials would expect, the Americans assumed, would be prisoners constructing a tunnel by night literally beneath where they worked by day.

"You others?" asked Talbot. "Do you agree with Dale?"

Most of the men nodded their assent.

"All right. But I must warn you: if the British find our tunnel, the black hole may be the least of our concerns. Each of us would go straight to the bottom of any prisoner exchange list. The Brits will have some say on who will be released and who won't, and those on the bottom of the list may have no chance of getting out before the war is over. Is this a risk you're willing to take?"

"For me, it is," a middle-aged privateer named Oliver Bartlett declared. He had been involved in four of the five previous tunnel attempts, and the effects of many weeks in the black hole on his body were clear. "I put no stock in what Thornton says. Hell, Silas, you know as well as I do that we're already *at* the bottom of the list."

"My sentiments exactly," said William Russell.

Talbot acknowledged Agreen Crabtree, who had raised a hand.

"I'd like t' comment on somethin' Richard Dale said. We have three months t' get the tunnel built, right? That's pushing everything mighty close t' winter. It'll be hard goin' then, diggin' up. Then, assumin' we do get out, we won't have the clothes we'll need for winter. Any one of us'd stand out in a crowd, dressed as we are. Five pounders'd be over us like bees on honey."

Men nodded silently in agreement. Agreen's points, they knew, were well taken, and his reference to the reward money got them to serious thinking. As British policy, any local citizen turning in an escaped convict to the Home

Guard was awarded five pounds on the spot. Five pounds was the equivalent of a year's salary for a farm hand. The generosity of the reward, and the speed at which it was delivered, made "five pounders" a serious threat to any prisoner attempting to escape. Especially during the early days of the war, it was not uncommon for a seemingly sympathetic guard to take an American into his confidence and offer to assist him over the wall, only to split the five-pound reward with a Janner waiting on the other side to nab the escapee.

"What choice do we have?" commented Bartlett. "Except maybe to speed up the process somehow."

"Or not dig so far," Richard said, so softly not everyone heard him.

"What was that?" Talbot inquired. His curiosity was piqued by the distant quality in Richard's voice and the furrows of concentration visible on his brow.

"Or not dig so far," Richard said in a louder, more confident voice. Shreds of an impossible notion were beginning to meld together in his mind.

"What are you talking about, Richard?" a perplexed William Russell asked. "We've always agreed we need to be fifty feet beyond the second wall before we can dig out."

"But we don't, William, that's the point." The notion was coalescing rapidly now. "We need dig only under the first wall. Gentlemen, we have only twenty feet left to go!"

"This is nonsense!" Joshua Barney scoffed. "Richard, have you taken leave of your senses? What are you suggesting? That we dig just to the Outer Yard? Hell, boy, we can walk out there any time we want, the gate's wide open till nightfall. What about the outer wall? We can't just walk out through the main gate, pretty as we please."

Richard grinned at him. "Yes we can, Joshua. Yes we can. Hear me out. Silas, how often do they rotate the guards out of here?"

"Every three months, from what we've observed."

"Exactly. And how often do they rotate the officers?"

"Every six months."

"Right. So when is the next time officers and guards are rotated out together? Most of them anyway."

Talbot gave that some thought. It was Russell who answered.

"The first of October, three weeks from now."

Richard nodded. "That's how I figure it." His right hand was working in quick chopping motions.

"So on October 2, we'll have a new batch of officers in our midst, plus a fresh rotation of militia guards, most of whom, we can fairly presume, will be strangers to each other. On that one day, an officer could walk in or out of this prison, pretty as you please, as you put it, Joshua, based on one credential: his uniform. Do you agree?"

The officers stared at Richard, digesting his train of thought.

"I think we can agree with that, Richard" Talbot said, scratching his head. "But where are you leading us?"

Agreen slapped his knee hard.

"I know where he's leadin' us, Silas! Jesus Christ, it's so obvious we should all have thought of it long ago. He's leadin' us into the prison office, the building right between the two gates where they keep the officers' uniforms. Our tunnel's headin' straight for it. Come up through the floor at night, don those uniforms, hide out till dawn, then walk out early before the *real* officers are awake. Bugger, but I'll look good in a lieutenant's uniform!"

He beamed at Richard. Richard beamed back.

Talbot held up a hand in caution.

"Steady on, lads. Steady on. Let's consider this."

Searching for the weak links, Talbot and the other officers ran their minds down the chain of sequential steps that under Richard's plan would take them from Long Prison under the inner wall, up into the prison office, and out through the main gate.

They could identify none until Eleazar Johnston asked, "How many uniforms do we reckon are in there?"

A former first officer on a privateer, Johnston rarely spoke without cause. Nor was he one to take lightly the consequences of a failed escape. After one attempt of his own, he had spent forty days in the dead of winter in the black hole. Then, not one month after he was out, he had made a second attempt. During a severe hail storm he had been shot in the arm by a guard while scaling the outer wall using a makeshift grappling hook. Dr. Ball had had to amputate the arm.

"I don't know," Richard confessed. "But there have to be quite a number. Every British officer is issued at least two uniforms in case one gets soiled."

"If we're caught wearin' those uniforms," Barney pointed out, "sure as hell we'll be hanged as spies."

Richard acknowledged that.

"Perhaps, Joshua. But it's a risk worth taking, don't you think? Once we're outside, we can get rid of the red dress coat. The rest of the uniform's pretty much the same as standard Continental Navy issue."

Barney pursed his lips reflectively.

"You're overlooking something," Richard Dale observed. "I grant you the sentries guarding the gate may be new, but so many officers leaving the compound so early in the morning would certainly arouse suspicion. They'd want to confirm everything with Cowdry before opening the gate. Don't forget, their ass would be on the line."

Discouraged agreement rumbled among the Americans. The weak link in the chain had apparently been identified.

Crabtree snapped his fingers.

"No, wait," he exclaimed, rising to his feet. "We've been thinkin' about this wrong. We don't all need t' be officers. Most of us can be what we are: prisoners. We only need a couple of us in uniform. We go in the buildin' at night, through the tunnel, just as Richard said. When we come out the next mornin', the prisoners are bound up, bein' led out by the officers. For further interrogation on *Yarmouth* we tell the guards at the gate. On orders from Admiral Digby himself, we say. What sentry, first day at his new post, facin' the prison brass, would challenge *that?*"

"He's right," Russell concurred, and everyone's mood brightened considerably.

And so the work continued. They had three weeks to dig the twenty feet to beneath the prison office. A foot a day was required, less than their average daily progress so far. With resolve rekindled, men set to work at night, while during the day they toiled over whatever artifacts they hoped to sell to Janners during the last three Sundays of September. The biggest need in any escape plan was the ability to buy clothes, food, lodging, and most important, passage on a ship bound for Europe, either on the deck of a neutral vessel or hidden behind a false bulwark aboard a British merchantman engaged in illegal commerce across the Channel in France. All this required money, lots of money, and since it was officers who normally had access to money, it was officers who normally made good their escape. Common seamen accepted this reality without much complaint.

"It ain't much, I realize, Mr. Cutler," Seth Gardiner said to Richard one day in mid-September, "but it's what I've been able to save from whittlin' things an' sellin' them to Janners. Please, sir, I want you to have it." He offered up a soft leather pouch heavy with coins. Richard had been walking with Richard Dale and Joshua Barney back and forth between the wooden gate and the prison office, as they did several times each day, silently measuring and calculating, when Gardiner approached them, doffing his woolen seaman's hat. "I wish you good fortune, sir," he concluded. "You've been good to me. You've been good to my mates. I won't forget you."

The bosun's mate came to attention and saluted Richard. He kept his right hand stiff at his forehead as Richard slowly returned the salute.

"Thank you, Gardiner," he said, reluctantly accepting the pouch. "I won't forget you, either."

Ten days shy of October, with the tunnel nearly finished, anticipation in the American compound became palpable, so much so that Talbot became concerned. He had experienced this sort of excitement before, and he knew it did not take much in the way of unusual behavior to arouse suspicions among the wardens and guards. He urged everyone not to even *think* escape or discuss any aspect of it unless it was in the guarded privacy of Long Prison at night. During the day they were to adhere religiously to the normal routine.

The prisoners obeyed his commands as best they could, aided to no small degree by a noticeable laxness in the guards' attitude as October 1 approached. Inspections of Long Prison became more cursory and no longer a daily event. Relations between the prisoners and their guards, always cordial, became downright friendly. Guards gave trinkets and mementos to favorite prisoners as parting gifts to remember them by, and paused often in their daily routine to chat with them and swap stories. Reminding themselves to remain vigilant, the American officers nevertheless found themselves drifting into a quiet lagoon of complacency, smug in the assumption that soon they would be free of this place and, God willing, back at sea.

Which was why it came as such a shock to them when, late in the afternoon of September 28, a senior warden of Old Mill marched into the inner yard followed by two armed guards. They came up to where a group of officers was strolling back and forth in front of Long Prison.

The warden strode right up to Richard. "Mr. Cutler, gather your belongings," he demanded curtly. "You are coming with me." His tone left no doubt he meant immediately.

"Where are you taking him?" Richard Dale demanded to know.

"None of your business," the warden snapped.

Richard, dazed, was given three minutes to stuff what few possessions he had into a makeshift seabag. Escorted out of Long Prison between the two guards, he shook his head in incomprehension at his fellow officers gathered outside in the yard and trudged off through the wooden gate to the prison office.

Two sentries at the door stiffened to attention as the warden and his party approached. Richard felt waves of despair and anger batter his insides. This could be no coincidence. There could be only one explanation for why he had been brought here. Someone had turned informer, allowing the British to unearth not only the tunnel but also its inspiration.

The warden knocked on the door of the prison keeper.

"Enter," grunted a voice from within.

The warden opened the door and stepped aside to allow Richard entry. Richard walked in hesitantly, scanned the room, saw the dour face of William Cowdry watching him, then froze as he recognized the man seated with his back to him. That man was now rising to his feet and was turning around to look at Richard, the emotion evidenced on his face as profound in its own way as it was on his nephew's. It was as though each was gawking at a mirror image of himself, at a considerably different age.

"Uncle William . . . !"

8

FAREHAM, ENGLAND

Fall 1778

*A*N AMERICAN OFFICIAL IN Paris, by name of . . . um . . ." The name seemed on the tip of his tongue.

"Franklin," Richard assumed. His glum tone persisted, though he was feeling a bit brighter about his situation now that he was recognizing familiar terrain. "Dr. Benjamin Franklin. He's an American commissioner in Passy."

"No, not him. I know of Dr. Franklin. He had lodgings years ago on Craven Street, near my club in London, and he had quite the reputation even then. No, the fellow who wrote the letter on your behalf was another commissioner, I believe." William Cutler tapped the tips of his fingers together, then abruptly held one up in triumph. "Aha. John Adams. He's the one. I have saved his letter. You'll want to read it." He grinned at his nephew. "I say, it's rather unusual for one your age to have such highly placed connections."

This show of genuine admiration had little effect on Richard. Not to William Cutler's surprise. Nothing else had been able to penetrate his nephew's sullen disposition since they had left Plymouth. He attributed that disposition, in part, to the way their fellow passengers had glared at Richard's soiled clothes and shrank from what he had to admit was his nephew's less than agreeable body odor, notwithstanding his furious ablutions of the previous evening with soap, water, and so many towels that the innkeeper had had no qualms tacking on an extra shilling to their bill. Now that they had transferred in Portsmouth from a public to a private coach, and cracked open the windows to allow air to circulate, they could, he hoped, relax and talk more freely.

"It seems," he continued, speaking slowly to keep a semblance of conversation going, "that your Dr. Franklin has taken a personal interest in your affairs. By coincidence, he and I have a mutual acquaintance in the British ambassador to France. I was introduced to Lord Stormont several years ago by my contacts in Westminster. Since then we have maintained a regular correspondence. We've even enjoyed a game or two of whist together at Barclay's. Well, perhaps the word 'enjoy' may not be quite the one to use. The ambassador is rather gifted at the game, you see, and insists on handsome wagers. He wins almost every round. No doubt that is why he remembers me so fondly. I have kept him in rather high style."

In spite of himself, Richard smiled at his uncle. It had all happened so quickly, in such a whirl and state of semi-awareness that he was not yet able to fully grasp what *had* happened. Minutes after being dismissed from the prison office, the two Cutlers had been whisked out of Old Mill Prison, to Plymouth Town to await the arrival of the noon post chaise that would convey them, first, to the Horse and Carriage Inn in Exeter, then on to Portsmouth the next morning.

There had been no time to gather his thoughts, to talk privately with his uncle, to fully absorb the conditions of what amounted to house arrest as they were rattled off to him by William Cowdry. Worse, by far, he had been denied leave to explain things to his fellow officers, to say goodbye to them. He had protested this decision, and he had vowed that under no circumstances would he honor the terms of his parole. So vehement were his protests, he nearly rent asunder the arrangements upon which his release depended. Were it not for the preeminence of William Cutler—or, more precisely, the preeminence of those he held in his confidence—Richard might have seen himself hauled back to Long Prison and his uncle gone. Which, at that moment, would have been his preference.

Now that they were on the road from Gosport and fast approaching the Georgian enclaves of Fareham, his mood began to brighten. Had it really been four years since he and Will had visited here? A week ago, in prison, it would have seemed an eternity. Today, it seemed a much narrower span of time.

"I'm glad your family is well, Uncle," Richard said suddenly. "I do look forward to seeing them."

It was a remark Richard should have offered the previous evening, during the first square meal he had tasted in months. He had picked sparingly at his generous serving of shepherd's pie as his uncle brought him current with Cutler family activities. Lizzy was home, her attentions focused these days on the whereabouts of Jamie Hardcastle, who, she had recently learned with a burst of joy, would soon be home on leave from his ship. Robin had sailed to the Indies to visit with his brother John in Barbados; from there he had gone to the island of Tobago where he would manage a second sugar plantation acquired by the Cutler family in much the same way they had acquired the first: by a loan default of the previous owner. The war was having a brutal impact on the revenues of English planters and merchants, and the two Cutler brothers were doing what they could to boost profits by reducing costs in production and distribution.

"I'm pleased to hear that, Richard," William Cutler said from the heart. "Your Aunt Emma and Lizzy are looking forward so very much to seeing you. And I believe there may be someone else equally delighted to learn of your stay with us."

Richard tried his best to appear nonchalant as his uncle patted the sides of his brocade coat, searching for something within. He withdrew what looked to be a letter, offering it to Richard, who immediately recognized the elegant script across one side naming him and the address of his family in Fareham. Turning the letter over, he found embedded on the other side, across the fold, a small circle of red wax on which the black letter H had been embossed.

"It came in a diplomatic pouch," his uncle explained, "along with several others. I selected this one as being the most . . . interesting."

Richard broke the seal and unfolded the letter. He read the brief message:

le 3 septembre 1778
L'Hérmitage, Passy, France

Mon Plus Cher:

Papa has just informed me that you are alive! And well! In a matter of weeks, perhaps days, you will be in the loving care of your family in England. I am beside myself with joy! To know you are safe and so near fills me with more than I dare express in this letter. Be assured, my love, that when God in His mercy permits us to be together again, I shall express my feelings for you with all the passion with which you have blessed my life.

Pray, come to me when you are able. Or bid me come to you. I am Swiss. I can travel at my pleasure. And I can imagine no greater pleasure, no greater desire, than to be in your arms again.

Je t'adore, à tout jamais,

Anne-Marie

"Good news?" William Cutler chirped.

Richard reread the letter, his very soul taken aback by the depth of emotion resonating in those few words. He knew she cared—but this!

"I suppose so," he said absently. "It's from a friend. In Paris."

"Just so," his uncle said impishly. "And is this 'friend' as lovely to behold as her handwriting?"

Richard was unaware that Lord Stormont had already informed his uncle about the intricacies of this case, the most intriguing being the presumed relationship between his nephew and a certain Anne-Marie Helvétian, *une belle femme du monde* ever in demand in Parisian social circles, but one who had been conspicuously absent from those circles in recent months.

Before Richard could answer, he realized with a start that their carriage was passing by the entrance to the Hardcastle estate. He slid as close as he could to the window, straining to look backward until the entryway was no longer visible.

"She is, Uncle," he said at last, settling back in his seat. "She's sort of an adopted daughter of Dr. Franklin. We came to know each other . . . quite well when I was in Paris last winter with Captain Jones."

"Aha. And is this relationship a, um, serious one? I don't mean to pry, mind you."

Richard stared out the window, his thoughts racing back to Passy and the words he and Anne-Marie had exchanged during those final few days together. However blissful that time may have been, and however more demonstrative in her desire Anne-Marie may have become as the hour of his departure drew near, he could not recall any of the solemn oaths or long-term commitments that serious lovers pledge to each other.

"Perhaps. We'll see," he said, and the rather dispirited way he said it made William Cutler grimace, no doubt saddened that Richard had not risen to his bait.

☆ ☆ ☆

A SHORT way ahead, the carriage made a sharp right turn onto the pebbled drive leading to the Cutler home. It was exactly as Richard remembered: the pond on the left, shrubs and banks of flowers on the right. Beyond, a great expanse of lawn, its color a rich green in these early days of October. Beyond that, a thickness of forest revealing the multi-colored splendor of fall. It was on that lawn, during those glorious days of remembrance, that he and Will and Lizzy and Katherine and Jamie and Robin had played games of bowls, or a match of cricket against teams of local youths, the rules bent here and there from those recently introduced by the Cricket Club at Hambledon. Gazing out at that field, Richard could almost hear her girlish squeals of delight whenever he stood at the wicket and slapped the ball with the flat of the bat, hobbling as best he could on his hurt leg over to the other wicket, past where his Uncle William and Aunt Emma and the household staff and neighbors watched and applauded. And there, always, was Katherine, smiling, laughing, clapping her hands in encouragement to him no matter if the bowler struck the wicket where he batted or the ball he hit were caught on the fly for an out. They were ever as one in those cloudless, sun-washed days, and it seemed their souls danced together whenever their eyes met.

The carriage shivered to a halt at the six-columned portico at the entryway to the Georgian manor. Lizzy was there to greet them and shooed away Harold, a longtime member of the household staff, opening the door herself on Richard's side. Immediately he saw her, Richard could not resist a smile, for she was a favorite of his. During the four years since he had last seen her, she had filled out strikingly into womanhood.

"You look wonderful, Lizzy," Richard said, stepping down from the carriage and clasping her gently by the shoulders, "the very image of Aphrodite."

Lizzy smiled but did not blush, the way she would have done profusely years before upon receiving such a compliment. In what seemed to him like one fluid movement, she embraced him, holding him to her, then kissed him on the cheek and stepped back.

"Lovely to see you again, Richard. Would that it could be under better circumstances."

She flushed with that remark, as though regretting she had said it. She glanced at her father. He shook his head briefly in reply.

Richard had no time to interpret that mysterious sequence. At that moment Aunt Emma came bustling out of the house to take command of the situation.

"Richard! Oh my dear, dear boy! You are truly here!"

She stepped quickly down the steps of the portico, holding her arms out before her. She embraced him hard, hugging him to her and patting his back like that of a baby.

"Oh my dear boy, look at you," she cried, with genuine concern, when she paused in her ministrations long enough to stand back and actually look at him. "How much weight you've lost! And these clothes! Well, we'll just have to get you properly fed and done up, won't we? Harold!" she said. "You remember my nephew, Richard. Please take his things upstairs. And draw a bath for him—the water should be hot from the fire—and lay out a fresh suit of clothes on the bed."

"Right away, Mum," Harold replied, bowing. Then, to Richard, as he reached inside the carriage for his seabag: "Nice to see you again, sir. Welcome." Showing no reaction either to the sordid condition of the duffel or its meager contents, he bore it into the house as if it contained the prized possessions of a duke.

"Now then, Richard," Emma continued in her matronly way, "you see to your bath and that sort of thing. Take your time, my dear, there's no hurry. We'll have a light supper in two hours, or whatever time you come downstairs."

Two and a half hours later Richard reappeared in the front hall, from all outward appearances a changed man. He had on clean charcoal breeches and matching linen socks to the knees, silver-buckled shoes, a pale blue shirt, yellow waistcoat, and a silk cravat of such exquisite texture it caressed his skin whenever he moved his head. He was freshly shaven, and he had washed his hair and pulled it back snug in a queue. He had, however, declined the black silk ribbon that a gentleman would normally wear on the queue at the base of his neck.

"Sorry I am late," he said, somewhat sheepishly. "I . . . um . . . fell asleep in the bath."

"First bath in a while?" his uncle chortled.

"Pish posh, my dear," comforted his aunt. "The wait was worth it. Just look at you, every bit the handsome country squire."

The "light supper" she had promised consisted of a roast pheasant, a fricassee of turnips, roasted potatoes, and freshly baked bread. Two bottles of French claret, a plate of various cheeses, and silver candelabra filled out the

Chippendale dining table where the four of them sat at the near end, two on each side, under Harold's attentive eye.

"Have you heard from my family?" Richard inquired, after he was seated and platters of impossibly rich food were beginning to make the rounds. It was a question he knew he should have asked yesterday.

"Infrequently, I'm afraid," his uncle replied, as he helped himself to a healthy portion of the bird. "I did receive a letter from your father some time ago, back in June as I recall. Hellishly hard to communicate with anyone these days, and that goes double for anyone in the colonies. Ah, excuse me, Richard. That is to say, in America. But be assured that he and the rest of your family are quite well. And safe. I am told there has not been a skirmish anywhere near Boston for more than a year. You should know, by the way, that I sent word to your parents immediately when I heard of your . . . situation. It went by packet boat to New York, so it should find its way to Hingham in good order. I told them you would be staying with us for the duration of the war. You can imagine their relief upon hearing that."

"Thank you, Uncle. I shall write them myself, tomorrow," Richard said. What kept reverberating in his brain was the phrase *for the duration of the war.* He downed a piece of bread with a slice of cheese but little else.

Emma Cutler noticed her nephew's lack of appetite. Concerned, she asked him if the food was not to his liking, and if so, was there something else the staff might bring from the kitchen?

"Thank you, no, Auntie," he replied. "Everything is delicious. It's just that I'm not used to this sort of food. It will take a while."

He could not explain to her that while it was true his stomach had shrunk and could not readily accept either the quantity or quality of food on his plate, the real reason he could not eat was, in a word, guilt. Guilt for abandoning his friends and fellow officers. Guilt for being here, in what was Buckingham Palace and Versailles combined compared to Long Prison. Guilt for the spotlessly clean, high-bred clothes he was wearing. Guilt for not inquiring earlier in the day about his family. Guilt too for the hot bath drawn for him by a servant and for the mere fact that a black silk ribbon had been set out for him to wear tonight. However gratifying it was to see the Cutler family and however much he appreciated their care and concern for him, this was not where he should be. Not now. Not at this moment in history. The tunnel came to mind, the escape plan he had conceived, and it tortured him to not know if it would succeed. Under no circumstances could he remain here, no circumstances whatsoever, even if, by some miracle, she . . .

"Richard?" interjected his uncle, sensing where his nephew's thoughts were tending. "You do realize, don't you, that you have no choice in this matter. You have acquitted yourself nobly in the war, and you have every reason to be proud of what you have accomplished. But the fact remains that henceforth, until the war is over, you are confined to this property. Until hostilities cease, you may not leave, even in my company. I have given my word on that. My word as a gentleman. You understand what that means, don't you?"

Richard pursed his lips. "I understand what you are saying, Uncle," he said, and William Cutler let it go at that.

"What was it like?" Lizzy asked. "The prison, I mean. How ghastly that must have been."

Richard shrugged.

"Actually, it wasn't so bad. The worse part was the feeling of marking time to no avail."

"Were they beastly cruel to you?"

"Not really. They didn't serve pheasant and claret for dinner, but they were quite decent to us as long as we obeyed the rules. The prison doctor saved the leg and quite possibly the life of a dear friend, a fellow midshipman aboard *Ranger*. So I have few complaints. American prisoners are treated much worse elsewhere."

"As are British prisoners," countered William Cutler somberly. "An inevitable consequence of war, I'm afraid."

Emma Cutler was not about to let a pall of gloom envelop the table.

"Richard, you must be exhausted," she said. "Please don't feel you need remain downstairs with us tonight. Tomorrow, after a good night's rest, we shall chitchat to our hearts' content and start putting some meat on those poor bones of yours." She stretched her right arm across the table. Richard took her hand in his and she squeezed it. "My dear, dear boy, do know that we love you so very much and want only the best for you. It won't be so bad here, you'll see. All wars end. This war will end too, and when it does, you'll be homeward bound, and you and John and Robin and Caleb can work together in the family business for years to come, if that is your wish. In the meantime you are free to eat, sleep, read, write, walk about, do just about whatever you want. Does that sound so terribly bad?"

"No, Auntie, it doesn't," Richard had to admit. "And thank you for preparing such a fine meal. You're right, I suppose I could use some sleep. But first, if she is willing, I'd greatly appreciate a few moments alone with Lizzy." He glanced at his cousin sitting beside him.

"Of course," she said softly.

After his aunt and uncle had excused themselves from the room, Richard got up, walked behind Lizzy, squeezed her right shoulder, and sat down at the head of the table.

"Better to see you," he explained, smiling. "I understand you and Jamie have become quite the couple."

For the first time that day Lizzy truly blushed, the young girl in her reappearing in the red of her cheeks and the twinkle in her blue eyes.

"I can't deny it, Richard," she gushed. "Nor would I ever wish to. I'm still not sure when or how it happened, but there came a day when I simply could not bear to be away from him. Jamie consumed my day and night. When he was here at home, I tried as hard as ever I could to be with him. When he had to leave, I so wanted him to be thinking of me while at sea, I stayed up nights before he left and wrote letters for him to pack. I numbered them, making him promise to read only one per week, on Sundays, after worship service, when he has time to himself. I just could not stop thinking of him. Miracle was, I learned, early on, that he could not stop thinking of *me* in exactly the same way."

Richard smiled. "It's no miracle, Lizzy. Remember our last conversation, back then? I predicted this would happen, despite your attempts to deny it."

"However did you know?"

"Jamie is not blind," he said simply. "He's coming home soon?"

"He is! We don't know exactly when. He's at sea, of course, but last we heard, his ship should be putting in to Spithead sometime toward the end of the month. Father has connections at Portsmouth Dock and they assure him of this."

"Your father has connections everywhere, it seems. Well, Lizzy, I'm very happy for you both. It's a perfect match. Jamie's a gem. I hope to see him when he's home."

"You shall. He'll insist on it. He remembers you so very fondly."

"And I, him."

With that, his mood degenerated. He reached for his aunt's near-empty wine glass and began twirling the long crystal stem between his fingers. For what must have seemed to Lizzy an agonizingly long period, he contented himself with watching the shallow red liquid slosh back and forth inside. When he spoke, it was to the glass, not to his cousin, and his voice held the subdued, carefully measured tones of one not entirely at ease either with himself or his position.

"Is Katherine here, Lizzy?"

The silence that ensued came as no surprise to him. He had expected nothing less. His stomach churned, and he felt the familiar throb high on his forehead.

"No, Richard, she isn't," she said at last. "She's away, at Burnham Thorpe."

"Where's that?"

"In Norfolkshire, East Anglia."

"May I ask her purpose in going there?"

Lizzy glanced down at her hands clasped in her lap, as though she were sitting in a pew during a church service. "She went with her brother Hugh," she replied, not looking up. "She is visiting someone there, an acquaintance. Actually, someone rather more than an acquaintance."

"A beau?"

"You could call him that."

"Well, at least that explains why everyone's been tiptoeing around me today. This beau . . . It's serious, isn't it, Lizzy."

Her eyes met his. "I rather suspect it is, Richard. She left to become engaged."

"Engaged." He half-whispered the word to himself, the finality and sacredness of it too overwhelming to repeat aloud. He poured out a dose of Spanish port and downed the contents in one swallow. "Did she know I was coming here, before she left?"

"No."

"And has there been correspondence to her since?"

"No."

"Well, at least there's that."

Lizzy made motions to leave but caught herself, apparently unable to walk away from such manifestations of grief.

"Richard, I realize this is very difficult for you. But do try your best to be happy for her. He's a dear young man, a Royal Navy officer with brilliant prospects, from a modest but respectable family. He's second cousin to the Earl of Orford, and his father is an Anglican min—."

"A Royal Navy officer!" Richard scoffed, doing nothing to hide his contempt. "Of course! What else could he be? Fate and her father would demand nothing less."

"That's not fair, Richard, and you know it," Lizzy countered. "And there's no use feeling sorry for yourself. Think on it. What choices did Katherine have? She had not seen you in years and had not heard from you in months. Yes, thank you, I know all about the war and the difficulty of getting letters through. And yes, I understand you were off at sea. But the truth remains, she had not heard from you for a very, very long time. And we were all so young then, not much more than children. People change, Richard. Look how much you've changed. Who's to say, were you and Katherine to meet here, right now, you could or even would want to pick up where you left off? Odds are you wouldn't, wouldn't you agree?"

THE DAY for departure for Barbados was drawing near, and however much he looked forward to being back at sea with Will and the crew of Eagle, he dreaded the coming of that day. It would mean the end of this, the beginning of the terrible missing of her. The last evening he and Will were in Fareham, the Cutler family was invited to the Hardcastle estate. Later that evening, Richard and Katherine walked in the back fields by the pond, where the crickets played while the swans slept. Conversation was unnecessary; they were content to be alone, together, in the privacy of shared thoughts. Ultimately they stopped at the small domed gazebo, an island of marble amid a sea of autumn bloom, where he turned to her.

"What will become of us, Katherine? I cannot bear to leave you. No one has ever . . . believed in me the way you do."

She raised her hand to his cheek and smiled. "Only good will come of us, Richard, if we believe in each other, as I shall always believe in you. Our time will come, if that truly is what we both want. And when it does, I will be there, beside you."

"Is it truly what you want?" Despite all, he could not believe it.

In answer, she raised her lips to his. He kissed her, awkwardly at first, for they were not used to each other that way. Their kiss lingered, longer than any before, until her arms came up around his shoulders and neck as he wrapped his hands tight around the small of her back, pressing her lithe body to his.

"Yes!" she whispered convincingly. "Oh yes, Richard, my love! Yes!"

☆ ☆ ☆

"THE ODDS may be slim," Richard groused, "though it seems you and Jamie have somehow managed to beat them."

"Bad comparison. Jamie and I have not been separated by three thousand miles of ocean these past four years. And however long Jamie is away at sea, I always know that, sooner or later, he'll be coming home. Katherine never knew that about you. She didn't know if she would *ever* see you again. Sakes, Richard, *you* didn't know you'd be coming here again until a couple of days ago."

She was right, of course.

"And Richard," she added, to drive her point home beyond exception, "can you honestly sit there and tell me that during all these years you have not . . . desired other women? And acted upon those desires?"

It was the final and longest nail in the coffin. He slumped down, felt a crushing wave of fatigue washing over him. He heard her chair scrape back, felt her kiss on the top of his head, caught her arm, stared up at her.

"Forgive me, Lizzy. I *am* happy for you, truly. Jamie is a fine fellow and, God knows, a very lucky man. You'll be great together."

She placed her hand over his. "That's sweet of you, Richard. Thank you. But if you don't mind, let's not count our eggs before they're in the pudding. In this topsy-turvy world nothing should be taken for granted."

It took Richard a week to develop something resembling a daily routine. Released from the confines and drudgery of Long Prison, and with no duty pressing, he succumbed to fatigue and the heaven of goose-down bedding by sleeping ten hours a night. Or more, during those mornings when driving rain or sleet splattered against windowpanes rattled by a moaning wind. Sleep was not only remedial, it allowed him to flee the guilt and despair hounding him, notwithstanding the kind attentions of both his family and their neighbors, people whom he had met years ago and who remembered him kindly, and people he had never met but who stopped by to visit with the young American naval officer whose deeds at Whitehaven had by now become part of the British psyche. As his strength returned, Richard welcomed these visitors as conduits to the outside world and, increasingly, as people who, to his surprise, seemed to respect more than disdain him.

"It was the same in Plymouth," he explained to his uncle one frosty morning in late October. They were taking their daily constitutional on icy grass that crunched under their step. "You wouldn't think from the way the local people treated us that we were their enemy. Some even helped prisoners escape from Old Mill."

William Cutler sidestepped a hole in the ground created by some burrowing animal. "That's no surprise, Richard," he quipped. "We British love our heroes, especially our naval heroes. Which is what you are to many people around here."

"Posh what people think," Richard scoffed, then caught himself, remembering, with a sharp pang of remorse, she who often used that phrase. "I'm no hero," he insisted. "Truth is, Uncle, I don't remember what happened on that beach. It's all a blur. I only know I managed to survive whatever it was I supposedly did."

His uncle chuckled, but he said nothing further until they had looped around by the edge of the woods and were heading home.

"I'd like to pick up on a subject we broached last evening," he said, the gravity in his voice reflecting the time he had devoted since then to clarifying his own views on the subject. "As you recall, I made several references to 'the war.' Understandably, to you and to most people in America, 'the war' means 'the revolution.' Fact is, England is currently engaged in *two* wars, each with an entirely separate purpose. The first war is to *maintain* our empire. That, sadly, involves the civil war in America. At the same time, we are fighting a second war to *sustain* our empire. That one is against our ancient enemy, France. At stake are the sugar islands of the East and West Indies: our islands, Richard, Barbados and Tobago among them. Whoever controls those islands controls the wherewithal to wage a hundred wars. Which is why I am convinced that Spain and Holland will soon enter this war. And other countries too, all allied against us. It then will become a world war, and England will be standing alone. Mind you, these other countries will not be fighting in support of American revolutionary ideals any more than France is. Why would Louis and his *chevaliers* support open rebellion against a king? No, they'll be fighting for the same reason they always do, for their own commercial self-interests, this time at the expense of Great Britain. Our navy is overextended and we're committing far too many resources to the civil war in America while paying scant attention to the *real* threat in the Indies. We can't defend our islands properly, and our enemies are aware of our weaknesses."

Richard walked on, pondering what his uncle had said. He had to admit, it made sense. "How would you advise the king and his council, were you able to?" he asked.

"I am able to, and in fact I have done so, through my contacts in Westminster. My advice to King George and Parliament is to seek reconciliation as quickly as possible with the former colonies."

Richard felt his eyebrows involuntarily shoot up.

"You'd sue for peace? Grant America her independence?"

"If necessary, yes," William Cutler said with conviction. "England would be far better off, in my opinion, with the United States as her ally rather than her enemy. After all, we share a common heritage and system of beliefs. Together, there would be no stopping us. And the civil war is simply not worth the cost. Our military and exchequer are being bled dry in America while we put our true source of wealth and prosperity at grave risk. Many Britons agree with me, which is why you've found so many people sympathetic to you both here and in the West Country."

Richard whistled softly. "What do members of Parliament have to say about this?"

"There's agreement there too, more than you might suspect. The problem is not with the Commons. The problem is with the king and certain of his ministers, particularly North and Germaine, and a fair number in the House of Lords, as well as some senior military officers. To such people, the notion of independence is intolerable. So we send more soldiers, more ships, more German mercenaries to America to fight a war that strategically is a disaster for England even if we should win it—which, frankly, I don't think we will." He stopped walking and put a hand on his nephew's shoulder. "It's hard for a crotchety old man to admit this, Richard, but that hell-fire brother of yours was right. When it comes to America, England has made too many tragic mistakes. And good people, Will first among them, have had to suffer because of those mistakes. Much of the wealth I once had is gone, and soaring taxes prevent me from replenishing my accounts. As bad as it is for me, I cannot imagine how men like your father are coping."

They finished their walk in silence, but the subject was brought up again ten days later when Jamie Hardcastle, in the company of his parents, paid a visit to the Cutler estate. He had a week's leave from his ship and had arrived home late the evening before. In contrast to his father, who was courteous but militarily stiff when he met Richard, Jamie greeted him with enthusiasm, their eyes and hands holding firm for several warm moments.

"Wonderful to see you, Jamie," Richard said with feeling, surprised at how the young midshipman had grown and matured. He was several inches taller than when Richard had last seen him, and his frame had filled out in a manly way. Everything about him bespoke strength and discipline, and he carried himself with a swagger born not of pride but in the knowledge and confidence of self.

High tea was served and began as an awkward affair for Richard. His aunt and uncle quickly became engaged in chatty conversation with Henry and Jane Hardcastle, while Jamie and Lizzy, seated together on a small settee and not having seen each other for many weeks, were engrossed in a more tender dialogue. He wondered if Jamie was purposely avoiding speaking to him, or if it was just his unease. There were certain questions Richard yearned to ask him in private.

When the midshipman broke off his conversation with Lizzy to reach for a tea cake, Richard asked, in the universal language of sailors, "Tell me about your ship, Jamie."

To a naval officer, that question referred principally to ordnance.

"*Serapis?* She's a heavy frigate, rated a forty-four but actually has fifty guns. Eighteen-pounders on the lower gun deck, nine-pounders on her main deck."

More than four times the firepower of *Ranger,* Richard calculated, and this a mere frigate.

"Where are you stationed?"

"Spithead. We're on convoy duty, shepherding ships back and forth between England and the Baltic countries. Rather boring work, really. I've put in for a transfer to a First or Second Rate."

"As well you should," his father broke into his son's conversation. Of everyone present, he had changed the least over the years. "Frigates may be the eyes and ears of the fleet, but the glory is in the fighting." He blew his nose, returned the handkerchief to his pocket, and reengaged William Cutler in conversation.

"The Baltics? Why there? Ships' stores?"

"Yes, lumber especially. We haven't enough here, and you chaps over there in the colonies have kindly denied us your supplies. Europe has turned her back on us, nothing unusual about that, so we're forced to go to those few places where we are still welcomed."

"Welcomed? Hah!" snorted Henry Hardcastle, interrupting a second time. "We're 'welcomed,' as you put it, James, because we're forced to pay a king's ransom for the stores we need. Were I in charge, I'd take the whole bloody Channel Fleet into Stockholm harbor, seize whatever we need, and pay our respects to those bastards with a round of broadsides. You'd see *that* lower the price, and quick!"

"Henry, you promised," his wife warned.

"Oh, poppycock, Jane," he harrumphed, his face growing redder by the moment. "I say, what has happened to this country? We have an army in America that can't decide when to fight and can't defeat a sorry lot of tailors and poets when it does. And we have a navy over here that refuses to fight the French. The *French,* Christ almighty! When have we ever not whipped the Frogs? And Keppel, here's an admiral—an admiral, mind you!—who informs Whitehall he won't fight against the Jonathans. They're his countrymen he says, and what happens to him? Nothing! Bloody *nothing!* 'That's all right, Admiral, don't you concern yourself. You stay right here in jolly old England and eat your roast beef. We wouldn't dream of asking you to fight our enemies.' Jesus Christ! No wonder the man was court-martialed!"

"Henry!" Jane snapped.

"Father," Jamie countered in more reasonable tones, "Admiral Keppel was not court-martialed for refusing to fight Americans. He was court-martialed for what happened at Ushant. And he was acquitted."

He was referring to events of the previous July. Admiral Keppel, with the Channel Fleet of thirty line-of-battle ships, had finally sighted the elusive Brest fleet of comparable size under the command of Admiral Comte d'Orvilliers. Due to light winds the initial engagement had been brief. The two fleets exchanged one round of broadsides as they passed each other on opposite tacks, neither fleet inflicting much damage on the other. After the two lines parted, Keppel signaled his ships to wear about in battle formation. But his signals were misunderstood, so claimed Admiral Palliser in command of the British rear division, who declined to engage anew so late in the day and under such fluky conditions. During the night, the French fleet sailed home to Brest. The failure of the British to sink a single enemy ship had led to outrage in the press and sordid charges and countercharges of gross misconduct between Admirals Keppel and Palliser. Though acquitted, Keppel refused to return to service so long as Lord Sandwich remained as first lord of the Admiralty, a decision supported by other British admirals.

"That may be," Henry Hardcastle sniffed, his voice calmer, "but it still proves my point of gross incompetence in the Royal Navy these days." He glared at the Cutler family. "Thank Heaven I have a son who is willing to fight England's enemies and not disgrace the family name. And as for my boy Nelson, he'll show them a thing or two, you just wait. Imagine! The rank of post captain at the age of twenty. Now there's ambition for you! Put Jamie and Horatio in the van of any fleet, I say, and by Jove, you'll see the Frogs showing us their heels!"

"Henry, that is quite enough!" his wife stated emphatically, and Richard wondered why. His opinions were not *that* outlandish. He continued mulling over the name mentioned.

"Nelson . . . Nelson . . . Horatio Nelson," he said half aloud to himself.

"You've heard of him?" Jane Hardcastle gasped, her hand at her mouth.

Richard nodded, his memory sufficiently jogged.

"Not only have I heard of him, Mrs. Hardcastle, I have met him. In Barbados. After I left here in *Eagle*. He was on the docks in Bridgetown, a midshipman at the time. His ship was . . . *Seahorse*. Yes, that was her name. I went up to him and asked . . ." He paused, aware that everyone in the room, save for Henry Hardcastle, was suddenly taking pains to avoid eye contact with him. Then it struck him a sickening blow. "Oh, I see," he said softly, having just made the connection of whom Katherine had gone to visit in Burnham Thorpe.

"I see," he said again, in a voice barely audible as he retreated deep within himself.

THE DRAB days and long, lonely nights of early November passed slowly for Richard. He got outdoors when he could, in the company of his uncle or Lizzy or perhaps a neighbor who happened by, seeking his company and an

American perspective on world events. Though flattered by everyone's attentions, Richard preferred being alone. He needed time to think, to hatch a plan that would see him to France and somehow back to sea. It would be no easy matter. Traveling incommunicado from Fareham to Portsmouth in the winter was a daunting challenge, and every facet of his plan had to be flawless. His leaving would devastate his family and bring into serious question his uncle's political and social standing. But if his plan failed, the ignominy would be infinitely greater.

He hated the thought of causing his family any sort of pain. They had taken him in when others under similar circumstances would have cast him out. But he had no choice, especially now that he had learned that his beloved Katherine, the only anchor that might have kept him afloat in Fareham, had crossed to the other side. And it was of no consequence that his uncle was sympathetic to the cause. He, Richard, was England's enemy. But how could he explain to his family and the good people of Fareham that his enemy was not them but the Royal Navy? First, Will. Now, Katherine. What other sacrifice would the gods of Whitehall demand of him?

Upon retuning home from a brisk walk during a dreary, cloud-thick afternoon that threatened southern England with the first significant snowfall of the season, Richard brewed himself a pot of tea in the kitchen and retreated into his uncle's study. Warming himself by the fire, he pulled down from the bookshelf volume 1 of Gibbon's *History of the Rise and Fall of the Roman Empire*. Although it had been published two years before, it remained the talk of English literary and political circles. Author and publisher were promising additional volumes. Volume 2 imminently and four others after that. Richard looked forward to reading the remaining five volumes as much as he was enjoying this one.

He sat down on a small couch facing the fire and opened the book to chapter 7, to where, the previous day, he had bookmarked a particularly intriguing passage: "Of the various forms of government which have prevailed in the world, a hereditary monarchy seems to present the fairest scope for ridicule." He made a mental note to ask his uncle if he had read this passage, and would it be permissible for Richard to send a copy of the book to King George, with this passage marked?

He smiled to himself. He would ask his uncle, just to see his reaction, and he would, he vowed, write Anne-Marie today or tomorrow, a real letter this time. He had written her a brief note after settling in at Fareham and had cursed himself ever since for the formality of it compared to what she had written him. She deserved better. None of his mess of emotions was her doing. To the contrary, her feelings for him were so . . . clear-cut, earnest, unconditional. What sane man would not beg for that from such a woman? Richard Cutler, he accused himself, not only are you a hypocrite, you are also an idiot. Drawing a heavy sigh, he picked up the book and started reading.

A while later he heard the door directly behind him click open.

"Richard," Lizzy called in, "you have a visitor."

"I'll be just a minute," Richard called back over his shoulder. He assumed the visitor was a neighbor he had befriended who wouldn't mind waiting a bit out in the front hall. He turned a page. "I just want to finish this section."

"Richard, it's Katherine. She's here, beside me."

9

FAREHAM, ENGLAND

Spring 1779

*T*HE DEEP GASH ON his forehead was not the only injury suffered by Richard in the fall from the horse. He had landed on his right side, his thigh absorbing the first hard blow from the ground. He hit so hard he had bounced several feet back up in the air and had landed a second time hard against his ribs. He would have broken several ribs, the doctors informed the Cutler family, had he not fallen the way he did, his thigh, in effect, cushioning the blow to his upper body. As it was, he had fractured two of them, and the muscle tissue in his right leg had been severely bruised. He would need to be bedridden for a few days. After that, he would have to go slow for another week or two, walking off the pain and avoiding serious physical activity. He was lucky, they said. Very, very lucky.

Richard did not feel lucky. It pained him to be laid up as he was, just as the joys of summer were approaching their zenith and there was always much to do within and around the Cutler household. Since almost the day of their arrival, Will and Richard had basked in the limelight at Fareham. The young ladies found them thoroughly engaging, so Lizzy claimed, and the young men sought their world views, their participation in games, and, Richard suspected, the attentions of Lizzy Cutler and particularly Katherine Hardcastle, who, often in the company of her younger brother Jamie, now made regular visits to the Cutler estate.

Richard found himself looking forward more and more to Katherine's visits. They became the centerpiece of his day, and it crushed him whenever she was unable to come. Will teased him unmercifully about this, his brother's feelings for Katherine almost painfully obvious since the time the two had first met, and sometimes Lizzy and Robin joined in the fun. Richard didn't mind. In those days it seemed as though the mere sound of Katherine's voice was enough to carry him forward, willingly, to whatever destiny awaited him.

There came a day when he was up and about but not yet able, he felt, to participate in the social goings-on his aunt and uncle were hosting in their home during the late afternoon. They had invited many of their neighbors, especially the younger ones. There were a number of people about, including several nobles. Richard sat alone in his uncle's study, feeling clumsy and boorish with his injured leg up on a footstool. He could clearly hear laughter—her laughter—coming from another part of the house, and he resented the young gallants so obviously circling around her. Far more, he resented the way she seemed to be enjoying their attentions.

When she found him sitting there, her cheery disposition did not have its normal effect.

"Richard, whatever are you doing in here alone? I've been looking everywhere for you. Come, join us. These are your friends."

"It seems they are more your friends than mine," he pouted, instantly regretting his words and tone.

She eyed him crossly, hands on hips.

"Oh, so that's how it's going to be, is it? You behaving like a bear with a sore head? Well, Mr. Cutler, in that case, I'm afraid you leave me no choice. I shall have to insist you leave this house immediately and walk with me alone, outside, in the garden."

He could not help laughing. "How can you always do this? Make me feel so good about everything?"

"I don't know why I bother sometimes, honestly I don't. Come on. Get up. We haven't all day."

"All right. If you'll just hand me my crutch."

"No, I shan't," she scolded. "You don't need your crutch. You need to start walking on that leg for it to heal properly. The doctor said as much."

He rose to his feet and took tentative steps forward. His leg buckled. She caught him, wrapping her arm around his waist.

"You can lean on me, if you'd like."

"Of course I'd like," he grinned sheepishly. "But what will they think?"

"Who? Them?" She gestured toward where the others were having a lively sounding time at tea. A young viscount named Pennington Sharpe had just told a joke that got everyone chuckling, his own high-pitched twitter easy to identify. Despite Sharpe's peculiar mannerisms, he was the one noble in that room whom Richard could stomach.

"Yes."

"Posh what they think!" The mock sternness in Katherine's voice had yielded to a very real frustration. "Posh what anyone else thinks. The only thing that matters, Richard, is what you and I think . . ."

☆ ☆ ☆

"I'M SO sorry about Will," she said, her voice as soft as the feathery snow beginning to fall outside. "I know how much he meant to you. And you to him."

He came around the couch, stood mute before her as the door to the study clicked shut, leaving them alone. She had changed remarkably little. Her hair was longer, fuller, with more curls than he remembered, but otherwise her facial features were almost exactly as he had secreted them away, long ago, in those innermost regions. She wore a purple velvet dress and about her was the faint scent of lilac. Draped across her shoulders was an off-white cashmere shawl, its soft woolen corners tied loosely together and hanging down. Richard noticed her lips quivering and her hazel eyes glistening, and he wondered if she could see those same traces of emotion in him.

Try as he may, he could not find the words. He waited, instead, until she came to him, so close their bodies touched when she laid her forehead gently against his shoulder.

"I'm so sorry, Richard," she whispered. "Please don't think ill of me for this. I could not bear to live with myself if you did."

He closed his eyes, breathing in her essence, brushing his lips against her hair. He felt himself falter, the urge to seize, embrace, reclaim proving too overpowering. He took a half step back.

"I could never think ill of you, Katherine. Don't do this to yourself. There's no blame here." He raised her chin. Wanting so to ease her sorrow, he brought

227

to bear a once-favorite phrase of theirs: "The jury finds you not guilty on the grounds that no crime has been committed."

She meant to laugh. What came out sounded more like a raspy sob. She wiped at her eyes with the back of her hand.

"Forgive me, Richard," she said. "I am so very happy to see you. I can't believe you're here. I can't believe I'm standing in this room with you."

He handed her a kerchief.

"How long will you be here? In Fareham, I mean."

"Oh, several months at least. Horatio . . ."

"It's all right, Katherine," he said when she hesitated. "You can talk about Horatio with me."

She nodded gratefully.

"As I'm sure Lizzy has told you, Horatio has been promoted to post captain and now commands a frigate, the *Hitchenbroke*. It's his first command."

"She did tell me. And I will say, it's an impressive rank for one so young."

"Yes. Thank you. It is. We're all so very proud of him." She dabbed at her eyes a final time and returned his kerchief, back in control of herself. "*Hitchenbroke* needs repairs, and they want to copper her bottom. She's in dry dock at Deptford, near London. Horatio insists on being there while that work is being done. Then there are the sea trials. As plans stand now, after the trials, he'll sail here to Spithead to receive his orders. We'll have some time together then. I'm not certain for how long. You know how it is in the navy." She gave him a feeble smile.

"Time enough for a wedding?" he asked.

He did not mean for his question to sound sardonic. By the way she flinched, that was how it must have sounded to her.

"Perhaps. It depends. Hugh wants very much to be in England for it. He's still in Barbados with the Windward Squadron. He and Horatio have been friends for years. And then there's Jamie. We don't know where he'll be come March or April. Probably in the Baltic somewhere. And then there's everyone else, my brother Jeremy of course, and all the arrangements that must be made. You can imagine, it's so terribly hard to plan anything like this in times like these. I . . . Pardon me, Richard," she said, her voice falling several octaves, calming the waters she herself had roiled up. "I'm prattling on like a silly goose, and I haven't asked a single thing about you."

He waved that away.

"Katherine, I must ask you something."

"Of course. You may ask me anything."

He held her gaze. She looked up, briefly, to the scar on his forehead. He waited until their eyes met again.

"Do you love him?"

"Why, Richard! What a question!"

"It's an easy question to answer, Katherine. I'm simply asking you to look me in the eye and tell me that you are in love with your fiancé. If you do, I swear I will never ask this sort of question again. And I shall be the first to congratulate you both."

She looked away, crossing her arms, holding them tight against her chest.

"It isn't quite that easy, Richard. In this life, things rarely go exactly as one might wish. Yet often there are silver linings. Horatio is a dear man. He's brave and kind and gentle and comes from a good family. He's ambitious, of course, but not like other naval officers I've known. His men adore him, even the most experienced ones. And his superiors hold him in the highest regard. There is something about him, they say, that will take him far in the Royal Navy. He loves me, he says, and I believe him. How very fortunate I am, compared to many other women I know whose marriages are arranged on their behalf."

"Without their consent?"

"Often without their consent. I have given mine to Horatio."

He could not take his eyes off her. Dear God, help me, he implored the Almighty. She is so beautiful, so very beautiful, and I have missed her so very, very much. He remembered the first time they met, when he had acted the fool, dumbstruck and tongue-tied in her presence. At that moment he would have sold his soul to Satan just to relive that one evening.

"I have no doubt all that is true," he said. "But you still have not answered my question."

"Haven't I?" She kissed him tenderly on the cheek. "I best be going," she said, "else that court of yours will surely find me guilty of something. I will see you again soon, Richard. I must. This I can promise you: there is a part of me that belongs only to you, and I swear on everything that is holy that I will never surrender that part of me to another."

☆ ☆ ☆

CHRISTMAS WAS a solemn affair in Fareham, as it was throughout the realm. Storm clouds were thickening throughout the empire and gathering ominously across Europe itself. Spain had not yet officially declared war, but British spies in the royal courts of both Madrid and Paris confirmed that such a declaration would be forthcoming by May, June at the latest. Gibraltar. Minorca. Jamaica. These and other possessions had been wrested from Spain during the past two centuries either by treaty or by brute force; together they formed the remnants of what had once been a vast empire stretching from Lima, Peru to Mexico City, to Cuba, and along the Spanish Main, all the way to Holland, where the Duke of Parma had successfully squashed an uprising by rebellious Dutch Protestants. Were it not for a perennial lack of money caused by annual plundering of his treasure fleets by Hawkins, Drake, and other English privateers, Philip II of Spain could have ruled an empire greater than that of Marcus Aurelius or Alexander the Great. The 1500s were the glory years of Spanish history. In 1779, Spain wanted some of that glory back.

It was solemn, too, because it was Jamie Hardcastle's last day in Fareham. His commanding officer had graciously granted his commissioned officers and midshipmen additional leave through Christmas. He was, however, scheduled to ship out on New Year's Eve day, and everyone was ordered to report back on board on December 26.

Christmas afternoon, Jamie paid his last visit to the Cutler home in the company of his sister Katherine. His father, he announced, was feeling under the weather, and his mother had decided to remain at home with him. Both sent their regrets and their warmest season's greetings. At that announcement, Richard breathed a heavy sigh of relief. He had not been looking forward to Henry Hardcastle scowling at him every time he so much as glanced in his daughter's direction.

Emma Cutler did her best to make this a memorable day for her family. The downstairs was festively adorned with pine boughs and Christmas ornaments, and a fire blazed in the parlor a short distance from a silver bowl of holiday rum punch and a tray bearing a wide assortment of freshly baked pastries. She even tried her hand at the piano, an instrument she played with some skill, but despite her best efforts to the contrary, the conversation drifted inevitably away from Christmas toward war—and the rumors, rife throughout the kingdom, that England's enemies meant to invade her once the weather turned.

"How can this possibly be?" Lizzy demanded, her concern more for Jamie than for herself or her country. "We're not even at war with Spain. And do the French really have the means to launch such an invasion?"

"They do," Jamie allowed, "if they are allied with Spain. Louis has been building up his fleets for years. So have the Dons. Combine the two navies and the House of Bourbon would have more than a hundred battle-line ships."

"How many in our Channel Fleet?" William Cutler inquired. Like many Britons, he was greatly disturbed that a well-established concept of naval strategy was about to be challenged and perhaps even repudiated. It was a concept known as "the fleet in being." At its core was the notion that the mere presence of a Royal Navy fleet permanently stationed in the Channel would ipso facto prevent any enemy from taking offensive action against England. Such a concept had ruled local waters since the Glorious Revolution a century earlier.

"At the moment, fewer than fifty. And many of them are in dire need of repair. You have no doubt read, Mr. Cutler, that a month ago a Third Rate sank at her mooring at Spithead. Just sank, right there, one afternoon. She had seen service in the Indies, and her bottom had been eaten away by teredo worms. Most French and Spanish ships are newer, and some of them are bigger than anything we have. The *Ville de Paris* and *Bretagne* have more than a hundred guns each. *Victory,* our largest ship, would be hard pressed against either."

"Does this mean your ship might remain in Portsmouth?" Lizzy asked hopefully. "In case?"

"I'm afraid not, Liz. England's need for ships' stores is greater than ever. No, *Serapis* will sail for Stockholm as scheduled. But this, I am sure, will be my last convoy duty. As soon as I pass my lieutenant's examination, which I will do the next time I'm in Portsmouth, I will be transferred to a First Rate. Captain Pearson, my commanding officer, has agreed to sponsor me."

"A much safer ship," Richard observed, to provide Lizzy some degree of comfort. "Few First Rates are ever sunk in battle."

"Very few," Jamie readily agreed. "Round shot bounces off their planking. It's why they serve as flagships to admirals. Can't have those worthies going under, now can we?" He gave Richard an appreciative look. "By the way," he said to him, to change the subject, "I've been meaning to ask about your Captain Jones. He has quite the reputation hereabouts, and I'd be curious to know your thoughts on him."

"What would you like to know?"

"Well, his character, for starters. Is it true he once killed a man in Tobago?"

"Yes. But it was not murder as many have asserted. He was threatened by a mutinous crewman demanding pay in arrears. Captain Jones had a full hold, was ready to sail, and did not want his crew paid off and leaving ship. He promised the crew that everyone would be paid in full upon their return to England. For whatever reason, this fellow became irate and attacked him with a sword. The captain defended himself with his own sword. There was no Admiralty court in Tobago to hear the case, and he was warned he would not fare well in civil court. Friends convinced him to flee the island."

"Is that when he decided to change his identity? By adding 'Jones' to his name?"

"Yes. He went to Virginia, where his brother owned a small plantation. When his brother died without heirs, Captain Jones inherited the property. He's a sailor, not a farmer, so he sold the property, freed his brother's slaves, and took two young Negroes with him to serve as powder monkeys aboard *Ranger*."

"But John Paul was not born a gentleman, was he? Did you know that the Royal Navy refused him a midshipman's berth? He lacked the proper heritage."

"No, I didn't."

"It's true. And might such a snub have caused him a certain resentment toward England, perhaps? I also understand he served as captain on a blackbirder."

"For one voyage, Jamie," Richard said defensively, adding, with a touch of sarcasm, "unlike the legions of British sea captains who have earned handsome profits from trading in slaves for years. Captain Jones loathes slavery. As I told you, when he inherited his brother's plantation, he freed the slaves."

It was a subject of conversation that caused English gentlemen to squirm in their cotton breeches. To many in England's more privileged classes, slavery was more an economic than a moral issue. The institution thrived because slave labor made Caribbean sugar so profitable—and taxable. The dirty secret was that it didn't matter under which flag a blackbirder sailed: slavery in the Western Hemisphere would have died a quick and natural death were it not for the global demand for sugar produced on Caribbean islands by white English planters and their black African slaves. Compared to the monetary value of what sugar plantations yielded in the British West Indies, American tobacco and cotton fields produced pathetically little.

"He may loathe slavery," Jamie replied, skirting the issue, "but not, apparently, the company of questionable women. His reputation in that area is really quite scandalous."

"I wouldn't know. We've never discussed that subject."

"Ah."

Katherine asked, "Is it not unusual, Richard, for a naval captain to share that sort of personal information with a midshipman? It would be rare indeed in the Royal Navy."

"It's different in the Continental Navy, Katherine. Captain Jones never saw himself in quite the same way as other American captains—he is, after all, British—but he did confide in me, on occasion, when we traveled together to Paris a year ago."

"Paris? I hadn't heard about that. Whatever were you doing in Paris?"

"I had the honor of serving as his military aide there. For most of the winter, I was in a town called Passy."

"Really! How terribly exciting, Richard! You must tell me about your adventures there."

"I will," he promised, before asking Jamie: "Does the Royal Navy know where Captain Jones is now?"

"We believe he's in France. At Brest. He captured and burned a brig near Belfast Lough a while back. After that, he vanished. The devil we're not able to catch him, though Lord knows we've tried. It's really quite an embarrassment to us."

"He's an excellent seaman," Richard said, adding, with a pride of ownership, "and *Ranger* is a fast ship."

Lizzy leaned close to Jamie and whispered something in his ear. He nodded, took her hand, and together they arose from the couch.

"I must take my leave," he said to her parents. "Duty calls. Mrs. Cutler, Mr. Cutler. Merry Christmas to you both and thank you, as always, for your kind hospitality. Pray forgive me for requesting a few moments alone with your daughter before Katherine and I must depart."

William Cutler approximated a salute.

"Permission granted, Mr. Midshipman Hardcastle. Else my daughter would see me flogged!"

"Good luck to you, Jamie," said Emma. "Merry Christmas and may God be with you in everything you do." She kissed him on the cheek.

Before leaving the room, Jamie Hardcastle excused himself from Lizzy and walked over to Richard, who stood as he did so. He offered his hand and stepped up close to him.

"Whatever else fate may have decreed for us, Richard," he said, their hands remaining tightly clasped, "I shall always consider you my dear friend. You mean so much to me and"—his eyes shifted meaningfully to where Katherine was talking with the elder Cutlers—"to those I love, who in turn love you. Very much. Do you understand what I am telling you?"

"Yes, Jamie. I do," Richard replied, though in truth he wasn't certain.

☆ ☆ ☆

WITH JAMIE gone, Richard and Katherine saw each other less frequently. They did manage to at times, however. Lizzy made certain of that. She and Katherine were what Jamie termed "the two women in my life," and she took great solace in Katherine's company. For her part, Katherine welcomed Lizzy's visits to her home. She had much to arrange, she told her lifelong friend, and what a comfort it was to have someone like Lizzy to help sort out the multifarious minutiae that underlie the pomp and splendor of what her father had come to call "a union of nobility." If he was stretching the truth, he reasoned, it was not by much. Horatio Nelson was bound for glory, he was convinced, and someday, all in good time, he would be awarded a noble title. In the meantime, rumor had it from within the corridors of Whitehall that as consideration for his many years of exemplary service to the Crown, a baronetcy was in the offing for Capt. Henry Makepeace Hardcastle, RN.

"No doubt," Richard growled to his cousin, "the crown jewel in Captain Hardcastle's career is the hand of his daughter given in marriage to one who someday will be of titled blood, a young British naval hero, no less." His mood was sour and his tone bitter.

"There is that," Lizzy acknowledged. "I can't deny it, Richard. But there's more," adding mysteriously, "something I can't quite put my finger on."

"What's that supposed to mean?"

She shook her head. "Nothing, I'm sure. The point is, Richard, you should not be ignoring Katherine the way you are. I understand why you're out of sorts, but it doesn't do to be so cruel."

That comment threw Richard completely off.

"Cruel? You consider me *cruel?* Jesus *Christ,* Lizzy! Do you have any idea how heart-wrenching this is for me, having her so close and knowing she is pledged to another? Sometimes I feel more in prison here than I did in Old Mill. I need to be free of this place and back where I belong."

"Well, dear cousin, that is not possible. And since we all must try to make the best of this situation, I have taken the liberty of inviting Katherine here to-morrow. I believe she has something for you."

☆ ☆ ☆

"Consider it a late Christmas present," Katherine said as they sat together by the fire in the Cutler study. "I had hoped to actually have it here by Christmas."

Richard gazed down at the rectangular package of white parchment paper wrapped with a single strand of crimson ribbon around its middle.

"You didn't have to do this, Katherine," he said, embarrassed both by the gift and by the fact he had nothing to offer in return.

"I know. Open it."

He removed the ribbon and separated the folds of paper. A leather-bound book came into view, the second volume of Edward Gibbon's treatise on the Roman Empire. He ran his fingers over the luxurious leather cover.

"How did you get this? I hadn't realized it was published."

"I know a bookseller in Portsmouth. He found it for me. It's one of the first copies in print."

"Well . . . thank you," he said lamely.

"It's inscribed, Richard. Have a look."

He opened the book to the title page. There, written by her hand, he read:

To Richard:
    For the memories of what was; for the faith of what is; for the dreams of what will be.

Katherine

"It's beautiful," he said, forcing himself to look at her. "They're your words?"

"No. I consulted the oracle at Delphi and asked, 'What are the words to use to make Richard Cutler flush the way he is right now?'"

He smiled, avoiding her eyes. "It's lovely, Katherine, thank you. I shall treasure it always. A gift from a true friend."

"A true friend indeed," she said. "Come, Richard. Will you walk outside with me? I need something from you."

It was an eerily mild afternoon for late February, in keeping with the better part of the entire winter thus far. Whenever a cold snap had invaded southern England during January, and however deep the snow accompanying those Arctic forays, prevailing winds had shifted soon thereafter to the southwest, bringing warmer, unsettled air from the ocean and inundating the West Country and Hampshire with dreary fog and rain. They could walk outside today with a light coat for warmth, though they were forced to remain upon the pebbled driveway; the grounds on each side were so saturated with water they appeared more as a Georgian swamp than a manicured English landscape. Patches of stubborn snow clung here and there to the edge of the woods as reminders of the season.

They walked along in silence until Richard asked, "What is it you need?"

"Your company," she replied, as she put her arm through the crook of his left elbow.

"Tell me about Paris," she said.

Her question startled him, not because she asked it, but because her voice seemed too off-handed, too devil-may-care, rather than simply eager to know. His suspicions aroused, he wondered just what she had been told and by whom. He shrugged off his concerns, realizing it could make no possible difference whatever the answers.

"It's a lovely city," he replied. "The people are a bit off-put, but that's the French for you."

"And the *jeunes filles*. Are they as pretty as English girls?"

"Depends on the English girl."

"Ah. A clever answer. You should be a diplomat. But seriously, Richard. Didn't you find their company . . . enjoyable?"

He glanced askance at her. "Why are you asking me this, Katherine?"

"I'm curious, that's all. Don't be cross with me. You needn't tell me anything you don't want to."

"It's not that I don't want to. It's just that there isn't much to tell. I was seldom in the company of French girls."

"Ah, well. That's their loss, isn't it."

At the end of the drive they turned round and began walking back to the house, their pace slowed as though by mutual, unspoken accord. Suddenly she said, "Richard, do you remember the day your uncle took you and me and Will and Jamie with him to Portsmouth? What a glorious day that was! You do remember, don't you?"

☆ ☆ ☆

WILLIAM CUTLER had to go to Gosport to transact some business in his shipping office, and he asked Will and Richard if they'd care to join him. Absolutely they would, they replied, and would it be all right, Richard asked, if Katherine and Jamie came along? After all, he told his uncle, he and Will would be leaving England within a fortnight, and this would be the only chance for the Hardcastle children to see *Eagle*. His uncle agreed, and the five of them set off for the port city.

The business transactions turned out to be more complicated and time-consuming than William Cutler had anticipated, and he was forced to excuse himself after a quick noontime meal. "I apologize," he said to his charges. "I had hoped to spend time with you here. I'm afraid you're on your own for the afternoon. Don't wander off too far and stay together. I'm here if you need me for anything."

"Don't worry, Uncle," Will said self-assuredly.

Just then Richard, scanning the harbor where *Eagle* was berthed, was struck with an idea.

"Uncle," he said, his face creased with excitement, "may we take out the tender?"

William Cutler stroked his chin as though contemplating the merits of his nephew's request.

"Think you can handle her?"

"Handle her? I should say! Will and I grew up in boats like that in Hingham. Please, Uncle," he pleaded as much with his eyes as his voice.

"All right. But stay on this side of the harbor. And don't go out past Burrow Island. Agreed?"

"Agreed!" Richard cried. He took Katherine's hand and began running with her toward the quays, feeling the pain in his leg hardly at all, so happy was he to be getting back under sail. *Eagle* had been warped up against the quay, her larboard side facing inward toward the port city, as all vessels were when either on-loading or off-loading. Tied to a bollard at quayside was her eighteen-foot, narrow-beamed tender, the single lateen fore-and-aft sail furled tight to the mast.

"Let's go," Jamie shouted enthusiastically. Will restrained him from leaping into the boat.

"Not so fast, squire," he said. "Let your sister and Richard have the first go. I'll take you aboard *Eagle* and show you the ropes. Maybe we'll go up to the maintop there. What do you say?"

"Well . . . ," Jamie grumbled, though he did cast an appreciative eye over *Eagle*'s top-hamper.

"Are you sure?" Katherine asked him. "There's plenty of room for us all."

"I know," said Will. "But first I want to show Jamie the workings of a brig. We'll go out with you later." He unraveled the clove hitch on the bollard as Richard released the sail from its stops. The loose-footed lateen sail spread out on a long yard attached at a forty-five-degree angle to the mast. The sail caught the wind as Will pushed the boat out from the dock, and Richard took the tiller and sheet in the stern.

"How marvelous!" Katherine sang out as the boat picked up speed in the greater wind and chop farther out in the harbor. Moored on this side of the massive harbor were numerous merchant vessels, and Richard had to concentrate on threading the small boat among them until they were in open water and heading for the narrow entryway between Burrow Island on the west shore and Whale Island on the east. In the far distance, they could begin to make out the Isle of Wight and the wooden fortress that was the naval fleet at Spithead.

"Richard!" Katherine shrieked with a mixture of fear and delight when a burst of wind sent the boat heeling. Instead of easing out the mainsheet, to bring the boat level, Richard trimmed it in, increasing the angle of heel. "Stop that this instant!"

A wave more menacing than the rest was fast approaching to windward, its crest up and, Richard sensed, about to break. At the precise moment, he jogged the tiller to leeward, swinging the bow more to windward. The wave slapped against the larboard bow just as it broke, sending up a shower of sparkling seawater that doused them both.

"You beast!" she cried, laughing. "You did that on purpose. What a horrid thing to do!"

"Beats riding a horse, hey?" he said, grinning, though he did ease off the wind and paid out the mainsheet until they were on a more comfortable broad reach. "Want to try sailing her?"

"Heavens, no," she snapped as she wiped water droplets from her face and brushed them off her clothes. "I wouldn't dream of such a thing."

"Well, in that case, since you insist on being just dead weight, at least sit where that weight balances the boat properly."

"Why? What's wrong with where I am?"

"Nothing, really. You're just too far forward. You need to move aft some, toward me."

She scooted a ways over. "How's this?"

"Better. Now just a little closer. A little closer. Just a bit more. There. That's it. Perfect."

"Richard Cutler, you are a cad," she sighed, as she nestled her back comfortably against his chest.

"Would you have it any other way?"

"No," she giggled, and they sailed on that way, back and forth across the mouth of Portsmouth harbor, until the warm September sun had dried their clothes, it was time to head in, and propriety dictated they assume more decorous positions within the cockpit.

☆ ☆ ☆

"Yes, I remember. Why bring it up now?"

"Why not bring it up now? I often think of those days, Richard. Do you?"

"I used to," he allowed, adding, though not before a pause for emphasis, "but not so much anymore."

"How terribly sad. I had hoped you would never forget them."

They were nearing the house and her carriage in waiting. "How are plans for the wedding coming?" he asked, trying his best to sound sincere and nonchalant. "I understand from Lizzy that it's been postponed."

She withdrew her arm from his. "It has," she confirmed. "Probably until June. I shall be leaving in several weeks to visit Horatio in London. We shall decide for certain then." She whirled around to face him. "Richard, I do so want you to come to the wedding. You will come, won't you? Promise me you will. I'm sure your uncle can get permission for you to leave Fareham just this once . . ."

It was the first time he had looked at her this closely that afternoon, and it greatly disturbed him to see just how sunken and bloodshot her eyes seemed to be, and how gray and puffy the skin beneath. She who had always seemed the paragon of self-assurance and buoyancy now stood before him the antithesis of a blushing bride-to-be. Again his heart yearned to embrace, protect, comfort her. Again his brain said no. It was her decision, willfully made, to pledge herself to another.

"I promise," he said, although he already had a plan in place that would have him long gone from Fareham come June.

THE LINCHPIN of his plan was Pennington Sharpe, a young man of impressive lineage who had befriended Richard years ago when he had first visited Fareham. Penny, as he preferred to be called, was a squirrelly, mild-mannered, often effeminate-acting fellow whose outrage, nonetheless, erupted whenever he had a podium from which to denounce King George and anyone else in the British government who sought to prolong the suffering in America. The war was an affront to the rights and liberties of Englishmen, he had confided to Richard, and he, for one, would act upon his principles. He would book passage on a merchant vessel bound for British-held New York and seek residence in Connecticut, a state that, for a reason he did not specify, he fancied more than the others.

Richard had subsequently learned from his uncle that principle was not the sole motivation behind Penny's bold decision to leave England. His family, on a downward financial spiral for generations, had gambled heavily in certain investments. Why, or just what these investments were, was very hush-hush, but it was known that Lloyd's had sponsored them, and they had gone belly up after ingesting most of what was left of the Sharpe family fortune. To Penny, emigrating to America to start a new life seemed a civilized alternative to living in disgrace in England—or fleeing to France as many of his countrymen in similar circumstances had done.

"Why not sail with me to New York?" he asked outright, soon after Richard had begun cautiously testing the waters. "We can share a cabin, or whatever space they provide passengers on those ships. It'd certainly make the trip a lot more enjoyable. You've really a mind to leave England, then?"

"I do." It was a throw of the dice; he had not been prepared to wade in this far this quickly. "But I must beg your indulgence, Penny. Under no circumstances must my family get wind of my plans. I will not have them involved in any way or hurt more than is necessary. And where I need to go is France, not America."

"Where in France?"

"Brest."

"Hmm." Penny tapped an index finger on the front of his chin, the sole area on his lower jaw free of mustache or sideburns. "That won't be easy to arrange, Richard, but not impossible. And of course you may rely on my discretion."

He went on to explain how he could use his family's "interests" in Portsmouth shipping circles to identify and approach a captain who would be willing, for the right price, to cross the Channel at night. "It will require money," he insisted. "A good deal of it. Do you have some?"

"Enough, I believe," Richard said. "I haven't had much occasion recently to spend what I have." They shared a smile, Richard adding that, for services rendered, he would expect to pay Penny whatever commission he stipulated, an offer Penny summarily declined.

"Nonsense, my dear man. It's an honor to serve the cause. Besides, you couldn't afford my commission. It'd cost you too pretty a penny."

Richard laughed along with Sharpe's high giggle.

A fortnight later, he was mentally reviewing the details of his plan while having a quiet dinner with his family. As usual, Lizzy was seated to his right, though as was her wont in recent weeks, whatever conversations she engaged in were directed at her parents across the table. A serious strain had intruded upon their relationship and Richard did not understand why. Although it pained him to be estranged from one he held so dear, he had decided to let the situation play out its natural course without getting further involved. A coward's way out, he had to admit, but God willing, there would be opportunities in the future for explanations and reconciliation. For the present, he had more pressing needs to consider.

"Richard," Emma Cutler said when they were well into their meal, "you know that Katherine is leaving soon for London. You will plan to see her before she goes, won't you?"

Richard laid his fork gently back on his plate. "I have been thinking about it, Auntie," he replied. "I want to. I'm just not sure I can."

"Well, I should think you would invite her to come over. Imagine her hurt if you didn't."

"We'll see, Auntie."

"'We'll see?' That's all you have to say? 'We'll see?' I don't mean to meddle in your affairs, Richard, really I don't, but in this case I do think–"

"It doesn't matter, Mother," her daughter interrupted, her voice low and dangerous. She was glowering down at the plate set before her.

"What? How can you say such a thing, Lizzy? Of course it matters. It matters very much. Why, the two of them . . ."

"Mother! Listen to me!" Her eyes shot up. "It doesn't matter because Katherine isn't going to London."

"Isn't going? Whyever not?"

"Yes, Lizzy," Richard asked, his senses suddenly alert. "Why isn't Katherine going to London?"

Her eyes swung to him, rage embedded in them.

"If you'd had the heart to talk to her just once this winter, Richard, I mean really *talk* to her *one time,* you'd have the answer for yourself. Since you didn't, you don't."

She excused herself from the table and balled up her linen napkin, nearly hitting Richard with it when she threw it down. She turned to go.

Richard was up, seized her arm.

"What is it, Lizzy?"

"You're hurting me, Richard."

"I'm sorry." He released her arm, then held her more gently by the shoulders. "What is it, Lizzy?" he said again, this time in a kinder, beseeching voice. "Please. I beg you. Tell me what you know."

She glared at him, her sea blue eyes wet with emotion.

"You've never seen Katherine cry, have you, Richard? Well, you wouldn't. She wouldn't let you. But I've seen her cry. I've seen her cry too many times these past few weeks. And it's all because of you."

"*Me?* What on earth are you talking about?"

She retrieved the napkin from the table and wiped away tears. She breathed in once, twice, to steady herself, as if she knew she was being melodramatic and not entirely fair.

"The wedding is off," she announced, in one long exhale. "Katherine is not going to marry Horatio."

"Why?" he heard himself say.

"Why? *Why?*" Lizzy was beside herself. "Lord, Richard, for an intelligent man you can be so ghastly *stupid* sometimes. The wedding is off because Katherine doesn't love Horatio. She never has. And if you weren't always so caught up in yourself and your silly notions of propriety and honor, you'd know perfectly well that the man Katherine loves is *you!*"

AT THAT moment, a mile to the south, a carriage-for-hire slowly wended its way northward, the driver reigning in a two-horse team now and again to request directions from another carriage traveling southward. Inside sat a lone occupant facing forward. He had no pocket watch, but from his estimation they had been on the road somewhere between an hour and an hour and a half. That would make it about 9:00. No later than 9:15. By 2:00 the next morning, in five hours, they had to be back at Portsmouth Dock. That's when the tide turned, and he suffered no illusions that the Dutch captain would cut him slack if they were late. He would simply sail without them. To be safe, they'd have to leave Fareham by 11:30. The question was, did he have enough time?

He gazed out the window at the estates passing by. He could not make out the buildings themselves, it was too dark, but he marveled nonetheless at their sheer size. That one there, he smiled to himself, the multistoried house with the flickering stretch of lights visible through the windows, that would be a village where I come from. Then his smile faded, the dark reality settling over him once again that this was not his land, these were not his people.

The carriage ground to a halt.

"We're 'ere, guv'nor," the driver called down to him. "That there's the Cutler estate. Want me to drive in?"

"No," the young man called back up. "What time is it?"

"I'd say about three bells," the driver announced, revealing his past service in the Royal Navy.

"Thank you. Wait here, please. I won't be long."

The young man disembarked. Though the weather was not cold, he pulled his borrowed boat cloak around him as he set off at a brisk pace on a mission, he knew, that would be decided, one way or another, within minutes.

At the front door he lifted the sturdy brass knocker in the middle and let it fall with a reverberating bang. From inside he heard footsteps. The door swung ajar and a liveried servant in a white peruke appeared in the open space.

"May I help you?" he inquired, stoically sizing up the young, freckled-faced visitor.

"I'm here t' see Mr. Cutler," the youth replied, summoning up his best official sounding voice.

"Which one, may I ask?"

"Come again?"

"Sir, there are two Mr. Cutlers in residence. Which one are you inquiring after?"

"Oh. That would be Mr. Richard Cutler."

The servant hesitated. He glanced inside then turned back: "I'm afraid Mr. Cutler is somewhat . . . indisposed at this moment. I . . . um . . ."

"It'll take just a moment," the footman was assured. "Please. It's important. And I've come a long way."

"Very well," he finally relented. "I shall tell him you are here. May I ask your name?"

"Agreen."

"I beg your pardon?"

"Agreen. That's my name."

"I see. Very good, Mr. Agreen. Please wait here."

Several moments later the door opened wide, and this time it was Richard in the doorway, a look of stunned disbelief on his face.

"Agee! How on earth . . . ? When . . . ?"

"Good t' see you too, Richard," Agreen grinned. He held out his hand, and Richard shook it warmly.

"This ain't a social call, Richard," he told him, leaning in confidentially. "We haven't much time. I have a carriage waitin' on the main road. It's takin' me, and if you're willin', you, back t' Portsmouth. There's a ship there, a Dutch trader, ready t' take us, for a pack o' money, t' France, t' Lorient, where I hear tell Captain Jones is outfittin' a new ship. I'm hopin' t' serve on that ship an' I'd be proud t' have you aboard with me. You must decide, though, and quick. The ship sails on the ebb tide, whether we're aboard or not, and that's in the second watch, at four bells. We must . . . Richard, are you all right? You don't look so good."

"What? Oh, sorry, Agee. I'm a little distracted, that's all. I'll explain later. What was that again? About the ship?"

"She sails in four hours."

Richard's mind was working furiously to make sense of these sharp turns of events and to attach some sort of order and discipline to the tangle of will and emotions coiling inside of him. It was to no avail. The tangle was too bewildering in its construction. Sensing no alternative, he succumbed to the hands of fate, which is what convinced him had brought Agreen to Fareham this night.

"Give me an hour, Agee. I'll meet you at the carriage."

Richard opened the door and stepped back inside the house. "Not a word of this to anyone, Harold," he whispered to the servant, "until tomorrow."

Harold stood at stiff attention, winked once.

"Who was it, dear?" Emma inquired from the dining room.

"Penny, wanting to play cards. But I told him I'm too tired. I think I'll retire early tonight, Auntie, if you don't mind."

"You do that, dear," she called after him, adding her usual dictum: "Things will be clearer in the morning, Richard, after a good night's sleep. You'll see."

Richard walked as casually as he was able up the stairway to the second floor. Quietly he opened and closed the door to his room. He lit a candle on his desk, then went to the closet and removed his refurbished naval uniform. This he crammed into his sea bag along with several pieces of civilian clothing and the book Katherine had given him. He went to the bureau, opened the bottom drawer, and withdrew the pouch of coins he had hidden there. This he buttoned up in an inner pocket of his overcoat and folded it, stuffing it too into the bag. He surveyed the room. Satisfied he had what he needed, he went to the desk and sat down. From the single drawer running the length of the desk he withdrew a quill, an ink well, and three sheets of paper.

He would write two letters, both of which he would leave in Lizzy's care, along with a note of explanation to her. They may have had their differences in recent weeks, but at her core she remained a staunch ally. She would deliver the two letters, of that he was certain.

The first letter was to his aunt and uncle. He wrote quickly, time was of the essence, but he had to express to them how much he appreciated all they had done for him and how his leaving was a matter of honor for him, a call of duty to his country, to his shipmates, and above all, to his brother.

The second letter was to Katherine. His heart beating relentlessly, he dipped the tip of the quill into the ink well, blew on it, paused for a moment in a desperate search for words, then wrote:

My dear Katherine:

Lizzy told me this evening that you have decided not to marry Captain Nelson. Because I don't have the ability to express how I feel at this moment, I shan't try. I only know that what you are doing you believe you must do, as I also must do. I am leaving Fareham and returning to the war. If I can find any solace in this, it is that I need not explain to you why I must go where duty compels me. You know me that well.

You once told me that you would always believe in me and you have been true to your word. It is I, dear Katherine, who failed to believe in you. I beg your forgiveness and I pray to whatever God controls this universe that you will not give up on me now. I am prepared to live without you, if I must because that is your wish. But I have no desire to live in a world where I cease to be the memory you hold so close to your heart.

For the faith of what is, for the dreams of what will be,

Richard

10

LORIENT, FRANCE

Summer 1779

BEGGIN' YOUR PARDON, RICHARD, are ye *sure* ye want t' be doin' this'? Either you're feelin' guilty as hell or there's a woman back there into you good."

Richard had a lost look about him as the coach-and-four drove southward in the dim light thrown off by two swaying lanterns outside and a gibbous moon suspended high above the horizon. They had minimal time to spare. If the driver were to keep on schedule and earn the balance of his fee, he needed to crack the whip. There was also the possibility, though slim on this well-traveled road, that a highwayman bent on robbery or worse might materialize out of the dark and seize a slow-moving team of horses. Greater was the probability of being waylaid by an inquisitive patrol of the Home Guard, civilian soldiers whose job it was to keep commerce-laden roads free of miscreants, a classification that included rebel midshipmen in violation of their paroles.

Richard turned his head from the window.

"I'm sure, Agee. Now tell me, what happened at Old Mill? How did the others take to my leaving?"

"They were confused at first, as you can imagine. But I helped set 'em straight. I knew you have family in Fareham, and considerin' the way you left, I told 'em you must've had no say in the matter. The guards said pretty much the same thing, so it didn't take much convincin' on my part. Though I didn't realize until tonight that your family is some kind o' royalty. I mean, *Jesus,* what a house!"

"They're not royalty, Agee. Not even nobility. My uncle's a sugar merchant."

"Well, t' this rube from Maine, it sure *looked* like royalty."

Richard changed the subject.

"What about the tunnel? Did our plan work?"

"*Your* plan, Richard. It was your plan, remember? And yup, she worked."

"You got out? All of you?"

"Yup. Walked out like we were on a Sunday stroll. Every officer and two mates, includin' Seth Gardiner. The guards weren't sure at first, but Dale an' Talbot, you get those two polecats warmed up, they sound like frickin' admirals. They put the fear of God into those guards."

What Agreen said both elated and depressed Richard. Elated, because the plan had worked. Depressed, because added to his already mountainous burden of guilt was the knowledge that Seth Gardiner had given him what he had earned in prison as an expert whittler. He must have assumed that as a lowly petty officer, he would not be included on the escape roster.

From topside came a cry of warning just before the twin right wheels of the carriage careened into a deep rut. The stagecoach driver yanked on the reins, causing both horses to rear up as the left wheels of the coach lifted up off the road. For several precarious moments the carriage balanced on edge. With the initial lurch to the right, Richard and Agee had lunged to the left, their weight helping to right the carriage, which fell back on all four wheels with a shivering thump.

The driver coaxed the horses back into forward motion with gentle, wavelike flicks of the reins and a gentle clucking sound. "You two all right?" he called down.

Agreen threw open the window. "Yes," he shouted up. "Now ease off the speed, driver. Let's at least *get* t' bloody Portsmouth!" He banged the window shut. "Thought for sure we're goin' over on our beam-ends," he muttered. "What a scrape we'd be in then."

"What happened next, Agee?" Richard asked, once they had settled themselves and their sea bags.

"After we got out, we split up into threes. I went with Richard Dale and Seth Gardiner as far as Devon. While Seth and I hid out, Dale made some inquiries in the local taverns, searchin' for someone t' take him and Seth over t' France. Took some doin', but he finally found one. I saw 'em off."

"Saw them off? Why didn't you go with them?"

"I had business in Portsmouth."

"What business?"

"Same as now, Richard. I was comin' for you."

"What happened? That was months ago."

"Well, I got there. But that's as far as I got, 'cause damme if I didn't do what Silas had warned me never t' do in public."

"What?"

Agreen grinned sheepishly. "Talk," he said. "Guess I don't sound much like a local gent or any other sort of folk around here. On the ride t' Portsmouth I got t' talkin' with this young lass. I couldn't help myself. Damn, she was pretty. She liked me too—a fellow knows that sort of thing—and we were gettin' along just fine, thank you, when this man sittin' next t' her, a much older gent and ugly as a horned toad, started asking me questions. He was suspicious. Or jealous. Or just plain ornery, who knows? Anyway, as soon we arrived in Portsmouth, he calls out the authorities. Before I knew it, I was back at home sweet home and lodged in the private suite."

"The black hole?" Richard gasped.

"The one and only. But it wasn't so bad. I caught up on my sleep and lost all that weight I'd put on eatin' those snails. I'm in fightin' shape now. Just need t' make me a new bow in France, and I'm back in business."

Richard leaned forward, put his hand on Agreen's arm.

"Agee," he said sternly, "why didn't you go with Richard and Seth? Why did you come here to get me, instead?"

"You saved my life, remember?"

Richard slumped back.

"What happened then? How did you escape a second time?"

"Turned out I didn't need to. Remember Thornton, the gent from Paris? Well, slap me blue if he didn't do just what he said he'd do. Captain Jones had a load of prisoners t' exchange. You want 'em back, Thornton informed the British agents, then you release every American officer held in England, pronto. So we were. Just like that. We were taken t' Portsmouth t' board a ship bound for France. That's how I got t' Portsmouth. Then I hired this coach with coins I had saved and what others in Old Mill gave me who knew my plans t' come for you. The men remember you fondly, Richard. They send their respects."

They were approaching the fields of northern Portsmouth, close to where an enormous mast pond had been excavated a century ago to season yards and spars within its scum-frothed waters before they could be properly installed aboard a Royal Navy vessel. Up ahead, at the city wall recently extended northward to incorporate a spate of new dwellings tending toward the naval dockyards, was the most dangerous segment of their journey. They would need to pass through Unicorn Gate at the western edge of Edinburgh Road to get inside the city proper, and their fate could depend on the whims of the guards stationed there. On his way north, Agreen had passed through without incident. But now, with French spies prowling about southern England in advance of a threatened invasion, entering the city had become more difficult.

At the gate, a guard holding up a lantern stepped out in front of the carriage. "Halt!" he demanded.

The driver reined in the horses. A second guard, similarly clad in the informal garb of local militia, strode around the carriage, searching for anything unusual or suspicious. In his left hand he held the strap of a musket slung straight down from his left shoulder; in his right, a lantern swayed to and fro as he made his inspection, the pendulumlike motion casting intermittent flashes of light into the interior of the coach.

"State your business!" he demanded of the driver.

"Carriage for hire, Portsmouth based, High Street," the driver replied, well versed in the intricacies of these situations. If it did turn out that one of his passengers was guilty of any sort of wrongdoing, that statement got him off the hook unless it could be proven that he had somehow abetted the crime. For that reason, he never inquired about a client's business, especially one paying so handsome a fee.

The guard swung open the coach door and thrust the lantern inside. "State your business!" he demanded of the two passengers. As he did so, Richard caught a sudden, unmistakable whiff of stale gin. "Hop to it!" he snapped, when he did not receive an immediate answer.

"Sir," Richard said politely in his most convincing British accent, "my name is Richard Cutler. My uncle is William Cutler, a merchant from Fareham. He owns a shipping office across the harbor in Gosport. My friend and I are here on his behalf to see a captain of one of his ships docked overnight at

Portsmouth Dock. He is sailing on the ebb tide for the Indies, so we haven't much time. If you will allow us to be on our way . . ."

Richard's upper-crust tone caused the guard to waver. "Prove it," he grumbled. "Show me your papers."

"Sir, we don't have papers. We had to leave in a hurry, and we forgot them. Now kindly let us through."

"What is it, Travis?" the first guard inquired, coming up. His speech was slurred, and his slight stagger confirmed that he, too, had pumped aboard a quantity of spirits during the course of the night.

"This fellow 'ere claims 'e's on business for 'is uncle, a merchant or some such. But 'e's got no papers. Forgot 'em, 'e says."

"Then we can't let 'em through," the first guard confirmed. He glanced inside the carriage. "My apologies, yer honors. New regulations, you understand. We 'ave strict orders. Now be good enough to step down."

"This is an outrage!" Agreen shouted. "I demand—"

"Sod off with yor demands, mate," Travis snarled. "An' get out of that coach quicklike if y' knows what's good for yer. If wot yer friend 'ere says is true, we won't detain you long."

"You got that right," Agreen declared, feeling for the pocket knife concealed in the inner lining of his coat. Richard grabbed his arm.

"My good sirs," he said, "certainly we do not wish to interfere with your duty, but can we reach an agreement here? We are all men of good will. If one of you would kindly hold out your hands, perhaps we can find a solution to our problem."

With that, he untied the string to the pouch of coins he had retrieved from his coat in the sea bag and flipped it upside down over the outstretched hands of the guard known as Travis. As silver crowns and gold guineas fell out and tinkled on top of one another to form a small pyramid, the liquor-dulled faces of both guards grew increasingly animated.

"Now then, gentlemen," Richard asked agreeably, "may we be allowed to proceed?"

The guard spoke to the treasure he held in his hands.

"Upon my honor, you may, sir. And may you and yer friend 'ere 'ave a most pleasant conclusion to yer journey."

☆ ☆ ☆

"WE COULD ransom frickin' King George for what we've spent so far," Agreen declared, "but at least it's got us here. And I have t' admit, I do kind of enjoy actin' like one of them street dandies you seem t' admire so much, Richard. I sure could get used t' spreadin' the money around like you rich folks do."

They were in the hold of a Dutch merchantman, shuffled aboard a half hour earlier and directed immediately belowdeck by the brig's master who hardly paused in his guttural commands to his crew as he transferred from Agreen's hand to his own pocket the outrageous fee that would persuade him to interrupt his voyage to St. Eustatius in the West Indies with a brief stopover on the west coast of France. Sequestered in their musty, cramped quarters, they could barely make out a stamp of feet on the deck above and the muffled voices of sailors preparing a ship for sea. Closer, they could hear coming from the capstan amidships the intermittent clicking of pawls and the grunts of men straining at the bars. The ship was weighing anchor; her topsails and jibs would be set momentarily, and the crew would be standing by in the waist to ensure proper headway out of Portsmouth harbor into the Solent.

"If you enjoy spreading the wealth, Agee," Richard bantered, "I've got good news for you. God and Captain Jones willing, very soon we'll be back in the employ of the Continental Navy."

"Earnin' our fifteen-dollars-a-month pay."

"In Continental paper, no less. We can spread that money around to our heart's content."

"Except in Congress. Don't try pawnin' those bills off in there."

"You got that right. Those worthies demand payment in gold or silver, no flimsy paper for them, thank you. Paper's for suckers like us, willing to put our necks on the line for them. What do we need money for? Our accommodations are luxurious and paid for by Congress. We get *le grand tour* of Europe, expense free. As for food, what dining establishment in London or Paris could rival the haute cuisine of a midshipmen's mess?"

Agreen grinned. "Glad to hear you laughin' again, Richard," he said. "Like old times. I have t' admit, I was gettin' a mite worried about you."

"No need to worry, Agee. I'm doing fine, no doubt as a result of your company. What say we get some sleep? I heard five bells some time ago."

"Whatever you say, Your Grace," Agreen bantered. He opened the small protective glass door of the metal-framed lantern resting on the deck beside them and blew out the flame inside. A residue of light remained, seeping through the cracks of the hatchway five feet above. "Ring for the butler, would you, my lord," he added, settling in amid a confusion of cordage and spare rigging and pulling his tricorne hat down over his eyes. "Ask him, if he'd be so kind, t' wake us for breakfast at two bells in the forenoon watch. It wouldn't do for highbrows like us t' be up any earlier."

Richard was using his fist to fashion his seabag into a pillow. "Right you are, your lordship," he answered. "See you at two bells."

The hold fell silent except for the faint shouts of sailors on deck and seawater gurgling along the hull's planking two inches away; then, a few minutes later, the heavy breathing of Agreen asleep. Richard lay on his back, willing sleep he knew would not come easily. It seemed impossible to him that earlier that same evening he had been with his family in Fareham, unaware that the course of his life was about to take so drastic a turn. He thought of Lizzy reading his note to her. What he had done would seem unimaginable to such a proper young woman. It would appear the same way to his aunt and uncle, though he convinced himself that after they read his letter, and realized what he had put at risk in leaving, they would find a way to forgive him. He thought, too, of his parents and what their reaction might be. Most of all, he thought of Katherine, and it was the prayed-for image of her reading and rereading his letter and holding it to her breast, her soul finally at peace, that consoled him through the darkest hours of the night until sleep finally settled him.

The two Americans were ordered to remain below in the hold throughout the passage, the one exception being when they had to use the head. Even then they were not allowed to go forward through the crew's quarters to the "seat of ease" at the prow of the ship; instead they were to use the officers' facilities in the after cabin. Otherwise they were to stay put, their rations brought to them by the first or second mate whenever the crew ate. Under no circumstances were they permitted on the weather deck.

Richard understood why such precautions were necessary. Though Holland and England were officially at peace with each other, behind official veneers serious trouble was brewing. Since the outbreak of hostilities, the tiny Dutch island of St. Eustatius had served as a willing go-between for French arms suppliers eager to sell their wares to American agents eager to purchase them. That trade, while creating enormous wealth for the island, had offended the British sense of fair play. Now, with France allied with America, with Spain on the threshold of war, and with even the Empress Catherine of the House of Romanov considering her chances against Britain, Holland felt emboldened to trade directly with all combatants, actual and potential, charging prices that its tight-fisted merchants conceded were designed to undercut the competition and create monopolies. Britain had expressed its outrage on land through strongly worded communiqués and at sea by firing warning shots across the bows of any Dutchman refusing to heave to for inspection before entering an American or French port. The brig Richard and Agreen were aboard had been on a diplomatic mission to England and carried no cargo; nonetheless, her master had been directed to dock near the naval base in Portsmouth Town, not by the commercial quays of Gosport, and British authorities had thoroughly searched her hold the day before for contraband weapons. Though it was unlikely a British cruiser would stop and board her at sea, the possibility existed, and from her master's perspective, the fewer visible reminders of the two Americans belowdecks, the better.

The route followed by the Dutch brig brought them along the French coast, south around Ushant Island off the western tip of Brittany, and into the Bay of Biscay. Seas became noticeably rougher there, a rapidly shallowing of the continental shelf allowing waves born of three thousand miles of fetch to roil up into steep-sided breakers. There, too, lurked the greatest danger of being sighted by a British cruiser standing off and on before the French naval station at Brest, forty miles southeast of Ushant. For years, the core of British naval strategy against its archenemy had been to blockade her two fleets based in Brest and Toulon. Bottled up, a French naval commander had essentially two choices: either sail out in the light of day and challenge the British, a rare occurrence indeed, or attempt to sneak out under cover of night, fog, or some other screen. That was yesterday. Today a French commander had more opportunities. With an allied invasion threatening, Whitehall had recalled most line-of-battle ships from its Mediterranean and western squadrons in defense of home waters, leaving British frigate captains on station to reconnoiter French naval maneuvers, and French sea captains more at liberty to sail as winds, tides, and foreign policy dictated.

On their third day out of Portsmouth, Richard and Agreen stepped onto the weather deck into a blinding sun. The Dutch brig was hove-to at the entrance to Lorient harbor, and a mate was directing them down into the tender as quickly as their cramped limbs would allow. It was not until they had been rowed ashore and left standing on the stone quays that their eyes finally grew accustomed to the dazzling light, enough to take in their new surroundings.

Lorient was a small, unobtrusive French seaport in overall appearance not unlike many seacoast towns in Cornwall or Devon. Its buildings were small and grouped together in intimate clusters, the majority constructed in typical Breton style, with white stucco walls and red-tiled roofs. Not coincidentally, the town was a few leagues south of the naval base at Brest and had been designed specifically as home port for the French East India Company, a mercantile enterprise that protected Gallic commercial interests in the Far East against two primary competitors: the British East India Company and the Dutch East India Company. Because piracy thrived in eastern seas, and because commercial relations with its European rivals often deteriorated into gunfire, the French East India Company had armed its merchant fleet with heavy guns and other military stores secured from the French navy. Over the years, the French government had invested nearly as much in this quasi-military facility as it had in the naval base at Brest, and the Lorient shipyards were admired throughout Europe for the beauty, speed, and durability of the ships they produced.

"Welcome t' France," Agreen said as they watched the tender hastening back to the brig. "Now what?"

"First thing, Agee, is to get some decent food. I have a few livres left over from when I was here, enough to buy us dinner and a night's lodging. After that, we'll just have to see . . . Hold on, I'll ask this fellow for a recommendation." He spoke in French to a stooped old man tending a clutch of thick-planked, brightly colored boats at quayside. The man nodded and spoke rapidly in response, jabbing his finger at what appeared to be a charming place where a waiter in a white apron was weaving among tables set out in front, deftly balancing a tray held up high by his right arm. The old man concluded with a kiss on his fingers bunched at his lips.

"*Merci, monsieur,*" Richard said.

"Understood that gesture," Agreen commented as the two of them set off to where the dockhand had pointed.

They were hoping to sit outdoors, the sunshine a blessing after being confined in a ship's hold for three days, but all tables there were occupied. So they went inside and stood near the doorway, adjusting their eyes to the cool dark and scanning the small, cozy alcoves for a place to sit. There appeared to be nothing available there either, and they were pondering their next move when, to his great surprise, Richard spotted a man he recognized in a nearby group. The man was staring back at him in equally startled recognition.

"Richard Cutler! Agreen Crabtree! My eyes deceive me!"

Richard Dale heaved his considerable frame up from his chair and strode over to the two midshipmen. As he did so, his left thigh bumped against the chair of another patron, causing wine to spill and a torrent of French expletives to erupt. Oblivious to what he had done, Dale, beaming, grasped Richard's hand, then Agreen's, and pumped it up and down. "My God, I never thought I'd see the day! Wait till the captain hears about this! Come, lads, join us, will you? The food is excellent, and God be praised, Congress is footing the bill!"

At the table Richard Dale made the introductions. The first man he introduced was clearly the host of the occasion. He was short and stubby with an almost perfectly round face, and he was dressed in tasteful yet plain brown breeches and coat, a pale yellow vest, and an ordinary white neckstock. Though he had a sharply receding hairline, sprouting out from the sides of his head were thick mounds of gray hair freckled with white, with bushy sideburns of identical color covering much of his ears. Under thin black eyebrows that nearly met above a prominent nose, a set of deep blue eyes glistened with a sense of vitality and intelligence that tended to subdue what was otherwise an austere demeanor. Rising politely to his feet beside him was a boy of about twelve, his facial features remarkably similar to those of the adult, including a slightly hooked nose that seemed too big for his face.

"Gentlemen," said Dale, "allow me to introduce you to Mr. John Adams. Mr. Adams is an American commissioner here in France. He is also a member of the Marine Committee and chairman of the Board of Ordnance. The handsome young man next to him is his son, John Quincy. They are returning to America aboard *Alliance,* a frigate of ours under the command of this gentleman, Captain Pierre Landais. Though Captain Landais is French, he is an honorary citizen of Massachusetts and holds a commission in the Continental Navy."

Adams shook hands firmly. The welcome proffered by Pierre Landais was more perfunctory.

"And this gentleman here," Dale concluded the introductions, "is Mr. Cutting Lunt, second lieutenant of the Continental ship *Bonhomme Richard.* She's anchored out there in the harbor. I am proud to say that I am her first lieutenant."

"And Captain Jones . . . ?" Richard inquired, after he and Agreen had shaken Lunt's hand.

"He is her captain. She's an East Indiaman. But as you'll see, she's undergone extensive modifications to bring her up to naval specifications. At King Louis's expense, I might add. Come, gentlemen, order up some food and waste no time telling us how you came to Lorient."

Agreen first, then Richard, recounted the events of the past few weeks. Those at the table listened with more than courteous attention, Lunt whistling softly every now and again as the accounts unwound.

Adams said, when they had concluded, "As you may recall, Mr. Cutler, those of us in Passy were made aware of your . . . family situation by the British ambassador. Dr. Franklin was ill at the time and asked me to intervene on your behalf. I remember him telling me that if an English prison could not detain you, an English country manor most certainly could not. He would be delighted to see you again, I assure you."

"Thank you, Mr. Adams," Richard said. "And of course I recall your kind intervention. How is Dr. Franklin? His health has improved, I trust?"

"I fear not, sorry to say," Adams replied, adding, with what Richard took to be mild reproach, "though I suspect his ill health has more to do with his free-spirited lifestyle than anything else. He's getting on in years, as you know, and has difficulty moving about. He suffers from gout and boils, among other maladies. He had planned to be here himself to observe the fitting out of the Indiaman, but his health, alas, would not permit. He sent me in his stead, a pragmatic decision since John Quincy and I had already planned to return to Boston by way of Lorient."

"Are you looking forward to the voyage?"

Richard had directed the question to the son; it was the father who answered.

"We look forward to getting home, of course, and especially to seeing John's mother. I confess to you, however, that I do not particularly enjoy a sea passage. There is nothing to see but sky, clouds, and water, one day to the next. I will concede that a sea passage provides me with ample opportunity to pursue my favorite activity, which is reading. I have long maintained that at sea, books are a man's best friend."

"We took a prize on our voyage here," young John Quincy chimed in. "And I have learned the name of every sail on a frigate. You can test me if you'd like, and after dinner I can show you my ship drawings." He looked eagerly at Agreen. "They're upstairs in my room."

"I'd be proud t' see them," Agreen said.

"Mr. Adams," Richard said, "I have with me a new book by Edward Gibbon. It's the second volume of his work on the Roman Empire. It was given to me by a friend in England. Have you by chance read it?"

"I have not, though I certainly enjoyed the first volume."

"In that case, sir, I would be pleased to offer it to you for your voyage home. When you arrive in Boston, if it's not too inconvenient, might I ask you to have it sent to my parents in Hingham? You would be doing me a great courtesy, as I would enclose a letter to them in the book."

"That is extraordinarily generous of you, Mr. Cutler. I accept your kind offer, and I will do better than what you request. I will take great pleasure reading the book on our voyage, and I will take equal pleasure delivering both your book and your letter to your family with my own hand. Hingham, you say? I'm a Braintree man myself. So I won't have far to go, will I?" He paused, a notion suddenly come to him. "See here, Mr. Cutler. Perhaps there is another possibility. Did you and Mr. Crabtree have a specific purpose in sailing to Lorient? One that might detain you in France? If not, might I persuade you both to join young John and me aboard *Alliance*? We would be most grateful for your company, and here is an opportunity for you to return to your home in Massachusetts. We sail in three days. Is that not so, Captain Landais?"

"*Oui, Monsieur.* I prefer to sail . . . how does one say, *tous les jeudis?*"

"On Thursdays," said Lunt.

"*Merci.* Yes, I prefer to sail on Thursdays. It brings *bonne chance* . . . good luck."

"Will you sail with us, Mr. Crabtree?" asked John Quincy hopefully.

"I'm afraid not, son," Agreen replied, bringing a frown of disappointment to the boy's face. "Mr. Cutler and I are here t' sign on as midshipmen with Captain Jones, should he have two berths available."

Dale slapped the end of the table. "I knew it! I knew that's why you lads had come here." He smiled broadly. "Well, gentlemen, that being the case, we must finish up and make haste to inform the captain of his good fortune."

From quayside *Bonhomme Richard* seemed an impressive ship, lying at anchor almost within hailing distance. From what Richard and Agreen had been told by Dale, and from what they could see for themselves, she was indeed a substantial vessel: 152 feet long from stem to stern, a 40-foot beam, 19-foot depth of hold, 900 tons burthen. That made her more than two times heavier than *Ranger,* Richard estimated, with a hull volume two and a half times greater. In design, she differed significantly from *Ranger.* Her quarter-deck extended almost to the mainmast at the center of the ship; astern of it, an old-fashioned poop deck rose high above the waterline. She was ship-rigged, though her foremast at the fo'c'sle was set apart from the main- and mizzenmasts stepped closer together farther aft. Jutting out at a forty-five-degree angle from the stem was a long, lancelike bowsprit secured under an even longer jibboom; at the other end of the ship, at the mizzen, was a fore-n'-aft lateen spar, its fore end extending past the mizzenmast almost halfway to the mainmast.

As Lieutenant Lunt stood facing the ship, slowly raising and lowering his arms to signal for a boat to be sent ashore, Dale reviewed the ship's ordnance.

"She carries forty guns total. In her main battery, we have sixteen twelve-pounders and twelve six-pounders. Her fo'c'sle has two six-pounders, and her q-deck, four. On her lower deck, toward the stern, you'll note the captain has had six gun ports cut out, three on each side. They're for eighteen-pounders, should they ever be delivered."

"You can't get them?" Agreen asked, curiously. "Why is that? Has the French navy no guns t' spare?"

"No. Not officially, at least. There are foundries nearby, at Nantes and Périgueux, but the folks seem more inclined to serve the navy. By hook or crook we've managed to secure the other guns we need."

"Why?" Agreen persisted. "It makes no sense, given what King Louis has spent outfittin' her."

"I agree," Dale said. "But beneath the surface, I suspect there's a good explanation for what's going on." He spoke confidentially. "Since you both know the captain better than I do, you perhaps will not be surprised to learn that he is having—how shall I put it?—a dalliance with the wife of the man responsible for procuring guns for French warships. And therefore, the guns for us."

Richard was in the midst of a mental calculation. From what Dale had told them, a broadside from *Bonhomme Richard* could hurl more than two hundred pounds of metal at the enemy, or four times *Ranger's* capability. Impressive as that was, it was child's play compared to the havoc a hundred-gun First Rate could wreak. Dale's last sentence sliced through his musings.

"Monsieur Chaumont?" he asked incredulously. "Is he the man you're talking about?"

"You know him? Yes, of course you would. You were in Passy with the captain, were you not?"

"Do I understand you correctly?" Richard asked in awe. "Are you saying that the captain has had an affair with Chaumont's wife?" He vividly recalled the indignation with which she had complained to Dr. Franklin last winter about the captain's advances toward her.

"*Is* having one, is more like it," Dale grinned. "He's been balling her for months. She's the real reason he's leaving for Paris. And from what I understand, she's the one insisting on it. It appears the society hen has taken a sudden romantic interest in the famous, all-conquering rooster." He spoke even more confidentially. "Between us, I suspect the *real* reason Chaumont is loath to give the captain what he wants for his ship is that the captain is giving his wife what she wants in her bed."

At the quay, a clinker-built ship's boat was gliding up alongside, its eight oar blades tossed to the vertical in one precise motion. At the tiller, a young man serving as coxswain saluted the two lieutenants. "Ship's boat as requested, sir," he said, his crisp military voice in keeping with a sharp naval appearance in spotless white breeches and smooth blue coat with a half-white, half-blue stand-up collar. Richard and Agreen felt glaringly out of place in their rumpled civilian clothing.

"Thank you, Mr. Fanning," Dale said, returning the salute. "We shall return to the ship at once with these two gentlemen. They served as midshipmen with the captain aboard *Ranger*. Mr. Cutler, Mr. Crabtree, meet Midshipman Nathaniel Fanning."

They exchanged handshakes and settled into the sternsheets. Fanning ordered the tender cast off and oars to give way. During the brief row over, Richard turned his attention to the ship, noting right away the three empty gun ports cut out close to the waterline near the stern that Dale had mentioned. As the tender pulled nearer, he noticed more and more how much this grande dame was showing her age, much like the way a country mansion may appear splendid from a distance but on closer inspection reveals years of neglect. *Bonhomme Richard* may be comparable to a Fourth Rate, Richard concluded, perhaps even a Third Rate. While the shipwrights may have done a commendable job of modifying her, at her core she looked every bit to be a slow and cumbersome merchantman. His sea instincts warned him that when it came to battle, she could not be relied upon for agility.

As the tender passed astern of the ship and to her larboard side, Richard's eyes took in the precision carvings in the mulatto-colored teak about her stern and taffrail, as well as the magnificent glass in her six square stern windows. The same diamond patterns of translucent opal glass graced the quarter galleries that wrapped around from the stern and bulged out from the ship's after sides like two giant tortoise shells. Midway down the stern, beneath a wooden balcony supporting a golden balustrade, the words BONHOMME RICHARD had been freshly gilded in stylish lettering.

A head peered over the poop deck railing by the ensign staff.

"Boat ahoy!"

"Aye, aye," Midshipman Fanning called up, signifying that an officer was on board the approaching boat. "Starboard side, toss oars," he commanded moments before the small boat bumped gently alongside the black hull of the mother ship. A bowman hooked on to the mainmast stays and, after handing the gaff to the foremost larboard oarsman, tied the gig's painter onto hardware bolted into the chain-wale platform. Secured, the tender bobbed alongside the built-in steps leading up to the entry port.

Richard Dale was first to go up, followed by Lunt, Agreen and Richard. Above, at the entry-way, a quickly assembled party of side-boys greeted them with salutes. Dale returned the salutes and saluted the quarterdeck before summoning the officer of the watch.

"Mr. Grombe," he said to the midshipman, "please give my respects to the captain and advise him that we have visitors aboard anxious to see him. I shall—" Dale stopped when he spotted the captain astern, coming their way. Jones was clad impeccably in full dress uniform of blue coat and white breeches and waistcoat, with a fringed gold-laced epaulet on each shoulder and gold trim outlining the entirety of his coat, including its button holes. His neckstock was of a rich material, and on his head he wore a large bicorne felt hat, a multicolored insignia of flag rank attached to the flat front above his forehead. He was ambling slowly toward the entry port with his hands clasped at the small of his back. As he approached, he glanced to his right and left and up and down the rigging, as though out for nothing more than a casual inspection of the weather deck. As he drew nearer, Richard discerned what looked like a glint of humor in the captain's eyes.

"Well, well," Jones said, stopping short before them and raising his eyebrows in mock wonder. "I do declare it is Mr. Cutler and Mr. Crabtree, come to pay us a visit. How very decent of you two gentlemen. We had assumed you so preferred the comforts of England that we would not again have the pleasure of your company until after the war is over."

Richard stood rigid, staring straight ahead. "Had not Mr. Crabtree snatched me from the lap of luxury, Captain," he said, "that would undoubtedly have been the case."

"Quite? Well, once again I see I am in Mr. Crabtree's debt. Pray, lads, will you come below for a glass of port? Mr. Dale, Mr. Lunt, please join us."

The captain's great cabin was of the type Richard had seen before, aboard HMS *Formidable* in Plymouth Harbor. Except that this space was larger, with greater areas of glass in the stern and quarter galleries, and with considerably more teakwork. Its furnishings, if anything, were even more elegant and commodious than those aboard the British cruiser. The brightly polished dining table and chairs in the starboard quarter gallery may not have been Chippendale by design, but they were, nonetheless, the kind of furniture one would expect to find in a fashionable chateau along the river Loire. As were the sandlewood desk, sideboard, and deep red leather arm chairs in the main cabin. Underfoot, the deck had been veneered with parquet, and in the middle of the cabin, under a long, narrow table of intricate carvings, was a plush oriental rug depicting ornate floral patterns. Oil paintings of pastoral French seascapes adorned the main cabin and private dining alcove and the captain's sleeping quarters on the larboard side astern.

"What do you think?" Jones inquired as he pondered the possibilities of ports and clarets arranged in expensive cut-glass crystal containers atop the Louis XIV sideboard. He made his selection and poured out the deep red liquid into five glasses. "A far cry from *Ranger,* what?"

"Indeed she is, sir," Richard agreed. "And I would be pleased to learn more about *Ranger,* when the time is appropriate."

"Right now is appropriate. But first, sirs, to your health. Welcome aboard." He clinked his glass against theirs and sampled the port wine. It was one of the few times Richard could recall the captain accepting any type of alcoholic beverage when not required by protocol to do so. He and the others joined in, drinking heartily.

"There is only so much I can tell you about *Ranger,*" Jones continued, his tone insinuating he did not care to dwell long on the subject. "Lieutenant Simpson sailed her back to Portsmouth in March with most of her remaining officers and crew. I had considered a court-martial, but that procedure requires three captains, and none was available. I did, however, take action against those six men who abandoned you on the beach at Whitehaven. Those traitors, I can assure you, will rot in a French prison.

"As for Simpson, the commissioners and I deemed it best to send him back to America. My orders were to remain in France to take command of a newly built Third Rate. As it turned out, that ship was awarded to the French navy. I was disappointed, to be sure, though I dare say, this ship has proven herself an acceptable alternative, despite what I can only describe as deficient sailing qualities. By the way, Mr. Cutler, her original name was *Duc de Duras*. She was renamed *Bonhomme Richard* not for you, alas, but in honor of our mutual friend, Dr. Franklin. You will recall that 'Poor Richard' was the pen name he used when writing in his almanac. Such an appellation would hardly apply to you."

"It would these days, Captain," Agreen grinned, and Richard nodded his head in agreement.

"Yes, well, sadly that is the case for many of us these days," Jones said, the irony of his words amid the grandeur of his surroundings apparently lost on him. "Tell me, just why *did* you lads come to Lorient?"

Agreen glanced at Richard.

"Captain," Richard said, "we came here to sign on with you as midshipmen. We request the privilege of sailing with you again."

"I see." Jones paused a moment to reflect on those words. When he spoke, it was from the heart. "I must say, gentlemen, that I am both flattered and touched by your loyalty. Any commander would be. Unfortunately I am unable to grant your request. I already have ten midshipmen aboard, a full complement. I don't require more."

Hopeful expressions dissolved.

"We understand, Captain," Richard said, trying his best to appear composed. "Perhaps, in time, there will be another ship you might refer us to."

"However, Mr. Cutler," Jones went on, as though he had not heard that comment, "I *could* use the services of a third lieutenant. The one I had must be replaced. As to a fourth lieutenant, I had not considered the need for one on this cruise, Mr. Crabtree. However, I am persuaded to the contrary by the quality of the man who would hold that position. Mind you, officially you would both be acting lieutenants, serving without benefit of formal commissions. I credit, however, that your commissions will be approved by Congress if those eminences ever stop running from the British long enough to sign them. Is such an arrangement satisfactory?"

"Yes sir!" they replied.

"Capital. Mr. Lunt will see to the paperwork, your cabins, and other arrangements. Welcome aboard, gentlemen, this time in an official capacity." He consulted his watch. "And your timing is fortuitous. In three hours, at six bells, commissioned officers are assembling in this cabin. Mr. Adams will be present, as will a number of other individuals, one of whom in particular I believe you will find quite intriguing. In the meantime, go ashore and get yourselves properly uniformed. I can recommend a tailor every bit as good as Gieves and Hawkes in London, and I can advance you funds if necessary. Before you go, Mr. Cutler, I require a word with you in private."

Agreen saluted and departed the after cabin.

"By God, sir, it is good to see you again," Jones said to Richard, his sentiments unmasked with the click of the door being closed. "Please, sit down. Let me pour you another round." He refilled Richard's glass and brought it over to the upholstered armchairs. Richard received it with a nod of gratitude. "I thought for certain that you and Mr. Crabtree had died on that beach. Imagine my relief when I was informed to the contrary. Imagine the joy of others in Passy."

"Thank you, Captain. It is good to see you as well. And thank you for the honor of rank you have bestowed on me and Mr. Crabtree."

Jones brushed that off.

"It's the least I can do. And I am not being kindhearted. You have earned your rank, as have all my officers. You will find on this ship, Mr. Cutler, that we have a crew of almost four hundred men representing twelve nations. All officers are American and most of them, like you and Mr. Crabtree, have served time in English prisons. That's a good thing, to my mind. I like for an officer to have a chip on his shoulder when sailing into battle. It gives him focus. And this time around I have been able to handpick every one of my officers, from Lieutenant Dale down to the youngest midshipmen. Unfortunately, that is not true of the other ships in my squadron."

"Other ships, sir?"

"Yes, there are four others. It will become clear to you later this afternoon, during the meeting. My reason for speaking with you in the meantime is to inform you that I am leaving on Friday for Passy. I have . . . certain matters to attend to before we sail in July. I am hoping I might once again prevail upon you to serve as my aide-de-camp."

Richard had a sense of what was coming the moment he heard the word *Passy.* He downed a generous swig of port, painfully aware that Jones had just conferred upon him a rare and intensely personal honor.

"I appreciate the offer, Captain," he said. "But from what Mr. Dale has told me, *Bonhomme Richard* is scheduled to begin her shakedown cruise within the week. I submit with respect, and gratitude, that my duty is to remain aboard ship, to participate in that cruise."

"Admirable," said Jones, in a way that suggested he was not at all convinced it was. "I will never fault an officer for doing what he believes is his duty. But these trials are perfunctory, Lieutenant. I already know how this ship performs. I warrant you do as well, having just come aboard. Hell, man, any sailor worth his salt can predict her ways just by *looking* at her. And you will have ample opportunity to see to your duty once we're at sea. We'll be on an extended cruise."

"I understand, sir. Nevertheless, with respect, I request permission to remain aboard."

Jones leaned in toward Richard, his voice conveying astonishment mixed with mild disgust.

"Let's dispense with the formalities, shall we, Richard? Good God, man, have you forgotten who's waiting for you in Passy? *What's* waiting for you there?"

"No sir, I haven't. That's the point."

"*What* bloody point?"

Richard hesitated, debating how much of himself to reveal.

"Captain, may I just say at this time, that I am unable to oblige the lady's feelings for me."

Jones laughed out loud. "Could you possibly loosen up a little, Richard?" he scoffed. "You look like you're about to soil your pants. What is all this? We're both aware of Anne-Marie's feelings for you, and by God you're a damn lucky man to have it so. Isn't that enough? What else is there? Matrimony?"

He meant to use the word in a lighthearted, humorous sense. When

Richard seemed at a loss to respond, Jones leaned back in his chair with a look of mild shock, apparently having drawn a wrong conclusion.

"Richard," he began, in the explanatory tone of a father to his son, "let me give you some advice. I had not realized you had come to this point with Anne-Marie. I can assure you that she has not come to this point with you. Nor would she ever."

"I'm afraid I'm not following you, Captain."

"No, I'm quite sure you're not," Jones sighed. He formed a steeple with his fingers beneath his chin and remained that way in silent contemplation before continuing. "Richard, it appears I must be blunt. You are living, I fear, in a fool's paradise. You are aware, are you not, that Anne-Marie is a young woman of noble blood? Her fate, for better or worse, is to marry another of her social status, I would wager someone here in France, a viscount or marquis perhaps, of which, I can assure you, there are many straining at the bit to pay court to her. A woman like Anne-Marie would never consider marrying a man like you. Whatever else about you she might admire, or find attractive, you, sir, lack an inherited title. As a suitor, therefore, you are disqualified, ineligible. As I was in my youth, merely because I lacked the social standing that comes with noble birth. Anne-Marie may have given you her heart, but under no circumstances would she give you her hand. Do you understand what I am telling you?"

"I believe so, Captain," Richard said, after a moment of his own. "May I ask a question I fear will sound naive? When does love enter the equation for a woman such as Anne-Marie?"

"For Anne-Marie, it already has."

"And yet she would marry another?"

"Now you *do* sound naive, Mr. Cutler, upon my word. In a marriage of nobility, love rarely is a factor. A woman like Anne-Marie must marry someone of her own class, and may, at the same time, carry on a relationship with another man—or men—for years. Her husband will almost certainly be doing the same sort of thing. Don't be shocked. Believe me, it's the rule more than the exception." He regarded Richard not unsympathetically. "So, bearing that in mind, I ask once again: will you accompany me to Paris? This is an invitation, not an order."

Richard shook his head.

"Thank you, Captain, but again I respectfully decline. For personal reasons."

"Personal reasons?" Jones asked, bewildered. "Another woman, perhaps?"

"Perhaps."

"Must be one *hell* of a woman."

Jones arose from the chair, went to his desk and began rummaging through some papers. "Very well, Mr. Cutler," he said, his voice all business. "You shall remain in Lorient and assist Mr. Dale in the sea trials. I shall ask Midshipman Grombe to accompany me in your stead. Be back in this cabin at six bells. And Mr. Cutler," he added, not looking up, "if you are determined to end your relationship with the lady, I strongly advise you to tell her that. I am prepared to act on your behalf in Passy, should you so desire."

"Aye, aye, sir. Thank you, sir."

"And please dine with me tonight, you and Mr. Crabtree. I look forward to learning more about your . . . affairs in England."

At 2:45 that afternoon a flotilla of small boats began arriving alongside *Bonhomme Richard*. John Adams was first to be welcomed aboard. He was greeted at the entry port with a shriek of pipes and a roll of drums and by a side party smartly dressed in loose-fitting white duck trousers, blue frocks with open collar, red neckerchiefs, and yellow straw hats encircled with a blue ribbon above the brim. He was immediately followed by a man clearly of lofty pedigree and wearing, in addition to a raised black felt hat sprouting a monstrous white plume, a blue dress coat with the epaulets and trappings of a senior military officer. After him came four French sea officers, one behind the other, dressed in identical, nearly all-white uniforms.

In the after cabin, Captain Jones made the introductions on behalf of the new arrivals, all of whom, except for John Adams, were chatting amicably in French.

"Gentlemen, may I introduce you to Mr. Richard Cutler, my new third lieutenant, and Mr. Agreen Crabtree, acting fourth lieutenant. Mr. Cutler, Mr. Crabtree, I believe you have met Mr. Adams and Captain Landais. This is Captain Denis-Nicolas Cottineau of *Pallas*, frigate, twenty-six guns; Lieutenant Philippe-Nicolas Ricot, captain of *Vengeance*, brig, twelve guns; and Ensigne de Vasseau of *Cerf*, corsair, eighteen guns. These men hold commissions in the Continental Navy and command the four other ships in my squadron. This last gentleman I shall ask to introduce himself. The full treatment, if you please, *mon général*."

The man wearing the blue officer's coat was above average height with the graceful, sinewy build of a young man of twenty years in prime physical condition. His head was oval shaped and his facial features gentle, yet suggestive of someone with a highly inquisitive nature who would not easily tolerate incompetence or frivolity, and who was not in the least self-conscious about his appearance or his lofty rank. His hair was long and brown and pulled back straight in a perfectly plaited queue extending halfway down his back.

He stepped up with a flourish. In what was no doubt choreography well rehearsed since childhood, he doffed his plumed hat and placed his left leg forward. He bowed low before the two young Americans, keeping his right hand over his heart as he swept his hat out from his left side, raising it high above his bent-over torso.

"*Bonjour, messieurs,*" he said. "*Je m'appelle Marie Joseph Paul Yves Roch Gilbert du Motier, le marquis de Lafayette.*" When he surfaced, he was smiling at Agreen.

The grandiosity took the young lieutenant aback. "Agreen Crabtree," he said, returning the gesture with an awkward bow. "Pleased t' make your acquaintance."

"And I am Richard Cutler, *Monsieur le marquis,*" Richard said, awed as well by the courtly display, though he had seen it performed many times before. "*Vous parlez anglais, je crois?*

"*Mais oui.* Of course."

"Then may I ask, is that a uniform of the Continental Army you are wearing?"

"*Oui, monsieur. Je suis* . . . I am a major general in the army of His Excellency, General George Washington. It is the title of which I am most proud."

"Richard," Agreen whispered into his friend's ear as they were settling in for the start of the meeting, "that fellow's no older'n we are. A frickin' major general?"

"I've heard of him," Richard whispered back. "His wife is related to King Louis."

"Ah."

"Gentlemen, welcome," Jones intoned, standing at the foot of the table. "Please make yourselves comfortable. We have much to discuss. I shall speak slowly for the benefit of our French allies. If any of you does not understand what I am saying, please raise your hand. Several of us Americans speak French, and several of you French, *le marquis* for example, speak better English than most Americans. So we should have no trouble understanding one another.

"To the first item of business, as most of you know, Spain has finally declared war on England. Within the week, the Bourbon fleets will begin joint naval maneuvers off Cape Finisterre. Admiral Comte d'Orvilliers has overall command of the fleet. You should know that this alliance between France and Spain does not extend to America. Spain has decided, at least for now, not to recognize American independence."

"*Quels poltrons, les Espagnols,*" Pierre Landais muttered, his observation setting off a titter of laughter among the other French sea captains. Adams cleared his throat loudly, the tittering ceased, and Jones continued.

"Second item: our orders have changed. We will not be attacking Liverpool, as we had assumed. It appears the English have caught wind of our intentions and have reinforced their defenses there. In addition, the Marquis will not be joining us. He is returning to America in *Alliance* to rejoin General Washington's army. Questions so far? Does everyone understand what I just said?

"Good. To continue, when Captain Landais returns to France in July, *Alliance* will join our squadron and we shall set sail. Our destination is the North Sea by way of Ireland and Scotland. Our objective is to cause so much mayhem and chaos along the way that the Royal Navy is forced to give chase, thus drawing ships away from the Channel Fleet and the allied invasion force."

"A wise strategy," the marquis cut in enthusiastically. He spoke to Richard and Agreen, his views on the subject apparently expressed on previous occasions to the others in the cabin. "I approve and I am certain His Excellency would approve as well. You put terror in the minds of *citoyens* . . . citizens . . . and you can use these citizens for your own purposes. They demand their government do something and the government must . . . *apaiser,* um, appease their fears, even if they are then at a disadvantage with the enemy. You comprehend? The British are doing this in America, in your South. *Chef d'escadre* Jones, you did this at Whitehaven, with excellent results."

"Thank you, General," Jones said, clearly pleased to be addressed as *commodore* even though it was a courtesy rank only. "You may assure His Excellency, when you see him, that we shall ensure an encore performance."

"Captain," Richard asked, "what about the invasion? Do we know what the Bourbons intend?"

"I was coming to that, Mr. Cutler. Yes, we do know their plan. They will sail for England with a substantial fleet sometime between late July and early August. D'Orvilliers will, we trust, neutralize the Channel Fleet and land on the Isle of Wight with heavy artillery to bombard the British naval base at Spithead. With that base out of action, the French will ferry over an army of forty thousand from St. Malô. Their destination will be Portsmouth. From there, they will proceed north to link up with—I say, Mr. Cutler, are you quite all right? You look rather pale, of a sudden."

"Sorry, sir. Must be something I ate. Please, continue."

"I was about to say, link up with an Irish army advancing from the west. Whether or not the Irish actually fight is, fortunately, not critical to the outcome. With a sizable and well-equipped French army marching toward London, with the Channel Fleet gone, and with most of the British army and navy overseas, England will have no choice but to sue for peace. And then, gentlemen, the war will be over."

Murmurs of excited agreement spread about the cabin.

"Captain," Agreen asked, "what about the war in America? Is anything happenin' there that might affect this plan?"

Jones deferred the question to Adams.

"There's not much news from America, Mr. Crabtree," Adams said. "We received dispatches from Congress a week ago. To our knowledge, there have been no major battles in recent weeks. Washington's army remains camped in White Plains, north of New York. He has sent two of his best generals to the South, which is where we believe the British are planning their next offensive. The British have apparently convinced themselves that there are thousands of loyalists in the Carolinas and Georgia eager to join their banner. With a British army on the march under the command of General Cornwallis, the time seems right, from their perspective."

"How convinced are you, Monsieur Adams," Lafayette asked, "of the strength of these so-called loyalists?"

Adams shrugged.

"Many of them, General, are nothing more than backwoods Scots. Their loyalty is to their family and friends, not to King George. Personally, I am pleased that the British high command believes what it does. Their so-called southern strategy splits their army in two and allows General Washington to deploy the same tactics that the Roman general Fabius Cuncator used against Hannibal. As you recall from your history lessons, Fabius prevailed against the numerically superior Carthaginians because he never exposed his army to a pitched battle, and thus a catastrophic defeat. It seems that His Excellency has learned two of history's most valuable lessons: that in times of crisis, patience can be a virtue, and what goes hand in hand with that, the best way to win a war is not to lose it."

With the principal points covered, further discussions focused on the details of the upcoming shakedown cruise in the Bay of Biscay. Captain Jones would participate only during the latter part of that cruise. He was departing for Paris at the same time *Alliance* was departing for Boston, and he would be accompanied by Midshipman Beaumont Grombe, a pleasant young man from Newburyport, Massachusetts, who had a working knowledge of French. The meeting was adjourned shortly before a supper of creamed cod and fresh vegetables was served in the dining alcove of the great cabin. Richard ate little and said even less, although Lafayette and John Adams kept the conversation continuous and interesting.

☆ ☆ ☆

"You're thinkin'" about what Captain Jones said about the invasion, aren't you," Agreen probed early the next morning, a dawn that found Richard as withdrawn into himself as he had been the previous evening. They were in the bowels of *Bonhomme Richard,* exploring the nooks and crannies of the orlop deck where lingering scents of tea and cloves recalled her days as an East India merchantman.

"I am, Agee. I never thought I would be saying this, but the Royal Navy *must* stop the Bourbon fleet. We can win this war without French and Irish soldiers rampaging across England."

"Especially across southern England," Agreen finished the thought for him. "But you needn't worry, Richard. Your family is in no danger. Neither is Katherine. Fareham has no military value, so why would the French bother with it? Besides, from what you've told me about Katherine's father, the French army will give him a wide berth on their march t' London. Nothin' else makes sense."

"There is that," Richard conceded, though his silence on the subject in the hours, days, and weeks that followed confirmed that, try as he may, he could not quite convince himself that, yes, there was that.

II

THE NORTH SEA

September 1779

RICHARD AWOKE THAT MORNING as he had every morning since their departure from Lorient, not with a gentle shake on his shoulder or the hum of a ship coming to life, but with the unpleasant feel of sweat running in haphazard patterns across his face and of salt stinging his eyes. As if by rote, he reached for the towel he kept at his bedside. Folding the damp fabric, he settled it over his brow and forced himself to lie perfectly still. It was to no avail. Tiny beads of water sprouted up like minuscule springs through the pores of his skin, merged forces, and fanned out anew in an unrelenting assault.

Cursing under his breath, Richard stripped the towel away and hurled it across the seven-foot width of his cabin, where it hit the hard canvas wall with a dull thwack. Yielding to the inevitable, he swung his legs over the edge of the bunk and sat there, rubbing his temples and running his fingers through his shoulder-length blond hair. Slowly, a subtle consciousness began to take hold. He opened a tinderbox and combined flint, steel, and tinder to light a candle on a sea chest serving double duty as a bedside table. He checked his watch: 2:45. An hour before he was required on deck. Forty-five minutes before a cabin boy assigned to the lieutenants' quarters on the lower deck would slip into his cabin to awaken him.

He rose to his feet. Swinging his arms back and forth to get his blood flowing, he padded over to a pewter bowl half filled with tepid water. He dipped his hands into the bowl, then splashed water onto his face. After a quick shave using soap as lather, he pulled on a pair of white cotton knee-high stockings, white breeches, and an off-white linen shirt, its three buttons open at the neck and its cuffs already rolled up to the elbow. In this stultifying humidity, Captain Jones forgave even himself the neckstock, waistcoat, and dress coat normally required of a naval officer.

Rubbing his eyes with the thumb and index finger, he opened the cabin door and stepped out onto the gun deck, colliding as he did so with the chief gunner.

"Sorry, sir, so very sorry indeed," Henry Sawyer gushed, stepping back deferentially and knuckling his forehead. "I didn't expect you up and about so early, sir. Upon me honor I didn't."

The jolt brought Richard fully awake. "No need to apologize, Sawyer," he assured him. "The fault is mine. I didn't expect to be up so early myself. It's hard to sleep in this godforsaken weather."

"Aye, sir, it is," Sawyer said, much relieved. "It's bad enough up on deck. Down here there's nary a breath of air, sir. Opening the ports don't 'elp much, I don't care 'ow cold the seawater is. I'm 'ardly moving and look at me. It's loike some churl threw a bucket of water over me 'ead." He demonstrated his point by peeling the front of his soaked cotton shirt away from his skin. "Never seen the loike 'round 'ere, sir. You'd think we was in the Indies."

"Or some place like it," Richard agreed. He respected Sawyer. After six years in the Royal Navy as a gunner's mate, Sawyer had been swept up in the passion of the American Revolution. Having no family in England except for what he termed a "bitch of a mum, most o' the time stinkin' o' gin an' ruttin' with damn near anyone wearing breeches," he had come over to the American side and *Bonhomme Richard,* bringing with him a troop of like-minded British tars. He was a first-rate gunner, his career as a petty officer assured in any man's navy, did he believe that was his calling. But he did not. A fisherman's life was his dream. After the war, Sawyer told his mates, he would swallow the anchor and put in a stake somewhere along the basin of the Choptank River in Maryland, "a place I 'ear tell where a man can settle down an' raise him a family, an' where the crabs run as thick as London 'ores near me 'ome in Wapping."

In the dim light of lanterns hanging from the deckhead, Richard could make out the forms of three cannon, eighteen-pounders, the largest guns, it was claimed, on any Continental ship. He could not see the three other eighteens directly across on the larboard side. Erected in the middle of the lower gun deck aft were makeshift officers' cabins that created, in effect, two separate batteries.

"What do you make of these?" Richard asked. It was a question he had asked himself many times since the big guns had finally been hoisted aboard. When Jones returned from Passy three weeks earlier to discover that the big guns had not been delivered, he had exploded with such outrage, it was claimed, that even the royal couple in Versailles had felt its tremor. As a result, King Louis had moved Monsieur Chamont into swift action.

"Don't roightly know, sor," Sawyer confessed, giving the guns his professional once-over. "They're old, that's for damn sure, and you can see fer yourself they 'aven't been kept up in any decent sort o' way. The Frog navy don't want 'em, and you 'ave to ask yourself why. Captain's roight not to fire 'em during gun drills. We may need 'em in a fight, and I doubt those old barrels 'ave many shots left."

"Perhaps," Richard said, "though with any kind of sea running we won't be able to use them at all. To my mind, their ports were cut too close to the waterline."

"Can't argue with that, sor. 'Course, we can't do nuthin' 'bout it now. So I guess we'll just 'ave to 'ope for loight winds, won't we, sir?" He gave Richard a weak grin.

Richard tapped the side of his head with a finger. "Think steady winds, Sawyer," he said. "Cool, steady winds to fill our sails and clear out this godforsaken gunk. Think you can manage that?"

"I'll try me best, sir," Sawyer promised.

Richard climbed up a ladder, through a hatchway, and on to the main gun deck. He returned the crisp salute of the French marine sentry guarding the door to the captain's cabin and watched as men in various stages of consciousness and dress began making their way up from forward hatchways to their assigned stations beside the guns. *Bonhomme Richard*'s crew was indeed international in pedigree, as Jones had indicated. Americans and English comprised the majority, with a liberal sprinkling of Irish, Scots, Swedes, and Norwegians, along with four Portuguese, two Malays, and an Italian: men motivated by principle or prize money or perhaps a narrow escape from the arms of the law or those of an erstwhile lover come fertile with child. Also on

board, more than a hundred French marines, three times the normal complement for a ship this size, most of them crammed into quarters amidships on
the lower deck between the crew's hammocks in the forecastle and officers'
bunks astern. So great was their number that fully a third of them was forced
farther below onto the orlop deck to scrounge whatever free space they could
find forward of the midshipmen's berth. The mere thought of conditions on
that lowest deck was enough to convince Richard that, of all the privileges of
rank, having his own cabin, however dank and cramped it might be, was the
one he valued most.

It was 3:45. On the quarterdeck he was met by Nathaniel Fanning and,
on duty by the binnacle, the sailing master, Samuel Stacey, a grizzled old seaman who reminded Richard, every time he saw him, of David Callum. The
two ships' masters had physical attributes in common, though to Richard's
mind Stacey lacked the tact and unassuming nature that made Callum so effective a senior warrant officer.

Stacey had little to do this morning. *Richard* was making scant headway in
the fluky wind. Her listless square sails sucked in what anemic breezes there
were, then forced them out with a loud thwump as the ship rolled in the oily
seas. Directly above him, the fore-and-aft spanker was sheeted in to prevent
its lateen spar from swinging. Blocks aloft creaked forlornly as ropes passed
back and forth through them, the wind too feeble to give them purpose.
Above, the moonless night was as black as *Richard's* hull.

"Good morning, Mr. Fanning," Richard greeted the senior midshipman
and current officer of the watch. "All is well?"

"No sir," Fanning informed him. "I must report that *Alliance* appears to be
gone. Mr. Mayrant concurs," referring to the midshipman serving as junior officer of the watch.

"What do you mean, 'gone'?"

"Parted company, sir. Near as I can determine, it must have been sometime during the past two or three hours. I counted the beacons at four bells.
When I counted them again at five bells, and at six, three were missing. I
could tell it was *Alliance* by the distance between the masts."

Instinctively Richard glanced up to where three beacons, one hanging at
each of the flagship's mastheads, glowed as night recognition signals to the
other ships in the squadron. Each ship out there shone three in reply. "Is there
fog ashore?" he asked.

"Yes sir, there is," Fanning informed him, "and that's what I assumed at first, that *Alliance* was swallowed in fog. But it's a wispy, early-morning type of ground fog, hardly thick enough to conceal the lights on a ship. *Alliance* must have doused hers. And, sir, there's something else. See those lights over there?" He pointed eastward. "That's the coast of Ireland. It's three miles away. We can make out those lights clear enough."

"Which brings up a more serious problem," Stacey gruffly chimed in. "See that brightest light ashore? Yes, that one. It ain't on the charts, but I figure it's got to be a navigational device of some sort. Trouble is, it ain't movin', relative to us. It's been on the same compass bearing for the entire second watch. And it's gettin' brighter."

"What are you suggesting, Mr. Stacey? That we're in some sort of current taking us ashore?"

"I'm more than suggesting, Lieutenant."

Richard detected a hint of sarcasm in Stacey's voice that he did not appreciate.

"Shall I inform the captain?" Fanning asked. "I was waiting until you came on deck, sir. I wanted your opinion."

Richard paused to think. If they were caught in an onshore current, which was certainly possible according to the charts, they would need to take action soon, else they would find themselves perilously close to a lee shore. But as the senior watch officer, barring an emergency or an obvious decision any cabin boy could make, it was his duty to work through his decisions and not rely too readily on the advice of others. He was, after all, the officer who would be held accountable for whatever happened next. And there was the matter of *Alliance*. During the shakedown cruise, Pierre Landais had proven himself time and again the antithesis of a model sea officer, but would he so blatantly disobey the captain's orders? Captain Jones would believe it; his contempt for Landais was exposed more than once. Still, Richard could not. *Alliance* must be somewhere within sight, and dawn, breaking soon, would reveal where.

"Not yet, Mr. Fanning. We'll wait until one bell. If conditions haven't improved by then, we will inform the captain. If there is nothing else, I have the watch. Please send Mr. Mayrant below to locate Mr. Grombe. Tell him he is demanded on deck and . . . belay that. I see him coming aft."

Fanning saluted smartly and pivoted in military fashion as Beaumont Grombe stepped up to the quarterdeck, rubbing sleep from his eyes.

"Good morning, sir," he yawned.

"You're five minutes late, Mr. Grombe," Richard snapped. "I need not remind you that that is unacceptable for an officer of the watch. Were the captain here, he'd have you kissing the gunner's daughter. Be late again, and I'll cane your backside myself. Understand? Now get forward to your duty by the guns. *Walk,* if you please," he called after him.

"Sorry lot, that one," Stacey smirked when the young midshipman was gone. "He'll never make much of a seaman, much less an officer. Too molly-coddled as a child, you ask my opinion."

Richard removed a long glass from the rack by the binnacle and trained it on the Irish shore. "Mr. Stacey," he said, squinting through the glass, "I did not ask for your opinion. While I have great respect for your skills and experience as a ship's master, I would ask you, please, to refrain from offering personal opinions about this ship's officers." He glanced up at a cloud cover as dark and unruffled as the sea. "What do you make of the weather?"

"Storm's brewing," Stacey responded, his tone grudgingly more congenial. "Could be a big 'un by the look of it. Though I'd say it's more likely to be a heavy downpour, then clearing. It'll get the wind up, for certain. Question is, will the storm hit us before we hit Ireland."

"You're convinced we're in a current, then."

"No doubt in my mind, Lieutenant."

"Very well, Mr. Stacey. You're probably right. But before we inform the captain, I'm going aloft to have a look around."

Richard stepped up onto the larboard bulwark, into the mizzen rigging, up to the futtock shrouds below the mizzentop. Lacing an arm in and around the thick hemp cords, he extended the glass to its full length and raised it to his eye.

He scanned the southern horizon first, as was his habit, searching for a tiny speck of white, or better, though fearing he'd see it, a forest of tiny specks that would confirm a fleet under sail. From his vantage point, bearing in mind the curvature of the earth and depending on weather conditions, he should be able to spot a royal more than twenty miles away. Today, as with every day so far during this cruise, the southern horizon held no clues as to the whereabouts of the Bourbon fleet. That the fleet was long overdue in the Channel was an undisputable fact. Whether that fact implied good news or bad, Richard could only speculate.

He swept the glass to his right. *Pallas, Vengeance,* and *Cerf* stood a ways ahead off to larboard under reduced sail to keep pace, more or less, with the slower-moving flagship. The three smaller ships were making respectable headway in the skittish breezes, any onshore currents having less influence on their lighter frames. Richard could not see dead ahead: the sails blocked his view. Unless *Alliance* was there, he would have to concede she was gone.

Richard scanned the horizon eastward, to where the assumed navigational fixture was clearly visible and closer than before. Stacey was right. They *were* in an eastbound current. And the western sky was getting darker. Much darker. He collapsed the glass and made his way quickly down to the quarterdeck.

"Mr. Coran," he called to a midshipman, "please give the captain my respects and inform him he is requested on deck. Mr. Linthwaite," he said to a second midshipman lolling about, "summon the bosun."

With the summons, a broad-shouldered giant of a man hurried up to the quarterdeck. He was dressed informally, his rank signified by a tall black-rimmed felt hat and a silver bosun's whistle at his chest attached to a fancy lanyard of knots and braids hanging from his neck. "Sir?" he inquired, saluting.

"Sway out the boats, Mr. Burbank. And take in all sail to foretops'l, jib, and spanker."

"Should I relieve the men from the guns, sir?"

"Yes. Have everyone not on sail duty standing by to man the boats."

"Aye, aye, sir."

Burbank yelled for his mates. Shrieks of bosun's whistles echoed about the ship as Jones strode up the short flight of built-in steps from the weather deck to the quarterdeck. He had dressed in a hurry: strands of red-tinged brown hair had escaped a hastily formed queue and hung straight down on each side of his face.

"Good morning, Mr. Cutler," he said, buttoning up his shirt. "Is there a problem?"

"Good morning, Captain," Richard greeted him. He told him of his two immediate concerns—the current and the gathering storm—and what steps he had taken in response. Jones studied the sky and the distant shore as Richard spoke.

"Very well, Mr. Cutler. I approve of your actions. Is there anything else?"

"Yes sir. *Alliance* has left the squadron."

Jones's reaction was less than what Richard had anticipated.

"Bastard," Jones said under his breath. "That son-of-a-bitch Frog no doubt has gone after prizes for his own account. So be it. We're better off without him." In a louder, more authoritative voice: "Order the boats lowered, Mr. Cutler. If they can't pull us out of this blasted current, they can at least keep us from drifting in farther."

Richard strode to the quarterdeck railing amidships and signaled to the bosun to lower two of the three ship's boats, one on either side of the vessel. Eleven men scrambled over the starboard side and down into the jolly boat. Seventeen others took positions in the launch, the coxswain at the tiller and sixteen at the oars. Each boat had attached to its stern a five-inch-thick hawser, the other end bent to the ship's bows. At the coxswains' commands, men in both boats strained on the oars. Slowly, ever so slowly, *Richard's* bow turned northward.

Lightning flashing in the far western sky followed by ear-splitting cracks of thunder added to the confusion of what happened next. From *Richard's* bow a sailor yelled out in warning. Then came the cries of other men in the bows and the curses and splashes of men being heaved overboard.

"What the devil?" Lieutenant Dale exclaimed, just on deck.

"Bosun, report!" Richard shouted through a speaking trumpet.

Burbank came running aft. "They've cut the cable on the launch, sir!" he cried in disbelief. "And they've thrown the coxswain and t'others over the side! They're makin' for shore!"

"Who?" Dale demanded to know.

"Fucking Irishmen," Jones spat. "With a hankering for home."

"Shall I signal *Cerf* to give chase, sir? She's closest in."

"Yes, do, Mr. Cutler, though I doubt it'll do much good in this wind. Get my gig over the side. Americans at the oars, if you please."

The light, narrow gig had taken the strain on the hawser rope and was dragging *Richard* northward along with the jolly boat when the storm raged in with a speed and violence no one had anticipated. Big round droplets of water spawned tiny volcanic eruptions as heavy rain began punching the glassy sea to westward.

"Get those boat crews back on board!" Richard shouted to Bosun Burbank through the trumpet. "Lines over the side to larboard! Roundly now, men! Leave the boats! We'll retrieve them later!"

Sailors heaved out hempen lines to windward as the jolly boat and gig hurried back to the mother ship. In as rapid a sequence as possible, oarsmen grabbed hold of the lines and clambered up the side of the hull as if they were scaling a fortress wall, exploiting the slight leeward list of the ship in the strengthening wind to claw their way up. The last few had barely scrambled over the bulwarks when the full fury of the storm struck with a vengeance.

It was a screaming gale, pounding *Bonhomme Richard* with such rage her massive oak bulk heeled sharply to starboard, spilling men on deck and capsizing the empty boats. Cursing and stumbling, sailors fought their way to sheets and braces to ease the strain on the top-hamper. Gradually the ship righted herself, her heavy canvas flailing and thundering as her crew wrestled the unruly beasts into submission. Miraculously, none of the crew was killed or maimed, save for a captain of the top named Hanson whose foot slipped off a supporting rope just before his hands slid off the slick canvas in a last desperate attempt to save himself. He plummeted into the sea, his head bobbing up on a high wave, down into a trough. When the wave rose again, he was nowhere to be seen, a life extinguished in a matter of seconds. Men watching in horror from the yards barely had time to cross themselves before resuming their backbreaking work with the sails.

Within a half hour the storm had blown eastward, and a sense of order was gradually restored. Above- and belowdecks, topmen conversed quietly among themselves about the mate they had lost as the ships of the squadron stood off and on the Irish coast, waiting for *Cerf* to rejoin them. Evening fell without a trace of her.

"Are we to remain here till morning, Dick?" Cutting Lunt asked in the informal address the lieutenants used when they were alone with each other. Though it was the blackest of nights, Jones had ordered lookouts to remain aloft at their posts. In addition, the four lieutenants continued to search the sea to the east for three lanterns sailing toward them.

"No," Dale replied with finality. "We'll sail north once the captain has finished his supper. Something has happened to *Cerf*. What, we may never know."

"You got t' figure she's either been taken," Agreen commented, "or wrecked in the storm. Else we'd've seen her by now. We're in too close for her t' be lost. An' the Brits must know we're here."

"There's always Cape Wrath," Richard said, with a note of resignation. He was referring to the area off the northwestern tip of Scotland that was the designated rendezvous point in the likely event a ship became separated from the squadron during the long cruise north. It was as far away as one could get in the British Isles from Portsmouth.

But *Cerf* was nowhere to be seen at Cape Wrath when *Bonhomme Richard* and *Vengeance* arrived there on the first day of September, though *Alliance* was anchored in the bay and *Pallas* sailed in a day later with two prizes in tow: English brigs laden with canvas and fine cloth and hogsheads of rum. The squadron would requisition ten barrels, Jones informed Captain Cottineau—four for the flagship and two barrels each for the other ships—before Cottineau appointed a skeleton crew to sail the brigs to prize agents in France. As for Pierre Landais, Jones did not ask where he had been, nor did he extend the normal courtesy of inviting him aboard the flagship for dinner. He communicated with Landais through messages dictated to his clerk and delivered to *Alliance* by a midshipman in a ship's boat, a modus operandi Landais found insulting in the extreme. He expressed his displeasure in hand-delivered messages of his own to the commodore.

The squadron did not tarry long off Cape Wrath, a quiet, brooding place of picturesque sand dunes and heather-clad moorlands that seemed, to Richard, to belie its name. From there they sailed east to the Orkneys, then southeast through Pentland Firth, between Pentland Skerries and Duncansby Head, and into the North Sea. Their destination: the port of Leith on the south shore of the Firth of Forth and nominally under the protection of Edinburgh Castle, a massive stone fortress perched high upon volcanic rock that had once served as the seat of Scottish kings. Though it overlooked the firth, its great guns, Jones knew, could not be trained to seaward; thus they could not prevent Jones from doing to Leith what he had done to Whitehaven. What did prevent him was an unrelenting west wind that kept the squadron at bay for three days, finally forcing Jones to bear off southward in search of more accessible prey. Which Jones maintained should be Newcastle-on-Tyne, in Northumberland. A successful assault there, he argued to his squadron leaders, would disrupt London's coal supply and create havoc among consumers there. The French captains disagreed, arguing that since Newcastle was so obvious a target, the city and its environs would likely be heavily defended.

Jones did not press the point, so the squadron continued sailing southward along the Scottish coastline into English waters, with Jones weighing his opportunities. Not yet satisfied with his successes at sea, he was delighted with what he observed on land. Clearly the British people were aware of his reputation. Wherever the squadron brushed close to shore with American colors flying, local citizens made a dash for their homes or to a fortification if one happened to be nearby. Not since the raids of the Vikings, Jones boasted to his officers, were the British people so terrified of foreign vessels off their coast. Which begged the question, Where was the Royal Navy? Why had they not spotted a single British warship since they left Lorient? The answer was unknown to the Americans, and it was unknown to an English pilot venturing out to *Bonhomme Richard* in a small pilot cutter. He had assumed the ship was British since at that moment she was flying the red ensign; he assumed further that her captain required assistance, for a fee, in guiding his vessels into a Yorkshire port, Hull perhaps, located a short ways up the shoal-laden Humber River. He was welcomed aboard, then seized by a bosun's mate and strong-armed over to Jones, who drilled him on recent British naval activity in the area.

"Cap'm, I ken tell y' naught, upon me honor I kent," the man whimpered, his large owlish eyes blinking in agony as the cutter he had come out in beat a hasty retreat toward shore. "I 'aven't seen a British warship in weeks, I swear upon me mother's grave I 'aven't."

"Is it because of the invasion?" Richard demanded to know, once Jones had had his fill of the man. "What news from Portsmouth?"

The pilot's pitiful expression went to Richard. Nervously he twisted the felt material of his tricorne hat in his hands. "Invasion, sir? Portsmouth?" He appeared utterly baffled.

"Yes, damn it, man! France and Spain. The invasion fleet. Have they landed?"

The pilot shrugged and shook his head in the same motion. "Dunno a thing 'bout an invasion, sir," he said respectfully. Then, with a flash of understanding, "A fortnight past there was Frog ships in the Channel, sir. I ken tell y' that. An' they had the Dons with 'em, one 'ell-fire number o' ships. Some say t'was sixty. Others say t'was more like a 'undred. I dunno fer certain, sir. I wasn't there, and I kent read naught but charts. So I'm just tellin' ye what I've 'eard people say."

"Yes, yes, go on," Richard snapped.

"Well, sir, it was like this: Admiral 'ardy, 'e gave 'em a warm reception. A *right* warm reception." The pilot smiled with relaxed pride, caught up, for the moment, in the telling. "Them Frogs didn't make it far up the Channel. When 'ardy gave 'em whot for, they wore 'round fast as kiss me hand and showed us their 'eels, they did! Like whipped pups they ran 'ome, throwin' their dead overboard, 'undreds of 'em, some say thousands. Whot a sight that must've bin! E's a first-rate 'ero, that Admiral 'ardy. I wish I *'ad* bin there, damme!"

Richard's long sigh of relief was so soft it was heard only by Agreen Crabtree standing right next to him. So what if the pilot had embellished the story. The allied threat to England was over.

"Take him away," Jones said.

Two days later Jones was dining in the great cabin with his lieutenants and two other senior officers: Antoine-Felix Wybert—lieutenant colonel of French marines, a man with drooping eyes and spindly legs whose blue military coat with red facings and cuffs seemed deliberately oversized to add bulk and authority to his frame—and James O'Kelly—sublieutenant of Irish Volunteers, a handsome and well-liked young man whose waggish disposition and ease of manner had been severely strained when men under his command had deserted in the launch.

The day was clear and fresh and warm, a soporific sun reinforcing the effects of a red Bordeaux served with dinner. Winds were gentle, far too gentle: *Bonhomme Richard* was close to drifting on a glassy surface where few vestiges of wind beyond the occasional cat's paw pestered the smooth sea, nudging the ship forward with apparitions of waves rippling out from her cutwater. Their position was at approximately fifty-three degrees north latitude, off Flamborough Head, a honeycombed mass of chalk cliffs rising hundreds of feet into the air from thin strips of sand at their base and visible a half league away through the starboard gun ports. Dinner over, Jones had invited his guests to join him in the main cabin for a round of port. A cabin boy had poured out the liquid and distributed the glasses. As he began clearing dishes from the dining table, the officers sipped the sweet dark wine, waiting for Jones to speak and lost for the moment in the privacy of their own thoughts. Suddenly, from high atop the rigging, came a lookout's cry, then a second, then a third, then a fourth.

Dale was up beneath a skylight raised at one end on the deckhead by an iron bar. "Deck there!" he bellowed up to the quarterdeck.

"Fanning here, sir," came the familiar voice.

"Report, Mr. Fanning."

"Ships on the horizon, sir!" Fanning announced, his voice overwrought with excitement. "Standing to the north, northeast. Lookouts report they're hull-down," he added, aware that approximate bearing and range would be the first two pieces of information Dale would want first.

Jones and his lieutenants lost no time in getting to the quarterdeck. Quick glances to the northwest confirmed a clear horizon. "Mr. Cutler," he said, handing Richard his glass. "Light aloft and tell me what you see."

"Aye, aye, Captain."

Richard slung the heavy brass device over his shoulder and stepped down from the quarterdeck to the weather deck, up onto the larboard channel, and into the mainmast shrouds. With determined, uninterrupted motions he climbed up the ratlines. As he came up through the lubber's hole at the main-top, a lookout posted there took the glass from him and offered a hand up. Richard aimed the glass to where the man was pointing. Yes, he could see top-gallants, with a royal mixed in here and there. How many ships, what kind they were, what course they were on, these things he could not determine without a better view. Without a word exchanged with the lookout, he hauled himself out onto the narrower shrouds leading up to the crosstrees at the juncture of the topmast and t'gallant mast. Near the spreaders abaft the crosstrees he braced himself in and readied the glass. He glanced sternward. Lookouts aloft in the other ships also had their glasses trained eastward, none as high up as he. He glanced down. A hundred feet below on a toylike weather deck, clusters of tiny heads craned up, watching him, waiting.

From this height he could determine that the ships, whatever they were, were sailing west toward the coast. There were many, merchant vessels from the look of them. They were on a larboard tack six, maybe seven leagues away. If they and *Richard* were sailing directly toward each other, they would converge in—he lowered the glass, calculating—four hours or so, toward the end of the first dogwatch. But they were not sailing directly toward each other. *Richard* was sailing at an angle to the other ships. Add an hour, two at the most, to his estimate, depending on wind conditions out there. He raised the glass again. The ships were just now coming hull up, to him, though their masts would still be invisible from the deck. Yes, merchantmen. Easy prizes. Fat prizes. The captain would be pleased. He swept the glass back and forth, then paused, focusing the lens on one ship that bore a yellow stripe down the entire length of her hull. Whatever cargo these merchantmen were carrying, it was deemed worthy enough to warrant a Royal Navy escort in waters that were, for the most part, free of enemy cruisers. He had seen enough.

Back on deck, Richard reported on what he had seen. Jones displayed no emotion as he continued scanning eastward.

By the next clang of bells the first set of sails became visible from the quarterdeck, "bearing north-northeast, a half east" Stacey informed Jones. He was stooped over the binnacle, sighting a bearing from *Richard's* compass to the lead vessels.

Jones studied the sails through a glass. "Ease her off a point," he ordered the helmsman. To his first lieutenant: "Make ready the stuns'ls, Mr. Dale. We have to assume the shepherd will take position between us and her flock, while the sheep run for cover to the barn." The "barn" he was referring to was a fort north of them by the coast, a stone fortress of imposing walls well defined in the clear September air despite its distance from Flamborough Head. It was Scarborough Castle, whose great guns, unlike those at Edinburgh, were most definitely trained out to sea. From its highest turret a huge red flag of warning hung listlessly in the light breeze, raised soon after the local pilot was captured. "We need to get farther out, gentlemen, away from these inshore currents in case we're dismasted."

"Make ready the stuns'ls," Dale ordered Agreen Crabtree, officer of the deck, who relayed the order to the bosun, who relayed it to his mates. The shrill of pipes at a practiced cadence directed topmen to lash on the studding-sail booms on the yards aloft and alow on the fore- and mainmasts, to secure the narrow, rectangular sails that added roughly a third more sail area and, perhaps, in these conditions, an extra knot of speed.

"And bring me the pilot," Jones said.

The pilot, his wrists bound behind him, was brought to the quarterdeck. He stood stock-still with eyes cast down until Jones said, "At your ease, man. I have no intention of harming you. I just need some information." He ordered the pilot's wrists freed and handed him the glass. "Out there"—he pointed in the general direction—"is a fleet of merchant vessels coming toward us. My lieutenant estimates forty-five ships. There is at least one escort among them, a frigate we believe. What ships are they?"

The pilot took his time squinting through the glass.

"What ships are they?" Jones asked again, impatience entering his voice.

"That there's the Baltic fleet," the pilot said. "An' yer officer's roight 'bout the number o' ships."

"And the man-o'-war?"

"She'd be *Serapis*, Cap'm. A frigate, aye. An' there'll be another," he volunteered. "She'll be the *Countess of Scarborough*, rated sloop o' war."

"No other escorts?"

"No, Cap'm. Not to my knowledge."

"The frigate, how many guns?"

The pilot shook his head disconsolately. "On me mother's soul I don't know, Cap'm. I've never been aboard 'er. Or *Countess*, for that matter. They're Portsmouth-based. But a frigate her size likely has thirty t' forty guns. As ye know, Cap'm," he quickly added.

"Very well," Jones said, convinced the pilot was telling the truth. He asked him several more questions, then turned to the bosun. "Give this man a tot of rum for his trouble," he instructed. "He's harmless. Just make sure he stays below and out of the way."

Jones ignored the pilot's cries of gratitude and focused on what he could see ahead, turning over in his mind both the choices at his disposal and the likely consequences of implementing each one. His problem was simplified when Richard walked over to him.

"Sir, I know this frigate *Serapis*."

"*You*, Mr. Cutler?"

"Aye, Captain. A young man I befriended in Portsmouth served as midshipman on her for a time. She's rated a forty-four, but carries fifty guns. As I recall from what he told me, she has twenty eighteens on her lower gun deck and smaller guns on her upper deck, nines and sixes, I believe. She is—at least was—commanded by a post captain named Pearson. And she carries the standard complement of marines," he added, meaning one marine per rated gun.

"That is extremely valuable information, Mr. Cutler, thank you," Jones exclaimed. He gave Richard a curious look. "The midshipman you mentioned. You must have endeared yourself to him in a very unusual way. That's not the sort of information one normally shares with an enemy."

Richard grimaced.

"I believe he considered me more his friend than his enemy, Captain."

"Well, whatever the circumstances, thank you for telling me this, Mr. Cutler."

It was approaching midafternoon, and they were nearly three miles off Flamborough Head, sailing north-northeast. From *Richard's* quarterdeck, one could make out tiny flecks of white and spars of black lining the eastern

horizon, the image of ancient Greek warriors advancing in horizontal formation from across a wide expanse, their shields and spears up, poised for
slaughter. Except that these ships, save for two, were unarmed. With what
wind there was alternating between a southerly and westerly direction, those
ships would be sailing close-hauled on an erratic course, intending, Jones
suspected, to get as close in as possible to the Head to capitalize on the split
of the incoming tide at sandbars there known as the Smithies. The pilot had
advised Jones of this phenomenon that allowed a ship to ride a strong south-
bound current, bucking even a moderate wind unless a captain came inshore
north of a massive reef known as Flamborough Steel, in which case he would
be caught up in an equally strong northbound current.

The British naval captains had plied these waters often, Jones assumed,
and no doubt they had spotted his squadron sailing toward them. Most likely
they were aware of Jones's reputation in British waters, and soon they would
detect the red flag atop Scarborough Castle. With possible danger looming,
they would signal the merchantmen to follow the most direct route to the
Steel and the northbound current, a faster route, in these fickle winds, to the
safety of the fort. For their part, *Serapis* and *Countess* could be expected to do
what duty required them to do, whatever the odds.

As *Bonhomme Richard* inched forward, Jones grew increasingly frustrated
by the agonizingly slow pace: a knot, a knot and a half, perhaps two knots
whenever a feeble puff prodded her on. Out there, coming at him at an
equally slow pace, lay his destiny: fame, fortune, and glory were he able to
fight his way through the escorts and wreak havoc among the merchantmen,
taking the fattest of them as prizes. His officers, too, sensed that fate had finally decided to play her hand. Their challenge was to keep the crew charged
and active amid sea and weather conditions more conducive to languor and
sleep. It was too early to beat to quarters. But there was much work to be
done belowdecks to prepare the guns and aloft to secure nets and chains in
the rigging to prevent severed spars from crashing on deck once the fighting
began. Jones ordered the bosun to clear the decks for action, allowing his
mates free rein, for the first time on this cruise, to lash with the knotted end of
a rope any sailor caught idling.

His lieutenants were ordered below to stow personal gear in sea chests and
otherwise clear out their cabins before sailors dismantled the hard canvas walls
and took everything movable down into the afterhold on the orlop deck. Alone

in his cabin, Richard exchanged his informal attire for a full dress uniform that included a three-foot-long officer's sword, its hardened steel honed to a razor edge from its tip up to an exquisitely crafted gold haft in the shape of a lion's head. It was a gift from Anne-Marie Helvétian, presented to Richard by the captain upon his return from Passy. Richard had admired it in front of Jones, but had stowed it away until this moment. He attached the sheath to his belt, and after testing the edge of the blade with a finger, slid it into place, taking satisfaction in the metallic ring of tight-fitting steel. He then gathered his personal belongings together and opened his sea chest. As he began moving the items around inside, his gaze fell upon a portrait sketched in pencil that Captain Jones also had brought back with him from Passy. It held an endearing likeness of the face of Anne-Marie, her head atilt under a flourish of thick dark curls as it often was when she had played the coquette with him. Beneath the sketch, written by her own hand, were the words: *Je n'oublierai jamais ce que nous avons partagé, cher Richard. Je suis la tienne, pour toujours.*

His gaze lingered on the sketch and the words beneath it. Then, with lips pursed, he placed the portrait protectively between soft fabrics of clothing and closed and locked the chest, slipping the key into an inside pocket of what once had served as a midshipman's dress coat, but now displayed the white facings, gold fouled-anchor buttons, and gold lace trim of an American naval lieutenant.

Outside, on the deck, a stream of sailors went about their work disassembling the officers' cabins and wardroom. A rap on Richard's door, and a hulk of a man entered the cramped space. He knuckled his forehead in a perfunctory way, seized the heavy chest by a leather handle on each end, and hauled it aft as other sailors began disconnecting and taking down the canvas panels. Within the quarter hour there would be nothing remaining on this portion of the lower deck save the six big guns and the men and equipment required to serve them.

Richard stepped up the ladder. The captain's cabin had already been cleared: the bare parquet floor and sparkling colored glass in the stern and quarter-galley windows stood in marked contrast to the red-painted deck and jet-black cannon on the rest of the main gun deck. Twenty-eight ports were open, fourteen on each side, and Henry Sawyer and his mates were carefully inspecting each piece. Cutting Lunt and Agreen Crabtree were with them. Agreen spotted Richard and came over.

"We're required up on the q-deck in ten minutes," Agreen advised. "I was just comin' below t' tell you."

"Thanks, Agee." Richard poked his head out an open port and glanced forward, noting how much closer the Baltic Fleet had drawn in the past hour. Even at this level he could see the frigate's topsails. "Will the other captains be joining us?" he asked, his casual tone concealing a mounting anxiety. He felt unnaturally warm. High on his brow, the old wound began to pulse.

"No. The captain refuses t' heave to. He claims there's no time."

"No time?" Richard was stunned. "No time to make certain the other captains understand his orders and signals? What do we lose if we delay here for half an hour? It's going to be dark in any event by the time we engage—*if* we engage."

"We're engagin', Richard. One look in the captain's eyes is all it'll take t' convince you."

Richard did look into the captain's eyes a few minutes later on the quarterdeck. They were rudely bloodshot, with crescents of black beneath, and it came to Richard how much the captain had appeared to age since that day they had met in Hingham. But he remained in every respect the man Richard had admired then, and his voice was ice-calm as he walked his officers through his battle plan. To larboard, an orange sun edged closer to the horizon, its soft hues highlighting the ship's brightwork and gilded transom against the brilliance of a chilly indigo sea. Above and astern, gulls and fork-tailed terns glided slowly about or hovered at a standstill, greedy for any refuse heaved overboard in the ship's wake. Ahead to starboard, the frigate *Serapis* and her smaller consort *Countess* were hull up, three miles away.

"Good evening," Jones said to those gathering before him. He had two pistols thrust into the waistband at his belly and had clipped two others to his belt, one against each thigh. "I estimate we have now"—he glanced seaward—"less than an hour until we engage. May I say, to each of you, that you have served your ship and your country with courage and honor, and you have acquitted yourselves as gentlemen. For that you have earned my undying gratitude and respect. It is my great privilege to serve with you."

He let the sincerity of those words sink in, then: "You know as well as I that we cannot fight this frigate *Serapis* gun to gun. According to Mr. Cutler, she has twenty eighteens to our six; thus overall, twice the weight of our broadside. At the same time we may assume that she is the more maneuverable vessel, which puts us at her mercy even in this light wind. So what is our advantage?" He bowed in the direction of Lieutenant Colonel Wybert. "We have a hundred thirty-seven marines to the enemy's forty-four. And we have the rifles brought to us from America in *Alliance.* As you have discovered for yourselves, these rifles are far superior to muskets. If we are to prevail in the upcoming battle, it will be as a result of small-arms fire. What I intend to do is grapple the enemy, sweep her decks from the tops, then board and take her."

"Sir," Dale put forth, raising a question on behalf of every officer, "you mention *Alliance.* What of her and the other ships? Add their guns to ours and we hold a clear advantage."

Jones shot Dale a hard look.

"Under normal circumstances, Mr. Dale," he said, "I would agree with you. But these are not normal circumstances. I put no stock in Captain Landais obeying my orders. How could I believe otherwise? We shall signal *Vengeance* and *Pallas* to engage the British sloop. As for *Serapis,* we are on our own, unless I am proven wrong about Captain Landais. If I am, I shall happily retract what I just said.

"As to stations, to repeat, gentlemen, here are my orders: Mr. Dale is in charge on the main gun deck with Mr. Coran. Mr. Lunt, you will be stationed on the lower gun deck with Mr. Linthwaite. Mr. Cutler, you will be in the maintop with Mr. Mayrant and twenty marines. Mr. Crabtree, you will be on the mizzentop with Mr. Tremain and ten marines. And Mr. Fanning, you and Mr. Meyers will be in the foretop with fifteen marines. Colonel Wybert, at his discretion, will station the remaining marines elsewhere in the rigging and along the bulwarks. Lieutenant O'Kelly will deploy his Irishmen as directed by Colonel Wybert. The rest of you midshipmen will remain with me and Mr. Stacey on the quarterdeck. Are there any questions?"

There were none.

"Very well, gentlemen. We shall beat to quarters."

"We shall beat to quarters!" Dale shouted out. Immediately on the two upper decks, drummers launched into a thundering staccato tattoo.

"Good luck," Dale said to each of his fellow officers over the din. He shook each man's hand, lingering a moment with Richard and Agreen, the bond among them the strongest.

Richard and Agreen shook Dale's hand but said nothing to each other. What they would have said, their eyes spoke for them during a brief, final salute.

Richard and young Midshipman Mayrant assembled their small company at the base of the mainmast. The twenty French marines assigned them were dressed similarly in white breeches, blue coats with red facings, and white crossbelts, their black spatterdashes extending from ankle to knee. Each carried a silver St.-Etienne musket and a long-barreled dragoon pistol, along with the cartridges, powder horns, and shot to service them.

Richard had two English flintlock navy-issue pistols pronged onto his waistband in front. Slung across his back over his right shoulder were two rifles handcrafted by Swiss gunsmiths in Pennsylvania. They were muzzle-loaded, unlike the breech-loaded Ferguson rifle the British had recently come out with, and while they took longer to load than a standard-issue musket, they were a good deal more accurate and had four times the range. Mayrant carried a third rifle to the main top, where he huddled low on his knees, his eyes peering above the wooden railing of the platform.

"Stand up, John," Richard whispered in his ear, his hand at the midshipman's armpit. "The men can't see you like this."

"Yes sir; very sorry, sir," Mayrant flushed, springing to his feet. "I was just getting my bearings."

Richard smiled sympathetically. "I understand getting one's bearings," he said confidentially. "For me, as a midshipman, it was that bloody snake inside. It kept slithering through my innards, forcing me to lie low. I swear that beast could have fed this entire ship's company had I been able to lure him out."

Mayrant forced a laugh. "Yes sir. Thank you, sir. I believe your snake has made my acquaintance. May I ask, sir, when does it take its leave?"

"It never does, John."

French marines were coming up one by one through the lubber's hole, crowding the top. Richard ordered two of them up to the crosstrees. Four others sat with their feet dangling through the hole, ready to drop to the futtock shrouds at the outbreak of battle. From the mizzentop, Agreen held up the bow he had hand-fashioned from the wood of a yew, its creation a source of shipboard gossip throughout the cruise. Although he had tested it by firing at objects tossed out to sea, tonight, Richard mused, would be its first test on live targets.

In reply, he held up a rifle in his right fist.

Jones, on the quarterdeck, had ordered the squadron farther off the wind, on a course that would bring them on a broad loop from the east around to the west-northwest, on a parallel course with the British warships. He had read Pearson's mind perfectly, Richard observed. *Serapis* was close-hauled on a course that would put her between the oncoming squadron and the merchant vessels now making all possible speed for the northbound current and Scarborough Castle. The British captain could not yet know for certain that *Bonhomme Richard* was an enemy ship. She was, after all, flying the red ensign. But he must have had his suspicions. He had opened his gun ports, and from across a dwindling expanse of sea the Americans could hear the distant, measured rat-a-tat of a marine drummer's call to arms.

Assuming the faint wind held, they were now less than thirty minutes from engagement. Richard kept his men occupied cleaning and recleaning the two swivel guns and two Coehorn mortars mounted on Y brackets bolted onto the top's larboard and starboard railings.

"*À l'aise, mes hommes,*" Richard ordered the marines when there was nothing left for them to do. With her yards braced around to a close haul, *Richard* nudged up toward *Serapis* from astern.

She had her courses clewed up, as did *Richard,* and her t'gallants hung loosely furled on yards lowered to their caps. A reduced sail plan allowed *Richard* to catch up to windward. *Countess* was on a more northerly course, with *Pallas* in pursuit. *Vengeance* had backed her sails and was drifting in the quiet sea as *Richard* went on ahead. To Richard's disgust, *Alliance* had sailed off on a southeasterly course, on an opposite tack from the pending engagement.

Overhead, a harvest moon, two days short of full, hovered above two ships that, after almost five hours of crawling toward each other, were now separated by a river-wide expanse of dark water. The British captain spoke first.

"I am Captain Richard Pearson of His Majesty's ship *Serapis,*" came the crisp English accent through a speaking trumpet. "What ship is that?"

"*Princess Royal,*" Jones answered, calling out the name of an East Indiaman the pilot had mentioned.

"Who are you, sir, and what is your cargo?"

Jones did not immediately respond. In the rigging, blocks squeaked for lack of tension, topsails fluttered in the fitful wind, crews on both ships stared silently across at each other. Pearson repeated his demands.

"Who are you, sir, and what is your cargo? Answer me, or I shall fire a broadside into you."

Jones raised a hand to Midshipman Grombe, a motion that sent the red ensign down the signal halyard; up went the Stars and Stripes in its place. Below, on the two decks, gun ports creaked open.

"My name is John Paul Jones," he shouted across the expanse. "I am captain of this vessel, a ship of the United States Navy. The cargo we carry is grape, round, and double-headed shot."

Just then the American's starboard battery erupted in an instantaneous broadside. *Serapis* immediately responded with a broadside of her larboard battery. Sailors struck deaf by the savage ear-splitting discharge of forty cannon fired at close range found their throats stuck closed and their eyes watering from a yellow-white shroud that quickly enveloped the area with smoke as acrid and insufferable as anything spewed out by a South Seas volcano.

The impact from two hundred pounds of metal slamming into *Richard's* hull sent men reeling. A marine crouched high up in the main crosstrees lost his balance and fell, screaming. He careened past the maintop, his cry cut short when he crashed onto the deck below. Richard watched as two sailors rushed to his body, picked it up, and threw it overboard.

Marines in the top fired blindly into the smoke.

"Cease fire!" Richard yelled at them. "*Cessez-le-feu! Que pouvez-vous voir?*"

Both ships paused to reload their guns. Slowly the smoke began to clear. Through a lightening haze, dark forms of ships loomed. Again the commands of officers, again the guns vomiting orange flames, again the staggering impact, again the choking smell of burnt powder, again the screams of men struck and dismembered, again the officers' cry for men to stand to amid the savagery and butchery of flying splinters, ricocheting grapeshot, and decks becoming unwieldy with the spilled blood of the dead and dying. Then, from *Richard's* lower gun deck, came the loudest explosion of all, followed by another of equal, horrifying volume.

"What was that, sir?" Mayrant asked, his voice shaking.

Richard leaned over the rail, aft to starboard. "I can't see," he said, "but I'd guess that two of our eighteens have blown themselves up." He dared not dwell on the horror in that corner of hell: hot metal exploding violently into pieces, flying in all directions, upending the other guns, ripping into ribbons the flesh of Cutting Lunt, Joseph Linthwaite, and the sixty men at their stations.

"Then we're taking on water!" Mayrant cried, aghast.

"Probably. But that's not our concern now. The smoke's lifting, Midshipman Mayrant. There's our target. She's pulled ahead of us."

Richard shouldered a rifle and took careful aim at a red-and-white fleck high in the enemy's mizzen pyramid. Gently he squeezed the trigger. The flintlock snapped forward and down, sending up a spark in the frizzen, igniting powder through a touchhole and into the heart of the gun, setting off the main charge, propelling a ball down a spiral-grooved barrel that caused it to rotate and fly true and strike the royal marine down, off the spar on which he had been perched, onto the quarterdeck, dead.

"Nice shot, sir!" Mayrant cheered.

"Reload this." Richard handed Mayrant the rifle and took up another. Aboard the frigate, a seaman was scrambling down the mizzen shrouds. Richard took aim and fired. The man threw his arms into the air and fell backward into the sea.

Serapis had raised her t'gallants to pull ahead of *Richard.* Jones backed his fore and main topsails and ordered the helm up, anticipating Pearson's tack southward. Whatever advantage *Serapis* enjoyed in weight of broadside, a considerable one now that *Richard's* lower gun deck was largely out of commission, it was better, to Jones, to take this unmerciful pounding than to risk being pulverized by a lethal rake from the bow or stern. The battle with *Drake* had taught that horrible lesson. Jones shadowed Pearson's moves as best he was able, his ship taking a horrific beating as he waited for his opening to strike, to grapple, to fight his enemy man to man.

An opportunity came when *Serapis* shot ahead and again tacked southward, her intent to rake *Richard* from the bow. Instead of shadowing Pearson's tack south, as he would have before, Jones maintained his westerly course and aimed *Richard's* bow at the enemy's stern. In the lackluster wind, *Serapis* was unable to avoid a collision. With a great thud the two ships banged together. *Richard* hung there listlessly, unable to bring her cannon to bear. Her topsails blocked the view of sharpshooters in her rigging; on her weather deck, French marines and Irish soldiers fell in ranks as British swivel guns and musket fire took their deadly toll.

"Have you struck?" Captain Pearson called over from his quarterdeck.

Richard heard the question clear enough. Pearson had shouted through a trumpet. But he could not make out what Jones said in reply through a hand cupped at his mouth. He shook his head to stop his ears ringing from the explosions of guns and asked Mayrant if he had heard the captain's response.

"I believe I did," Mayrant rasped. He moved close to Richard. "What the captain said, I believe, sir, was that he has not yet begun to fight."

Richard gave the midshipman a dull look. "Well, that's inspiring," he said. Glancing down to the quarterdeck, he saw Jones by the helm, a pistol in one hand, his sword in the other. He was ordering the topsails backed, to reverse his ship away from the enemy. Gradually, with the groans and snaps of splintering wood, *Richard* slid apart from *Serapis*, which turned, bringing her guns to bear, disgorging another crippling broadside into her enemy's hull at point-blank range, shattering metal, wood, and bone on her main gun deck, sending a shudder through the very core of the ship as though the firmament itself were being rent asunder. *Richard* answered, but with sporadic, undisciplined fire from a dwindling number of serviceable guns. Richard Dale and Henry Sawyer crossed Richard's mind, as did many of the others he knew on the main gun deck. Many would already be dead.

Stacey was having trouble managing her course. Braces and sheets had been blown away on all three masts, rendering it difficult to trim the yards. Inadvertently *Richard*'s stern turned, exposing her starboard quarter. A broadside from *Serapis* ripped into her heart, shattering the gilded artwork and decorative galleries that seconds earlier had graced the after quarters, leaving in their stead an ugly, vacant cavity.

Ashore, high atop the chalk cliffs of Flamborough Head, citizens of Yorkshire had come running with the first echoes of gunfire. They were clustering around a series of fires constructed, no doubt, for warmth and food and the communality of good cheer. Now *this* was entertainment.

A league out to sea, *Bonhomme Richard* was in increasingly dire straits. Much more of this unmerciful pounding, and she would be reduced to a floating hulk, limited to musket balls and grape to respond to an adversary whose gun batteries remained largely intact. It was as though *Serapis* could smell the blood awash on *Richard*'s decks and spilling out from her scuppers. She maneuvered about like a cougar teasing its prey, circling, circling, ready to streak in, lash out, kill. She held back, as if goading *Richard* to come forward, then turned on a westward tack, her starboard guns loaded and run out, the black void at *Richard*'s stern their aim, her very bowels their target.

But *Serapis*, too, had suffered damage to her rigging. And the wind dropped abruptly just as she commenced her final maneuvers. *Richard*'s midships loomed; on *Serapis* the rudder would not respond adequately to the helmsman's frantic efforts to avoid a second collision. With shouts and curses and exchanges of musket fire, her jibboom speared *Richard*'s starboard mizzen

296

rigging, securing her there as *Serapis* pivoted slowly with *Richard* in the awakening breeze, clutching each other as in some sort of macabre dance, the guns on both ships, for the moment, silent, unable to bear. The embrace was sealed when, with an almighty crack of her jibboom, *Serapis* swung free to bump against the side of her foe, her starboard bow at the American's stern, held there as a fluke on her spare anchor caught hold of the mizzen chain-wale on *Richard*'s starboard quarter. The two ships lay side by side, starboard to starboard to each other, the bow of the American facing north, the bow of her foe facing south. On the poop deck, Jones and Stacey seized a broken forestay swinging back and forth from the enemy's topmast and wrapped it around the base of *Richard*'s mizzenmast. Under covering fire from French marines in the top-hamper, *Richard*'s sailors hurled grappling hooks over the enemy bulwarks and drew her in snug, the two tumble-homes and muzzles of cannon jamming up against each other.

With *Serapis* roped in, *Richard* brought her swivel guns, mortars, rifles, and muskets to bear, battering the enemy's weather deck and peppering her exposed gun deck. *Serapis* unleashed another devastating broadside: round shot smashed through *Richard*'s starboard hull, across her gun deck, killing anyone in their way, then ripped out her larboard side, skipping across the sea two cable length's distance until finally expending themselves in a swirl of seawater.

On the frigate's quarterdeck Captain Pearson, his sword drawn, ordered a troop of marines to the weather deck with axes. Small-arms fire blazed from *Richard*'s top-hamper and bulwarks. The first wave of British marines fell. The rest retreated, not one reaching the bulwarks to hack away at the grappling lines. Pearson ordered his main anchor dropped, on the larboard bow, apparently hoping that the tension on the hawser would keep his ship in place while forcing *Richard* apart from her. He was wrong. Neither current nor wind proved strong enough. *Richard*'s death grip remained steadfast.

American sharpshooters kept the enemy below, away from the ten sixes positioned on the weather deck. Belowdecks, the frigate pulsated with life, her eighteens pumping ball after ball into the soul of *Richard*. Throat-burning, eye-watering smoke was everywhere, held captive in the battered hulk. Men gasped for air, their faces blackened with soot as dark as any pure-blooded African. So jammed together were the ship's hulls that crews preparing cannon for refire thrust the shafts of sponges and rammers out through a gun port of one ship and into a gun port of the other. *Richard* was fast becoming a doomed hulk. One by one her guns were upended, until all that remained were three sixes on her quarterdeck under the direct command of Captain Jones.

"Quarter! Quarter! In the name of God, quarter!"

It was Beaumont Grombe, his uniform tattered and stained with blood, screaming and gesturing wildly from the splintered rail of the quarterdeck. Richard stopped pouring powder into the barrel of a rifle and watched as Jones leaped from where he was sitting on an empty chicken coop and ran over to Grombe, striking him with such force on the side of the head with a pistol that he knocked the midshipman senseless.

"Do you strike?" Pearson demanded a second time through a trumpet.

In reply, Jones brought a slow match down on the touchhole of a six-pounder, igniting the flannel cartridge, rocketing the ball into the frigate's mizzenmast, blowing away a chunk on its right side, filling the air with lethal wooden javelins.

At that very moment, from *Richard's* stern, the dark shape of *Alliance* loomed in the moonlight. One after the other, in a perfectly timed sequence, she fired into the grapple-locked ships, her guns belching orange fire and vomiting white sparks as she glided past. She inflicted minor damage on *Serapis,* but *Richard's* gun deck was swept clean with cast-iron grapeshot and canister, the effect of ten titanic shotgun blasts. Screams of men belowdecks rent the air as *Alliance* slid off into the night, her work apparently done.

"Fuckin' Frog traitor!" Richard heard Agreen yell from the mizzentop. "What the hell is he *doin'*?"

"This is madness!" cried Midshipman Mayrant, crouched low behind the wooden railing, officer decorum be damned.

Off to the north, in a ray of encouragement for the beleaguered Americans, the *Countess of Scarborough* was lowering her colors to *Pallas.*

Richard laid down his rifle, his eyes glued on the cartridges he had spotted earlier on the frigate's weather deck, stacked in short piles on the steps of a forward hatchway ladder leading down to the main gun deck. Powder monkeys had left them there when musket fire and swivel shot had driven them away from the sixes mounted on the frigate's fo'c'sle. Richard had tried lobbing a grenade into that hold, first with the mortar, then by tossing them sidearm. Each time he had missed his mark. What pitiful shred of hope his ship and crew might have lay there, he was convinced, in those piles of cartridges.

Richard's futtocks and knees and deck beams and stanchions, hammered relentlessly by the frigate's guns, were being reduced to not much more than kindling. Any moment now, the lower decks might collapse, unable to sustain her masts and rigging and upper deck. The decks would cave in on top of one another, transforming what had been a proud ship of war into a battered, sinking wreck littered with the charred remains of battle.

Leaning against the railing, Richard took out his pocket knife and cut a thin strip of cotton from his shirt. Then, picking up a coil of slow match, he cut off a piece approximately two and a half inches in length with a quick upward slice of his knife. This short piece of oil-soaked oakum he carefully tied to a two-inch length of fast match attached to his last grenade. Satisfied that the fire on the slow match would transfer uninterrupted to the fast match, he held a small linstock to the tip of the slow match. Instantly it sizzled to life. Now there was no time to think, just do. He had four minutes until the slow match set fire to the fast match; after that, twenty seconds until the grenade exploded. Gripping the sizzling grenade firmly in hand, Richard climbed over the railing and out onto the footropes of the main yard.

"Where are you going, sir?" Mayrant cried in horror.

"To end this, John, one way or the other. Cover me."

At the end of the spar, Richard transferred his footing to the starboard main yard of *Serapis*. British marines spotted him and fired. Richard soldiered on, bullets humming and whining around him as he sidestepped along the footrope as fast and steady as he was able, the slow match now an inch above the fast match. He had a minute more—maybe. From *Richard's* top-hamper, a torrent of covering fire lambasted the frigate's weather deck.

On the enemy maintop, a few feet ahead, a wounded British marine was struggling to his feet, leaning on his musket as a crutch. With an evil curse he heaved himself upright and brought the weapon up to his waist, the barrel wavering at Richard's chest. Below, a lieutenant, realizing the danger to his ship, braved the hail of shot and stepped out on the weather deck. He raised his pistol, taking careful aim at Richard.

What happened next would be forever seared as individual images in Richard's brain. In the lambent light of a near-full moon, and the harsher light of fires above deck and in the sails, what appeared as no more than a flicker of a shadow against the backdrop of white topsail struck the marine full in the chest. He fell backward, dead in an instant, the white-feathered arrow sticking up straight. Richard tore his eyes from him to the officer on deck. In his hand the fast match burst to life. Almost as a reflex motion, he dropped the grenade down into the forward hatchway just as another officer, one wearing a midshipman's uniform, hurried up onto the weather deck amidships, then stopped, staring wide-eyed up at Richard who stood gaping down at him, a moment frozen in incredulity for them both.

"Oh, sweet Jesus!" Richard cried aloud. *"Jamie!"*

The effect of the grenade on the gun deck was catastrophic. Powder cartridges piled up by the hatchway and down each step on the ladder ignited, setting off a chain reaction of explosions onto the main gun deck as one supply of gunpowder exploded, igniting another and another, on down the line of closely packed guns. Screams of men being consumed by flames and scalding fragments of iron were lost on Richard. He stared down at Jamie, watching trancelike as the midshipman suddenly lunged to his left, hurling himself at his superior officer. The pistol went off. A burst of light flashed between the two men. Jamie sank to his knees, his head down, his hands at his stomach. He slumped onto his back, the white of his linen shirt giving way much too rapidly to a spreading stain of red.

Leaping to a backstay, Richard slid down to the frigate's main channel and jumped onto her weather deck. The British officer, stunned by what had just happened, recovered his senses when he spotted the enemy aboard his ship. He drew his sword. Richard drew his. From behind the officer a marine corporal came charging at Richard with an eight-foot boarding pike capped with a slice of sharp silver steel. His piercing cry of attack was reduced to a sickening gurgle when an arrow struck his neck, impaling it, the tip through on the other side. The marine twirled in agony before collapsing on deck, the pike he bore clattering forward.

The British officer came at Richard. There was a clang of steel as Richard raised his weapon to parry, another clang as the officer parried Richard's thrust. Slash and hack. Parry and slice. Stamp, slash, balance, parry, slash. Both men knew the drill, the American the more determined, the Englishman the more skilled. He saw his opening. Sidestepping Richard's thrust, he hacked across horizontally, striking Richard's forearm, tearing cloth and flesh, drawing blood, knocking the sword from Richard's hand. The officer lunged. As he did so, his right foot slipped in a pool of blood, momentarily throwing him off balance. Richard seized the boarding pike from the deck. Ducking low from a wild swing of the sword, he surged upward from a crouched position, summoning all his strength to impale the officer and thrust the steel tip deep into his belly. Richard took one step forward, forcing his adversary one step back, his mouth twisted in agony, his hands wrapped around the shaft of the pike as though engaged in a gruesome game of tug-of-war.

Richard released his hold on the weapon and ran to where Jamie lay. British marines and sailors watched from the shadows, spellbound by what they were witnessing, doing nothing to help or hinder. Richard knelt beside Jamie and gently lifted his soaked shirt, swallowing hard as the extent of the wound was revealed to him.

"Surgeon! Surgeon! Is there a surgeon here?" he demanded of the faceless forms, knowing all too well that were the Royal College of Physicians to act in emergency concert, it could not save his friend now. He cradled Jamie's head in his lap and looked down into eyes growing dull with oncoming death. "Why, Jamie," he managed, choking on his words. "Why did you do it? *Why?*"

"Richard . . ." It was a wisp of a voice, nothing more. His eyelids fluttered. Blood oozed from his mouth. He reached up, curled his hands around Richard's neckstock. With what strength remained, he pulled the American down to him. "Richard . . ."

"I'm here, Jamie," Richard pleaded. "I will always be here. I will never leave you. Not ever."

"Richard . . . I must . . . you must . . . promise me something."

"Yes, yes, Jamie, I promise," Richard said, wiping away tears with his bloodied hand as Jamie's faint whisper faded away to nothing. "I promise," he vowed again, emphatically, and he brought Jamie's head to his chest and held him close, his tears freeflowing and mingling with Jamie's blood as Captain Pearson above on the quarterdeck called for quarter. The great guns fell silent, and the standard of the United States of America was transferred from *Bonhomme Richard* to *Serapis,* First Lt. Richard Dale in the vanguard, followed by every officer and sailor and marine able to walk or be carried over onto the British ship.

Richard held Jamie still, with Agreen beside him on one knee, long after what remained of both ships' complements had filed past them; Captains Jones and Pearson had toasted their battle with a glass of wine on the quarterdeck; British and American sailors working in unison had released the two ships from their fatal embrace; fires on deck and below were extinguished; Dr.

Lawrence Brooke of Boston had confirmed the death of Midshipman James Henry Hardcastle; and the bow of *Bonhomme Richard* had slipped quietly beneath the waves astern, taking the grand old lady and those dead who had served her loyally down to their watery graves twenty fathoms deep on the floor of the North Sea.

12

FAREHAM, ENGLAND

October 1779

*T*HE FRENCH MARINE PRIVATE posted outside the captain's cabin snapped to attention when he recognized Richard stepping down the broad wooden ladder leading to the main deck. When Richard reached the bottom rung and turned aft toward the captain's cabin, the marine stamped the butt of his musket hard on the oaken deck and swung his right arm across his chest, his hand flat and palm down by the muzzle, all the while maintaining a stoic stare ahead. Richard gave him a perfunctory salute in return. Such parade-ground formality went beyond required protocol and annoyed Richard. But he let it pass. Since the battle with *Serapis* he had become accustomed to deferential treatment from both officers and enlisted men.

"*Bonjour,*" Richard said. "*Je suis ici pour voir le capitaine.*"

"*Oui, lieutenant Cutler,*" the marine responded. "*Un moment, s'il vous plaît.*" He rapped sharply on the cabin door and announced the visitor.

Inside the frigate's great cabin, a smaller but equally accommodating version of the equivalent space aboard *Bonhomme Richard,* Captain Jones sat before a long glossy table conferring with Captain Pearson. Jones glanced up from his study of the Thames estuary as his clerk seated nearby made careful note of what Pearson had to say about the chart spread out on the table. Richard entered and saluted both captains.

"Good morning, Mr. Cutler," Jones said casually. "Please join us. May I offer you coffee or tea? Some toasted cheese, perhaps?"

"Thank you, no, Captain," Richard said. He sat down and laid his tricorne hat before him on the table. He looked at Jones, who stared intently back at him as a father might to his son before either punishing or praising him.

"Might I assume," Jones asked, though the answer to his question had already passed silently between them, "that my efforts to dissuade you from leaving us have not had their desired effect?"

"Yes, Captain," Richard said. "But may I again say how grateful I am for your—"

Jones held up the flat of his palm.

"There's no need for that, Mr. Cutler. It is I who am in your debt. Were it not for your shenanigans the other night, I doubt I would be in a position to consider anyone's request. More than likely I would be on my way to the Tower and a date with the axman. Would you not agree, Captain Pearson?"

"I daresay, Captain," the British captain answered. A flicker of a smile creased his lips. "Though I rather suspect it would be to Newgate Prison where you'd be going," referring to the institution where the dregs of society were incarcerated before being carted off to the gallows. "And your assignation would be at Tyburn Tree."

"Quite so," Jones parried good naturedly. "I quite forget myself, Captain, thank you. No lordly beheading for this dastardly pirate, eh?"

His tone turned serious, his eyes again on Richard.

"So be it, Mr. Cutler. Understand, if I believed for an instant there was *any* hope of finding another American ship in these waters, I would deny your request. I could not afford to lose so fine an officer, no matter what else might be involved. But unfortunately that is not the case. Like it or not, our service to the Continental Navy is apparently over. I suspect my last service to my country will be at the court-martial of Captain Landais." He indicated the chart on the table. "I had thought of standing in toward the Thames, but have decided against it. Captain Pearson is right. There are too many shoals and reefs in there for a ship in our condition. So we shall sail on to the Straits, where this evening we shall put you and Captain Pearson ashore at Dover."

"Captain Pearson, sir?" Richard said, his gaze glancing off the Englishman.

Pearson answered rather than Jones. Despite a calm confidence and easy congeniality, the handsome and superbly uniformed officer sat as a Whitehall portrait of how a Royal Navy post captain should appear. "Quite right, Lieutenant," he said. "Captain Jones has granted me the honor of accompanying you to London. Alas, I fear his gracious decision has deprived him of his last and most valuable bargaining chip."

Pearson was the sole British prisoner remaining aboard *Serapis*, save for those seriously wounded plus two seamen claiming to be Americans. Beginning early in the morning the day after the battle, what remained of the enemy ship's complement was shuttled ashore under a white flag. It was grueling work: only two of the ship's four boats were serviceable, and the offloading had to be completed during the incoming flood tide. Jones had ordered American crews at the oars relieved after each trip ashore.

More than magnanimity was involved in the decision to free enemy survivors. *Serapis* was a battered ship, brought close to the point of total wreckage by the chain reactions detonated by Richard's grenade. She remained afloat and could be sailed, in a fashion, her captain's cabin the one area of the ship unscathed from the battle. Barely enough food and water remained aboard to provision one ship's crew, let alone two, and many on both sides had been cruelly bloodied. In such conditions, with men subject to disease packed in tight against one another, there was a real danger, Jones knew, of deadly plague running amok aboard what was now his command.

Captain Pearson had refused to go. He had ordered his officers and men ashore, but he insisted on remaining aboard to preside over the burial of his dead.

Richard inclined his head to him.

"Your servant, sir. I shall be honored to travel in the company of so distinguished a sea officer."

Pearson inclined his head, in turn, to Richard.

"Thank you, Mr. Cutler. Let us hope the lords of the Admiralty concur with that most gracious assessment."

"And you shall need this," Jones said. He picked up a gray canvas bag from the floor and placed it on the table.

"What's in there, Captain?"

"Change of clothes. A boat cloak, overnight necessities, those sorts of things. And I have put some pounds sterling in there for you: back pay plus, shall we say, a small bonus for a job well done. Hardly a fortune, but enough to get you to Portsmouth, which is where I assume you are going?" Richard nodded. "I regret I have no travel papers for you. But I am assured by Captain Pearson that not only will he honor his parole, insofar as you are concerned, he will provide what he can to assure your safe passage. Would there be anything else you might require?"

"No sir," Richard said, raw emotion causing his voice to catch in his throat. Such generosity went beyond anything he had anticipated. "Thank you, Captain."

"Very well. You may return to your duties on deck. Should this wind hold, we will have you in Dover for supper."

The weather deck and top-hamper of *Serapis* remained in various states of disrepair, though American shipwrights, carpenters, and riggers were doing a commendable job putting her to rights. She had no mainmast. It had gone by the boards when *Serapis* had been freed from the death grip of *Bonhomme Richard*. Just a stump remained, three feet high, capped with jagged white teeth of torn New Hampshire pine. Her foremast, however, was completely intact, its rigging rerove and its broken spars replaced. On the mizzen, a hastily patched fore-'n-aft spanker was sheeted out to catch the northerly breeze, with nothing above it save a small jury-rigged topsail.

It was here, just yesterday, that the service for the dead had been administered by Captains Jones and Pearson, standing together at the quarterdeck railing. One by one, the names of the dead had been called out to the ship's company assembled below in the waist and the appropriate passage read. With each "We commend his soul to God," a body sewn tight in a canvas shroud weighted down with round shot had slipped out from a plank covered with either the Union Jack or the Stars and Stripes and splashed into the sea, disappearing quickly in the white bubbles of the wake astern. Long before Pearson had called out the name of James Henry Hardcastle, Richard was beside the dead midshipman, as he had been during most of the preceding night, standing vigil beside him and others on the American side he had come to know and respect: among them, Lt. Cutting Lunt, Midshipmen John Linthwaite and Jonus Cornan, and chief gunner Henry Sawyer, whose dreams of a life along the Choptank had been extinguished the instant the eighteens on *Richard's* lower gun deck had exploded into scraps of searing metal. As Jamie's corpse was placed on the plank under the Union Jack, Richard stood behind the plank in rigid salute. He remained that way until some time after the plank was tilted up, the shroud slid outboard, and Jamie's body had been committed to the deep.

"So you're goin', Richard? Tonight?"

"I am," Richard replied. His voice was stiff, unwelcoming, as he stared out to starboard where a pencil-thin line of snow-white chalk glittered above the cerulean sea.

Agreen exhaled a breath. "In that case, my friend, I will miss you sorely."

"And I will miss you, Agee. But at least we're alive, aren't we? We've survived, haven't we? Others were not so lucky. Dead men tend not to miss each other." Instantly he regretted the bitterness in his voice. "I'm sorry, Agee," he mumbled. "You don't deserve that."

"Don't apologize, Richard. I can't feel your sufferin' because I haven't lost what you have in this war. I'd have t' lose you, t' feel that. And you're right, we are alive. And some day we'll have occasion t' be together again." He leaned against the bulwarks, his hands clasped before him. "I'm not much of a churchgoin' man, Richard. And I don't spend much time readin' Scripture. But I do believe in a father spirit, like my friends the Penobscots do in Maine, an' I'll pray t' Him for that occasion. And I'll pray t' Him t' watch over Will, as I believe Will has been watchin' over you all this time. And I'll pray too for Katherine, that she finds peace, together with my best friend."

Richard felt a warm glow soothe his ragged emotions. "You're a true friend, Agee," he said from the heart. He rested a hand on the man's shoulder. "And our friendship will not end here. We have many more campaigns together, you and I. This war won't last forever. When it's over, I'll be coming to see you. I know where you live in the Eastern Province, as we highbreds from Boston prefer to call it."

They smiled together, recalling a long-ago conversation.

Northerly winds picked up during the afternoon and drove *Serapis* southwestward toward the South Foreland off Dover. By the first dogwatch, they had sailed within striking distance of the ancient Cinque Port dwarfed by an enormous citadel presiding high above the town on the chalk cliffs. More imposing, to Richard, than Edinburgh or Scarborough Castle, this fortress, he knew, dated to the Iron Age, its construction continuing through the Roman,

Norman, and Plantagenet eras. Its massive stone walls and a huge four-square crenulated turret rising up in the middle served as the centerpiece of southern England's coastal defenses, keeping watch over her commerce, her enemies, and her history.

Lookouts aloft in the foremast rigging remained vigilant for any flutter of red or white upon the strait that might signify a Royal Navy ensign. They saw none, though considerable water traffic scurried about, small vessels mostly, traders plying their wares along the English coast. Still, these remained dangerous waters. A jury-rigged top-hamper on what was clearly a British frigate could raise questions and bring out an official vessel from a coastal port to investigate. It was time for Richard and the British captain to depart.

Serapis was hove to, her captain's gig swung out and lowered. Twelve sailors took position at the oars, six per side. Midshipman Fanning was at the tiller. Up on deck, his seabag strapped over his shoulder, Richard forced himself to concentrate on the simple mechanics of getting down the built-in steps into the gig. More than anything he wanted to avoid an overly emotional send-off. But it was not to be. As he approached the open entry port and turned to salute the quarterdeck a final time, a roll of drums and shrill of pipes rent the air as the entire ship's company, from Captain Jones on the quarterdeck to the youngest cabin boy on the fo'c'sle, stood at stiff attention, saluting him in silent tribute.

"God be with you," Richard said when the din had abated. "God be with all of you." Quickly his gaze passed over individuals and groups of men who were like kin to him: Captain Jones, Richard Dale, Lawrence Brooke, so many others, finally to Agreen, their eyes locking together a final time before Richard dropped his salute and turned, resolutely, to make his way into the boat. He took position in the sternsheets as the drums and pipes struck up again to honor Captain Pearson, the last to step down.

Twenty minutes later, they were on the docks of Dover, watching the gig return to *Serapis,* its oars dipping and rising, dipping and rising in perfect rhythm with each other.

Captain Pearson broke the silence. "I say, Mr. Cutler. Your fellow officers and crew hold you in rather high esteem, do they not? I have rarely seen such affection and respect in the service. And I must allow that your captain, aside from that rather foul temper of his, is a gentleman and a very fine seaman. Quite the opposite of how he is portrayed in England."

"He'd be proud to hear you say that, Captain," Richard said, distracted by what he could just make out aboard *Serapis*. The gig had been hoisted up and she was coming off the wind, on a course for the Dutch island of Texel, which was to have been *Bonhomme Richard's* ultimate destination. On the ensign halyard astern, the Stars and Stripes fluttered above the Union Jack, the first time the American flag had been raised over the British ship. That fact did not go unnoticed by Pearson.

"There, Lieutenant, go the spoils of war," he sighed, watching as *Serapis* sailed away eastward into the gathering night. "It seems we have both lost a ship this day. I, for one, will be court-martialed for my loss. Standard procedure, I'm afraid."

They began walking toward the center of town. Citizens afoot and on horse gave them scant notice as they strode along.

"You will be vindicated, Captain. How could you not be? You fought bravely and you protected your convoy. And by surrendering, you avoided needless bloodshed. Far from reprimanding you, your king should honor you."

"I say, Mr. Cutler, that is most considerate of you. Most considerate indeed. You seem just the man to have in my camp." Mirth twinkled in his sea gray eyes when he asked, "Might I then prevail upon you to serve as a character witness in my court-martial? I doubt I could find a more compelling witness. Or a more convincing one."

Richard smiled. "With respect, Captain, I must decline. I have spent quite enough time in an English prison, thank you."

"Yes, well, quite. I have to agree, you make a wise decision."

Their relationship had grown comfortable enough for Richard to ask, later that evening over a dinner of mutton stew in an inn with few other patrons, "Captain, if I may, why was Jamie Hardcastle serving as midshipman aboard *Serapis?* I thought he had transferred to a First Rate. He was quite convinced of that when I last saw him."

Pearson sipped his beer contemplatively. At first, Richard thought he was not going to answer him.

"I was equally convinced of that," Pearson said. "But when it came time for his examination, we discovered that two of the post captains assigned to administer it had been called away to sea duty. The French fleet, you may recall. I had orders to sail to Stockholm, and I asked Mr. Hardcastle if he would care to join me on one final convoy. Predictably, he agreed." Pearson signaled the serving girl to refill the glasses. He went on in dull, melancholy tones. "So you see, Lieutenant, I have no difficulty blaming myself for what happened. Mr. Hardcastle could have declined my request. He could have remained in Portsmouth and awaited his exam. That was his right. But instead he did what he saw as his duty and signed on with me." He drank deeply, replacing the glass hard on the table. "Damn it to hell, I wish he hadn't! Hardcastle was a fine officer. And a superb sailor. And a gentleman. He would have gone far in the service and every man jack who sailed with him would have been the beneficiary. I confess to you, sir, I miss him more than any other. And that includes that lieutenant of mine you so handily skewered."

Richard covered the top of his glass with his hand when the serving girl came by for refills. Fatigue and fond remembrances had him by the throat. "He held you in the highest esteem, Captain," he said. "He told me that on more than one occasion. He sailed with you on that convoy because he wanted to serve with you."

"And you, sir," Pearson went on, as though oblivious to that remark. "How he gave his life to save yours, wasn't it? And how you risked yours to save him, fighting your way over to him, holding him the way you did long after he died. By God, sir, I tell you, I have never been so moved! I've seen much in my years at sea. Too bloody much. But never, never shall I forget what I saw that night." He choked with emotion, then coughed to cover it up. "Nor shall anyone else who was there."

☆ ☆ ☆

THEY WERE up early the next morning, booking passage to London. They had no trouble finding a post chaise to convey them, although Captain Pearson had to pull rank to bump off the coach two rather elegantly dressed and none-too-pleased civilians to make room for himself and the young man he introduced as his lieutenant. It was a warm and humid day for late September, overcast with showers threatening. Though to the common eye the uniform he wore could pass for that of a Royal Navy officer, Richard kept his uniform coat stowed in his sea bag and his boat cloak on. As uncomfortable as it was to wear, it concealed everything he wore except for his white breeches and a pair of silver-buckled shoes.

He kept to himself as the coach rattled along ancient Watling Street, an almost perfectly straight road that ran from Dover through Canterbury in the heart of Kent into the old City of London. There it linked with the original Watling Street, running northwest from London through central England to the coast of Wales. Roman engineers had built these roads centuries ago to tie together this distant outpost of the great empire. Today it remained the mainstay of England's highway system, providing rides so smooth along its ancient slabs that one could nap undisturbed along the way, which is what Richard was now pretending to do.

But he was listening intently to the discussions going on among the other passengers. At one point, Pearson asked a citizen of Dover (judging by his repertoire of local knowledge) about the large number of English soldiers he had noticed in the area. Was not the threat of invasion over?

"Aye, 'tis, my lord," the man replied deferentially, overreacting perhaps to the gilded grandeur of a post captain's dress uniform. Most, though certainly not all senior Royal Navy officers had roots in England's peerage. "For now, leastways. But the army's stationing troops permanently along the south coast, just in case."

Pearson prompted him and his companions for their version of the failed allied invasion. What they told him differed somewhat from the pilot's account aboard *Bonhomme Richard.* The number of French and Spanish ships involved was about the same, but according to those in the coach, Adm. Sir Charles Hardy had not defeated the enemy ships in a pitched battle. Rather, he had employed at sea the same tactics General Washington was employing so effectively on land in America. Outnumbered and outgunned, Hardy had kept the Channel Fleet positioned between the allied fleet and the southern ports, leading the enemy up into the Channel as far as Portsmouth, then leading them back out as far west as the Lizard, tempting the allied ships, taunting them, picking off stragglers, but never presenting a formal line of battle. Ultimately, what defeated the Bourbons was not superior tactics but the pox. As if carried on an Old Testament wind of pestilence, it had swept through an enemy fleet too long at sea, its meager provisions of fruit and vegetables long since depleted, its sailors and soldiers dying of scurvy even before the scourge ravaged what remained of decimated crews. What had once been the pride of the French and Spanish navies had plummeted disastrously into wards of diseased men rotting aboard hospital ships. So many French and Spanish dead had to be tossed overboard, it was reported that citizens of Cornwall and Devon had not eaten fish since. Finally, his stores of men and supplies running out, Adm. Comte d'Orvilliers called off the initiative and sailed home to ignominy.

As to the war in the colonies, either there was little of note to discuss or these passengers didn't much care. The Americans had tried to recapture Savannah, it was reported in the press, but the English garrison there had repulsed a rebel army under the command of a general named Lincoln and a French fleet commanded by an admiral called D'Estaing. General Cornwallis, meanwhile, was laying siege to Charles Town, as the man talking kept referring to the South Carolina seaport, and the city was expected to fall any day now. Most likely it already had. Again the name of Lincoln came up, as the rebel leader in charge of the city's defenses.

Richard's eyes flew open with the first mention of the name Lincoln. Gen. Benjamin Lincoln was a close friend of the Cutler family; it was in his home in Hingham where he had first met Captain Jones. It was possible, though unlikely, that there were two generals in the Continental Army with that name.

They spent the night in a quaint little place near Canterbury, a surprisingly small town—or city, as Captain Pearson had explained to Richard, since the English called any community a city if it contained a cathedral within its walls—which this one certainly did. The next morning they were off again, making good time to London, where they arrived in late afternoon, picking their way through the squalid tides of humanity ebbing and flowing across the latent hazards of the East End. As he peered out through the coach window at the goings-on about him, and at the bewilderment of shops, homes, and official buildings set against running streams of human and animal refuse, it occurred to Richard that Paris seemed, in contrast, a remarkably civilized place.

"Your first visit?" Pearson asked, grinning. He had spoken little to Richard since morning, even after other passengers began disembarking at stops along the way, leaving the two of them alone in the coach.

"Yes," Richard replied, his gaze now absorbed in the snarl of water traffic on the Thames: heavy barges, naval cutters, flotillas of small sailing craft, and barges cluttering and churning the pewter gray waters from Greenwich Hospital and Deptford Naval Yard far downriver up to the eastern edge of the Old City at the Tower and at London Bridge, where a drawbridge had been raised to allow a large vessel to pass through. Onward upriver to a second bridge, longer and wider than London Bridge, its entire twelve-hundred-foot span boasting timbered homes set one against another, one home distinguished from its neighbors by a different slant of timbers or a different color scheme. A series of stone arches beneath permitted only the smallest of vessels to pass through to the other side.

"That's Westminster Bridge," Pearson explained, following Richard's gaze. "It was completed just a few years ago. Quite a marvel, what?" He made ready to disembark. "It's our, I should say, *my* destination. I trust you'll find this area a bit less chaotic than what you've seen thus far. One can only hope." He reached inside his dress coat. "I have this for you, Mr. Cutler." He gave Richard a sheet of paper with words hand-printed on it and personalized at the bottom with a signet seal.

"It's your safe passage," he explained. "Should you be detained, you may show this to the authorities and be on your way. Mind you, I would be ever so grateful if you would not bandy this about. It's all rather delicate, isn't it, you being my enemy." He smiled at Richard.

The carriage clattered to a stop close by the river Thames, a short walk to the government buildings of Westminster.

"Thank you, Captain. May I say again how much I have appreciated your kind hospitality. I wish you the best."

"You are most welcome, Lieutenant. I have enjoyed your company as well. As I said to Captain Jones on the quarterdeck that night, since ours was a fight between British and Americans, it was, after all, a battle in which diamonds cut diamonds. Would you not agree?"

"I cannot disagree, Captain," Richard replied. "But there were many French marines involved, plus Irish volunteers and sailors from other nations."

"Yes, quite," Pearson allowed. "My point is, I take no shame in being cut by a diamond such as your Captain Jones. Nor, for that matter, by one such as yourself. Good luck to you, Mr. Cutler."

He offered his hand, and Richard clasped it firmly.

Pearson said, "Charing Cross is where you need go if you are wanting to book passage to Portsmouth. It's just beyond the park there. Quite an interesting place, really." Pearson indicated the general direction. "And Mr. Cutler, you may want to have a look at that building over there. Yes, the rather pretentious chap. That's Whitehall. Your nemesis, what? My next port of call is on the west side, at Admiralty office."

The captain said good-bye and went on ahead. Whitehall was indeed a pretentious building, a huge rectangular structure gray on the bottom half, red on the top half, its construction a marriage for the centuries of stone, brick, glass, and sets of perpendicular gray columns, five to a set, extending from the base to the roof. A square stone observatory rose close to each end, three perpendicular windows per side and a dome on top capped by a sky-scraping steel pole on which flags of the realm fluttered in the warm breeze. These marble halls of power had once represented everything Richard despised. Now, as he strode across St. James Park, an oasis of serenity on this late autumn afternoon, he discovered that his feelings for His Majesty's navy were not quite as hateful as they once were.

Charing Cross was not so very different from what he had observed on the East Side, just more stylish and impressive in layout. Humanity in its most magnificent and sordid forms, and everything in between, abounded in this more privileged section of London. Here, a hurdy-gurdy man cranked out his droning tunes as he walked among offal sellers, wig makers, ragged news-boys, dandies dressed in outlandish styles and colors, pretty young women in revealing dress selling nosegays, memorandum books, or in some instances, risqué sketches to male customers that suggested an easy transition from sell-ing one's wares to selling one's body. And there, a man pushed a wheelbarrow. Heavy leather straps looped around his shoulders to support it as he used his hands to sprinkle sugar on pudding cakes he was peddling to bystanders watching what looked to be family members dressed in rags acting out a bal-lad of some sort, all but begging the more affluent onlookers to flick a farthing or ha' penny in their direction. Everywhere, hawkers were selling and people were buying the goods and services of the empire, their transactions eased by spirits poured out in nearby gin houses or, for the more fashionable set, in street-corner coffeehouses that had become popular in London society.

For all its uneasy charm and rank commerce, Charing Cross was a place where a young rebel naval officer could blend in without difficulty or undue notice, biding his time until he could board a coach for Plymouth with stops along the way, including one in Portsmouth.

☆ ☆ ☆

RICHARD WAS fortunate. He was able to book passage for the next day in the Portsmouth Mail, a coach providing comfort and speed to passengers who could afford such luxuries. Though the premium price of the ticket drained most of the sterling Jones had given him, he deemed it a good investment. It would be a faster journey and, given the coach's priority status and upper-class clientele, it would be far less likely to be detained.

The trip to Portsmouth started out uneventfully. As was his custom since arriving in Dover, Richard maintained an aloof demeanor that discouraged others from inviting him in to their idle conversations. On the last leg of his journey, he found himself in the company of a rather heavyset young woman with a pleasant face and long auburn curls who looked to be about twenty years of age. With her was an older relative, Richard presumed, since her hair was equally long and red, her frame as stout, and her features as becoming. The women rarely spoke to each other. Since boarding the coach, the younger of the two seemed quite content to sit and stare at Richard.

"Hello," she said at length. "My name is Hester. But you may call me Nessie. All my men do."

She said it with the green of her eyes boring into the blue of his, before once more roaming appreciatively over his body. Richard noticed her travel companion turning toward the glassed window, shaking her head and staring out at the meadows, streams, and copses of knotty oak.

"What's your name, love?" Hester encouraged.

"Richard."

"Richard, is it. A manly name. Where are you from, Richard-love?"

"Portsmouth"

"A sailor, are you?

"Yes."

"Going to sea? Or . . . coming?" She smiled coquettishly.

"Just returning."

"Just returning, is it?" she gushed. "So you've been away at sea all this time? Confined in a little ship, with just men to keep you company." Richard nodded, and her smile broadened. This was getting better all the time. "In that case, surely you must be looking forward to those . . . certain comforts a woman can provide?"

"Indeed I am."

"Hmm." She pursed her lips, as though pondering a matter of serious consequence. "Well, Richard-my-love, here's a proposition for you. Auntie and I are on our way to Exeter. We are hoping we might appeal to your gallantry and persuade you to extend your journey a day or two to accompany us there. It would be ever so comforting for us to have a man of your . . . build, so to speak, to protect us in the event . . . well, you know how things are these days. Ne'er-do-wells and enemy agents behind every tree. So what do you say, Richard-my-love? Will yon chivalrous knight attend these two poor damsels and see them safely home?" She assumed a mock businesslike air. "You will expect some sort of compensation, of course. So state your terms, and be not timid about them. Be assured I shall not cringe from whatever you might demand of me."

Richard smiled inwardly at what "auntie" must be thinking.

"Ah, Nessie," he said, doing his best to sound disappointed, "I'm afraid the fates are aligned against us. However much I am intrigued by your proposition, my business in Portsmouth is really quite urgent. We shall just have to make it some other time."

"Pity," she said, though that last sentence sounded hopeful and her eyes sparkled with the possibilities it portended. From her carry-on she withdrew a pencil and paper and wrote out her address. She folded the paper and handed it to him. "For you, Richard-my-love. For when you are next in Exeter and in need of . . . anything."

Richard tucked the paper in a shirt pocket inside his cloak, grateful for the blare of the coachman's post horn above, signaling the approach to Portsmouth Town. Grateful, too, for the much-needed diversion pretty Hester had unwittingly provided.

☆ ☆ ☆

RICHARD DISEMBARKED from the coach, bowed low in gentlemanly fashion to Hester and her aunt, then made his way quickly to the city docks adjoining the naval shipyard. There he hired a small boat, six pence paid in advance, and took a seat at the stern. As the wherry man began rowing across the entrance of Portsmouth Harbor, in the same waters where he and Katherine had once sailed together aboard *Eagle's* tender, he scanned the docks at Gosport and the shipping offices interspersed on the incline behind. Yes, there it was. The dark blue private coach he had come to know so well, the outline of the Cutler coat of arms emblazoned on the side door.

At the door to his uncle's office, Richard hesitated, then knocked boldly.

The door came ajar, and a heavyset, agreeable-looking man Richard did not recognize filled the open space.

"Yes?" the man inquired, peering around the door. From what Richard could see, he was dressed gaudily in orange breeches, light blue shirt, and egg-white vest and neckstock. In his right hand he held a short-stem clay pipe.

"Is Mr. Cutler in?" Richard asked.

"He is, young sir, but unfortunately not available at the moment." He took a pull on his pipe as he sized up the visitor and blew the smoke out slowly. "Might I ask you to come back in . . . shall we say, two hours? Our business ought to be concluded by then."

Richard ignored that.

"Please tell him that his nephew Richard is here to see him."

"His nephew, you say? Well, I, um . . ."

The door swung wide. William Cutler stood there, his mouth open, as two other men came up behind him, glancing inquisitively at each other.

"Richard! Dear boy! This is highly unexpected!"

"Hello, Uncle," Richard greeted him. He felt uncomfortable and flushed in the hard stare of the four men. "I don't mean to intrude. I've just arrived in Portsmouth and . . ."

"No, no, no," William Cutler countered. "I need a minute, that's all . . . Gentlemen, this is my long-lost nephew, Richard Cutler. Richard, these gentlemen are business acquaintances of mine. We were discussing . . . Never mind that. Lord, Richard, I can't believe it is really you." He turned to the others. "Gentlemen, I must apologize, we shall have to conclude our business some other day. Let's see. Today is Wednesday . . . My schedule . . ." He glanced at Richard. "We'll carry on next Tuesday. Ten o'clock. Here in my office."

"Tuesday?" the man with the pipe challenged. "William, this is highly irregular, to say the least. We've waited a long time for this meeting, and we have much to discuss."

"I understand that, but I'm afraid all this will just have to wait a little longer." William Cutler stepped back from the open door. "Good day to you, gentlemen." When the three men had reluctantly filed out, he closed it.

"Richard!" his uncle exclaimed. "How are you, dear boy?"

"I am well, Uncle, thank you. I . . . I was hoping you would be happy to see me. I left you and Aunt Emma not under the best of circumstances."

"No, you did not. And I will admit to being quite disappointed in you after you left. But I finally came to my senses. Lizzy helped me sort things out, as she often does."

"How is Lizzy?" Richard asked.

His uncle gave him a sorrowful look. "You know about Jamie."

"Yes."

"And you know about the . . . circumstances."

"Yes. I was there, Uncle. I had no idea Jamie would be there too. I thought he had transferred off *Serapis*. I was on the American ship."

"We feared as much," his uncle acknowledged. He motioned to his desk where recent copies of the *London Chronicle* lay stacked in a neat pile. "It's all in there, including quite a bit about a young American officer who held Jamie in his arms, weeping, as he died. I must say, those accounts are quite moving and are causing quite a stir throughout the realm, including in Parliament. The Whigs are holding them up as antiwar fodder, among other things. It seems most Englishmen agree with them." He tilted his head inquisitively at his nephew. "By the way, you wouldn't happen to know the identity of that young American officer, would you?"

"Later, Uncle, please," Richard answered. "How is Lizzy?"

William Cutler sighed. "Taking it rather badly, I'm afraid. She spends her time alone or with Katherine. I've never seen her like this. Thank the Lord God above that Katherine is able to be there with her.

"And how is . . . Katherine?"

"The same as Lizzy on the inside, I suspect. A bit more stoic on the outside. A family's navy background has its influences. Sadly, you come to expect this sort of thing when in the service.

"See here," he exclaimed into the ensuing silence, "I quite forget myself, Richard. Get your cloak and bag, and we'll be on our way to Fareham. It will do wonders for everyone to see you. I'll have the horses harnessed."

"You would do that for me, Uncle?"

William Cutler put his arm possessively around his nephew's shoulder. "Of course I would, Richard," he said, without compromise. "I am so grateful to see you here safe and sound. Never should you doubt that. And you have no idea how thrilled your aunt will be to see you. But first, unless I have totally misjudged why you have come home, I suggest we plan a stop along the way."

☆ ☆ ☆

THE RIDE north was made mostly in silence, William Cutler taking it upon himself to answer the one question he thought Richard would ask but did not, the question he believed nonetheless deserved an answer.

"Those three men in my office, Richard," he said, once they were well under way. "They are business acquaintances, as I indicated. They run a shipping company much like ours, and they trade in West Indies sugar, as we do. In years gone by we were fierce competitors. I suppose we still are, though in these difficult times we're all just trying to survive. They have approached me with a business proposal I find I must seriously consider."

Richard tried to sound concerned. "You're not looking to sell out, are you?"

"No. They're looking to buy in. They're proposing a business combination of some sort, claiming that economies of scale would benefit both our companies should we merge them."

"Would they?" Richard asked, more to be polite than anything else.

"Depends on the terms, doesn't it?" his uncle answered. "That's what we were in the process of negotiating when you knocked on the door."

"I'm sorry, Uncle. I hope I didn't jeopardize anything."

"Jeopardize? Hardly. As I said, your appearance is quite fortuitous. You have bought me some time, Richard, and I intend to put that time to good use. I have misgivings about all this, despite what seem to be economic necessities. What decisions I make may not affect me much, but they will affect my children, not to mention you and your family. Any sort of merger we put together would mean the end of our business as a strictly family enterprise." A deep sigh escaped him. "How I wish John and Robin were here so I could seek their counsel. Alas, they are away in the Caribbean."

"What does father think?"

"I have been waiting a long time for your father to respond to my last three letters. It's this blasted war. We wouldn't need to be even thinking along these lines were if not for our loss of earnings since it began." He shook his head regretfully. "So you see, nephew, I have been drawn kicking and screaming into circumstances I otherwise would have dismissed out of hand."

Richard was having trouble envisioning his uncle being drawn kicking and screaming into anything under any circumstances. But it didn't matter. His mind was drifting irretrievably away from matters of commerce.

"Do you want me to come in with you?" William Cutler asked as the carriage turned into the semicircular drive of the Hardcastle estate.

"No, Uncle, thank you," Richard said, opening the door of the carriage before it had come to a full stop. "I need to go alone."

He walked up to the front door and knocked loudly using the solid brass rapper in the shape of a ship under full sail. The door was opened by a liveried servant who backed one step away when he recognized Richard.

"Good afternoon, George," Richard said. "Is Miss Katherine in?"

"Who is it?" a deep demanding voice boomed from the hallway.

Richard pushed the door fully open and walked in past the astonished servant.

"Richard Cutler!" Henry Hardcastle cried from the vestibule. It sounded more like a curse than a greeting. "What in God's name are you doing here, boy? Haven't you caused enough grief for this family?"

"I'm not here to cause grief, sir," Richard said, his eyes darting about the downstairs of the household, up the stairway to the second floor. "I'm here to see Katherine."

"Well, by God you shall not see her. Not if I have anything to say about it. I demand that you leave this house immediately! And be quick about it! I have half a mind to summon the sheriff."

"Oh be quiet, Henry!" Jane Hardcastle strode briskly forward from down the corridor. "Leave the poor boy alone." She lifted the hem of her blue embroidered dress as she hurried along in determined steps, her eyes frigid on her husband. "I swear, half a mind is all you seem to have these days." Her expression softened considerably when her eyes met Richard's. "She's in the garden, Richard. With Lizzy."

"Thank you, Mrs. Hardcastle."

They were sitting with their backs to him, side by side on a stone slab bench within the gazebo. Lizzy had a shawl wrapped about her shoulders despite the warmth of the day. Her long, curly hair glistened gold in the sun; nothing else about her seemed at all cheery or healthy as she stared out at the pod-cluttered pond. Katherine had a hand on Lizzy's back and was rubbing it gently in small circular motions when she heard Richard approach. Lackadaisically she turned her head, saw Richard, was up in an instant.

Lizzy followed her stare, rose, inhaled sharply.

"Richard! You've come back! Does father . . ."

"Yes. He's waiting out front in the carriage."

His eyes went to Katherine, taking her in as if to his soul, pleading for her understanding, her acceptance. She nodded as if in recognition of his plea and walked slowly toward him, drawn irresistibly by a bittersweet conviction she had held close to her heart and never for one moment doubted.

"It *was* you, wasn't it?" she asked, her voice thick with emotion. "I knew it. I *knew* it was you. I told Father, but he didn't believe me. Mummy did. So did Lizzy."

"Katherine . . ."

She was there, a few feet away and coming closer. He held out his hands to her. She took them in hers, the wonder, the beauty of her, mesmerizing him, rendering him speechless.

"You have come, Richard," she said softly, inquiringly, as if the image of him were too fragile and would vanish if she spoke out of place. Lizzy had come up beside her. "Why? Was it to tell us about Jamie?"

"Yes," Richard managed. "I promised him I would come. At his last breath I promised him. I would be dead were it not for Jamie, Katherine. He sacrificed his life to save mine. So I could come here to you. And to Lizzy."

"What did he say, Richard?" Her voice seemed distant, as if in echo from a faraway place. Yet here she was, so very, very close. "I need to know exactly what he said."

"He said . . ." He swallowed, the pain of memory weighing on him. "Jamie said, 'Go to Katherine, Richard. Go to her. Promise me you will. She needs you so very much.'"

Richard's voice trailed away as he spoke. Katherine closed her eyes. Tears formed at the edges and rolled slowly down her cheeks. She made no effort to wipe them away.

"Did he say anything else?" He could barely hear her.

"Yes." He looked at his cousin, her eyes wide with anticipation and dread. "His final words were: . . . 'Give my undying love to Lizzy.'"

She turned from them, her hands covering her face, her body wracked with sobs.

"Richard," Katherine said, her eyes now resolute on his during a passage of time impossible to gauge, "was it to fulfill a promise to Jamie you came here? Or is there another reason?"

His hands went to her shoulders. His grip was gentle, his eyes moist, his voice unsteady. "There *is* another reason, Katherine. I have come to ask . . . to *beg* for your hand in marriage. I love you, Katherine. I have loved you from the moment I met you, and I shall love you with my last breath. Marry me, Katherine. Tomorrow. Today. Now. Marry me." Despite himself, he closed his eyes, as if witnessing so much as a flicker of hesitation on her part would be a rejection he could not endure.

She brought her arms up and around his neck in a tender embrace, and her lips gently to his ear. "I *will* marry you, dearest Richard," she whispered. "I once told you that a part of me will forever belong only to you. That part of me is my heart."

He took her full in his arms, clasping her to him with such strength of purpose it was as though God in all His omnipotence could not have wrested her away.

"You will not go, Richard?" she implored. "You will not leave me again?"

"No, my love. I will not. I have lost two brothers in this war. First, Will. Now, Jamie. It's enough. I will not lose you."

Part 3

13

BARBADOS

1780

SHE STOOD ON THE deck by the starboard quarter, anticipating the rise of the jibboom with the wave and the ship's hesitation on the crest. Instinctively she braced her legs, then yielded to the roll of the ship as it dove down into the trough, tossing white water off to the sides and up into the air before rising again to repeat the process. This rhythmic plunging of the ship did not trouble her. She reveled in it, had not been seasick once during the long voyage, to everyone's surprise including her own. With her hands on the bulwark railing, she gazed out at the great press of sail: transports, supply ships, and five ships of the line, three of which she had identified as Seventy-Fours on her own, thanks to Jamie's patience with her years ago in explaining how it was done without having to actually count the guns. Most vessels were nonmilitary, much like her own *Sparrow* that had become their home, their refuge, during these past few weeks. On the outer fringes of the convoy, frigates raced about the fleet like sheepdogs yipping at an errant flock, exacting order from their charges now that land had been sighted from the crosstrees. Land! The prospect thrilled her because it represented something new, something full of promise and adventure. At the same time, it saddened her, because never in her life had she experienced such carefree rapturous bliss as she had aboard this ship.

Sparrow was not her ship, of course, nor was it technically a Cutler family ship. But it was one with a master who had become sufficiently prosperous over the years as a result of Cutler commerce that he had, without hesitation, placed his private cabin at the disposal of Richard Cutler and his bride. The "honeymoon cuddy" he had jokingly referred to it whenever he spotted the two on deck.

She removed her straw hat and lifted her face to the soothing warmth of an early morning tropical sun. The breeze upon her was so fresh, so clean and inviting, she felt caressed with velvet as the light blue of her linen dress billowed out about her in puffs. So *this* is why sailors love the sea, she thought, not for the first time. She felt his presence behind her and waited for him to come closer.

"Look at the sea, my love," she sighed, leaning her head back against his chest as she felt his arms come around her waist. "So powerful. So eternal. So very beautiful. It *is* beautiful, isn't it?"

"Yes, Mrs. Cutler, you are."

She closed her eyes, luxuriating in the wonder, the sheer miracle of it all. "I shall never tire of hearing you call me that," she murmured.

"I should hope not. Cutler men do not take kindly to floozy wives."

She looked up at him. "Oh, really? I had thought that floozy wives were the only kind you Cutler men could get. Until I came along, to save you from your fate."

At the fo'c'sle, a seaman cried out. His mates about the ship craned their necks forward. Yes, there it was: a dull strip of brown and gray on the distant horizon just off to starboard. Hovering above it was a mass of smoke gray clouds that made it hard to distinguish land from sky.

Richard held her close. "For that insult to my family name," he whispered, "I shall have to demand satisfaction from you. Tonight."

"Tonight, my lord?" she pouted. "You really mean to make me wait that long?"

He kissed the top of her head. "Behave yourself, my lady."

"Joy o' the morning to ye, Mr. and Mrs. Cutler. I trust I'm not interrupting anything?"

It was a question that ship's master Julian Tobias had asked often since they left England. At first, he had asked it seriously, obsequiously, as though fearful of treading where he should not. By now, friendship and respect had turned the question into a joke and a bond among them. During many evenings in the after cabin, before retiring to the more Spartan quarters of the first mate's cabin, this jovial old sea dog had regaled the newlyweds with tales of his life at sea: fascinating accounts of far-off places and the exotic, sometimes dangerous people he had encountered there. Richard and Katherine had not once dismissed him, even when he had forgotten himself and dragged the evening well into the night, so absorbed were they in the telling.

"Good morning, Captain," Richard said, reluctantly dropping his hands to his side. "It appears we shall be arriving in Bridgetown shortly," adding, simply to make conversation since he knew the answer, "It's been a fast voyage, hasn't it?"

"Indeed it 'as, sir. Indeed it 'as." It was a topic custom-made for Tobias. "One of the fastest in my memory. Per'aps *the* fastest. Being a seaman yerself, Mr. Cutler, ye know that trades are fair and predictable winds. But these! My God, it's been since Cape Verde that we've 'ad to man braces and sheets. Yer lovely wife 'ere will think we sailors do naught but sit on our rumps and gaze out at the sea."

"It's what I've always suspected," Katherine put in, "except for the part you left out about rum and women." She smiled affectionately at Tobias. "Tell me, Captain: will my husband and I have the pleasure of your company aboard *Sparrow* whenever it is we are to sail from Barbados to Tobago?"

"T'would be my fondest 'ope, ma'am," the master replied. He glanced about inhaling the salt air deep into his lungs. "It's 'ard to imagine, isn't it, 'ow many more ships we 'ad sailing out o' Portsmouth. I wish we knew how Sir George fared at Gibraltar."

When the great fleet had weighed anchor five weeks earlier in a January mist and snow, a vast armada of three hundred ships had set sail southward. Due west of Cape St. Vincent on the Iberian Peninsula, Adm. Sir George Rodney had parted company in his flagship *Sandwich,* sailing due east with twenty-one other ships of the line, fifteen frigates, and a flotilla of smaller military vessels and supply ships. His destination was Gibraltar and the five thousand redcoats under siege from Spanish troops on land and Spanish ships at sea intent on recapturing this prized British possession. The remainder of the fleet had sailed to the Indies, where, a hundred miles east of Antigua, they had separated into two convoys. The main body had sailed west to Antigua and the naval base at English Harbor holding sway over a six-hundred-mile chain of islands on the eastern edge of the Caribbean, stretching from St. Kitts in the north to Tobago in the south. From this Leeward

Station, more than half of these same ships were ordered to continue sailing westward the thousand miles to Jamaica, to resupply and reinforce the largest British naval base in the Caribbean, at Kingston. *Sparrow* and those thirty ships bound for Barbados remained on the more southwesterly course they had followed for the past several days.

"I'm sure he fared well," Richard remarked. "He's an excellent sea officer, from what I've heard. Even if he failed to break the blockade, he will try again. England will not yield so vital a base. And the threat of another attack from sea should keep Spanish warships at home, away from these waters."

"See 'ere, Mr. Cutler," Tobias grinned. "Yor soundin' more like a Whitehall admiral every day. 'Aven't decided t' switch sides on us, 'ave ye?"

"Hardly that, Mr. Tobias." Richard was at once afraid he had sounded horribly pompous, since common sense told him there was no offense intended. "I love my country," he went on, his tone conveying more remorse than resentment, "and if I can help her cause here in the Indies, I assure you I will. But Spain is not an ally of the United States. The Dons refuse to recognize our independence. Nor have they offered us any sort of military assistance. They're fighting purely for their own interests."

"That's why every country goes to war," his wife pointed out.

"I realize that, Katherine. And so does every man who signed our Declaration. But in an independent United States, not all things will be done the way they always have been. Many people believe that. I, for one."

"May it come to pass," Tobias said. "Now if you two fine people will excuse me, I 'ave my duties to attend to. Land's approaching. Ma'am. Mr. Cutler." He touched the edge of his tricorne hat.

"Yes, of course," Katherine said. "And thank you again, Captain, for the use of your cabin. You have been most kind to us."

"You certainly have," Richard agreed. "I shall not forget it."

"My honor, I assure ye," said Tobias.

When the master was out of earshot, Katherine said, "You needn't have been so cross with him, Richard. He was just making merry. He meant nothing by it."

"I know he didn't. And you're right, of course. It's just that . . . sometimes I feel . . . sometimes I'm not sure what I *should* feel," he confessed.

"Let me see if I can help. You feel sometimes that you should be back at war, doing your duty, whatever that is, since you had no ship to serve on and no prospects of ever finding one. And whatever else might be involved, you sometimes feel guilt for the . . . pleasures you are enjoying at sea while others suffer on land. Am I correct?"

He shrugged. "Perhaps. Is it possible you understand me *too* well, Katherine?"

"No, my love, that is not possible. But I do know this and I will say it to you again: you have done your duty, Richard. To your country, to your shipmates, to the memory of Will and Jamie. What more can anyone ask of you? What more can you ask of yourself?"

He stared at her, said nothing.

She cocked her head and smiled back at him.

"Your lady does not please you, then?"

He knew why she had said it: to escape the gravity of the moment and recapture the bliss of their time together. But he could not restrain himself. Emotion had overcome him.

"Katherine," he said, grasping her by the shoulders, "listen to me. When I came back to Fareham that day and saw you there with Lizzy, I thought I would come undone at the mere sight of you. I thought I could never love anyone more than I loved you at that moment. But I was wrong. I was so terribly wrong. I love you more with each day that passes, each hour. Whatever I may have felt for you back then, I did not know that anything like this existed, that anything could be this so God Almighty wonderful. Whatever truths I may hold in my life, Katherine, my love and need for you will *always* be first among them. You *must* believe that."

She bit her lower lip. "I do, Richard. I do believe that. It's the same for me."

"Then you must also understand that what I feel about the war has nothing to do with *me* and everything to do with *us*. I want us to live together in a new country, *our* country, and to build our future and the future of our children in a land free of the abuses of our ancestors. Will spoke those exact words to me, about what he wanted for himself. It's what I want too, for us."

"I know, my love. I know. It's what we both want for us." She held his gaze, then turned toward Barbados. "Look, darling. We can see land clearly now."

What before had been dull colors and obscure forms had opened up to gray cliffs, clusters of multicolored shrubs, pink-tinged beaches lined with palm trees, and field upon field of rich green stalks waving in the morning breeze. Barbados. Chief among the necklace of Caribbean islands embellishing the British Empire, its stones were not diamonds or rubies or emeralds but something equally precious: sugar crystals. It was here on these gentle slopes of green that outrageous fortunes had been made for the planters whose slaves worked the fields and mills; for the distillers who processed rum; for the merchants who shipped molasses, sugar, and rum to domestic and foreign ports; and for the Exchequer in London, whose steep taxes imposed on sugar profits fueled Britain's war machine and spread its hegemony around the world.

"Will your cousin be in Bridgetown to greet us?" Katherine asked as *Sparrow* hauled her wind for the first time in three weeks to round up past the parishes of St. Philip and Christ Church on the southern edge of the island.

"You may rely on it," Richard replied, cheery now and as captivated as she with the lush tropical scenery passing by them off to starboard. "If John is anything as I remember him, he will have seen to the arrangements long before the first sail was sighted. He's a man who likes to see things done properly."

"Very much like my husband," she mused, "so marriage has taught me."

She said it off-handedly, staring straight out toward land, though she did allow him one quick sideways peek.

☆ ☆ ☆

WIND IN the West Indies carried with it both a blessing and a curse. On these paradise islands of warm sand and swaying palms, of flowers and bushes bursting with unimaginable colors, delicacy, and fragrances, fatal disease could strike a man down without warning. Within hours of first feeling ill, his skin turned a sickly yellow and his body shook with dry heaves, having disgorged every ounce of bile from his belly in a vomit so black and viscous it looked like liquid tar. What caused this horror remained a mystery, though medical evidence was mounting that the lowly mosquito was responsible. Whatever its cause, this much was certain: the higher up one lived and worked on an island, the more exposed to the cleansing southeasterly trades, the less likely he was to be stricken by a disease that concentrated its virulence in the lowlands during the wet summer months, with few cases reported during the drier seasons.

At the same time, the higher the elevation of one's plantation, the more exposed it was to the risk of being battered to pieces by a hurricane. About every six years or so, one came shrieking in from the Atlantic in late summer or early fall, throwing about windmills and curing stations and three-story houses as though they were children's toys, causing more damage to an island and its sugar treasure within a twenty-four-hour period than the combined effects of drought, war, shipwrecks, and slave uprisings over many decades. Later, after the raging fury had howled its way westward, it would take several years and immense amounts of money, toil, and endless negotiations for more money to coax sugar production back to prehurricane levels.

Which is why the home of John Cutler, in keeping with architecture now standard on most English plantations on Barbados, was a one-story affair constructed of coral stone and brick, its windward side built in a circular design to resist the effects of strong winds while allowing gentler breezes and flickering sunlight to caress the inner sanctuaries through a series of jalousie windows mounted in the walls with three sets of complex hinges, two vertical and one horizontal.

"Actually, I got the idea for these windows from our slaves," John Cutler explained to Katherine, when she asked about their origins. "They've used them for years in their houses, though we English have tended to stick with what we know. These are far more efficient, as you will observe when I move these levers up and down." Alternately, as he did so, the room was as light as noon or as dark as evening. "See? You can let in all the air and sun you want, or close everything up tight as a drum in a blow."

"Imagine," Katherine mused. "A Cutler taking a lesson from a slave."

John retuned her smile. He had taken immediately to Katherine, a young woman he had not seen since she was a little girl. "Yes, well, I prefer in this instance to think of them not as slaves but as local people with local knowledge. It doesn't do, does it, to ignore what has been learned over the centuries by others, no matter what their station in life. But we English are famous for doing just that, aren't we?

"See here," he said apologetically, after a pause. "You must be exhausted from your trip and I imagine you will want to freshen up before supper. I propose to put you and Richard in what I call the West Room. It's a self-contained area. Very private. As you'll see, there's a garden just outside, and the windows open up on three sides. Look out to the west and there's the sea. I trust it will do?"

"It will do just fine, John," Katherine said.

"Splendid. George here will see to your baggage. If you'd like, his missus will draw you a bath. Just the thing after so long a voyage at sea, what? Now then, supper is at seven o'clock sharp. Be prompt. No dillydallying. I just may have a surprise in store for you."

As a servant dressed in pure white gathered her baggage and led the way down the polished stone hallway, John turned to his cousin with genuine admiration.

"She's lovely, Richard. My, how lovely. And what questions she asked on our way up here! Who would have thought anyone but a naturalist would care so much about bloody flowers and birds? I couldn't answer half the questions she asked, though I've lived here for, what, eight years now, since I was sixteen. I've never seen a woman—or a man, for that matter—so inquisitive and eager to learn. You must be very proud. And happy."

"I am both, John," Richard said softly. His eyes lingered on the sway of her hips as she followed the servant down the hallway, her sea legs, like his, not yet accustomed to the constancy of land. Incredible, he thought: five weeks confined with her in a small cabin in a small ship, and it pained him so to see her walking away from him. He snapped to, aware that his cousin was waiting.

"So tell me," he said. "What about you, John? Given your class and those outrageous good looks of yours, you must cut quite the swath around here."

"Well. Ahem, ha. I wouldn't know about that, dear cousin," John flustered. "There just might be a young lady I fancy, we'll see. Business first, I always say. Speaking of which, shall we take a short stroll around? I can give you a brief tour of the grounds. If you're quite up to it, after so long a sea journey."

"Lead the way, John. I'd welcome a chance to stretch my legs."

John Cutler selected a light cotton cloak from a closet and drew it over his shoulders, buckling it at the neck. It was eggshell blue in color, complementing the darker blue and yellow of his breeches and waistcoat. A silk neckstock completed his wardrobe, a jeweled pin securing it to his white linen shirt frilled at the neck and cuffs. He offered Richard a cloak, but Richard declined, feeling wonderfully at ease in the cooling breeze in his plain white breeches and white linen pullover shirt.

Outside, the setting sun cast long shadows from the mahogany and palm trees and other foliage set strategically about the complex to provide maximum shade to rooms in what John called "the great house." The term was a throwback, he explained, to the days when plantation homes reflected the grandeur of English country mansions: three or four stories high and of wood construction, their white pillars and sculptures out front reflecting the personal taste of the owners, most of whom, in Barbados, actually lived on their plantations. Which, John explained, was not always the case on other British-owned islands in the Indies. On Jamaica, for instance, plantation owners were more apt to live in England.

"Who manages operations there?" Richard asked.

"The owner's agent, or agents, depending on the size of the plantation. We employ an agent here too. He lives with his family in that cottage you see down the road there, to the right. We'll pass by it, then loop around for a view of the cane fields."

"What does he do?"

"The agent? Basically, manages everything day to day. He works with the overseer of the slaves and those in charge of various processes. He also represents our interests in trade and shipping matters. Which have become more critical now that we are denied use of your father's ships. These days we must pay dearly for shipping our sugar. Alas, much of my own time, it seems, is devoted to money matters."

"Does the agent have assistance? From anyone besides yourself?"

"Yes. He has help from the overseer, of course, and from the bosun, what we call the chap who actually runs the mills. 'Bosun,' get it? Everything here runs by the wind, you see, just as on a ship. The agent also has help for the more menial tasks, of course, from slaves he trusts. Those would be Creoles, the lighter-skinned Negroes you see. Most of them were born on Barbados or on nearby islands, and on the whole they're quite dependable and hard-working. We import few slaves from Africa here. We may sell them in Bridgetown, but they tend to go elsewhere, mainly, before the war, to Charleston, in South Carolina. Now they go mainly to Kingston, though we send a number to Tobago and other islands nearby. Good riddance to them, I say. In my experience, African slaves are much harder to manage than local Creoles."

Probably, Richard thought, because Africans have known freedom.

"Ah, here's just the spot from which to observe," John said, as they came to rest at the top of a gently sloping rise. Legions of bare-chested slaves were in line-abreast formation, hacking and slashing at the cane with machetes, their thick muscular arms swinging back and forth in pendulum motions through the sea of green. Other Negroes trolled in their wake, picking up the severed stalks and carrying them over to mule-drawn carts reined in along dirt roads. In the center of it all, in a multi-acre area cleared of all vegetation, stood two windmills, each with its four great sails rotating four or five times per minute in the diminishing wind of late afternoon. Slaves carried bundles of slashed cane from carts to inside the mill through one doorway, while from a second doorway other slaves carried what appeared to be flattened stalks outside, stacking them in neat piles along the perimeter of the cleared yard. Richard asked what that was and why they were doing that.

"It's what we call bagasse," John explained, "or stalks after they've been pressed twice in the mills. We use them as fuel in the furnaces of the boiling house, the building that's right over there, the one with the open front and smoke coming out the top. In the mills, the cane juice drips from the rollers into a large tank. From the tank, it passes through an underground pipe to the boiling house."

"What happens in there? Something is boiled, I presume."

"See how quickly you learn, Cousin! Father said you were a quick study." John was enjoying himself. "Yes, the juice of the cane is boiled in there, in copper pots. The boiling causes sugar to crystallize into large chunks. Then everything goes to the curing house, that building you see over there." He pointed to an unassuming stone building that resembled the boiling house and complemented the three other structures within the cleared area. "In there we drain away whatever has not formed into sugar crystals. That's what you know as molasses. We then load sugar and molasses separately into hogsheads to be shipped out. Sugar goes to any market where we can sell it, while most of the molasses goes to distilleries to make rum. Quite the efficient operation. Though in my estimation it does not go quite far enough."

"What do you mean, 'not far enough'?"

"Let's defer that topic, shall we? Until after you've been here awhile and had a chance to learn the ropes, as you sailors like to say. You will be here quite a long while, is my understanding?"

"I believe so. Your father also wants us to spend time in Tobago with Robin. But based on what I've seen so far on *this* island, I suppose we'll stay put until you finally come to your senses and throw us out."

"Oh no, Cousin, I would never do that," John said, his words coming quick in protest, as though Richard had meant his words to be taken seriously.

"You're family, Richard. You and Katherine are welcome here as long as you wish to stay. I will say, though, that Tobago is quite a lovely island. A lot like Barbados, except it has much thicker rain forests. A very romantic spot, I might add. And I know Robin and Julia are looking forward to seeing you both. Robin remembers Katherine as fondly as I. By the bye, his is a smaller plantation, about two hundred acres. This one is closer to six hundred, about average for Barbados."

"Seems big enough to me," Richard said, as they began strolling back toward the house.

"Actually, it's not so big. Not when you compare it to plantations on Jamaica or Antigua, for instance. Those can be several thousand acres in size. But as I said, ours is typical of what you find here on Barbados . . . So what do you think?" he asked, in a way that made it sound as though Richard's first impressions truly mattered to him.

Richard glanced about, shaking his head. "I'm a sailor," he said, "not a businessman or planter like you, John. But I promised your father I will do everything I can to learn this business. I owe it to him and to my own father. I owe it to you too, for being so kind in taking us in."

"Nonsense, Richard. As I said, you are family. I remember you and your brother Will quite fondly from your visit here in '74. He may have been a trick to handle, but Will was so full of life and promise. I greatly missed you both after you sailed for Boston. As for 'owing,' if you ask me, what you 'owe' is to yourself. And to Katherine and to the children you shall have together. You'll fashion quite a comfortable living from sugar, once this wretched war is over and we can start making real money again."

"So I've observed," Richard said.

☆ ☆ ☆

Back at the main compound Richard took leave of John. He went down the hallway to the west room, tapped lightly on the door so as not to startle Katherine, and walked in. She was sitting before a mirror, dressed in her underclothes, combing and brushing her shoulder-length, damp hair. On the bed lay a fetching linen dress, light yellow in color with white at the belt and cuffs. When Richard entered, she paused in her ministrations.

"Did you have a nice tour with John?" she asked.

"Yes, very," he said, coming over and kissing the top of her head. "We strolled around a bit. This island's really quite the place. You'll enjoy exploring it. I missed you."

"I missed you too. And I can't wait to explore this island. Which I intend to do just as soon as I can find a young, dashing escort from Hingham, Massachusetts, who knows how to pleasure a lady."

Richard bowed low, grinning. "Your servant," he said in formal fashion. Straightening, he rested his hands on her shoulders and inhaled deeply. "What is that marvelous fragrance you're wearing?"

"Mist of frangipani. Or some such. George's wife, Sarah, gave me this little bottle, to keep. Then, oddly, she patted my hand and gave me quite the wink."

"I think I know why."

The aroma *was* intoxicating. And there she sat, seemingly immersed in it, already half undressed. He felt the familiar stirrings.

"Don't get any ideas," she said, reading his thoughts. "John told us to be prompt at seven, remember? I wonder what surprise he has in store for us. You'd best hurry if you want a bath and change of clothes before dinner. I recommend it. It's heavenly." She went back to combing her hair, rubbing here and there with a towel and working the comb to dry it and to fashion some semblance of curls. "Besides, my lord, if you remember, on the ship this morning you promised me satisfaction tonight."

He answered her reflection in the mirror.

"I did no such thing, my lady. As I recall, it was I who demanded satisfaction from you."

"You forget yourself, my lord," she chirped. "We're married now. It's all one and the same, isn't it?"

☆ ☆ ☆

THE DINING area of the plantation house encompassed what in a larger Fareham or Hingham home would have been two rooms. There was the dining table itself, a long rectangular affair made from imported East Indian teak, with two silver-branched candelabras in the middle and four matching chairs on each side and one at each end. A separate sitting area was set off at one end, encompassing a couch and three chairs all in mahogany, each piece decorated with matching blue and red cushions. There were no rugs or mats on the floors, just polished marble and stone. The windows and doorways, like those throughout the house, were designed to minimize the negatives of searing heat and gusty winds, while maximizing the benefits of cool breezes and light from sun and moon. Above the sitting area was a skylight of thick glass that could be raised at one end or covered completely with a curtain set flat against the ceiling and worked back and forth with a complex system of ropes and pulleys that reminded Richard of a ship's running rigging.

Richard was studying a centuries-old wall map of Barbados, and Katherine the inner workings of what John had earlier identified as a seventeenth-century John Fromanteel wall clock, when John made his entrance, dressed as he was before. He was followed close behind by a servant bearing a tray with four glasses on it. The servant carefully placed the tray on the table in front of the couch, wiped away a spot of something he noticed on the table, and departed without saying a word.

"Well, I must say, you two look rather refreshed," John said happily. "A bath does the trick, doesn't it? Though I will admit, I sometimes prefer a splash in the sea to clean off. You must walk down to the beach tomorrow and see for yourself. It's a marvelous place." He motioned to the tray, his words coming quick, in a keyed-up, staccato fashion. "Please, sit down. Do have a drink. It's a mixture of rum, fruit juice, and lime, with a sprig of ginger lily as garnish. If you'd prefer something lighter, Katherine, a glass of wine perhaps, I shall have Howard fetch it for you. We shall have wine with supper, of course."

"This will do fine, John. I'm getting used to rum, being married to a sailor."

"What's that? Oh yes. I see. Ha. Well said."

"There's an extra glass there, John," Richard pointed out. "Is someone joining us?"

John held up a finger, his ears pricked to the muffled sounds of a carriage arriving. Moments later there was a knock on the front door.

"Ah, yes," he beamed. "My 'surprise' for Katherine has arrived, punctual as always." He gave her a jovial wink.

Richard and Katherine gave each other a blank look. The servant George walked hurriedly across the hallway and opened the door. They heard a firm, authoritative voice speak in greeting. It was a voice, incredibly, that Katherine recognized.

"Hugh?" she gasped, rising from her seat. "Hugh!" she cried out, as a tall, attractive man bedecked in the full regalia of a Royal Navy officer strode confidently into the room.

"Oh, dear God, I can't believe this! Dear, sweet Hugh!" She ran to her brother, who took her in his arms and lifted her off her feet, twirling her around, laughing in joy with her. "I can't believe this!" she kept saying. "It's been . . . How many years? Here, look at this uniform! What are you, some sort of admiral?"

"No," he laughed. "But I am a flag lieutenant to one. Admiral Parker, here with the Windward Squadron. And you, Katherine! Look at *you!* You've changed not at all. Ever the fair princess. I've always said, show me your most beautiful, your most alluring, and I'll outclass them all with my younger sister."

"You shameless flatterer!" she giggled, slapping his arm. "You've never said any such thing." She went to John and embraced him. "Thank you, John," she said with heartfelt sincerity. She planted a kiss firmly on his cheek, a buss that seemed to give John Cutler a sudden case of sunburn.

"Yes, well, ahem," he managed. He shook Hugh Hardcastle's hand. "Welcome, Hugh. I'm glad you could come tonight."

Katherine went to Richard. "Hugh," she said, her right hand on the small of Richard's back, "I have the joy of introducing you to my husband. Richard, this is my brother Hugh."

Hugh bowed. "So *this* is the young naval officer who won the heart and hand of my darling sister," he said, sizing up Richard before offering him his hand. Richard took it, glad that Hugh seemed so open.

Given his own six-foot height, it was unusual for Richard to have to look up at someone. Now he did. Hugh Hardcastle was taller than Jamie, taller than either of his parents, and he cut an imposing figure standing there in his uniform. He was handsome, in a manly way, as one who had seen his brothers or father would expect. His face was clean-shaven and well-proportioned, with a square patrician chin and blondish brown hair snipped short around the edges, longer on top and combed back on the left side in waves of tiny curls. The tint of the hazel eyes scrutinizing Richard matched Katherine's almost perfectly.

"I am honored to meet you, Hugh," Richard said. "Katherine has told me much about you. Among other things, she credits you for teaching her how to handle a pistol. On our voyage down here, she hit just about every target thrown out to sea. She outgunned everyone, myself included."

"Did she now!" Hugh Hardcastle beamed with pleasure. "How well I remember those days. I was home on leave, as was Jamie, and for some reason this little sister of ours wanted to learn how to shoot. Mother was aghast, but Jamie and I agreed to teach her. Father found it all rather amusing. That is, until he observed how well she handled firearms. She put on quite a show for us. Not one to forget. So here's a piece of brotherly advice, Richard. When Katherine flares up, as I can assure you she will once the newlywed bliss wears off, avoid her at all costs if she has a pistol in her hand."

"Kindly remind my husband of that," Katherine said amid their shared laughter, "when I get old and fat, and he starts swooning over young doxies."

They finished their drinks and moved into the formal dining area, where two servants, a Creole couple, were busying themselves with the evening meal. Richard held out Katherine's chair, but deferred to her brother the honor of sitting next to her. He sat across the table from his wife, next to John, as a servant introduced the main dish.

"What is this?" Katherine asked, after sampling the tender white meat. She placed her fork down thoughtfully on the white china plate. "I have never tasted anything so delicious."

"Pompano," John replied, pleased with the compliment. "A local fish. Sarah prepares it rather well, doesn't she? She sprinkles a little coconut and nutmeg and God knows what else on top to give it that special flavor. Locals around here know how to use spices to bring out the best in foods."

"Do you eat fish a lot?" Richard asked.

"Yes. We're rather forced to, aren't we, Hugh? Mind you, there's plenty of arable land on Barbados, but almost all of it goes to planting cane. The profits, you understand. There are a few head of cattle and sheep about, and we have some plots where we grow vegetables and fruits and whatnot. The slaves have their plots too, but for as long as I can remember, the staple of their diet has been salted fish. Before the war, we imported that fish from America. Now it comes from the Grand Banks, mostly. So we take what we can, fresh, from local waters. I insist that my overseer allow slaves time off from their work in the fields to fish for their own purposes. Keeps them healthy and happy, though I must admit, my fellow planters don't always agree with my methods."

"I could live on this," Katherine said with reverence, savoring another forkful.

"Tell me about the wedding," Hugh said. "I've heard only a little. Was it at St. Stephen's? Reverend Fenton presiding?"

"Yes," Katherine replied. "I so wish you could have been there, Hugh. It was a heavenly day: warm and lovely, with lingering colors of autumn. Hundreds of people came, most of whom knew Richard and many quite curious to see him. His family was so very gracious to everyone, as you would expect. Especially Lizzy, my maid of honor. And Daddy looked so very handsome in his naval uniform."

"I'm sure. Well, at least you two have been blessed by the best. The Reverend Fenton has always been a favorite of mine. By the way, what was Father's reaction when you told him you were going to marry Richard?"

"I've seen him happier."

"Yes, I can imagine. How did you bring him around? Enough to attend your wedding, at least."

Katherine glanced at Richard. He offered no clue as to how he'd prefer this conversation to proceed.

"Hugh," she continued, "you know about the battle involving *Serapis*. And you know what happened to Jamie, and how Richard risked his life trying to save him."

"Yes," he allowed, his tone subdued. "It's been all over the papers, even down here. Though I did not know it was you, Richard, with Jamie, until I received a letter from Mother. I am forever indebted to you, for the care and love you gave my brother."

"I wish I could have done more, Hugh. I would not have been in that fight had I known Jamie was aboard *Serapis*."

"That's a noble statement, sir, truly. But with respect, I doubt its veracity. You are a naval officer. Fighting on the wrong side perhaps, but a naval officer nonetheless. You had your duty to consider."

There was a pause before Katherine went on.

"After the battle, Richard requested leave of his ship from his captain. He was granted that leave, in part because Captain Jones did not believe he would find another ship to command. There are no American warships left in Europe. Captain Pearson, of *Serapis,* accompanied Richard to London. Along the way he gave him a document for safe passage for the remainder of

Richard's journey, but it also contained words about Richard that were quite complimentary. Richard didn't want me to, but I showed that letter to Father, after he told me he would not attend the ceremony if I went through with the marriage. I was very angry with him. I told him I didn't understand what he had to gain by being so obstinate, though I was quite clear on what he had to lose."

Hugh Hardcastle whistled softly. "That would do it," he agreed, admiring his sister. He had never heard anyone talk to their father in that manner and could not imagine his reaction. "So you decided to come to Barbados. Why?"

Katherine deferred to Richard.

"It was a family decision," he explained. "As you know, there are many people in England who disagree with this war. But my aunt and uncle did not believe we could remain in England for long, though we did stay in a gardener's cottage on my uncle's estate for two months after the wedding, while the ships were making ready to sail. As more and more Whigs in Parliament are demanding peace, Tories are digging in and becoming more recalcitrant, especially in and around the naval base in Portsmouth. My family, and yours, feared there might be retaliation against me, an American, that could also put Katherine in danger. So staying in England long term did not seem a wise choice."

"I would agree. But could you not have sailed to America? Mind you, I am merely asking. I am delighted you are here. But many of our countrymen—*my* countrymen, I suppose I should say—have gone to America over the years. Katherine would be in no danger there."

"No, she wouldn't. And we seriously considered that. The trick was how to get there. Parliament has decreed that only military vessels are allowed to sail from England to America. To board one, I would have had to accept service in the Royal Navy, something I am not prepared to do under any circumstances. Even if I did, Katherine never would have been allowed to accompany me. So we decided it would be best for us to come here, to the Indies, to wait out the war while learning the family business as best I can—excuse me, as best *we* can. Katherine is very much a part of this."

"I see. I have to admit it makes sense. But are you truly prepared to sit out the war in Barbados? Come what may? I grant you, it's a rather delightful place in which to sit. But will you be content here?"

Richard held his gaze. It was Katherine who answered, looking directly across at her husband.

"We are prepared to do what circumstances dictate, Hugh. As for Richard, he has served his country with courage and honor. I love him for that and for so many other reasons. When this war is over, we plan to live in Massachusetts. In a town near Boston where Richard grew up. He has told me a great deal about it, and it sounds the perfect place to raise our family, in a land of hope and opportunity."

"I say," Hugh chuckled. "I mean no disrespect, Richard, but it seems to me you have converted my sister into quite the rebel patriot. I doubt your Dr. Franklin would be as eloquent on the subject." He looked hard at her and asked, in tones that seemed only half in jest, "Have you quite forgotten your roots, Katherine?"

Her eyes remained fixed on Richard's.

"No, dear Hugh," she said softly. "I have not forgotten my roots." She reached her hand across the table. Richard took it in his. "I have found them."

THE DAYS lapsed into weeks, the weeks into months, and the seasons changed from winter to spring, though it seemed like perpetual summer to Richard and Katherine as they blended into a routine that became as constant and captivating as the wind on Barbados. If the wind during the night maintained its easterly flow, dawn ushered in a peace and quiet so intense it magnified the early morning call of tropical birds that for most people, planters and slaves alike, served as an orchestral alarm to wake and get on with their day. Between nine and ten in the morning, like clockwork, the breeze picked up, freshening to fifteen or twenty knots by early afternoon, when thick white billowing clouds came scudding across the sky to cast intermittent sequences of sunlight and shade along the island's cane fields, plantations, and sandy beaches. By late afternoon the wind eased, and by nightfall the sea was again at peace and the sky clear, with the last tinges of red fading into night.

Daybreak was their favorite hour. If not too worn out from the previous night, they arose early and stole out of the house before anyone else awakened. Their destination: the nearby beach, where they would walk along the water's edge as sandpipers, terns, and other shorebirds afoot scurried off before them. Alone together, they splashed their feet in the blood-warm sea and waded out to view the odd fish and sea anemones attached to inshore rock formations clustered here and there in what seemed impossibly clean water compared to Boston or Portsmouth harbors. Unlike most sailors, Richard had learned as a youth to swim quite well, he and Will dismissing the commonly held superstition that a seaman's ability to swim merely denied him a quick and merciful death in the event his ship sank at sea. In these waters, he took pleasure in diving down to rock formations farther out from shore, snatching the occasional lobster from the seabed and surfacing quickly, his eyes stinging from the salt. It was one of the few activities he enjoyed that Katherine chose not to pursue. She was perfectly content to stand knee-deep in the gin-clear water and watch her husband glide effortlessly beneath the surface.

Later in the day, between ten and four, Richard often accompanied John or Robert Graves, the burly Cutler agent, around the grounds and various outbuildings to absorb as much as he could about sugar planting and processing. The more he saw, the more impressed he became. In one week, he learned, each mill could crush approximately two hundred tons of cane within its three vertical iron rollers. That amount of cane should produce fifty-five hundred gallons of juice that, in turn, yielded twelve tons of sugar crystals. Of course, John explained, that level of output depended on favorable winds and the ability of slave labor to clear and cart to the mill sixty to seventy loads of cane per day, about two acre's worth. It was the job of the overseer, acting in concert with John Cutler as the final arbitrator, to ensure that the one hundred twenty slaves in the fields maintained that level of production.

Days and weeks swept on like the endless swells rolling in from far across the Atlantic and breaking soothingly on the pink-white sands of Barbados.

"You're not cruel to them, are you?" Katherine asked one day, in reference to the slaves. She had accompanied Richard and John as she had on many previous days, fascinated by the processes involved with sugar production though unsettled by the sight of so many black men hacking and slashing and loading the carts from dawn to dusk, in such backbreaking and sweltering conditions.

"We make every effort not to be," John replied, drawing a kerchief from his coat pocket and mopping his brow. He offered them a seat, to rest a while, on a bench outside the great house in the shade of palm trees and beside a ten-foot-high century plant, its yellow blossoms in full bloom and throwing off a distinct and pleasing aroma. "Sometimes we have no choice, but that's the exception. Local authorities are rarely summoned up here. As I have told

Richard, I do not believe in whipping slaves unless it becomes absolutely necessary. To the contrary, I believe, and I know Robin believes, that by keeping slaves content, and allowing them certain privileges here and there that most other plantations do not, we keep their spirits up as well as their production levels. You've seen their homes. They're not so very bad, are they?"

"Much better than I feared," Katherine admitted.

"Well, it's the least we can do for them. After all, it's their labor that makes sugar so profitable. Mind you, it's not entirely free labor, despite what many people seem to think. We don't pay them of course, but we do provide decent food and shelter. That cost is no small matter. Study the books. You'll see that last year we had expenses totaling almost nineteen hundred pounds, against revenues of thirty-six hundred pounds. The vast portion of those expenses went to maintaining our people. Not just the slaves; we employ some poorer whites—'Redlegs' as they're called locally—and one or two freed Negroes to work the mills and such."

"That still leaves seventeen hundred pounds in profit," Richard calculated. "A tidy sum for one year's output, wouldn't you say?"

"It may appear so," John allowed. "But bear in mind the taxes we must pay. Each year the government demands more and more from us. And the scrutiny they give us! It seems to me sometimes that the king's agent in Barbados lives up here with my bookkeeper. Taxes are suffocating us, and exposing us to considerable risk, should we get hit by a hurricane for instance. And the 'profit' you mention does not take into account any distributions to Cutler family members. Nor does it consider what improvements and repairs we must make, nor what absolutely must be put aside each year in reserves. Without these reserves, we could be wiped out overnight by a hurricane. Consider that these days it costs fifty-six hundred pounds to establish a small, one-hundred-acre plantation. Imagine what it would cost to establish one this size from scratch." He spread out his arms expansively.

"Is there no insurance to protect against losses?" Katherine asked.

"Unfortunately, no. Insurance comes available only when goods are loaded onto ships bound for England. Lloyd's won't touch hurricane insurance, nor will local companies like Lascelles or Maxwell. And because of the war, the rates they charge once goods *are* aboard ship are outrageous." He said this with some agitation.

Richard asked, "On our first day here, John, when we took that walk, I recall you saying that you don't believe the process here goes far enough. I'm curious. What did you mean by that?"

"You have a good memory," John said, calming down. "And I'm pleased to see you're paying such close attention. The issue you raise is a very important one. And yes, I'd be delighted to share my thoughts with you. But first, let me see if I can scour up some refreshment for us. Some light rum, with lime perhaps, and a few sandwiches, as I understand they are now called in England. After our first lord of the Admiralty, correct? A rather good idea, I must say. At least he accomplished *something* while in office."

As John hurried off to get things going in the kitchen, Katherine rested her head against Richard's shoulder and closed her eyes.

"Sleepy, are we?" he murmured, a tinge of sarcasm in his voice. He put an arm around her shoulder to draw her in, make her more comfortable.

"Mm, yes. It's the sun. And sea air." Her voice was fast fading. "And the fact that my husband, whom I love dearly, could not keep his hands off me last night."

"*Me,* was it? Aren't you the jolly one." He soothed back strands of chestnut hair blown free by the trades and kissed her forehead. "Not exactly how I remember things . . ."

It had been a rapturous night of lovemaking, more typical of the early days of their marriage, from that very first night when he had thought to withdraw from her, for he was hurting her and there was blood. "No!" she whispered, clutching him to her, one hand gripping the flesh of his back, the other guiding his essence back toward her own, urging him, commanding him, in, ever deeper. There had been no embarrassment and little awkwardness since their first time together, their passion steeped, in the beginning, in a savage intensity, an almost animal-like need to have, to hold, to utterly possess. With the passage of time their movements had become more artful, when, secure at last in the certainty of their union, they experienced the uniquely human desire to protect, to caress, to discover and tease his pleasure points, to more intensely trigger her release by deferring his own, to love comfortably, confidently, unconditionally.

Last night, lying naked together in the tender afterglow of sweet outpourings, she had snuggled up against him in the soft light of flickering candles, satisfied, but not yet entirely fulfilled. She kissed his neck and shoulder as her hand kneaded the hard muscles of his abdomen, trying her best to arouse him, to bring him back from the abyss of slumber into which she knew he deserved to go, but loath to have the night end just yet.

"Richard, wake up," she whispered. "Please wake up, darling. I have something to ask you."

He flopped an arm over his eyes. "Lord, woman," he groaned. "You are insatiable. Don't you *ever sleep*?"

"Why sleep when I have you to play with? Seriously, Richard, I have a question for you. Are you awake?"

When his response was a low pitiful moan, she ran her hand high up his inner thigh, gathered him in, and squeezed gently. "Are you awake?"

"I am now."

"Good." She let go. "Richard, there's something I want to ask you, something I've been meaning to ask for some time."

"Well, ask it."

"It's of a rather . . . personal nature and I don't wish to embarrass you."

He turned on his side and propped himself up on an elbow. "What?" he asked warily.

She kissed his lips, then lightly pecked at the lobe of his ear. "How did you get the nickname 'Dubber'?" she whispered.

"*What?*" He slapped her bottom.

"I'm serious," she squealed. "I want to know. How did you get that nickname?"

He lay on his back, his hands under his head, staring up at the ceiling.

"From my little sister, Lavinia. That's what she called me when she first started talking."

"How did she end up with 'Dubber' from 'Richard'?"

"I haven't a clue." He looked at her. "How did I end up with such an inquisitive wife? And an high-bred English prude, to boot?"

She nestled up over him, her long chestnut hair curling down upon his chest as she looked into his eyes and ran her tongue over her lower lip. "Oh, so now I'm a prude, am I? Is *that* what you think? Well, my lord," she purred, her lips moving slowly, in exquisitely soft, moist steps, down from his face to his neck, chest, stomach, and beyond. "I must try my hardest to dispel that notion, mustn't I."

Richard closed his eyes, the moans emanating from the core of his being no longer ones of protest but of encouragement . . .

☆ ☆ ☆

"**O**H DEAR, oh dear," John fussed, returning from the great house with a newspaper folded under his arm. "I see Katherine has fallen asleep. I really must apologize. It's my fault. I should not be keeping you two up so late, however much I enjoy your company. Please do forgive me."

"Of course I forgive you, John," Richard said. "But I daren't speak for my wife. She tends to hold a grudge for some time."

"What? Oh dear. You're not serious. I had thought . . . Oh, ha, I see. Ever the cracker, aren't you." He sat down, relieved, on an adjacent stone bench. After mopping his brow with a kerchief despite a pleasant and unexpectedly cool breeze on the shaded patio, he said, keeping his voice low, "Well, I say let the poor girl sleep. It will do her good. And I do promise to be more considerate henceforth. Though sadly, I don't know for how much longer that should be."

"What do you mean?"

"Here. Have a look. A post rider delivered it this morning."

It was the current issue of the *Bridgetown Gazette*. Richard took the newspaper from John with his free hand and unfolded the front page on his lap. There were several headlines featured in bold black on that page. The first one to catch his eye was a herald of bad news.

CHARLESTON SURRENDERS! Charleston, South Carolina, 18 May 1780. Generals Clinton and Cornwallis are victorious! The City of Charleston has fallen! Following a long siege the southern citadel finally has surrendered. In what has been described as the worst defeat for rebel forces since the start of the war, the rebel general Benjamin Lincoln and 5,000 Continentals have laid down their arms. This force, according to British military sources, comprised almost the entire Southern Command of rebel general George Washington. In addition, the British military seized three rebel warships in Charleston harbor: two frigates, Boston and Providence, and a sloop of war, Ranger. These ships will soon see service in the Royal Navy. As a result of capturing these three ships, what Whitehall has never considered a significant naval presence has all but ceased to exist. Lord Cornwallis and the British Army are now firmly entrenched in the American South. With his victory, coupled with what are now confirmed reports of a recent mutiny of two regiments in Washington's army in the colony of New Jersey, the War of Rebellion is expected to reach a satisfactory conclusion in the near future.

"*Ranger.* My first ship. And General Lincoln . . . A mutiny . . . Oh dear God . . ."

"What?" John got up and came over to where Richard was sitting. "Oh no, dear chap," he said, peering over his shoulder. "*This* is the notice I was referring to."

He pointed at a short notice printed entirely in bold black, with a thick black border.

YELLOW FEVER REPORTED. Bridgetown, Barbados, 24 May 1780. Several cases of Yellow Fever, also known locally as the Black Vomit, have been reported in Bridgetown and outlying areas. Citizens are urged not to panic and to follow normal procedures to limit the spread of the disease. Government House will issue frequent communiqués to alert citizens to developments as they occur.

☆ ☆ ☆

"WHAT ARE 'normal procedures'?" Richard asked absently, his mind absorbed in the terrible news contained in the first article he had read.

"For us up here on the plantations, it simply means staying put. Not going down to Bridgetown or other low-lying areas unless it's quite necessary. The disease rarely affects us up here. It happens, but it's rare. Which is why, by the way, I happen to believe the disease *is* carried by mosquitoes. Breezes up here tend to keep them at bay."

"And you believe Katherine and I should leave Barbados? Because of this?"

"Not just because of this. You are planning in any event to spend time in Tobago. Now might be just the time to get cracking. As a precautionary measure, you understand. For reasons I cannot explain, Tobago is not as susceptible to the fever. Also, we are fast approaching the hurricane season, and hurricanes tend not to trouble that island. Please understand that I do not want you and Katherine to leave, Richard. But maybe it's something you should consider."

"We will, John, thank you. I'll talk with Katherine about it as soon as she wakes up. And John, for the moment, I'd appreciate your not mentioning anything to her about what's written here about Charleston and the war."

"Mum's the word, dear cousin."

"**WILL HUGH** be all right?" was Katherine's first question when Richard informed her later that afternoon of the outbreak of fever and John's recommendation that they start making preparations to sail to Tobago.

"I'm sure he will be. Government House and the fort are built high up, no doubt for this very reason. And who knows. Perhaps they'll cancel his shore duty and put him back aboard ship until the danger has passed."

Which is precisely what the Royal Navy did, as they were to discover the next day. A message came from Hugh Hardcastle requesting their company for dinner in the snug little bungalow that served as his living quarters ashore while attending to the administrative needs of Adm. Hyde Parker, an obscenely overweight and pretentious windbag as Katherine had earlier described him to Richard after the first time she had met the admiral in the company of her brother. Parker was apparently a seaman who preferred the comforts of Government House to the confines of a ship, no matter its size, though he appeared quite keen to put to sea once reports of sickness began to circulate. He had desired his staff to join him, and they would be departing Carlisle Bay in two days, in the company of five other ships of the line and two frigates.

"Where are you sailing?" Richard asked him, after finishing off the remains of a surprisingly tasty beef pie. He took a sip of a fruity red wine and wiped his mouth with a napkin.

"On patrol, to nowhere in particular," Hugh replied. "See here, would either of you care for another round of pie? I'm afraid it's not what you're accustomed to on the plantation. It's more like wardroom fare."

Richard shook his head no. Katherine asked, "If you're not going anywhere in particular, Hugh, why go? Is it just to escape the fever? You told me you felt quite immune to it up here. And what if one of your crew has already been infected? While on shore leave? Would he not endanger everyone else aboard ship?"

Hugh smiled affectionately at his sister.

"He would, if that were to happen. But it won't. Everyone sailing tomorrow, except for the admiral, myself, and two other officers, have been aboard ship for two days. If a sailor was infected, we'd know about it. As to leaving Bridgetown, it's partly to escape the sickness, I suppose, though the fever seems not to be spreading much.

"But there *is* a reason for us to be putting to sea," he went on, "and I must confess to looking forward to being on a quarterdeck again. No doubt I will be back on shore duty in another month or two. I've already been informed that I shan't be returning to England with the squadron during hurricane season. I have been ordered to remain here, in Bridgetown."

"What's the reason then for putting to sea?"

Hugh gave his brother-in-law a thoughtful look.

"As you no doubt have learned while living in Barbados, Richard, today the theater of war is more here than in America. There's a good reason for that. At stake are the sugar islands, any one of which means a great deal to a European nation. We go back and forth with France, capturing one small island here, giving up another one there. Sometimes bigger islands are involved, as when France captured Dominica in '78, or we captured St. Lucia in '79. I was in that battle, by the bye, as fourth lieutenant aboard *Alarm* under Rear Admiral Barrington. We took St. Lucia right from under the noses of the French naval base on Martinique. They tried to take it back," he added defiantly, caught up in the memory. "D'Estaing landed five thousand soldiers on the other side of the island and attacked our fifteen hundred redcoats holding position on a rise. That battle was rather like your Breed's Hill, though this time around the gods of war were apparently with us."

He gave Richard a smug grin before continuing, "Up to now there has been a balance of power in the Caribbean. We have a number of first and second rates at our base here in Bridgetown, as well as English Harbor and Kingston. The French have had more or less an equivalent number at Fort Royal and other locations. But the French apparently are intending to increase the number of their ships in these waters. By quite a large number, if our intelligence is correct, and it normally is. We know, for instance, that D'Estaing recently arrived in Martinique with twenty ships of the line. And with twice the number of soldiers crammed into transports than we have in service throughout the Indies. Spies also tell us the Dons have finally decided to make their move. They're on their way here with a sizable fleet, with designs on Jamaica, so the rumor goes. Jamaica? Ha! My opinion? They're coming here to snatch up the crumbs of war and to protect Cuba, their main base in the Indies."

"I thought Admiral Rodney defeated the Dons at Cape St. Vincent. I read in the *Gazette* that the entire Spanish fleet besieging Gibraltar had been either captured or destroyed. Certainly Rodney's arrival here in March created quite a victory spectacle."

"Rodney did defeat the Dons. Quite handily, as the article described. But the Dons and Frogs have been building up their fleets in recent years. Combined, they have a good many more ships than we do, and theirs are new and fast, whereas ours . . . well, let's just say ours have seen their share of sea duty over the years. Ships without copper bottoms rarely last more than seven years in these waters."

"You're scaring me, Hugh," Katherine said. "Where are you going with this?"

Hugh covered her hand with his. "You needn't be concerned," he assured her. "France and Spain may have more ships, but we have far superior admirals and sailors and battle tactics. I don't have time now, but remind me at a later date to explain to you Admiral Rodney's new theory of concentrated firepower. It's brilliant. Absolutely brilliant. My grandest wish? To be serving in his fleet when next he engages the enemy. Talk about a victory spectacle, Richard . . .

"So you see, you cannot compare a D'Estaing or a De Guichen or Solano with a Rodney or a Hood. Our officers and gun crews are second to none. I'll take one British tar to five of the enemy any day. I mean no offense to you, Richard."

"None taken, Hugh."

"You speak of brilliant admirals," Katherine said. "I have met Admiral Parker."

"Aye, so you have. He's an administrative type, really, not a fighting admiral like Rodney. He's also my superior officer, so you shan't cajole me into speaking ill of him, however hard you try."

The hour was getting on. If the Cutlers were to make the four-mile journey back to the plantation in any hint of daylight, they would have to take their leave soon. Out the wide rectangular window that comprised fully a third of the harbor-facing wall of the bungalow, they could see the outer stone edges of Government House and the fort a short ways below it. Soldiers in red and white uniforms patrolled back and forth along the parapet, their rifles up and aslant on their left shoulders, the burnished steel tips of their bayonets gleaming in the late-day sun. Far below, in Carlisle Bay, what seemed like an army of ants on model ships was swarming over the weather decks and rigging of the squadron, making ready the warships that would sail on the morning tide.

"Richard," Hugh Hardcastle suddenly interjected, "may I speak bluntly to you? Time is short, and there are things that need be said."

"Of course, Hugh."

"Thank you." He cleared his throat before launching in. "Before I met you, Richard, I was not inclined to like you. Yes, I had heard Jamie speak favorably of you many times over the years. And I had a strong hunch even then about how Katherine felt about you. But you had, after all, taken up arms against my country. And you had wooed my sister away from my best friend. On top of that, I will admit, I was perhaps overly influenced by my father's opinion of you. So when your cousin John extended the invitation to come to dinner at his house that first night, I was happy to accept. I so wanted to see Katherine. But I was not especially looking forward to meeting you."

"Hugh . . ." Katherine began to protest. Richard quickly put his hand on her arm. "Go on, Hugh," he said.

"Thank you. This is not easy for me." He downed the remainder of his wine in one long uninterrupted drink, then placed the glass gently down on the table. "I must say, however, that in recent weeks I have come to change my mind about certain things. Katherine is largely responsible for that. She loves you very much, Richard. Very much indeed. More than ever I thought she would love any man. She was never one to easily yield her affections, you understand. How often I used to tease her about her high standards when she would send home one suitor after another, some with impeccable credentials, with their tails between their legs. She was never cruel to them, but she made her point. So when she spoke to me about you, which she has done whenever she has come to Bridgetown to visit with me, I have listened carefully to what she's had to say. The long and short of it, Richard, is this: whatever it is you two have found together, Lord knows this topsy-turvy world of ours needs a great deal more of it. Which is a roundabout way of telling you that I could not approve more of your marriage to my sister. I do hope that some day, when this war is over and your side has won, that you and I can find together some of that special relationship you had with Jamie."

"When our side has won?" Katherine asked, as moved as Richard by Hugh's words and as stunned by that surprise announcement. "Is that truly what you believe?"

"It is. In the end, principle will triumph over greed and corruption. Sadly, our military and government are rife with both. As bad as General Howe might have been, General Clinton is worse. He refuses to fight, even when the odds are overwhelmingly in his favor. Lord Cornwallis is an excellent soldier, and he holds Clinton in such contempt he won't communicate with him, much less take orders from him, though Clinton is his superior officer. He has said publicly that he will take orders only from Lord Germaine, the American Secretary in London. As for Admiral Marriot Arbuthnot, the new commander in chief of Royal Navy forces in America, let's just say he makes Admiral Parker look like Julius Caesar."

"But just a moment ago you sang the praises of British admirals."

"I did, Katherine. And I meant what I said. British admirals are worthy of such praise, those that are stationed here in the Indies. That's my point, don't you see? England has lost her heart for the war in America. It's been hard for me, but I've come to realize that if we don't stop fighting men like you, Richard, our brothers, England is in danger of losing her soul. Things will continue as they have in the Indies, because our *real* enemies are here and because there is so much more at stake. But in America it will come down to one final, glorious battle in which the military genius of your General Washington, together with his French allies, will be pitted against our corrupt and incompetent generals, most of whom, except for Cornwallis, have lost their will to fight. Then, God be praised, this godforsaken war in America will be over."

14

TOBAGO

1780–81

VICTORY IN SOUTH CAROLINA. Bridgetown, Barbados, 21 October 1780. General Cornwallis has won a major victory at Camden, in the colony of South Carolina. In his march northward to clear the Carolinas of rebel forces, Lord Cornwallis was confronted by Continental regulars and local militia under the command of rebel general Horatio Gates, the self-proclaimed "Hero of Saratoga." In the ensuing battle the rebel army was routed. It is reported that Colonel Banastre Tarleton and his Royal Dragoon Guards chased the fleeing rebels northward and would have annihilated them had his cavalry been able to ford a river across from which the retreating rebels had dug in to return fire. Captured rebel soldiers confirm that the Southern Army of George Washington has been all but destroyed, a favorable circumstance that leaves the door open to Lord Cornwallis to quickly subdue the colonies of North Carolina and Virginia. Thousands of Tory sympathizers are expected to rise up in those colonies in support of their British brethren. Rebel general Washington is not expected to march south with his main army as long as General Clinton retains his iron grip on New York City. The "southern strategy" framed by American Secretary Lord Germaine and carried out by British commanders in North America appears to be succeeding.

ROBIN CUTLER waited patiently as Richard Cutler reread the lead articles in the *Bridgetown Gazette*. It was frustrating, he knew, for Richard to have to wait for the mail packet to arrive in Scarborough twice each week, bearing mail and the most recent editions of the *Gazette*. News from America was old by the time it was printed in Bridgetown. Pity his cousin had to endure another week for that same news to reach Tobago.

Richard skimmed through the remainder of the ten-page newspaper, folded it, and laid it down on the stone bench on which they were sitting.

"Anything in there I should know?"

Richard smiled in a resigned way that his cousin had come to expect in such circumstances.

"The usual," he answered. "The British continue to march through the Carolinas. Whatever opposition the Continentals are able to muster comes to naught. According to the *Gazette,* it's only a matter of time until Cornwallis has conquered the entire South. When that happens, it won't be long before General Washington is forced to capitulate."

"So this foolish war is coming to an end. Hip, hip . . . ?"

There was no immediate reply. They had dissected this topic more than once.

"I suppose one's reaction, Robin, depends on one's allegiances. As my acquaintance Dr. Franklin said to Congress at the start of the war, 'We must all hang together, or surely we will all hang separately.'"

"Well, cousin, that's one thing you needn't fret about. You're welcome to hide out in the curing house as long as need be, until King George and his chums are through meting out their punishments. However, I'm afraid Katherine shan't be joining you. Julia would not have it. Hanging would be a merciful sentence for me should I do anything to take your bride away from her."

Richard grinned. He liked his cousin Robin in ways quite different from his feelings for John, since the two were so different from each other. About the only thing similar about them was their stocky build and their brownish blond hair streaked almost white by the sun, hair that Robin had tied back tight in a club-shaped knot, the one bow to fashion he allowed. He explained it was simply to keep his hair out of his eyes and was easier to fashion than plaits. As a rule, Robin wore elegant but plain clothes, avoiding the silk neckstocks and gaiters and other, more garish accompaniments preferred by many English planters. Even the straw hat he wore had none of the colorful ribbons and bands sported by his neighbors. It was simply a wide-brimmed hat, frayed around the edges, meant to keep the searing noonday sun off his face.

When he walked about with family or friends, he carried a plain bamboo walking stick, much like his father did in England, using it to point out a mango hummingbird here or a crab-eating raccoon there, should one scurry across their path. Unlike John, he was able to answer most of Katherine's questions about life on this exotic tropical island.

Robin had settled on Tobago in '77, when the Cutler family acquired a modest sugar plantation there through the bankruptcy of the former owner whose mortgage the Cutler family held. Robin had brought with him a bride, née Julia Fletcher, a handsome woman with mahogany-tinged hair, ruddy complexion, and blue gray eyes. She had grown up in Barbados, enjoying the social privileges of one related to the Mount Gay Rum families, but with few of the restraints normally imposed on a young lady of breeding in Britain. She had taken to Katherine immediately, delighted to host a young woman her own age and of similar background. Katherine found Julia's company delightful, especially when she discovered, to her joy of joys, that Julia was an avid rider. The plantation contained a small herd of horses and a smart array of English leather saddles. Each day, either early in the morning or later in the afternoon when the sun was less intense, the two women rode together to explore another of the island's glorious nooks and crannies, mindful of Robin's stern admonition not to stray far from the plantations on the flat, southwestern end of the island. During the previous decade there had been four slave uprisings on Tobago. With a recent influx of African slaves increasing the ratio of blacks to whites to nine to one, he wanted them taking no chances.

"Is that why you're not keen to maintain this plantation?" Richard asked him one evening soon after their arrival, when the two men were alone and discussing the possibilities of another insurrection. "I can understand if the answer is yes."

"No, not really," Robin had replied. "Sugar production can yield wonderful profits, Richard, but along with those profits come commensurate risks. No island is immune. Planters on Barbados may not fear their slaves, but they have hurricanes to contend with and a greater fear of plague. Fact is, planters on Tobago *must* import African slaves since there aren't many native borns here. A few Arawaks and Caribs is all."

"Then you support John's contention that the Cutler family should consolidate its holdings on Barbados and extend the family business to include a distillery?"

"Yes. John and I are in complete agreement on that. Father is too, though it took some doing to convince him. He's quite traditional, you know. Maintain one line of business and do it well has always been his philosophy. Irony is, even when he said that, we were actually engaged in *two* lines: shipping as well as lending money to the planters whose products we ship. When we acquired our plantations by default, he was not pleased at first. He had thoughts recently of selling part ownership in them. I understand you met the three gentlemen involved."

"I did. At your father's offices in Gosport."

"Much to my relief, and John's, Father has decided against doing that. Don't misunderstand. We as a family are not making the money we used to, and there is no question we will require considerable funding if we are to establish a distillery on Barbados. One way to raise the necessary funds, I should think, is to sell this plantation, perhaps to those same three gentlemen. You've heard the expression in England, 'Rich as a Tobago planter?' No? Well, that's the perception back home. It's a misconception in today's world. But it will serve us well. This piece of property will fetch a handsome price."

"There *is* one thing, Robin. If the Cutler family produces and sells its own label of rum, would we not then be in direct competition with Julia's family? John seems not the least concerned about that. Are you?"

Robin shook his head. "I agree with John. We could both have fifty distilleries on Barbados and still not meet world demand for rum or sugar. As you know, John has met with the Mount Gay families. Not only are they not concerned by our venture, they have proposed ways we might work together to our mutual profit. In fact, it was their enthusiasm that finally brought Father around."

"Well, Robin," Richard smiled, "I must say, you seem to have done quite well for yourself. In business *and* in marriage. Or perhaps I should say, in the combination of the two. Julia's a love. And she brings with her some of the richest sugar plantations in the Indies."

"Yes. She does. Though, man to man, Richard, I would not have married Julia had I not fallen for her as I did. When we first met, at a ball in Bridgetown, I was not aware of her family connections. Nor was I made fully aware of them until after I had proposed. She didn't tell me earlier, I suppose, because she wanted to be certain I was marrying her for the right reasons. I respect her for that." He touched Richard's arm. "I must say, Cousin, you have fared rather well yourself in that area. I was delighted to learn of your marriage to Katherine. I remember her as a pretty little thing running about with ribbons in her hair, chasing after butterflies and squirrels while her nurse huffed and puffed chasing after *her.* What mischief she and Lizzy used to get into! She was always hatching some scheme with my sister, the more so as they grew older. 'What a handful that child is!' my poor mother would complain, though always with affection." He grinned at the memories. "Your Katherine is very much like my Julia, which no doubt is why they have taken so to each other. We're lucky men, eh?"

"We are indeed, Robin," Richard said, relishing his cousin's anecdotes of Katherine as a young girl. Then, he added, "So we sell this plantation, use the proceeds to establish a distillery on Barbados, and ship out sugar, rum, and molasses in vessels owned by the Cutler family whenever possible. We would then own the entire process, one end clear to the other, on an island protected by the Royal Navy and a fort with a sizable garrison."

"That's it, in brief. That last part you mention is critical. We are not well protected here on Tobago. From our own slaves or from the French or Spanish. Which is why we planters decided some time ago to form our own militia. I have the honor of being appointed captain of militia. The Royal Navy rarely patrols these waters and maintains few ships in Scarborough harbor. The garrison at Fort King George has only fifty soldiers. And their commanding officer . . ."

"Yes, I've had the privilege of meeting your Major Butterworth," Richard said, his expression turning sour. "Quite full of himself, isn't he? When Katherine and I registered at the fort as Americans on *his* island, I thought he'd have us arrested on the spot. No doubt it was our kinship to you that has kept me, at least, from being hauled into prison. And the way that slimy bastard kept ogling Katherine . . ."

"Does remind one of those miniature alligators one sees slithering about," Robin had to admit.

BRITISH SETBACKS. Bridgetown, Barbados, 9 November 1780. Rebel forces have declared victory at a remote location in the colony of North Carolina known as King's Mountain. The battle would hardly be worth reporting were it not for the capture of the British Commander, Major Patrick Ferguson, renowned in England as the inventor of the breech-loading rifle, and as the soldier at the Battle of Brandywine who had rebel general George Washington in his sights but declared it "not good form" to fire upon a man who had turned his back to him. The rebels refused to fight on open ground. As has been their custom since the defeat at Camden, they hid behind trees and ambushed the British regulars, then ran away through dense undergrowth before the British soldiers could return fire. Comparisons of this battle to the Battle of Trenton in 1777 seem far-fetched, though no doubt rebel morale has been given a boost.

In another development, it is reported that the Comte de Rochambeau and his son, the Vicomte, have landed in Newport, in the colony of Rhode Island, in command of 4,000 French soldiers. What Rochambeau intends to do remains uncertain, though sources speculate he will eventually seek to join with Washington's army encamped north of New York City. The French force would effectively double the size of the rebel army, proof positive of how few colonials support this rebellion.

☆ ☆ ☆

"RICHARD? WHERE are you, darling? Are you ready to go?" Her voice echoed pleasantly down the hallways.

"I'm downstairs in the study," he called up to her. "And yes, I'm ready." He put the newspaper, folded, on the desk. Here was good news for a change. Hardly anything worth celebrating, but good news nonetheless. His spirits brightened considerably.

Two sets of footsteps clicked hurriedly on the brick stairway. A moment later, Katherine appeared in the doorway of the study alongside Julia Cutler. During the months the newlyweds had spent in the tropics, the color of their skin exposed to the sun had deepened from a light pink to a dark red to a rich brown. Julia stood in marked contrast to them both, her Scottish heritage reflected in a perpetual sunburn that defied a natural tan.

"Good morning, Julia," Richard greeted her.

"Good morning to you, dear Richard," she replied with equal affection, a hint of a highland brogue in her speech that always reminded Richard of Captain Jones when they first met in Hingham. "I understand you and Katherine are about to set out for a ride. I have packed a bite for you to eat, and some wine. And you needn't worry about your horse. He's a gentle old swayback. Katherine told me how you received that scar on your forehead."

"A mark of honor," Katherine sighed, in a teasing sort of way. "A gallant squire out to win the heart of his fair maid."

"Don't believe a word of it, Julia. It was nothing like that. There I was, minding my own business, when suddenly that dumb old hack heard the dinner bell and tore off as though bitten by a snake. I doubt a royal hussar could have remained in the saddle."

"All right you two," Julia reprimanded them with mock sternness. "That will do. Be off. And Richard, I have a strong hunch you will quite enjoy the spot Katherine and I have picked out for you today. We came upon it a few days ago, during one of our rides. You'll want to spend some time there." She raised her eyebrows and cocked her head in Katherine's direction.

"Thank you, Julia," Richard said mystified. "I'm looking forward to it . . . I think."

Outside, two horses were tethered to a post near a semicircular stone wall marking the top of the drive and carriage turnaround adjacent to the great house—which to English planters on Tobago was a term of greater relevance than on Barbados. Tobago was a small island lying in the horse latitudes close to the equator. Here prevailing winds were as likely to be light and capricious from the northwest as they were to be strong and steady from the southeast, as in Barbados. There being minimal threats from hurricanes or other damaging winds, planters on Tobago felt more at ease in reflecting their personal taste, and financial resources, in their houses. The Cutler house was modest compared to others in the area, and it was built in the widely adopted T shape, its upper end incorporating an outdoor porch facing north to the paved drive and whatever breezes were available. Living and sleeping quarters were stretched out below on the stem of the T. At its base, detached to shield the house from the heat of cooking fires, was the kitchen.

"We're not going to the beach?" Richard asked. He was guiding his horse beside Katherine's on a down-sloping dirt road winding northeastward alongside a riverbed. Across the river they could see a slave village, a cluster of modest but well-maintained huts with palm-thatched roofs, coral-stone walls, and shaded cooking pits interspersed among them. Few people were about. It was midmorning, and all but the youngest and oldest of the slaves would be at work either in the cane fields to the southwest or in the mills adjacent to the river. On Tobago, where winds were often capricious, water was the preferred source of power to turn the rollers that crushed the cane.

"No," she said. "We're staying inland on this trail. Did you see that forest up ahead, just as we were starting down? That's where we're going. It's five, maybe six miles from here."

"Katherine," Richard said sternly, "you and Julia have ridden up-island that far? It's almost halfway to the other end. Robin has made it clear he wants you two remaining close to the plantation. I agree with him. There are far fewer settlers up there."

"I realize that. But do you remember the planter we met from one of the big estates up north? The one you liked so much? Tirpin, I believe his name was. He's the chap who told Julia about the place I'm taking you. He swears it's quite safe. You'll see, darling. We'll be fine. Besides, I always have my faithful pistol, just in case." She patted the folds of her ankle-length linen culottes, where a slight bulge indicated where a small pistol with a large bore lay concealed in an inner pocket. Robin had given it to her and insisted she always take it with her on her rides, as a precaution, when he learned from Richard how well she handled firearms.

They were riding bareback, there being no need on this slow, winding path through thickening, jade-colored foliage to burden their horses with saddles. As he had from the time he first observed Katherine ahorse, Richard found himself admiring the easy and confident way she coordinated her movements with those of her steed. Only when forced by constraints of genteel society to ride sidesaddle did she seem at all out of her element. Fortunately for her, such constraints had been rare in the privacy of her family's estate in England and nonexistent here on Tobago.

At a point where the trail veered upward along the spine of undulating hills and peaks running down the center of the island, Katherine nudged her horse left onto a path so narrow it was almost hidden in the dense underbrush of leafy ferns, bamboo thickets, and tree-climbing philodendrons. She went on ahead, Richard following close behind. Here, the growth was a more seasonal mix of deciduous rain forest compared to the lush, almost impenetrable jungle higher up. This same forest, Robin had told them, had years ago covered almost the entire island. After 1763, and the treaty by which France ceded Tobago to Great Britain, many English families had settled on the island, hacking down whatever was in their way to make room for fields of sugar cane. They had started on the southwestern end of Tobago and worked their way northeastward into the steeper interior, cutting down so many trees that some planters became alarmed. Ten years ago, a dedicated group of them sent off the first of several petitions to King George, asking him to take royal action to preserve what forests remained on the middle and northeastern parts of the island. Although coming late to the cause, Robin Cutler supported it as avidly as any planter, and he celebrated along with the others when Parliament enacted a law creating, for the first time in England's history, a Crown reserve.

"Where in God's name are we going?" Richard called ahead, as he blocked the backlash of a branch with his arm. "Into your jungle lair so you can take advantage of me? Is that what you and Julia were chortling about?" From overhead he heard a heavy flap of wings; to his right, he noticed a trio of brown-spotted tree frogs clinging to the bark of a yellow-flowering acacia tree, giving him a poker-faced, bored stare as they passed by. "Cheer up, chaps," he chided them.

"Not much farther, darling. Just a little way ahead."

He heard it before he saw it: the pleasing sound of water tumbling down, gurgling and splashing in ever louder patters as they approached a hidden lagoonlike body of water surrounded on three sides by steep granular volcanic rock and a myriad of aromatic flora. Richard knew or cared little about flowers, but he readily recognized the scent of orchids, and there were hundreds about, tiny white ones attached to limbs of small trees lining the perimeter of the lagoon. Directly across from them, from a summit many times the height of the Cutler house, a river turned white as it spilled over the edge of the cliff and cascaded down the sides of the great stone wall, splashing into shallow pools where tantalizing shrouds of mist and vapor hovered over exposed rock.

Katherine slid off her horse and looped the reins low around a tree trunk, allowing ample scope for the animal to munch on whatever it could find. Richard walked to the edge of the lake. He kneeled and swirled his hand in the delicious warmth. Removing his linen hat, he flipped it over and filled it with water. He offered a drink first to his horse, then, after a subsequent trip, to Katherine's.

When he walked back to the water, he found Katherine rapidly peeling off her clothing.

"My lady," he clucked. "This is really quite shocking. What are you doing?"

"What does it look like, silly," she replied happily. "I'm going swimming. And so are you. Ever since I first saw this place, I've fantasized about standing naked under that waterfall with you." She waded into the water hip-deep. "Come, darling," she called to him, when she noticed him hesitating, searching the woods behind them and the top of the cliff. "There's no one around for miles. We're quite alone." Slowly he pulled his shirt over his head and stood there, grinning sheepishly at her. "That's a good start," she encouraged. "Now drop your pants, Dubber, and get your bony arse in here!" Giggling, she launched into an ungainly dog paddle toward the falls.

Richard stripped, waded in, and dove down into the clear liquid, swimming underwater with fluid, turtlelike motions until he was directly beneath her. Glancing up at her struggling form a few feet above, he planting his feet firmly on the pebbly bottom and pushed off hard. He shot straight upward, catching her around the middle, lifting her, shrieking, out of the water, maintaining his hold on her from beneath as they plunged down together, going underwater himself to keep her buoyed up with both his hands, preventing her the scare of being totally immersed.

"You ogre!" she spluttered, laughing, when he surfaced a short way away. She splashed water at his face.

He splashed back.

"Don't tread water so fast," he cautioned her, when he noticed her struggling with her legs. "You'll wear yourself out. Slow, easy strides do the trick. Here, watch me . . .

"I'll swim us both over," he said, when she couldn't quite seem to get the hang of it and was breathing hard. He breaststroked over to her and held her firmly by the rib cage. "Relax, Katherine. Relax. Just relax, darling . . . That's right. There you go . . . Now grab hold of my shoulder. Hang on and kick your feet when I do."

He wrapped his left arm around her waist, kicked hard once, twice, reaching out with his right arm and sweeping it back in repeated sidearm motions. When they reached the base of the stone cliff, he stopped swimming, felt for the bottom, and stood up. He took her hand; together they waded in increasingly shallow water to the falls. Tilting their heads up, they luxuriated in a drenching so pure they could hold their mouths open and drink it. After they had their fill, they waded close to where slabs of ancient rock worn smooth by millenniums of roiling water rose up from the bottom in steplike formations.

Katherine draped her arms around his neck, locking her eyes on his. "You swim the way you make love, Richard," she said evenly over the plash of falling water. "With smooth, powerful strokes ever so delightful to experience."

He kissed her eyes, nose, and forehead, the seductive aroma of pure water and tropical flora scenting the air about them. "Flattery will not serve, my lady," he murmured in her ear. "I am wise to your ways. Confess. You say the same thing to all your men."

"I am found out!" She affected despair, but then opened her mouth, her tongue seeking his. "I do confess, my lord. But can you blame me? What better place to lure my men?"

"*All* of them?"

She held him tight, her breath coming short, her tongue dueling his. "No, not all of them," she managed between breaths. "Just the married ones."

"Married ones, is it?" His hands and fingers moved up and down, kneading, exploring, teasing the ins and outs of her soaked body. "You like bringing married men here?"

"Oh yes," she panted. Her breasts heaved, water dripped off them. Richard kissed the aroused tips. Her hand probed his groin, fondled his strength. "Raw pleasure is what I'm after. No nasty entanglements for me. Just give me a lord who enjoys a good rut with his lady." She inhaled sharply as his fingers went between her legs and began gently massaging her there.

"*Now,* Richard," she implored, moments later, when she could no longer tolerate his being outside her. "Take me now or I will explode!"

He retreated backward to the slabs of rock and lowered them both onto a top step. He drew her to him, ready for her, no further prompting required. She rolled on top of him, and as he entered her, they cried out together in the rapture and sanctity of their union, in the mystery and magic of this wild, secret, primitive place, their breath coming in long, drawn-out moans as she began moving in a smooth, deliberate pattern, up and down, up and down, slowly, unabashedly, beseeching the moments to last, to be as one, inseparable, in the cooling mists, the blood-warm water, the hot sun, until it was all too much, they could no longer withstand, either of them, the pressure cresting within. In a sudden, final, almost violent outburst, the wave broke over them, immersing them, overwhelming them, before gradually receding, leaving behind, in its wake, blissful exhaustion, spasmodic trembling, and streams of tender, undying emotions.

"Dear *God,* I love you so, Richard." She was on the verge of weeping, so absolute was her ecstasy. She clutched him to her as yet another blissful tremor assailed her. "Whatever would my life be without you?"

"Don't think on that, dearest Katherine," he said, his hands caressing her, his lips kissing her over and over. "Don't ever, ever think on that."

☆ ☆ ☆

ENGLAND DECLARES WAR ON HOLLAND; MORE REBEL VICTORIES. Bridgetown, Barbados, 24 May 1781. In a long-anticipated development, England has formally declared war on Holland. As a result of this declaration, the Dutch island of St. Eustatius is expected to quickly fall under British control.

In America, reports confirm that the British army suffered two major setbacks earlier this year. At a location known as Cowpens, a newly raised army under the command of rebel general Nathaniel Greene and his subordinate Daniel Morgan surprised the army of General Lord Cornwallis as it was marching north through the colony of North Carolina. The main body of Lord Cornwallis's force repelled the attack, sustaining modest casualties, though British supply wagons were captured or burned. Many Dragoon Guards, however, were killed. Cowpens marks the first significant defeat in the war for Major Tarleton's dragoons.

Subsequently, the British army engaged the enemy at a site known as Guilford Courthouse, in northern North Carolina. Both sides suffered heavy losses. As a result of the battle, the British army was cut off from its supply lines. Lord Cornwallis has therefore curtailed his advance into Virginia. He is marching southeastward through swamps to the port city of Wilmington (see map, below), where the Royal Navy is expected to resupply his army. What General Clinton and General Cornwallis intend next remains a military secret. It is widely speculated, however, that General Clinton will not relieve Lord Cornwallis until he is certain of the intentions of rebel general Washington and his ally the Comte de Rochambeau. The French army, based in Newport, Rhode Island, was recently reinforced by the arrival of Admiral de Barras and nine ships of the line.

Most distressing to Lord Cornwallis, as reported by a high-ranking aide, is the failure of local Tories in the South to rise up and join the British forces. Most of those that have come forward refuse to take orders and appear to use a soldier's guise to perpetrate crimes of rape and pillage on their American brethren.

In another development, it is reported that Brigadier General Benedict Arnold has advanced into Virginia with his American Legion to confront a rebel force under the command of the Marquis de Lafayette.

He felt her hand on his right shoulder. He took it in his left hand while keeping the newspaper spread out on his lap.

"I know this man Lafayette," he remarked. "I met him in Lorient. Agee and I both did. He held the rank of major general."

Katherine peered over his shoulder to read that part of the news story. "He's a marquis," she observed. "General Washington has a French marquis as a general in his army?"

"That's not unusual. A number of Washington's senior officers are European. I've told you about Baron von Steuben. The officer at Valley Forge who taught the Continentals how to drill properly? He's Prussian, can't speak a word of English. I could give many other examples."

"What about the other fellow mentioned there? Benedict Arnold. I thought he was on our side."

"He was," Richard responded bitterly. "He was an American officer so respected by Washington he was offered command of the left wing of Washington's main army, the position of highest honor. Arnold refused. Turned traitor instead. Irony is, he is the real hero at Saratoga. Congress may have given Gates the credit, but had it not been for Arnold, Gates would have retreated without a fight. I heard that even before leaving New Hampshire on *Ranger*."

"Why did he change sides, do you think?"

"Who knows? Money? Power? Resentment, perhaps."

"I'd wager there's a woman involved."

"That's the romantic in you, and in this case you might be right. He married a society woman in Philadelphia, a daughter of a prominent Tory family. I don't recall her name. Quite possibly she persuaded him."

"Yes, well, we both know what evil spells a woman can conjure up." She started massaging the base of his neck. "Speaking of which, what say you and I take a ride down to the beach of palms. I have something to tell you."

"Couldn't you tell me here?"

"I could. But I'd ever so much prefer to tell you there. It's our special place, and, well, what I have to say suits it."

There was a quality to Katherine's voice that Richard had not often heard. It conveyed a sense of suppressed urgency, but not the sort that portended anything bad. He turned around to look at her. To his surprise, she had her hair done up fetchingly, in eye-catching rolls of chestnut curls. And he noted a thin gold bracelet on her left wrist, the same one she wore the evening they had first met in Fareham.

"Can it wait a while? I promised Robin I'd meet with him at ten o'clock, on what I've learned from some planters about the new horizontal presses from Jamaica. These fellows have already installed them in their mills. I must say, they're quite the thing. On the first go, they can extract more juice than . . . Yes, well I can see how thrilled you are with *this* conversation."

"Oh, posh the mills, Richard. Just this once and just for an hour or so. My subject is *far* more interesting, as you'll agree once you hear me out. Which you will, of course. I've already asked Charles, would he please saddle the horses."

Richard looked up and sighed.

The beach they had frequented during their months on Tobago had indeed become a favorite place of theirs. A stub of land sticking out into the Caribbean on the southwestern end of the island, it had as yet no official name. Katherine referred to it simply as the "beach of palms" because rows of soaring coconut palms lined the mile-long beach with a wall of gray bark capped with a swaying green mantle of fronds. There were even palm trees growing close to the water's edge, sculpted by wind in their youth, their trunks running almost parallel to the sand before rising up majestically a hundred feet into the air. Walking along the beach on this side of the gray wall and the thick tropical growth, they had the impression of being stranded on an island in the Great South Sea, though the capital city of Scarborough was not far away, a comfortable ride due east across the southern tip of the island.

The day seemed to grow brighter as they approached the sunstruck sand at a slow trot. The sky was cerulean blue, a perfect match with the color of the sea. Puffs of pure white cloud scudded above them. To the south a larger and denser mass was forming. It was June, the start of the rainy season on Tobago. But as Robin explained, even during the wet summer months, rainstorms were normally limited to brief, heavy downpours during the midafternoon hours, when the sky would darken to a leaden gray and the sea would become eerily calm.

At the edge of the beach they dismounted, removed their heavy silver-buckled shoes, and padded across the powdery white sand to where an endless array of gently breaking waves purled onto the beach and teased their bare feet. They held hands as they walked, their horses following behind on slack reins. For a while they exchanged not a word, Richard content to let Katherine bide her time and bask, as he always did when he was here, in the tropical splendor of this secluded cove. A short way out to sea, flying parallel with their route, a pair of white pelicans skimmed over the surface of the water, their eyes keen for an unwary school of mullet or ballyhoo or other small fish to gather in their massive, fishnetlike maws.

They had walked a quarter-mile when Katherine said, "Richard, do you remember when we were on this beach and we found ourselves in that thicket over there?" She pointed at a break in the wall of palms where a snug, semishaded area offered a good deal of privacy, in addition to a soft blanket of undergrowth on which to lie.

"How could I forget?" he grimaced. "I woke up later that afternoon with a nasty burn on my derriere. It was painful sitting the next couple of days."

She suppressed a giggle. "How cute your bottom looked all in pink," she said. "I don't recall you protesting much when I rubbed on that salve Robin gave you. I wish I could have been there when you asked him for it." She assumed a more reflective air. "Anyway, I've been doing some thinking, and I wouldn't be surprised if that's where it began."

"Where what began?"

"Of course," she rambled on, "having a rogue husband like you I suppose it could have been just about anywhere on this island. Pick your spot."

He stopped walking and looked at her. "Katherine, you're talking nonsense."

She smiled at him. "I know I am, my love. I'm a bit giddy, that's all."

"Giddy about what?"

She flung her free arm around his neck and kissed him full on the lips. "That's for everything," she told him, her voice very serious, when she pulled herself away. "For everything you have given me."

He searched her eyes. "I'm not complaining," he said, "though I am confused here. What is it you're trying to tell me?"

"Just this, my love. You and I, we . . . What is it, Richard?"

He had suddenly stiffened, his senses alert.

"Listen."

"I don't hear anything," she said after a pause.

He brought a finger to his lips. "Shh. Listen."

There it was. A distant but distinct rumble followed by angry, rolling echoes.

"It's thunder, Richard. A summer storm brewing."

"That's not thunder, Katherine. That's cannon fire. And it's coming from the fort."

Quickly they put on their shoes. Lacing his fingers together, he gave her a leg up onto her horse, then jumped up and swung onto his with a single, swift motion Katherine had never seen him do before. Together they rode at a good clip back up the trail they had followed down, to the top of the rise and the Cutler estate where men, women, and children were already gathering—English families that had left their plantations nearby to seek leadership and counsel at the home of Robin Cutler. Men bore arms: double-barreled muskets, pistols, blunderbusses, swords.

Richard reined in near where Robin and Julia were conferring with another man ahorse, lather foaming at the stallion's mouth.

"Robin?"

Robin Cutler stopped talking to look up at his cousin.

"A French squadron is attacking the fort, Richard. According to Justin"—he indicated the rider—"they have landed marines at midisland near Glamorgan. They are heading this way."

"How many marines?"

"A few hundred, maybe."

Richard wheeled his horse.

"Where are you going?" Robin asked him.

"To Scarborough. To see what I can see. I'll report back."

"Wait. You'll want these." He held up a pistol in each hand.

"No, Robin. If I stray near the fort, it's best I'm not seen carrying weapons. Just make sure your men don't fire on the marines. They're not poorly armed slaves in rebellion."

He urged his horse forward on the southward trail.

"I'm coming with you, Richard," Katherine called up behind him.

He reined in, turned in his saddle. "No, Katherine," he said to her. "Please stay here. It may be dangerous down there."

"That's *why* I'm coming with you."

It was a statement not open to debate.

Scarborough, the administrative center of Tobago, was a small town by Caribbean standards, perhaps one-fifth the population and geographical size of Bridgetown. What gave it strategic importance was a deep, well-protected harbor with an entrance facing south. What gave it authority was a recently constructed fort on the highest stretch of land on the eastern side of the harbor. Fort King George had its great guns trained in every direction. A double line of cannon faced west toward the harbor and another double line faced south toward the Atlantic. Newly erected buildings in Scarborough had tended to gravitate toward the fort, which is why if one studied the area from a rise to the north on Plymouth Road, as Richard and Katherine were now doing, the fort *was* the town of Scarborough.

"What do you think?" Katherine asked. She watched as haphazard streams of humanity flowed toward the outer portcullis.

Richard was studying the sea beyond the harbor. He counted eight ships: five line-of-battle ships, the biggest surely the flagship, a Second Rate, perhaps eighty guns. Four he judged to be Third Rates, sixty to eighty guns. Two others were frigates, and the eighth a smaller vessel, either a naval supply ship or transport vessel. The squadron was sailing off and on under reduced canvas, a cable-length in distance from the entrance to the harbor, apparently in no hurry to resume its attack on the fort.

In the harbor itself a number of vessels rode at anchor. Most were brigs or other small merchantmen. Two were British warships: a frigate and a sloop of war. Though Richard noticed activity on their decks, he could distinguish few men aloft in the rigging. For once, he thought, their captains had placed common sense above typical Royal Navy bravado. Any foray by those two ships against that French squadron had only one possible outcome.

"I'm not sure," Richard replied. Silently he asked himself if the French ships could elevate their guns sufficiently to strike the upper reaches of the fort, and if so, what damage they could inflict firing from such a distance. He decided "yes" to the first question, "not a great deal" to the second.

"What concerns me," he said as much to himself as to Katherine, "is what the French marines are intending. They must know they cannot take the fort without a siege. So they must have something else in mind."

"What, do you think?"

Richard shook his head slowly. "I can't imagine."

At that moment, six seaward-facing guns in the fort erupted one after another in perfectly timed, five-second intervals. Richard stood in his stirrups, shading his eyes with his hand. He counted six plumes of water, each a different distance between land and ships, one punching the sea a mere fathom from the flagship.

"Ranging shots," he explained. "And a warning to keep away." He sat back in the saddle.

"Whatever the marines have in mind," Katherine observed, "I doubt the garrison knows they have landed."

It was such an obvious and critical point, Richard cursed himself for not having already considered it. Of course they would not know. How could they?

"Right," Richard said, his mind made up. "I'm going down to the fort. Go back to the plantation, Katherine. Tell Robin what you've seen here. Try to keep everybody calm. The French may have their quirks, but they do not wage war on women and children."

Katherine shook her head.

"I'm not leaving you, Richard. Think. If you intend to warn the major, he's more apt to trust me than you. I'm English, or so he believes. You have to agree, he doesn't much care for you."

Richard had to agree with both her logic and her statement of fact. He nodded at her, then nudged his horse forward, Katherine following close behind.

Activity in and about the fort had intensified with the roar of cannon. Civilians were bolting toward the double iron doors as Richard and Katherine dismounted, tethered their mounts, and joined the last of the throngs running inside. The outer doors were open to everyone; two inner doors leading to the heart of the citadel were shut tight and guarded by two musket-wielding redcoats. Roughly two hundred people who had elected to seek shelter inside the fort were crowded together in a musty-smelling, dimly lit area. It would not be long, Richard suspected, before many of them sought permission to leave, preferring the relative comforts of home to this dank and dreary place, whatever the risks.

Richard approached the two sentries. "We need to speak to Major Butterworth," he said to them.

"For what purpose?" the taller of the two asked. He spoke to Richard, though his eyes flickered over to Katherine.

"We have information concerning the French squadron."

"What information?"

"French marines have landed, soldier," Katherine snapped at him, "and they'll be here shortly. I should think your commanding officer would be pleased to have this information."

It was the quality of Katherine's voice, more than the threat it conveyed, that persuaded the sentry.

"Follow me, please." He sounded almost humble.

Richard and Katherine followed the sentry down one corridor, up a flight of stairs, down a second corridor that dead-ended at a cross-corridor running north and south along the entire western side of the fort. Six massive cannon were housed on this platform, trained on the harbor approaches. Five redcoats were pacing back and forth and peering occasionally through one of the gun slits. Directly above them, outside on the parapets, a second tier of thirty-sixes was similarly aimed at the harbor entrance.

This Richard took in while they waited to be allowed entry into what he assumed was the fort's command post. When the sentry reemerged, he left the door open and stepped aside, indicating they should enter.

Once inside, Richard quickly scanned the room. There were two official-looking men standing by a table. One he instantly recognized. Three soldiers stood at ease nearby, the burliest of them a bearded man with the three gold chevrons of a sergeant emblazoned on the sleeve of his dress uniform coat.

"Well, if it isn't Mr. and Mrs. Cutler," a man called out in sardonic greeting. He had a surprisingly patrician accent for one so short and stout. His nose was red and bulbous, and he had a receding hairline and a thin, curling, Spanish conquistador–style moustache. His hair was crimson-colored, close in match with the red of his uniform jacket, and his skin was white, too white, suggesting he either was sickly or loathe to expose himself to the equatorial sun. Richard recalled his initial impression of the man; London tailors must have had a time stitching together a uniform to conform to this stubby frame.

"To what do I owe this unexpected pleasure?" The man's tone remained cold, unwelcoming.

Richard fought a rise of blood. He had expected Butterworth to taunt him. Don't give him cause, he warned himself.

"Major," he said, with as much respect as he could muster, "we've just come from the Cutler plantation. The militia is gathering there. A rider from the north has informed us that a force of French marines, perhaps five hundred in number, has landed at mid-island and is marching on Scarborough."

"Do tell. And why should I believe you?"

"Because it's the truth, Major," Katherine answered him. "Why else would we have come here?"

He leered at her.

"You too, Mrs. Cutler? You too have turned rebel on us?" He glanced at the other individual by the table, a tall, somewhat aloof man, obviously of authority, wearing expensive civilian clothing and one of the few powdered wigs Richard had seen on the island. He had never met Lieutenant Governor John Graham, but formal introductions were not necessary.

"Sir," Butterworth said to Graham, "this gentleman, and I use the term loosely, is Richard Cutler, cousin of our highly esteemed Robin Cutler. Not only is he an American, he has served as an officer in the defunct Continental Navy, in ships under the command of a certain Captain John Paul. Does that name ring true?"

"Oh my, indeed it does," Graham sniffed. He dabbed at the side of his nose with a kerchief, similar in color and finery to the wide lacy neckstock bulging out from his blue-checkered waistcoat and red velvet jacket. "In fact it was I who first interviewed Paul after he brazenly murdered a sailor aboard a brig named . . . *Betsy,* if memory serves. He added 'Jones' to his name, didn't he, after he fled justice on this island. I have read about his exploits at sea, and I must say, he is nothing but a damnable pirate. You served under him, Mr. Cutler? How very, very unfortunate."

Richard was hard put to show no reaction to these blatant lies.

"Quite so," Butterworth agreed. "And this young woman is his wife. She is English, the daughter of a distinguished Royal Navy officer, Captain Henry Hardcastle by name. Her brother Hugh also serves in the Royal Navy, as a flag lieutenant for Admiral Parker in Bridgetown. Oh yes," he said to her startled expression, "I have done some checking up on you two. And the more I learn, the more disgusted I become. You, madam, are a disgrace to your family name."

"How terribly disappointing," the lieutenant governor allowed. His look of anguish was so profound, Richard almost felt sorry for him. "I do so hate dealing with matters of treason."

"Major," Richard said, struggling for self-control, "we're wasting valuable time here. My wife has nothing to do with any of this. And whatever you may think of me personally, it has nothing to do with what is happening here. Everyone on this island is in danger, the garrison included."

"The garrison, pray?" Butterworth's voice was high in disbelief. "I hardly think so, sir. The French squadron out there poses no threat to us. And I don't care how many Frogs have landed. They cannot take this fort without a siege. A very long siege. And at that they will fail."

"That may be. But there are hundreds of men, women, and children out there who cannot get to the fort. What of them? You can't go to their aid. You haven't enough soldiers."

Butterworth eyed him closely.

"So what would you have me do? Surrender? Ah, yes. Wouldn't *that* just suit you! Remind me, are not the French your allies?"

Richard took a deep breath, praying for patience. "It's hardly my place to recommend surrender, Major. But I do urge you to negotiate. Before the French marines get here. Speak to the commodore under a flag of truce. Buy as much time as necessary to get as many people as possible to safety. My family is out there, Major. My first loyalty is to them. It's why I came here. Robin may not be able to control the militia. They're undisciplined. If one man opens fire on the marines, many innocent people may die as a result. Does it not make sense to at least talk to the French and find out their intentions? What is lost by doing that? You and Governor Graham can then determine where your best chances lie."

"I know *bloody well* what the goddamn Frogs intend," Butterworth burst out. "They intend to take this fort and capture this island. In that, as I said, they will fail. As for you, sir, this conversation is over. You made a grave mistake coming here, Cutler. I have no choice but to detain you both as spies. We shall deal with you later, at the proper time. Seize them!" he ordered the sergeant. "Lock them up!"

"Richard! Watch out!"

Two guards came for Richard, one for Katherine. Before they could reach him, Richard lunged out at the redcoat approaching Katherine, striking him on the side of the face with such authority that the man went careening against the table, sprawled head-first across the top, and slumped over on the opposite side at the feet of the recoiling lieutenant governor. Richard wheeled about to face the other two, his fists up.

"Corporal!" Butterworth bellowed.

The door opened. An army corporal hurried in, sized up the situation, yelled for his men on the gun deck. Encouraged, the first two soldiers laid into Richard. He thwarted one blow with his left forearm, gave the man two swift punches in the solar plexus, jerked up his knee when the soldier bent over, sent him reeling backward. The other soldier, the sergeant, lashed out, connected, sent Richard crashing to the floor on his back. Richard rolled over 360 degrees with the momentum, came up hunched down, threw himself at the sergeant, tackled him around the waist, and hurled him backward into the five soldiers hurrying into the room. Flailing with his fists, he took a heavy toll, sending two soldiers against the wall, one with a mangled nose spurting blood. From behind, a pistol butt glanced off Richard's head, dazing him. From the front, a soldier wielded the barrel of a musket as he would a cricket bat, striking Richard full in the chest with the butt end, forcing air from his lungs. He dropped to his knees, one hand on the floor, the other over his stomach. A redcoat came up and kicked him hard in the abdomen, taking the fight completely out of him.

"Hold him up," Butterworth hissed, after a semblance of order was restored. Two soldiers yanked Richard to his feet and held him firmly at the sides. Butterworth calmly began unbuttoning his uniform coat. "I shan't be denied a go at this traitor," he sneered as he removed the coat and began rolling up his right sleeve. He advanced toward Richard, who could only challenge with his eyes, their sea blue essence flushed with hate.

The lieutenant governor looked away, aghast. As Butterworth made ready with his fist, he heard a soft double click and turned toward the sound.

"'Ere, what the bloody 'ell is this?" he blurted out at what he saw.

"Release my husband."

Her voice was as steady as the short barrel of the pistol she pointed at Butterworth's chest, its hammer up at full cock.

"*Are you out of your mind?* Do you realize what you're doing? 'Ere, give me that gun."

He advanced one step. She raised her sights to between his eyes. He stopped.

"Release my husband," she demanded again. "And back up against the wall. You and your men."

"Why?" he scoffed. "Because of that peashooter? You have but one shot. What then? My soldiers will seize you."

"Yes. They will. And you will be dead."

Stunned by her resolve, unsure what to do next, the two redcoats holding Richard eased their grip on his arms. With one angry shrug he shook himself free. "I'd do what she says if I were you, Major," he said, running the back of his hand across a bloody lower lip. "She's rather handy with that thing."

Silent moments ticked by in the stalemate. From down the corridor they heard the sudden, sharp rap of boot heels on stone. Someone was making his way rapidly toward them in the controlled, determined gait of an officer. When he appeared in the open door, his expression was one of dire emergency mixed with incredulity at the scene before him.

"It's all right, Lieutenant," Butterworth assured him. "Report."

The Royal Army lieutenant saluted.

"Sir, French marines are marching toward Scarborough. Our scouts estimate six hundred to seven hundred men. They are heavily armed."

Butterworth waved that information away. "We know that," he said, giving Richard a grudging glance. "Tell me, Lieutenant, are they bringing siege equipment with them?"

"No sir," the officer replied. "They apparently have no intention of attacking the fort. They have let it be known that they will set fire to one plantation every half hour until the fort surrenders."

"*What?* The *bastards.* They wouldn't dare."

"With respect, Major, I believe they would. The Coates estate is already ablaze."

"*Jesus Christ!*"

Butterworth stood quiet. All eyes in the room were upon him, and Katherine still held her pistol. She had it pointed down, at the floor, prepared to bring it back up again quickly. Butterworth glanced at the lieutenant governor. Graham turned his head, avoiding Butterworth and any responsibility for his decision.

"Very well," Butterworth said dejectedly. "I will speak to the commodore. See to the arrangements."

The lieutenant saluted.

"A wise decision, Major," Richard said, after the lieutenant had gone and he had relieved two soldiers of their pistols. "Now if you please, I would appreciate your handing over the key to this room. You have my word I shall give it to your lieutenant as soon as the French commodore arrives.

"The key, Major," he repeated, advancing toward the wretched man. "I advise you not to make me ask for it again."

Butterworth motioned with his head toward the side drawers of the table. On his second try, Richard found a set of three keys attached to a large ring of iron. "It's the middle one," Butterworth said, the last traces of obstinacy gone from his voice.

Outside the room, in the corridor, with the door locked behind them, Katherine leaned against the stone wall, her hands over her stomach as if she were about to vomit. Her color was pale, and she was trembling.

"What is it, Katherine?" Richard asked with concern, coming over to her.

She inhaled deeply, exhaled slowly, once, twice, three times.

"That gun, Richard," she managed, looking up at him in anguish. "It wasn't loaded. It never has been."

☆ ☆ ☆

MAJOR BUTTERWORTH and the others in his company were released from the command post an hour later, after a small flotilla of ships' boats glided up to the quays at the harbor, the Bourbon white flag centered with three golden fleur-de-lis fluttering from astern the lead gig. Once Katherine had recovered sufficiently, Richard walked with her out of the fort, the key tucked away in a pocket of his breeches. No one thought to challenge them. The garrison seemed resigned to its fate. English forces were hopelessly outnumbered and outgunned, and thus incapable of defending the island and its rich, landed gentry. Surrender was inevitable. When Commodore de Bougainville strode up to the fort from the quays, with squads of officers and French marines trailing behind, Richard approached the Royal Army lieutenant who had appeared earlier in the command post and who had now the dubious honor of greeting the enemy at the gates.

"The decision of whether or not to release the major is yours, Lieutenant," he said with a wry smile as he handed over the ring of keys. "I do not envy you that decision."

Terms of surrender, as announced later that afternoon, were generous though not atypical for such *affaires de guerre*. Transfers of power and control on islands in the West Indies were by now so commonplace that unwritten rules of procedure and civility had become more or less accepted by all parties. France would appropriate the two British warships in the harbor; British military personnel would be sent to Martinique as prisoners of war for the duration; and the Bourbon flag would fly above the parapets of what would still officially be known as Fort King George. No harm would come to private citizens, and their property would not be confiscated. In addition, civilians who so desired were free to leave Tobago in one of two merchant vessels commandeered for that purpose. One vessel would sail to Bridgetown, the other to Kingston.

"We will sail for Bridgetown," Katherine said with finality that evening in the Cutler home. A family conference had ended, and Robin and Julia had retired for the night. "I will hear no more about it, Richard. You *mustn't* worry about me. You heard Robin. He and Julia are coming with me. Robin is convinced it's the right time to make the move to Barbados. We can all stay with John. Hugh will be there too. I will be surrounded by family and in excellent care."

Richard shook his head, not yet convinced. "It's not that," he said. "I know perfectly well you'd be safe and well treated. And there was a time I would have leaped at such an opportunity. Now, I just don't know how I can leave you."

"Richard, look at me."

He did. She took his hands in hers from across the span of table between them.

"Richard, my darling, ever since we set foot on Barbados, I have watched how you pore over every newspaper, how you perk up whenever anyone mentions anything about the war in America. You think I don't notice, but I do. Understand, it's no threat to me. I love you for many reasons. But I love you most of all because principle and honor matter to you and because you *care*. Not just about me; about your family in Hingham, my family, friends like Agee and Richard Dale and Silas Talbot and Captain Jones—men you hold so dear I feel they are my friends as well, though I have never met any of them. I know you, Richard. I know what's in your heart."

"*You* are in my heart," he said defiantly.

"I know I am. And knowing that is the single-most joy in my life. But if you are to love me as much in ten years, you must be free now to do what you and I both know you must do. You must finish what you have started. You must see this war to its rightful conclusion, because now you *can*. Richard, you *must* accept the French commodore's offer to serve as lieutenant on his ship. Else, for the rest of your life, you will regret not having done everything you could for the cause you and I care so deeply about. Eventually you would become angry with yourself. Then, inevitably, you would become angry with me. Correct me if I am wrong."

He looked down, not daring to say anything.

"Besides," she said, her voice suddenly much cheerier, "I have it all figured out."

"Have what figured out?"

"Well, let's see. It's now June. The commodore made it quite clear that Admiral de Grasse has no intention of remaining in America beyond the end of the hurricane season, in mid-October. So that's—" she began counting on her fingertips for emphasis—"one, two, three, four months from now. Four months is nothing for the wife of a naval officer. Jamie was often away at sea for more than a year. Now, let's assume it takes De Grasse two weeks to sail from America to Martinique, and another week for you to sail to Barbados aboard some neutral ship. Even allowing another week or two for the unexpected, that would still give us a month together before our child is born."

He was listening intently, but those last words hit him like a thunderbolt. He gaped at her. She smiled back at him. He came around to where she sat and dropped to a knee.

"Katherine, you are with child? Are you certain?"

"Yes, quite certain," she said. She put her hand in his hair, gently coaxing back the thick blond mass. "Women have a way of knowing such things. It's what I was trying to tell you on the beach before the French cannon so rudely interrupted." She looked deep into him. "Richard, you're going to be a father."

He laid his head on her lap, unable to speak.

"Our child is another reason you must go, Richard," she said, her hand continuing its gentle, loving stroke in his hair. "The most important reason of all. If it's a boy, and a mother's instinct tells me it is, you will have much to tell young Will about his uncle and namesake, and what you did in the war to avenge him."

Not since holding Jamie in his arms on the deck of *Serapis* had Richard felt such an inexorable welling of tears. He held her tight around the waist with both arms, his face buried in her lap. After a long while, he lifted his head and looked at her with watery eyes.

"What is it I have done, Katherine," he begged to know, "to have God love me so much, He sent me you to be my wife?"

That night they made love with a fury of passion, as though it could have been their first time together, as though it might be their last.

15

YORKTOWN, VIRGINIA

October 1781

*T*O RICHARD, IT SEEMED like a monarch's reign since he had last seen America. His view from *Ranger*'s quarterdeck that day almost four years ago had been of the rockbound Isles of Shoals off the coast of Portsmouth. His view this morning from a roost in the foremast trestletrees of a French Second Rate framed a landscape quite different, though he noted some comforting similarities with the outer reaches of the South Shore of Boston and Cape Cod. The shoreline was low-lying and sandy, with what looked like tall, scraggly pines clustered close to shore. And the land seemed sparsely populated. Cruising along the North Carolina and Virginia coasts, he had observed few signs of human activity.

Richard leaned forward amid the tar-blackened shrouds and trained the spyglass northward to where the sharp-angled jibboom of the eighty-gun *L'Auguste* was pointing. Again he focused the lens on what the lookout in the mainmast crosstrees had spotted minutes before: two ships. One, clearly a frigate; the other, a smaller two-masted corvette. Both flew the red ensign of the Royal Navy and were wearing around fast in a broad figure-eight pattern, having apparently seen what they had ventured out from the Chesapeake to see.

His pulse quickened. Within an hour, two at most, they would have the answer to the question every French officer had been asking since they set sail from Cap François on Santo Domingo three weeks earlier. Was the British fleet that had left Antigua for America, waiting for them here? De Grasse had sailed west from Santo Domingo to Cuba, then north, guided by local Spanish pilots through the tricky shoals and sandbars of the Old Bahama Strait. From Florida northward, he had kept to the western edge of the Gulf Stream, past the shore-lines of Georgia and the Carolinas to the Outer Banks. Farther out to sea, Rear Adm. Sir Samuel Hood had presumably followed a more direct northwesterly course bound for—where? The Chesapeake? New York? Charleston?

New York—Richard remained convinced as he explored the empty waters north of Cape Henry. His reasoning was simple. Hood could not know what De Grasse knew. A month before, a swift American privateer bearing dis-patches for De Grasse had found the French fleet anchored off Cap François. The dispatches were from General Washington and contained what was es-sentially a plea to the French admiral to sail as quickly as possible to the Chesapeake to rendezvous in mid-September with an allied army com-manded by Washington and Count Rochambeau. Without access to Washing-ton's strategy, and not having sighted the French fleet along the way, Hood could reasonably be expected to sail to New York to report to his superior, Sir Thomas Graves, rear admiral of the Red. But also there was the possibility that Hood was behind them, a circumstance Richard deemed unlikely. The two fleets had left the Caribbean at about the same time, and while the British fleet did not have the advantage of the northbound Gulf Stream, it had a much shorter distance to sail on the hypotenuse of a right triangle. And it had not dropped anchor off Havana.

"*Lieutenant Cutler? Le chef d'escadre veut parler avec vous. En dix minutes.*"

Richard glanced down at the blue-jacketed midshipman staring up at him by the catharpings under the foretop. Even at that distance, he could sense in the young lad's expression the same aversion he had once felt to climbing far-ther up the ratlines than duty required.

"*Merci, M'sieu Bourneuf,*" he shouted down through a hand cupped at his mouth. "*Envoyez mes hommages au chef d'escadre. Je serai en bas actuellement.*"

The midshipman saluted and retreated down the ratlines. As he picked his way to the weather deck, Richard took in the majesty of the vast fleet stretched out about him in the Atlantic: twenty-eight ships of the line, the smallest among them the sixty-four-gun *Reflechi* and *Solitaire* sailing off to larboard. Sev-enty-Fours comprised the majority, plus several Eighties and the mammoth three-decker 110-gun flagship *Ville de Paris,* the most powerful and, to many, the finest ship ever built. Four frigates raced about, acting as screens and re-connaissance for the fleet and the two hundred supply and transport vessels conveying military stores, ordnance, and detachments of the Gâtinois, Tour-raine, and Agénois regiments of foot: the elite of French West Indies garrisons, three thousand strong under the command of a no-nonsense general, le mar-quis de Saint-Simon.

Richard found Commodore de Bougainville on the quarterdeck in tradi-tional naval pose, staring straight ahead, his slender legs spread slightly and his hands thrust firmly behind his back. Even standing beside the diminutive Captain Castellan, the commodore seemed the antithesis of a military com-mander, quite the opposite of the huge bull of an admiral, Francis Joseph Paul, le comte de Grasse. Richard had met the admiral and had immediately sensed a man born to the sea. He was a full three inches taller than Richard and considerably more stout, though not fat, and he bore a dignified look about him that, to Richard's mind, forbade familiarity from all but his closest intimates, while at the same time inspiring awe and respect, even love, among those who served under him. In contrast to De Grasse, Bougainville offered a first impression of one more at home in a wig shop, content to pass along the latest gossip with a perfumed clientele while fussing over the proper fit of a newly purchased peruke.

It was a false first impression, as Richard was to learn. The third morning out from Tobago, he had received an invitation to dine that evening with the commodore and Captain Castellan in the grandeur and haute cuisine of the stern cabin. During a memorable dinner of freshly caught dolphin and fine Rhenish wine, Bougainville had expounded further on why he had offered Richard a lieutenant's berth on his ship. During an interview at Fort King George after its capture, Bougainville had discovered, more from what Kather-ine had said, that Richard had played a key role in the fort's surrender. In ad-dition, he spoke fluent French, a rarity among Americans, thus in addition to sea duties he could serve as a liaison officer between the fleet and the allied force on land. Of most significance was Richard's record of service with Cap-tain Jones, a sea officer revered throughout France. If Jones saw in Richard Cutler an officer worthy of promotion, that alone was enough for Louis An-toine de Bougainville.

Later during the dinner, when Richard politely inquired about the com-modore's life at sea, Bougainville had demurred. It was left to Captain Castellan to recount how the commodore, fifteen years earlier, before Captain Cook had set sail on his first expedition from Plymouth, had passed through the Strait of Magellan into the Pacific, exploring the Great South Sea from Tahiti to the archipelago of Tuamoto, all the way to the Great Barrier Reef and Dutch-held Batavia, claiming many of these lands in the name of His Most Christian Majesty, Louis XV. Along the way, Bougainville, an amateur naturalist, had amassed an admirable collection of plant and animal life, taking careful note of the island from which each leaf or rock or piece of molted skin had been taken. It was his curiosity in the world around him that allowed Richard to open the door to a discussion about Katherine and her own enthusiasm for all things zoological and botanical. Bougainville listened with keen interest, his penetrating ice gray eyes and empathetic expression encouraging Richard to speak freely.

"*Votre épouse n'est pas seulement très belle, lieutenant Cutler,*" he said when Richard paused for a sip of wine. "*Elle est tout à fait une femme accomplie. Elle a beaucoup de chance d'avoir un mari qui l'aime tellement. Ce qui est rare de nos jours.*"

"*Merci, Monsieur le chef d'escadre,*" Richard replied, moved by the commodore's kind and, unfortunately, true words. It *was* rare these days to find the joy in matrimony that he and Katherine had discovered together. Robin and Julia had. He prayed for the same for his cousins John and Lizzy, and for Caleb, Anne, and Lavinia.

Bougainville grasped the stem of his wine glass. "*Vive les États-Ûnis!*" he exclaimed, smiling at Richard as he raised his glass. "*Et vive l'amour.*"

"*Vive le roi!*" Richard said in proper response. As their three glasses clinked together, a liveried cabin servant stepped forward as if on cue, opening another bottle of Rhenish in anticipation of a long evening ahead. "*Et vive l'amour, toujours.*"

MIDSHIPMAN HENRI Bourneuf was not quite correct. Commodore Bougainville did not wish to speak with Richard. He simply wanted him on the quarterdeck beside his three other lieutenants should the British fleet be sighted in the Chesapeake. A cable distance ahead, the frigate *Glorieux* stood off and on between the fleet and Cape Henry, ready to relay signals from her sister ships *Aigrette* and *Diligente,* which were probing the waters of the Chesapeake.

Finally, word came.

"*Les Anglais ne sont pas ici!*" the lookout in the crosstrees called down.

"*Merde!*" the first lieutenant muttered under his breath. He had his fists balled up, eager for a fight.

Bougainville gave Richard a brief nod.

Richard walked to the quarterdeck railing amidships. "Bosun!" he called out in French. "Ready the longboat and assign oarsmen. Stand by to sway out."

A strapping hulk of a man with a flaming red beard saluted and drove his mates into action. He needn't have hurried. They had ample time to prepare the ship's boat for launch. Cape Henry lay several miles ahead. In obedience to the dispatches, the fleet would stand off the entrance to the Chesapeake until the situation ashore was understood. Determining that situation was Richard's responsibility as fleet liaison officer. The British navy may not be in the Chesapeake, but a British army most definitely was. Its being there was what had brought De Grasse more than a thousand miles from his base in Martinique.

A bosun's mate pegged the wind at ten knots, from the west southwest. The day was warm and sunny, with surprisingly low humidity for the last week of August. There being no concern of a lee shore and the charts showing deep water off Cape Henry, the crew of *L'Auguste* maneuvered close in before heaving to and lowering the thirty-foot longboat. Oarsmen clambered down into her, each attired in duck trousers, a red-striped, short-sleeved shirt, and a straw hat. A midshipman followed, serving as coxswain. Then it was Richard's turn. At the entry port he saluted the quarterdeck before swinging his body around and grabbing hold of the side ropes. Quickly he stepped down into the longboat to take his place aft in the sternsheets.

"*Avirons en haut, du côté gauche,*" the midshipman ordered in a high-pitched, authoritative voice of aristocracy. On the left side of the cutter, eight men raised their oars. "*Le bon côté, défendant au loin!*" On the right side, crew pushed off from *L'Auguste*. "*Tous, menez!*" he commanded when the cutter was clear of the hull. Blades dipped into the water, and the cutter surged forward toward a point of land cleared of trees and underbrush where a field tent had been pitched. Out in front of that tent, the flags of the United States and France fluttered side by side at equal height. So far at least, everything was going according to plan.

Richard stepped ashore at a makeshift landing of smooth rock and rough-hewn planks laid against each other down to the low-tide mark. He was met by two officers: one, a squat, rather plump man with a sharp nose, who introduced himself as Colonel Gimat; and the other, a considerably taller, sinewy man with a strong jutting jaw who was dressed in none of the French officer's finery. He wore instead a fringed calf-length hunting shirt and soiled brown cotton leggings, shaped to the leg and fastened at the ankle with four buttons. He had a sheathed knife tucked in front behind a belt, and on his feet he wore soft deer-leather shoes resembling moccasins. Richard could distinguish no insignia of rank anywhere on his person, his being "of rank" indicated only by the fact that he was standing next to the French colonel. Behind them, a squad of twenty men milled about lethargically, many of them leaning against their muskets and watching with faintly amused expressions as the officers introduced themselves to each other.

"*Est-ce que je peux* introduce, Lieutenant," the French colonel said, mixing his languages with a heavy Gallic accent, "*Monsieur* John Mercer, *capitaine* of Virginia militia."

The two men shook hands, Mercer without much enthusiasm.

"You speak English well, Colonel," Richard said. "Please use French if you prefer. *J'ai suivi le français depuis sept ans.*"

The colonel inclined his head. "That is *plus aimable* of you, *Monsieur Cutler*," he said gratefully. "But I must—how you say?—decline your courtesy. Le marquis—*c'est-à-dire*, the major general—insists we officers speak English . . . *aussi souvent que possible* with our American allies." He motioned toward the cluster of tents. "Please, if you will join me? Captain, you as well?"

"Reckon not, thankee, Colonel," Mercer replied. "Less'n y'all need me fer somethin' in thar. If'n you do, y' jest need holler." He grinned, exposing yellow, tobacco-stained teeth.

"*Très bien,*" Gimat replied, having no idea what Mercer had just said.

"*Attendez-moi ici,*" Richard ordered the midshipman, who acknowledged with a salute.

The three officers walked toward the tent where two Continentals in blue jackets with red cuffs and facings stood guard. As they approached, they presented arms smartly, then stepped aside and pulled apart the flaps. Richard and Gimat ducked inside where two other senior officers were conversing at a simple wooden table on which was laid out a map. Both men wore the blue uniform dress coat with buff facings and gold buttons that identified the officer corps of the United States Army. Two silver stars on the twin epaulettes of one officer confirmed a high rank, in league with the black and white cockade on his tricorne hat resting on the table. But it was not the uniform Richard recognized. It was the tall, lanky body it contained.

"*Monsieur le marquis!*" he exclaimed. "*Me rappelez-vous?*"

It took several moments for Lafayette to respond. Whether from surprise or a lack of recognition or both, Richard could not be certain. "Yes. Yes, of course I remember you. In Lorient. Monsieur Cutler, is it not? Lieutenant Richard Cutler. You were with Captain Jones. And that marvelous fellow . . . Mr . . . um . . . Mr. . . . ." He snapped his fingers together, stimulating memory.

"Crabtree. Lieutenant Agreen Crabtree."

"*Oui! C'est lui! Lieutenant Crabtree,*" Lafayette grinned, losing himself for the moment in his native tongue. "*Quel homme charmant!*" He crossed over to Richard with arms outstretched, Richard thinking he was going to embrace him. Instead, Lafayette grasped him joyously by the shoulders.

"What pleasure comes to me this day!" he exclaimed, beaming like the young man he still was. "To finally see my country's ships in America! And to see old friends! You are the flag's liaison officer?"

"I have been given that honor, yes, General."

"*Bon.* You shall have much to report. I would go with you to visit my dear friend the admiral, but alas I must return to my command in Williamsburg. Colonel Gimat will accompany you in my stead." He bowed to Gimat, then indicated the fourth officer in the tent. "Lieutenant, the Colonel here has just come from General Washington. He brings good news from him, and from General Rochambeau and General Lincoln. I have the honor of naming to you Colonel Alexander Hamilton. Colonel Hamilton was once aide-de-camp to His Excellency and is his personal representative here."

Richard saluted a man an inch or two shorter than himself and a few years older. He was fair skinned with a long, thin, almost austere aristocratic face capped with thick brown hair swept back straight and tied in back with a small black ribbon, gentleman-style. Years ago, in Hingham, Richard had read Hamilton's earliest writings on the principles of responsible government, his views anathema to patriots such as Thomas Jefferson who distrusted *all* government power. He was as impressed then as he was now, face to face with the author.

"Is that not a Continental Navy uniform you're wearing, Mr. Cutler?" Hamilton asked. His voice was deep, resonant. "May I ask how you came by it? And how you came to Virginia in a French ship?"

As best he could, Richard recounted the highlights.

"Fascinating," Hamilton said at the conclusion. "Absolutely fascinating. Barbados? Tobago? I was born on Nevis and raised on St. Croix. As fate would have it, I too was employed on a sugar plantation, as a clerk in my youth. Now then," changing the subject, "a moment ago, General Lafayette mentioned the name Jones. Was he referring to Captain John Paul Jones?"

"Yes sir, he was. I served with Captain Jones as midshipman aboard *Ranger*. I then had the honor of serving with him as acting third lieutenant aboard *Bonhomme Richard*."

"Fascinating," he said again. "I am most pleased to make your acquaintance, Mr. Cutler. Your exploits over there provided those of us in the States with some welcomed reading during some tough times. I particularly enjoyed reading about your engagement with *Serapis*. I look forward to learning more, though for the moment, as I am certain the general will agree, we best get to the business at hand. Admiral de Grasse awaits your report, no? So let us dispense with formalities of rank. Speak your mind, Lieutenant. Ask any question you wish. It is imperative you understand our situation here."

"Thank you, Colonel. My first question is, have you sighted a British fleet offshore recently?"

"Yes, we have. Five days ago. From our count, there were fourteen ships of the line plus a few smaller vessels. A frigate came into the bay to rendezvous briefly with *Charon,* a Royal Navy frigate attached to Cornwallis's army. Then the fleet sailed northward, we presume to New York."

Richard scribbled a note to himself on a piece of paper. "May I also inquire, Colonel, on a personal note: You recently met with General Lincoln? I know the general. We are from the same town in Massachusetts. I understood he was taken prisoner at Charleston."

"He was. Six months ago he was exchanged for a British general named Phillips, captured at Saratoga. His Excellency has appointed General Lincoln second in command of the allied army. He is the one responsible for getting that army to Yorktown. I assure you, it is not a responsibility I covet." He directed Richard's attention to the map on the table. "This will help explain our position."

Depicted on the map was an area extending from the mouth of the Chesapeake west across the bay to Williamsburg, the colonial capital of Virginia and the commercial hub of the Tidewater. On the left side of the map was a series of fingerlike peninsulas, one on top of the other, running west to east and sticking out into Chesapeake Bay. At the knuckle of the middle peninsula, east of Williamsburg, was the town of York, bounded by the York River to the north and the James River across the peninsula to the south. North of Yorktown, across the York River at the arrow tip of another, much stubbier finger-peninsula ending in the shape of a crab claw, was the town of Gloucester. Between Yorktown and Williamsburg, a short way to the west, was the settlement of Jamestown.

Hamilton glanced at Lafayette. He nodded in reply, indicating he should carry on.

"Cornwallis is here, in York, or Yorktown as most people now call it." Hamilton pointed at the spot. "He also occupies Gloucester, across the river, with perhaps a thousand soldiers. He has been here for more than a month, digging in. We are informed by deserters that he has in his command about seventy-five hundred men. Many are Queen's Rangers, a Loyalist band of experienced fighters. He also has detachments of British light infantry and Royal Welsh Fusiliers, in addition to Hessian and Jaeger units. Plus however many marines are attached to the two frigates anchored in the river. Major Banastre Tarleton—I see you have heard of him?—is with Cornwallis with his legion of royal dragoons."

"What is your number?" Richard asked.

"At the moment," Lafayette answered dejectedly, "we have two hundred Continentals and eight hundred militia."

"What of British supplies?" Richard asked, studying the map. "Do they have ample provisions, do you think?"

"That depends, doesn't it, on how long Cornwallis intends to remain here. He is headquartered in the home of Major Thomas Nelson, the patriot governor of Virginia and the commander of our Virginia militia. The major says that . . . *les entrepôts* . . . the warehouses in Yorktown have much food, but for an army? The English have been plundering local farms for food, and they have exhausted that source of supply. So they can last . . . what? A few more weeks? That's just a guess."

Richard jotted more notes. "Admiral de Grasse will want to know the size of General Washington's army. And the date you expect him to arrive here."

"At a pace of ten to fifteen miles per day, we estimate that his Excellency is now near Philadelphia," Lafayette replied. "We have sent express riders north to inform him of the arrival of De Grasse. Colonel Hamilton can confirm the number of soldiers. I understand he brings with him six thousand Continentals and three thousand militia. General Rochambeau accompanies him with seven thousand soldiers of France."

"I can indeed confirm those numbers, Lieutenant," Hamilton said. "And you can assure Admiral De Grasse that General Washington is making every effort to get to the Chesapeake as quickly as he can. He understands that we may lose our opportunity to trap Cornwallis if he cannot get here fast enough. He also understands that we cannot prevail on land without supremacy at sea. And supremacy at sea means not only the French Indies fleet that, praise God, has arrived, it also means the French squadron in Newport. We don't know for certain if General Rochambeau was able to convince Admiral de Barras to sail here with his artillery and siege equipment. It seems likely he did, but we can't be certain. De Barras had been inclined to attack Newfoundland, and Rochambeau was forced to leave Newport before De Barras set sail."

"De Grasse is the superior officer," Richard pointed out. "Should he not send a frigate ahead and *order* De Barras to sail here?"

"You tell me, Mr. Cutler. You're the liaison officer."

Richard felt his face flush. Silently he cursed his naivete. De Grasse had four frigates attached to his fleet. He would not sacrifice one of them for what could well turn out to be a wild goose chase in British-patrolled waters.

He forced himself to concentrate instead on the arithmetic: sixteen thousand allied soldiers marching this way, plus three thousand in the West Indies regiments on board the transports, plus eight hundred French marines gave the allies a potential three-to-one advantage in troop strength over the British. No one in that tent knew precisely how many line-of-battle ships Graves had in New York. But the naval force of De Grasse combined with that of De Barras would at least be comparable in strength to anything the British could muster. As he studied the map again, he felt a stab of unease. The numbers worked overwhelmingly in favor of the allies, however daunting the odds against De Grasse and De Barras and Washington converging on Yorktown at more or less the same time to defeat the British military before mid-October, when De Grasse insisted he would sail back to the Caribbean. Why, then, was he so troubled? It all seemed so made to order. And that's precisely what bothered him. He asked why Cornwallis had allowed himself to be boxed into so defensive a position when even a child could see that all he had to do was gather up his forces and march out. There was little Lafayette's small force in Williamsburg could do to stop him.

"That is the question, is it not," Lafayette answered him. "You are not alone in asking it, Mr. Cutler. For two months I have . . . how do you say? . . . *shadowed* the English army through Virginia. At Petersburg, we saw Cornwallis joined by the army of General Phillips, the same officer exchanged for General Lincoln. From there we followed the British to Richmond. I am ashamed to inform you that Colonel Tarleton ordered his dragoons to burn the city and kill many old men, women, and children. *Alors,* we were powerless to assist those poor people. From Richmond, Cornwallis marched to Williamsburg, from there to Yorktown. Why did he come here? To repeat your question, Why does he now choose to stay here when he can clearly see the enemy at his doorstep? You are correct. We could do little to prevent him from leaving. *Encore,* there can be but one reason he chooses to remain. He expects General Clinton in New York to either reinforce or rescue him. In my opinion, whatever relief the British send will come soon, by sea. That is why haste is so critical, and why I must return to my command."

"I understand, General. What do you want Colonel Gimat and me to tell Admiral de Grasse?"

Lafayette deferred to Colonel Hamilton, whose hard facial features had softened into something resembling a smile. "You answered that question before you asked it, Lieutenant." He put the tip of his right index finger on the map directly on Yorktown. "We must do whatever is necessary to prevent Cornwallis from leaving Yorktown until General Washington arrives with his army. How many soldiers and how many ships does Admiral de Grasse have with him?"

"He has three thousand soldiers from the West Indies, plus eight hundred marines. His fleet has twenty-eight ships of the line, four frigates, two corvettes, and two hundred transports. And, Colonel, he also brings with him twelve hundred thousand livres, from Havana. These livres are for General Washington, to pay his soldiers when they arrive here."

Hamilton whistled softly. "De Grasse was able to do that, was he? God bless that man's soul." His voice was low, abstract, as if he were speaking to no particular audience. "There was another mutiny, Lieutenant. You could not have heard of it. It happened less than a month ago, before the march south began. Our soldiers haven't been paid in months, and some who have been with General Washington since the siege of Boston refused to leave New York without pay. Threats of a firing squad could not convince the mutineers. That is, until several leaders were shot for treason."

He went on, in the same tone. "Can't blame the lads, in my opinion. We ask them to fight and die for their country and in return we give them . . . what? Rags to wear. Knives and old muskets to fight with. What food there is, not fit for an animal to eat. And on top of that, we pay them nothing. Because Congress gives us nothing to pay them with. What does *not* surprise me is that we are no longer able to sign on new recruits. Every state is falling disastrously short of quota. People are sick of this war. They want it over, at any price, on any terms. What *does* surprise me is that, despite all, General Washington is still able to lead men who will fight. A few continue to follow him. A precious few: the true heroes of this revolution. But mark my words. If we lose this opportunity here in Yorktown, his soldiers will desert, and he will not be able to raise another army. Our cause will be lost."

His words cast a momentary pall on the conversation. Then Lafayette said, with some urgency, as if awakening from a bad dream, "Return to the flagship, Mr. Cutler. Report to Admiral de Grasse. Tell him what we have told you. Tell him we need his soldiers on shore and his ships in the rivers to deny Cornwallis any chance of escape."

☆ ☆ ☆

RICHARD AND Colonel Gimat made their report to the flagship. As a result, work began immediately to comply with General Lafayette's request. It was no small matter maneuvering the great fleet of transports toward Jamestown Island, where the troops of General Saint-Simon were to be disembarked over several days. Docks in the area were limited to those near the commercial establishments at the base of the Yorktown bluffs. As these docks were directly under British guns, transport vessels had to anchor out of range of enemy fire in the bay and ferry the troops and ordnance to Jamestown in small boats. As the transfer from ship to land began, *Valliant,* a Seventy-Four, ghosted in under topsails and dropped anchor at the mouth of the York River near her sister ship *Triton* and the frigate *Glorieux.* Across the peninsula, line-of-battle ships *Experiment* and *Andromaque* dropped anchor far up the James River, their cannon and swivel guns trained eastward across a stretch of peninsula stripped bare of trees and underbrush. Should Cornwallis attempt to flee, his army would be hard pressed to survive the fury that these two ships could unleash.

On the evening of September 4, as he was accustomed to doing every evening after supper in the wardroom, Richard retired alone to his small after cabin on the main gun deck. As liaison officer, he was relieved of watch duties and could expect to sleep the night through. Sitting on his cot and using his sea chest as a makeshift desk, he wrote in a diary by candlelight, recording the events of the day and inserting personal impressions he deemed appropriate. He kept the text factual, unemotional, for while he certainly wanted Katherine to read his words, the diary was intended as a gift to their child, son or daughter. When he was finished and had the diary tucked away in the chest, he dipped his quill and wrote a different sort of letter to be read by Katherine alone upon his return to Barbados. In these letters he allowed his emotions to run free, for he had found that expressing himself in such a way brought her close and eased the misery of missing her so. Though he refused to dwell on the possibility, at the back of his mind rested the comfort that, should he fall in battle, these letters would serve as memories of their time together.

The next morning, after a breakfast of bread, chocolate, and coffee, he was conveyed along with other naval officers to Jamestown Island by a ship's boat under sail. As the winds were favorable, it was a swift, enjoyable passage. Once ashore, however, he felt the same rough edges of anxiety that had vexed him at the close of yesterday. As the disembarkation process neared its conclusion, a sense of urgency mixed with anxiety had befallen the allied camp. Richard was not sure why, though he thought it may have had something to do with a corresponding sense of equanimity in the enemy camp. The British seemed utterly unimpressed by the looming danger. Last evening, so it was reported by army officers ashore, a band in Yorktown had struck up the tune *Rule Britannia* to the cheers of British soldiers. Was it simply bravado, Richard wondered, or had Yorktown become a seat of enormous self-delusion for the English?

Since Cornwallis was not one to suffer fools, Richard assumed it had to be bravado. And if bravado, it must have a cause. And that cause, he was convinced, was linked to whatever intelligence Hood's frigate communicated to *Charon* during their brief rendezvous in the Chesapeake. Lafayette was right: the British would return—in force. Should Graves and Hood prevail, consequences would be dire. Under no circumstances would De Grasse abandon the regiments of Saint-Simon on the Yorktown Peninsula. Whatever losses he might suffer in battle, he would remain off the Virginia capes as long as necessary to get them off. Were he to sail to Martinique without those soldiers, the coveted sugar islands of the French West Indies would be, as Saint-Simon put it, "spread wide open to the English rapists." Worse, from an American perspective, the British would then control the Chesapeake, with Washington and Rochambeau potentially trapped between the army of Lord Cornwallis already there and the army of General Clinton marching south from New York. If the United States had everything at stake here, Richard concluded, so did France. A British victory at Yorktown would spell disaster for the empire of King Louis XVI.

He sensed a presence behind him.

"Mornin', Lieutenant." The southern accent was unmistakable.

Richard turned to see Captain Mercer ambling up beside him, tamping down a bowl of tobacco in a corncob pipe as he watched with seeming disinterest the squads of French soldiers splashing ashore from a massive raft drawn up close to the beach. He was clean-shaven, unlike the first time they had met, and what passed for a Virginia militia officer's uniform was, today at least, in evidence.

"Good morning, Captain," Richard said. He waited for Mercer to open the conversation, which took awhile.

"Right pretty boys, ain't they, dressed up in them fine white uniforms."

Richard gave him a second glance. Mercer had struck a light and was concentrating on getting his pipe lit, sucking in hard on the stem until thin wisps of white smoke wafted up from the bowl. He studied the Virginian's profile. A grand air of indifference he had noted on Mercer had been replaced by the look of a man who had witnessed much sorrow and pain in recent days.

"They're good soldiers, Captain," Richard reassured him. "Some say the best in the French army. They will serve us well."

"Reckon they will," Mercer mused, exhaling a stream of smoke.

They watched together in silence as the pace ashore accelerated. More and more soldiers and ordnance were coming ashore from the transports, which were now in a frenzy to get the job done and march these men north to Williamsburg to join their brothers in arms erecting a barrier across the narrow Yorktown Peninsula. It was not yet midmorning, but already the sun was beating down on them with an intensity Richard had rarely experienced in the tropics. There the air was fresher, and dependable morning sea breezes tended to reduce heat and humidity to acceptable, often pleasant levels. Katherine came easily to mind. He wondered what she was doing at this very moment and found himself smiling at the thought of John with a pregnant woman in the house. How grateful he was that Julia was there with her, to attend to her needs. Grateful, too, that her brother Hugh was there. And, he had to admit, the Royal Navy.

He was wiping his brow with a kerchief and breathing in the sweet aroma of burning tobacco when Mercer spoke again. He was looking not at Richard but at the goings-on along the beach. His tone was off-handed, that of a reporter simply recording the facts.

"Two weeks back, my boys on patrol came upon a house down the road a spell. Farm house, you know the sort. They was thirsty, lookin' for water, so they knocked and yelled. No one answered, so they went inside." He paused to pull on his pipe, his brow furrowed, his mind seemingly tortured by wretched mental images. "Know what they found in there, Lieutenant? In the bedroom of that house? There'd been visitors not so long ago. Don't know if they was regular British or local Tories, though it hardly matters. What my boys found was a woman tied up with ropes against a closet door. She was nekked and pregnant. Had been, least ways. Her belly was slashed open, an' they had ripped out her young'un. It was there beside her, run through with a bayonet and pegged to the door. The 'bilical cord was still attached. On the door they wrote, in the mother's blood: 'Fucking rebel whore, ye shall bear no more.' My boys, Lieutenant, they've seen a lot in this war. But with this'un, they ran outside and puked their guts out."

Richard felt his sweat go cold. He gaped at Mercer. "What sort of barbarian does a thing like that?" he half whispered.

"That ain't the half of it. I've seen for myself things as bad. Heads sliced off and stored in kitchen cupboards. Girls younger'n my daughter Lucy, who's nine, raped every which way by God knows how many, till they're damn near dead. Rotted bodies of men an' animals dumped into wells to poison the water. You want more? I got more, Lieutenant. I got as much as you'd like. And it ain't just the Brits. Hell, they're holy men compared to what some of our so-called patriots are doin' t' them loyal to King George. Same damn thing: people fuckin' each other, people killin' each other, and I ask you, for what purpose? Where and when does this all end? It's been like this in the

South ever since Charleston fell an' the Brits started promisin' amnesty an' goin' 'round recruitin' local boys, white and nigger, to join their army."

A terrible silence fell.

"What's your point, Captain?" Richard mumbled at last.

Mercer spat on the ground.

"My point? Hell, Lieutenant, I jest done got through tellin' you: there *ain't* no point. To *any* o' this. For two years, my boys and I've been fightin' our own damn war here in Virginia. An' our war has nuthin' to do with yer gentlemen's rules and fine ways and codes of honor. That's all jest chicken shit to us. Do y'all think fer one moment that any of them fancy friends of your'n out there in them ships gives a hoot about the *real* war in Virginia? Or any o' these Frogs sashayin' ashore here? Or fer that matter, any of yer Yankee generals? I doubt it. I doubt it very much. I ain't ashamed to admit, there are times I don't give a rat's ass who wins here in Yorktown. Ask me an' I'll tell you: both sides've already lost."

It was not often in his life that Richard found himself lost for words. Now was one such time. He glared numbly at Mercer, sucking audibly at his pipe, as if the sound and motion could somehow exorcise the satanic images savaging his mind. It was then that they heard the first roar of cannon echoing from across the Chesapeake. Ten blasts in regular, short intervals, followed by another ten. Blank discharges fired from a French ship as a warning to all within earshot that a British fleet had been sighted, closing fast on the Virginia capes.

☆ ☆ ☆

CANNON FIRE instantly transformed Jamestown Island into a scene of bedlam. On shore duty were a hundred French naval officers and nearly two thousand sailors. With the blasts of the big guns, men began racing for the nearest boat. Out in the bay, empty craft on their way to the transports turned sharply, in a frenzy to get back to the beach.

In a knee-jerk reaction, Richard waded waist-deep into the river and clambered over the gunwale of a longboat that had just finished unloading a contingent of soldiers. Others waded in after him. He held out his hand to a barrel-chested sailor and pulled him aboard. Together they hauled up the man next in line, a lieutenant. Rank meant nothing. The objective was to get as many aboard as quickly as possible and shove off.

From across the Chesapeake, guns roared in sequence again. Oarsmen drew hard, propelling the longboat downriver. Once clear of the James, the sailors set the lateen sail and trimmed the sheets against a fair northeasterly breeze. The tide was slack; they could go no faster. Would it be enough? Richard stepped onto a thwart by the mast, next to another officer, the tall, fair-skinned, black-haired lieutenant he had helped aboard. He, like Richard, held a hand over his eyes, searching into the brilliant sunshine reflecting off the bay waters.

"*Qu'est-ce qui se passe?*" a chubby, self-important officer in the sternsheets demanded to know.

The lieutenant responded in words that were not encouraging. Richard's heart sank, knowing he was right. They were close enough to the great ships to see crew on the topsail yards unfurling and dropping canvas. At the bow of the nearest ship, *Le Marseillais*, two sailors were waging war with axes against the thick hemp of the anchor rope—to hell with the capstan—cut the cables and get out to sea. Richard glanced past Lynnhaven Bay into the Atlantic. Glints of white on the eastern horizon were bearing down on them.

"*Ces bateaux, sont-ils peut-être amiral de Barras?*" Richard said, hoping against hope, to the officer beside him.

"*Non.*"

The reply was terse and for good reason. It was known that Admiral de Barras commanded nine ships of the line. This fleet contained perhaps twice that number.

Ahead to starboard, near shore, a sleek two-masted schooner swung at her mooring. She was carvel-built and American-rigged, her two gaff sails and twin foresails furled neatly on their booms. More a private yacht than a fighting vessel, she was being kept in reserve to convey General Washington and other allied officers south from the Head of Elk on the northern edge of the Chesapeake. But she did have two swivel guns, one mounted on each side amidships, and she looked to be swift. She just might serve some purpose.

"*Ce bateau-là, lieutenant,*" Richard said, pointing toward the schooner. "*Y allons-nous?*"

The French lieutenant nodded. He ordered the coxswain to steer to starboard. Twenty minutes later the longboat glided up alongside the fifty-foot hull of *Princess Charlotte*. Richard deferred to the lieutenant, who had introduced himself as the Comte de Vioménil, first lieutenant, then scrambled aboard after him. Twelve hand-picked sailors followed. Quickly they made ready to sail. In the bow, a sailor attached a buoy to the bitter end of the anchor line and heaved it overboard. Another kicked the jib over to windward to put the schooner close-hauled on a course to the southwestern corner of the Middle Ground, an area of treacherous shallows lurking halfway between Cape Henry to the south and Cape Charles to the north. Once there, the helmsman brought her over onto a larboard tack. With a northeasterly breeze steady on her beam, she cleared the outer shoals of Cape Henry and knifed her way into the Atlantic.

Less than two miles northeast of the Middle Ground, making slow but steady progress in the five-knot wind, was the vanguard of the British fleet, close enough for Richard to see her raised gun ports through a spyglass. In the Chesapeake, the French fleet remained a confused muddle of ships struggling for open water. If the British brought their guns to bear as things stood now, they could pummel the French van as its ships emerged one by one from the bay. Which is exactly what Richard was anticipating as he swept his glass along the long line of battle cruisers running east to west.

From the third ship in line, a blue pennant fluttered from the foremast truck and a blue flag from the forepeak. Hood's ship: vice admiral of the Blue. Richard searched for the red pennant of Adm. Sir Thomas Graves flying from the main truck of the flagship positioned at the middle of the center division. He could not find it, but he knew it was there, as would be a white or blue pennant farther back at the mizzenmast of a ship at the center of the rear division. It was all preordained in the fighting instructions, for a hundred years the bible of the Royal Navy. If a British admiral dared violate the instructions, he had best emerge from the battle victorious on an epic scale. Nor could he follow the instructions at the expense of victory. As a schoolboy in Hingham, Richard had learned the ditty of Adm. Sir John Byng who, in an engagement in the Mediterranean during the French and Indian War, had followed the instructions to a T—and had lost the battle. As a result, the British naval base at Minorca was lost. As punishment for what was deemed a dereliction of duty, Byng was executed by firing squad on his own quarterdeck.

"*Combien de bateaux les Anglais ont-ils?*" Vioménil asked, scanning the waters north of them. "*Je compte dix-neuf.*"

"*Oui, dix-neuf,*" Richard agreed. Nineteen ships of the line, plus a few frigates. Assuming the Third Rates anchored in the York and James rivers remained on station, that compared to twenty-four ships of the line sailing with Admiral De Grasse. A five-ship advantage over the enemy translated into a four-hundred-gun advantage, a significant edge assuming all else was equal. But all else was not equal. The British held the weather gauge and could therefore dictate battle tactics. At this moment, ships in their van were about to bring their lethal broadsides to bear against the vulnerable lead ships of Commodore Bougainville tacking out from the Chesapeake. Those aboard *Princess Charlotte* braced themselves for an all-out, ear-splitting thunderclap of gunfire.

But . . . no. The British ships continued to wear in silence, nearly all the way around, each ship in line duplicating the evolutions of the ship in front until the British fleet was on a line running west to east, rather than east to west, and what had been the vanguard of the fleet now comprised its rear division sailing away, ever so slowly, from the Virginia capes in a southeasterly direction. In these fluky conditions, with the wind abeam, the lead ships were forced to back and fill their sails, as if gasping for breath while they allowed their own ships and those of the French to catch up and form a proper line of battle ahead, opposite each other.

"*Incroyable!*" Vioménil cried out. "*Les Anglais nous permettent pour à sortir et à combattre. Qui le croit?*"

Richard was as incredulous. In allowing De Grasse to sail out from the Chesapeake unchallenged, Admiral Graves had conceded a victory-defining tactical advantage. Had he ordered Hood to rake the French van under the prevailing conditions, the outcome of the engagement might already have been decided. But he chose not to. Why? To Richard's mind, it came down to respect, and not just for the fighting instructions. Graves had thrown down the gauntlet and, as the gentleman he was, would now permit his adversary to come out and fight.

It was midafternoon. Twenty-four French warships had formed themselves into a line of battle under topsails and jibs. They made cautious and haphazard progress forward, as much by design, Richard felt, as the effects of gentle breezes. De Grasse held the lee position by necessity and also by preference, since it would allow him to break off the engagement if necessary and prevent the British from maneuvering between his fleet and the Virginia capes and thus seize control of the Chesapeake.

For almost two hours the opposing fleets sailed parallel to each other on the same southeasterly course, a musket shot apart. At precisely six bells in the afternoon watch, the British van fell slightly off the wind on a bearing that put it on a long slanting line of interception with the French. Almost instantaneously, a solid yellow flag shot up the foremast signal halyard on *Ville de Paris,* followed underneath by a large, square blue and white flag. Signals from De Grasse to Bougainville: come to the wind and engage the enemy as closely as possible. Immediately the frigate *Glorieux,* on station by the flagship in the center division, dropped her t'gallants and trimmed sheets, surging forward to *L'Auguste* in the van to make certain Bougainville had understood the order.

He had. Slowly, ever so slowly, the vans of the two fleets converged in the shape of a giant sideways V facing southeast, its arms becoming more and more crooked as the center and rear divisions of both fleets struggled to maintain position. The center of the French line was drifting off to leeward, increasing the span of ocean separating it from its counterpart in the British fleet. A hundred yards south of the French line, *Princess Charlotte* maintained her distance.

"*Nous ne pouvons rien faire d'autre que de regarder,*" Vioménil said disgustedly, summing up the frustrations of everyone aboard the schooner. Vioménil was right. There was little they could do but watch and wait.

Suddenly the lead ship in the British van hauled her wind, came abreast of her counterpart, and opened fire. Bougainville responded in kind with all eight ships in his van. One massive broadside after another hurled an unimaginable weight of iron at the ship opposite in line, the powder charges reduced at close range to produce bigger and thus more lethal wood splinters. As was their custom, French gunners fired high, on the uproll, the quoins removed from their cannon trucks, their aim to shred rigging and topple masts in order to hamper enemy maneuvers. British gunners fired low, on the downroll, quoins all the way in, their aim to smash holes in enemy hulls: cripple the enemy, put her out of action, and finish her off later like a shark striking its prey, wounding it, then circling back for the kill. Aboard the schooner, it was impossible to confirm who held the upper hand. Spyglasses were useless. The arena of battle had quickly become enveloped in thick acrid clouds of smoke that hung over the fleets like a stubborn summer fog in Hingham Bay.

For two hours the battle raged on. Though the vans of the two fleets remained closely engaged, their center divisions were firing at each other from too great a distance to cause much damage. Rear divisions, on the tips of the wings of the great crooked V formation, had yet to engage at all. The thundering, rolling cacophony roared on and on, unceasing, echoing about the sea and capes as round after round of iron shot shrieked from one ship across to another. In the front lines, where fighting was fiercest, Richard noted a mainmast beginning to wobble. It teetered back and forth until finally it collapsed and disappeared into the thick ashen clouds below, taking with it the mizzen and fore topgallant masts. It was the same at sea as it was on land, Richard thought to himself, as he watched spellbound while the two great powers lined up opposite each other and pounded away until one side finally yielded, having endured too great a sacrifice of life, limb, and heart of oak.

Except that, in this battle, surrender was not possible. What finally permitted a cease-fire was not victory but the coming of evening and a shift of wind to the southwest. At the start of the second dogwatch, as if by pre-arranged design, the great guns fell silent. An eerie calm pervaded the Atlantic as the two fleets remained in a parallel line-ahead formation, assessing damage to its ships and attending to its wounded and dead. Pitiful screams and sobs of men breathing their last—or worse, maimed, disfigured for life—wailed over the quiet waters into the night.

Richard awoke the next morning before dawn after a brief, fitful sleep. He lay in his berth for several minutes, trying to remember a scenario his mind had constructed during those disjointed but often highly creative moments between sleep and full consciousness. Finally he gave up. With a sigh, he swung his legs over the side and stood up, pausing for balance before heading for the companionway.

On deck he was greeted by Lieutenant Vioménil, seated by the tiller between two bearded, red-striped-shirted sailors.

"*Bonjour, Monsieur Cutler. Vous aimez du café?*"

"*Oui, merci,*" Richard replied, his words sending one sailor hurrying below. Slipping on his uniform coat against the chill of a late summer dawn at sea, Richard used both hands to smooth back unruly strands of blond hair from his eyes as he scanned northward in the gathering light.

The two fleets were there, in plain sight of each other. The French fleet was closest to the schooner, the British fleet perhaps a half mile farther to the northeast. What wind there was had clocked around to the west during the night, raising ripples on the water's surface sufficient to propel *Princess* forward at a reasonable pace but scarcely enough to influence the behemoths in the currents. To westward, a strip of land shimmered atop the horizon. Exactly what strip of land, Richard could not determine, though he estimated from their rate of drift that they must be near Albemarle Sound off the coast of North Carolina.

"*Merci,*" he said to the sailor who handed him an earthen mug. He sipped the steamy black liquid, feeling its heat explore his throat and stomach as he reflected again on the image that had startled him awake. It was coming back to him now, stimulated perhaps by the coffee.

"*Lieutenant, y a-t-il un drapeau britannique à bord?*"

"*Je crois que oui.*" Vioménil replied. He eyed him curiously. "*Pourquoi?*"

Richard told him why. He spoke deliberately, as if to first convince himself of the wisdom of what he was proposing, then with a quickened tempo as Vioménil latched on to the idea and added his own contributions. Here, they agreed, was something tangible they could do that could perhaps make a difference. First, they needed the admiral's approval.

A half hour later *Princess Charlotte* was abeam of the immense *Ville de Paris*. Standing at the schooner's bow with a speaking trumpet in his hand, Vioménil had to shout to make himself heard above on the weather deck. He was not certain he had been understood until the imposing form of Admiral de Grasse appeared in the hollow entry port at the main gun deck three-quarters of the way up the hull. He stood there by the outer railing on the domed wooden platform, a hand cupped at his ear. When Vioménil finished speaking, De Grasse disappeared inside with his subordinates. A few minutes later he reemerged on the platform.

"*Bonne chance,*" De Grasse called down, as he touched the forward tip of his admiral's hat. He then turned on his heels and disappeared inside.

As *Princess* swung around toward land, Richard gave the French lieutenant a meaningful glance. He was grateful and not a little surprised, despite their strengthening relationship, that in his communication with De Grasse, Vioménil had insisted on giving Richard full credit as architect of the plan.

The course *Princess* followed brought them in toward the Outer Banks until a lookout sighted shoals ahead. She then hauled her wind northward, hugging the coastline as close as she dared, well out of sight of either fleet. When sometime later the lookout called back that the Virginia capes lay on the distant horizon ahead, Vioménil ordered her around on a southeasterly course, back toward the drifting fleets. Timing was critical. It was now almost two o'clock. Their plan called for sighting the British ships before sunset and using their stern lanterns as guideposts during the night.

To their relief, the wind freshened considerably during the early afternoon, as cloud formations had suggested it would. This, too, was a critical factor. Vioménil had not told De Grasse what the admiral should do as a result of their proposed action; it would have been impudent in the extreme for a lieutenant to make such a public recommendation to an admiral. Nonetheless he was confident that, under the circumstances, De Grasse would wear his fleet around under cover of darkness. To accomplish that, he needed wind at his heel. He also needed a decent head start. British ships were copper-bottomed and thus considerably swifter than wood-bottomed French ships laden with Caribbean sea-growth. Were Graves so inclined, he could easily beat De Grasse in a race back to the Chesapeake. Neither Richard nor Vioménil could fathom why he had not already done so.

They would have their answer shortly.

Richard was on deck before dawn, standing watch by the forward mast. Before them lay the British fleet, each ship a mass of black against an eastern sky now beginning to draw shape and proportion from the gloom. Surprisingly, the fleet maintained a credible formation in line ahead, though as dawn approached, they could clearly see that the ships in the van had taken a terrible beating during the battle. Rigging had been cut to pieces; sails on what yards remained had been shredded to strips of white rags that flapped uselessly in the morning breeze. One warship had lost her mainmast, another both her foremast and mainmast. A third was missing her main topmast and the spanker over her quarterdeck. Of greater significance, only eighteen ships were visible. The nineteenth was nowhere to be seen.

To the south, where the French fleet should have been, was empty water.

As *Princess* glided along the larboard side of unblemished warships in the rear division, Richard was reminded of Will and *Eagle* and their visit to the naval base at Spithead those many years ago. Then, as now, were a gunnery officer so ordered, he need but settle a slow match over a fuse to blow their little vessel to kingdom come, leaving behind few traces as evidence of where, moments before, men had lived and schemed.

Here and there a head appeared at the bulwarks, peering down at *Princess Charlotte* much as a child might gaze down at a water beetle skittering alongside a rowboat. She was making for *London,* the flagship at the center of the middle division where a Union Jack rolled listlessly from the main truck. As she approached the entry port, *Princess* feathered up in and off the wind as her crew, dressed in the nondescript togs of any ship's slop chest, shortened sail to match *London's* sluggish pace.

Richard was standing next to the tiller, beneath the British flag on the signal halyard, looking up at some significant damage done to the lower yards of the flagship. He raised a speaking trumpet. "Ahoy, *London!*" he shouted in his most patrician English accent.

No response. Were it not for the bang of hammers and the rasp of saws emanating from her bowels, *London* would have seemed a ghost ship drifting upon the waters. Richard strained his eyes up, but he could make out only vague forms moving about the weather deck. He was about to hail the ship a second time when a red-coated officer appeared on the entry platform together with two subordinates. He was middle-aged and appeared somewhat disheveled, as though he had just been awakened. He wore no waistcoat, and his shirt was not tucked in all the way.

"What vessel is that?" he called down through a small speaking trumpet. With his free hand he worked the gold buttons of his dress coat. "Who are you and what is your purpose?"

"*Princess Charlotte*," Richard answered the first question, adding, "captured from the Americans," lest her American rig arouse suspicion. "I am Lieutenant Richard Cutler, and this vessel is attached to His Majesty's frigate *Charon* in Yorktown. I carry a personal message from Lord Cornwallis to Admiral Sir Thomas Graves." As proof, he held up a thick square piece of paper folded over several times with what looked like a signet seal in the middle. "I assume he is aboard?"

"Admiral Graves is not to be disturbed," the officer stated unequivocally. "I am Samuel Tavington, *London's* first lieutenant. State your business. I assure you I shall relay any message to the admiral."

Richard dropped the trumpet to his side and glanced down at the deck, as though pondering his next move. He glanced at Vioménil who, like the others on deck, remained stone-faced. He raised the trumpet back up.

"My orders are to speak personally with the admiral."

"I don't doubt that, Lieutenant," Tavington replied, his voice becoming edged with irritation. "But the admiral has given strict orders not to be disturbed, as I have told you. And as you can see, it would be no easy matter bringing you aboard. You have no boat, and it would be rather difficult under the circumstances for us to sway out one of ours. Can you tell me, is the message you bear of a decidedly personal nature? Or one of extreme urgency?"

"No sir, it is neither."

"Then tell me what it is," he stated with finality.

"Very well, sir, if you insist." He paused for emphasis. "Please inform Admiral Graves that Admiral de Barras will soon be arriving in the Chesapeake with eighteen ships of the line. A packet boat sighted the fleet yesterday off the coast of New Jersey, making good speed."

There was a pause as Tavington conferred with his subordinates. "Again, please? How many ships did you say?"

"The packet boat claims eighteen, sir. Plus three frigates. These circumstances compel his Lordship to advise Admiral Graves not to return to the Chesapeake. He fears were he to do so, his ships would be in dire peril. Lord Cornwallis also desires Admiral Graves to be assured that he is well supplied with food and munitions. His position is impregnable, and he intends to affect a breakout within the week and return to South Carolina. Rebel forces here are local militia units and pose no threat to him. It is all here in this letter." Again he held it up.

Lieutenant Tavington huddled with the two junior officers, this time for a longer period. He shook his head once or twice, and at one point he seemed to be weighing something in his mind as he glared down at the small schooner keeping pace below him. It occurred to Richard, with a pang of foreboding, that against all reason someone aboard *London* might have recognized *Princess* yesterday feathering up to the French fleet. Or Tavington might order a heaving line or some sort of breeches buoy thrown down to bring the message aboard. In which case, Richard was prepared to accidentally drop it overboard and have the lead strips sealed in the letter take it to the bottom.

Richard called up, "Is my message understood, sir?"

Tavington slowly brought the trumpet to his lips. "It is, Lieutenant," he said, in what sounded like tones of resignation. "Thank you. I shall inform the admiral. One question before you depart: did you sight the French fleet on your way here?"

"Aye, sir, we did. Heading north, toward the Chesapeake." Where, by Richard's numbers, De Grasse would combine his naval force with that of De Barras, giving the French an overwhelming two-to-one superiority over the enemy. To Whitehall, no army was worth the potential loss of a fleet.

"Very well. Carry on, Lieutenant. Upon your return to Yorktown, please convey the admiral's warmest personal regards to Lord Cornwallis."

"Aye, aye, sir. I shall do so. Please advise Admiral Graves in return that Lord Cornwallis sends him his best compliments. God save the king!"

At Richard's command, the helmsman tacked the schooner around, back toward the Virginia capes. Once the British ships were hull-down on the eastern horizon, he brought her into the wind and ordered her hove to. There she remained until her officers and crew were convinced that Admiral Graves had indeed ordered his crippled fleet back to New York, leaving to their fate Gen. Charles Lord Cornwallis and his army of seventy-five hundred men. Only then did the little schooner hoist all sail and set a course for Lynnhaven Bay.

WHAT CONTINUED to astound Richard, as he left General Lafayette's headquarters, was how ragged and disorderly the American army appeared in contrast to the French.

Two weeks ago, the combined forces of General Washington and Count Rochambeau had arrived at the Chesapeake, two days after Admiral de Barras had sailed triumphantly into the bay with nine line-of-battle ships and French siege provisions, the same day that Admiral Graves had set off for New York. The white-uniformed army of France made quite a spectacle for the war-weary citizens of Williamsburg as it marched down the wide, tree-lined Duke of Gloucester Street, its regiments of foot tromping in perfect unison. In its impeccably arrayed ranks were two nine-hundred-man regiments of Bourdonnois, their uniforms marked by crimson lapels and pink collars; two regiments of Soissonois, in uniforms notable for their light blue collars and yellow buttons and rose-colored feathers on grenadier caps; a regiment of six hundred artillerymen; and six hundred cavalry of the renowned legion of the Duke of Lauzun: German, Swiss, and Polish mercenaries resplendent in amazingly unblemished sky blue jackets, yellow trousers, black boots, and towering black shakos pinned with fancy plumes of various bright colors.

In marked contrast, the American army had shuffled into Williamsburg dog-tired from the forced march, a motley herd of men including scarred veterans, a few freshly minted Americans from Europe, boys of fifteen and sixteen untested in battle, and especially in the New England militia regiments, hundreds of Negro soldiers purposely kept apart from their white brothers in arms.

Many soldiers went shoeless, including a number in the Continental regiments, and often what passed for a uniform was nothing more then a collection of threadbare rags sewn together so many times the effort itself finally became pointless.

Senior American officers were well outfitted. As were the divisions of artillery, the elite troops of this and every army, who looked every bit the professional soldier as they marched into Williamsburg in their blue dress coats with red facings and shiny gold buttons. A few regiments of Continental regulars were also handsomely attired, but these were the exceptions. Most American soldiers Richard had seen confirmed the oft-quoted description of the rebel army advanced years ago by Gen. Sir William Howe as a "ragtag mass of rabble."

With the help of sentinels posted along the way, Richard finally spotted the large gray tent he was seeking. Not far away to the north, between these officers' tents and the British defenses at Yorktown, he could hear sappers and miners begin their night work, digging a four-mile-long trench in the hard, sandy soil six hundred yards from the British lines. This first parallel, as this trench was called, was almost complete, and mortars and small cannon were already being hauled into position along its perimeter.

Getting to the tent had been no easy matter. Sentries wearing blue coats with the New England regimental white facings and cuffs had challenged him along the approach. At the flaps of the tent, a heavily armed guard was the last to demand to know his business. As he had with the others, Richard produced the letter of invitation and explained why he was there.

"My boy, welcome," a pleasant-sounding voice boomed from inside the tent. "It's all right, Corporal," Benjamin Lincoln said, grinning as he threw back a flap to the tent and beckoned Richard inside. "I know this young man. You have nothing to fear from him unless your wife or daughter happens to be nearby." He chuckled merrily at his own witticism.

"Well, well, well," he said, after they had dispensed with formalities and he had given Richard a thorough once-over. "I hardly recognized you, at first glance. You have changed, Richard. My, how you have changed. I left you a boy in Hingham. You return to me a man in Virginia. A married man, so I understand."

"You have heard from my parents?" Richard asked eagerly. He had no way of knowing, until this moment, if any of his letters had gotten through to his family. But he could see from the broad grin on the general's big, kindly face and the amused twinkle in his leaf-green eyes that one, at least, had. "Is everyone well?"

"Oh, I should say. Anne and Lavinia are cutting quite the swath among the young men. And Caleb, well . . . Caleb is counting the days until he can follow in your footsteps. As for your parents, they are as charming and as gracious as ever and delighted with the news of your marriage." He placed his hands on his hips and gave Richard a mock frown. "So, my boy, you've struck your colors and turned on us by marrying an English girl, eh? Is she the same lass Will teased you about back in Hingham? Christmas of '74, wasn't it?"

"Yes sir, it was," Richard said, astounded by Lincoln's memory. "Her name is Katherine. And yes, she's English, as I am, though she now considers herself as much an American as I do. We plan to live in Hingham when the war is over. It's her wish as much as mine."

"By Jove, *that* is good news!" Lincoln beamed. "How pleased your family will be! You will of course allow Mrs. Lincoln and me the honor of hosting a small get-together to welcome Mrs. Cutler to Hingham. Don't worry, we'll keep it intimate. Don't want to scare the young lady off, do we? We'll just invite over a few neighbors and . . . perhaps . . . three or four hundred of our closest friends?"

"Thank you, General," Richard grinned. "Mrs. Cutler and I are honored to accept."

"Excellent."

Lincoln found a bottle of Madeira and filled two glasses. "This calls for a celebration," he said, handing one to Richard. "It's the one luxury I can offer you, I'm afraid. You've eaten, I trust?"

"Yes sir," Richard replied, though in fact he hadn't. He took a sip of the clear gold liquid and felt its soothing burn slide down his throat. "You look well, General," he commented a moment later.

"You are as thoughtful as ever, my boy, whatever the truth may be." He let out a heartfelt sigh. "Fact is, I am fighting a losing battle on two fronts." He patted the area above his forehead where baldness was making shiny inroads into a raised bank of white hair farther back. Then he patted his stomach with both hands, its ample girth such that he had to leave unbuttoned the bottom three buttons of his white linen waistcoat. "This at least," glancing down at his hands flat on his waistline, "I can blame on Mrs. Lincoln. Her cooking is irresistible."

Richard gave the general a brief smile, waiting for him to raise the issue he had mentioned in the letter he had written inviting Richard to his headquarters. When silence ensued, Richard said, because he felt it had to be said, "I'm sorry about Charleston, sir."

Lincoln nodded appreciatively. "Thank you." He finished off his glass of Madeira and poured himself a second. "Unfortunately, my choices were limited. Admiral D'Estaing sailed away right when I most needed him, and even the South Carolina militia units refused to fight to save their city. General Clinton, for once, was itching for a fight, and he had the British army and navy at his disposal. We still managed one hell of a defense, and I shall always remember the Continentals who stood by me. They may not look the part, Richard, but I tell you that our soldiers are every bit as good and as brave as Europeans. Besides," he grinned weakly, "surrender gave me an opportunity to return to Hingham and tend to my farm. I confess it's what I most enjoy doing. Much like my dear friend, General Washington."

He lost himself briefly in personal reflection, then gave Richard a sudden solemn look.

"I am informed by General Lafayette that you have volunteered for the assault against Redoubt Ten five nights from now. May I ask why? Mind you, I am inquiring as a friend of your family, not as a superior officer."

Richard was prepared for that question. "I understand, sir. And of course you may ask me anything." He put down his empty glass and looked directly at Lincoln. "I did not leave the Caribbean, General, simply to observe the war in Virginia. That was my fate during the naval engagement, and it must not happen again. Commodore Bougainville understands this and has released me from duties aboard his ship."

"I see," Lincoln said, holding Richard's eyes with his own. He opened his mouth as if to say something, then apparently thought better of it. "Be careful, my boy," he said simply. "I beg you, take no unnecessary risks. There's no need, and you have much to live for. Many people are praying to see you safely home. Your bride is one. Your family and friends in Hingham, of course. Count me as one of them." He offered his hand.

Richard returned the handshake, swallowing hard. "Thank you, General," he said. "It is for those you mention and for others I have come to know in this war that I must do what I must do. Those people are not able to be here. I am."

☆ ☆ ☆

THE BOMBARDMENT of Yorktown began early in the evening of October 9. General Washington set off the first gun from the American artillery park, a howitzer that lobbed a projectile high into the air in a wide arc, its fuse sizzling white in its wake, before it came shrieking down onto the British defenses, exploding with an ear-popping crash that hurled shards of scorching metal in all directions. Shell after shell followed, more than a thousand that first night, a howling downpour of twenty-four-pound shot, canister, and grape that hammered everything in its path. The next morning the unmerciful barrage grew louder when fifty heavy siege guns in the French grand battery added their weight to the assault, reinforced by mortars and light artillery dug into the trench of the first parallel, sparing nothing in Yorktown including the ships anchored in the river. Late in the night of October 10, the Royal Navy frigate *Charon,* bottled up and unarmed, her guns ashore in the battlements, was struck on her weather deck by a red-hot shell. When the conflagration reached her magazine, an enormous explosion rent the air, sending a towering column of sparks high into the night. Silhouettes of soldiers of all stripes and nationalities stood mute, staring in awe at the fiery spectacle.

The British responded with everything they had, concentrating their aim on the stripped-clean area in front of Yorktown, where sappers and miners were advancing the American offensive line three hundred yards forward and beginning work on a second parallel. It was risky business. British guns were murderous at such close range. Along the eastern edge of the parallel, soldiers and engineers were cut down unmercifully, the gabions and fascines they had erected as protective barriers pulverized into wastes of dirt and grains of sand.

Then, suddenly, inexplicably, the British guns fell silent. Deserters confirmed that munitions in Yorktown were running low and that disease was savaging the British ranks.

Dawn on the fourth day revealed dead horses floating in the river. At noon that day, the British forced hundreds of Negro soldiers and servants stricken with smallpox out from Yorktown at a slow walk, with orders to infiltrate the enemy lines and infect as many American and French soldiers as possible. Muskets aimed at their backs ensured obedience from men who had fled the cruelty of their American masters in hope of British succor.

General Washington quickly ordered their isolation before any harm could be done.

On the morning of the fifth day, chief engineers informed Washington and his staff that the second parallel was complete. Frontal assaults on the outer defenses of Yorktown could commence at any time.

British "outer defenses" began north of Yorktown at a redoubt in the shape of a star a thousand yards from the center of town. Defended by Royal Welsh Fusiliers, it had been constructed on the west side of a shallow ravine that served the same purpose as a moat surrounding a castle. From the star redoubt, as this position was called, the defensive perimeter arced out several hundred yards in front of Yorktown and along the west bank of a small creek, before swerving up to the northeast where it connected with two adjacent redoubts south of Yorktown at the river's edge. These wooden fortifications were known simply as redoubts numbers nine and ten.

Earlier in the week, the British had abandoned three outer redoubts along the arc in front of Yorktown. Cornwallis apparently believed these positions were too exposed to enemy fire and had decided to draw in his defenses as one might draw in one's fingers to form a fist. But he refused to abandon the three remaining redoubts, and allied commanders understood why. Swivel guns and cannon positioned there would make short work of any frontal assault on the town. For the investment of Yorktown to succeed, these redoubts had to be captured and integrated into the second parallel.

During the afternoon of October 14, messengers relayed orders from Washington's headquarters to commanders in the field. Tonight was the night. A diversionary action would precede the three main assaults. At 7:00, on the Gloucester Peninsula, the Duke of Lauzun's calvary, supported by Continental infantry, would feint an assault on the British Legion defending the town. An hour later, at 8:00, le marquis de Saint-Simon would lead his West Indies regiments against the star redoubt. At 9:00 sharp, Guillaume, Comte de Deux-Ponts, would lead the charge against Redoubt Nine with four hundred French grenadiers. Col. Alexander Hamilton, commanding a similar-sized force of Continentals and Virginia militia, was responsible for the capture of Redoubt Ten.

During the day, the allies hammered all three redoubts with an unrelenting artillery barrage.

That evening, at 8:45, Lafayette addressed the one-thousand-man assembly lined up in crisp military array before his headquarters.

"Good luck, dear friends and fellow soldiers," he shouted through a speaking trumpet. *"Bonne chance, mes chers amis et soldats de camarade."* To his left, le comte de Deux-Ponts stood at stiff attention, his subordinate officers in a row between him and the blue and red squares of French grenadiers. To Lafayette's right, Colonel Hamilton stood before a line of officers that included Richard Cutler dressed in a lieutenant's naval uniform. He had a long-barreled dragoon pistol clipped to his belt and an army sword buckled at his side. In his left hand he clutched a lock of Katherine's hair she had given him shortly before she left Tobago for Barbados.

"The fate of this siege," Lafayette exhorted over the distant clash of battle, "the fate of this revolution, hangs in the balance tonight. May God be with you."

At nine o'clock the two assault parties, the grenadiers in the lead, were ordered at a quickstep into the ten-food-wide, four-foot-deep trench of the first parallel. Bent over at a crouch, they jogged along until they reached the zigzag lines leading northward to the second parallel. Wheeling right at the T, they made for the twin redoubts rising to the east. When Deux-Ponts and the allied officers reached the end of the trench, they dropped to one knee to allow those behind to catch up. He signaled down the ranks, pointing like a deaf mute at the fortification inland from the river fifty feet away: Redoubt Nine. When his officers relayed back that all was ready, Deux-Ponts shook Hamilton's hand, raised his right arm, swung his sword in a broad loop, and eased up from the trench onto the open field badly pockmarked from the shelling. Grenadiers followed behind at a fast walk, then at a trot, then at a full sprint when guards in the redoubt cried out in warning.

Hamilton waited until those in his command had filled the void in the trench left by the storming grenadiers. As the order "Fix bayonets!" was relayed down the line, Richard studied the walls of Redoubt Ten directly ahead. The fortification was about thirty yards square and constructed entirely of felled trees, their sharp, saw-hewn trunks pointing upward like so many giant upended pencils tied together in a row.

Hamilton raised his sword in the air and jumped up out of the trench. Richard and the others followed close behind. The element of surprise gone, there was no need for stealth. Hamilton let out a war hoop, taken up by those behind, and began running at full tilt, his sword pointing up the gentle slope to where a line of British defenders had taken position, their muskets cradled between the chest-high wooden stakes and aimed at the front ranks of charging rebels screaming like men gone mad.

It was a withering volley. Continentals were cut down by musket shot, momentum pitching their legs forward in a drunken stumble until they collapsed face down in the dirt or hurling them backward with their arms in the air.

Rebels held their fire. They had one shot, and Hamilton had ordered them not to waste it. The British had taken theirs and that line, at least, would have to pause to reload. Thirty yards of open incline separated them. Richard ran at a sprint, sword in hand, urging his men onward. The ground was rising now, leading up on a broad slant to the defensive wall where a second battery of muskets had replaced the first. From one corner of the redoubt, a swivel gun erupted, then another from the opposite corner as a volley of musketry cracked out from spaces in between. A ball whined past Richard's ear. Another, then another. On both sides of him men fell, screaming in agony as hails of grape fired at ten yards riddled their guts or blew apart their limbs. Ahead, to his left, an officer died in his tracks, unknowing, a bullet passing through his eye as another, larger projectile, grape probably, simultaneously took away part of his forehead. Richard paid no attention. There was no time to think, just do. He ran on in a raging desire to reach the crest, his heart pounding in an insane blend of exhilaration, panic, and fear.

"First rank, fire!" Hamilton screamed. On a dead run, those with an unobstructed aim fired from the hip at so close a range some found their mark.

They were at the wall, thrusting bayonet tips into chinks between logs, firing point-blank with rifles and pistols, clawing at the abatis, loosening them, rocking them back and forth, back and forth, a mob mentality at work determined to knock the boughs down. One abatis went over, pulled from its roots in the sandy soil like a dentist extracting a tooth from a diseased gum. Down came another. Here, there, the rebels gained entry. As the wall split apart, Americans stormed inside, jabbing and swinging at the enemy. British officers fought to restore order, to repel, as American officers impelled their men onward into the breach.

Trumpets sounded. A British countercharge. Redcoats and blue and gold jacketed Hessians and Jaegers responded to a man, straining against the swarming tide of rebel forces, compelling it backward, step by step, brawling ferociously in close-quarter, tortoiselike formation until they had pushed the enemy back outside the redoubt's collapsing facade, onto the slope, back down the hill. At the leading edge of retreating rebel infantry, Richard parried a bayonet lunge and thrust his blade deep into the bowels of a charging Hessian. He yanked it free, blood dripping, as the Hessian fell over dead.

"Fan out!" Hamilton screamed to those behind him. Officers took up the call. Militia units at the base of the incline fanned out to the right and left.

"Rear ranks, fire!" Major Nelson commanded. His Virginia militia units in the rear took aim at British and Germans exposed on the hillside outside the redoubt. They unleashed a slaughterhouse crossfire.

Two things happened almost at once. British still standing closest to the redoubt turned and ran for cover inside the shattered defenses. Those farther down the hill, mostly Hessian grenadiers, realizing they had been abandoned by their English allies, fought on with renewed and stunning ferocity, selling dear every drop of Teutonic blood.

Fighting close beside Richard, Hamilton suddenly cried out in anguish. A Hessian's sword slashed open his right arm, forcing him to drop his weapon. Another Hessian charged at Hamilton with a bayonet leveled at his chest.

Richard hurled himself at the grenadier, punching the haft of his sword against his jaw, sending him to the ground. He then jumped on him in a death struggle, until a Virginian slashed the Hessian's throat with a knife seconds before he was gunned down by a pistol-wielding Jaeger.

Richard stood, dazed. The Jaeger tossed aside his pistol and unsheathed his sword. Above, British in the redoubt rallied, inspired by Hessian grit, and came charging down the hill.

Richard parried the Hessian's sword thrust, lunged, missed, parried another thrust, forcing his body around with all the strength he had in a desperate swipe of his sword. The Jaeger jumped back unharmed, then he cut in savagely with his razor-sharp blade. It found its mark high on Richard's stomach, below the rib cage, slicing simultaneously shirt, waistcoat, and flesh. Richard glanced down in disbelief at the wound, the pain of it not yet registering. Blood oozed from the long, ugly gash staining his shirt red.

Dazed, terrified, Richard groped for his dragoon pistol. Somehow he found the strength to pull back the hammer, bring it up, fire. He could not miss at a distance of two feet. Nor could the British officer coming up behind the slumped-over Jaeger. For one brief moment of abject horror, the red-coated officer stared deep into Richard's eyes, as if searing in his brain for eternity the measure of the man he was about to kill. Richard stood transfixed, unable to react, staring blankly as the pistol pointed at his chest. When the officer squeezed the trigger, a grenade exploded nearby, making the ground tremble, spoiling his aim. He fired low, missed his primary target, Richard's chest, hit another, Richard's thigh, the ball tearing into muscle with searing pain that buckled both his legs. He collapsed to the ground and rolled over onto his back, staring up with dulled eyes at the star-studded sky above.

What happened next Richard would never be able to fully piece together. He remembered the call to arms of soldiers behind him and a surge of infantry sweeping past. He could remember also the British officer crying out, his eyes bulging as he was lanced by three bayonets at once. He recalled seeing a red and white striped flag fluttering uphill past him and then, after a passage of time impossible to measure for a man drifting away, he felt someone reaching under him, lifting him, ordering others nearby over on the double to assist. An unholy stab of pain brought him back to consciousness. Oddly, what he would always remember, at that moment, was the acrid smell of old tobacco.

"Easy, Lieutenant. Take it easy," he heard Captain Mercer say. He was standing guard over Richard and beckoning impatiently at four men running toward them with a litter.

With what little strength he had, Richard clawed at Mercer's shirt, his wild eyes beseeching the Virginian. "Please, Captain," he wheezed. "Don't let them take my leg. Dear God, don't let them do that."

"I won't," Mercer promised. "God as my judge, I won't." Carefully he laid Richard on the litter. "Get him to the field hospital," he ordered. "Quick now!" As the litter was lifted, Richard heard Hamilton say, "Sergeant, this man saved my life. Find General Lincoln. Tell him what happened here. Tell him Lieutenant Cutler is down, and we require his surgeon at the field hospital."

"Sir!" The sergeant saluted and was gone.

As great resounding shouts of triumph resounded from inside both redoubts, Richard continued his private battle for consciousness, helped along by the rough motion of the litter. In the field hospital, he came to with a start as he was transferred from the litter to a cot. Then someone propped him up, forced his head back and his mouth open, and poured a foul-tasting syrupy liquid down his throat. After the liquid had run its course, he was lowered back down onto the cot. A surgeon was there beside him, looking more like a butcher than a physician in his blood-spattered apron. He had the tools of his trade laid out on a table nearby and was rolling up his sleeve.

"Hold him steady," he ordered his mates. Richard felt firm pressure on his shoulders and shins.

He made to scream, to sob, to do anything to stop the abomination. What came out was a hoarse, squeaky "No!" as he braced against the unspeakable horror of a jagged-toothed instrument assaulting his flesh, cutting through skin and muscle until it reached the bone, sawing through it clean, all done in less than three minutes, the leg off and thrown aside, a piece of offal. What he felt, instead, was someone snipping at the skin around his leg wound, and someone else forcing the broken skin apart. Then he felt the cold steel of forceps entering his thigh . . . probing . . . probing. There was pain, a god-awful pain, but it was a pain that seemed to belong to someone else. Richard experienced it only vicariously.

"Missed the femur," he thought he heard the surgeon say; then, with more authority, "and the femoral artery too, by God!" Quite clearly he heard the surgeon cry out in triumph, then words of congratulations from the others in the tent and the faint metallic sound of a ball dropped into a bowl and rolling back and forth. "You're an extraordinarily lucky young man," the surgeon said matter of factly, his face fading into a blur as Richard watched him wiping his hands. "Once the laudanum wears off, you'll hurt like a son of a bitch, I can guarantee you that. And we'll need to keep a weather eye on those wounds for gangrene. But you should make it through just fine. And I'd wager you'll keep that leg of yours."

Richard choked back tears. Weakness overcoming him, semi-awareness slipping away, he blinked up at those standing near his cot, nodding and smiling at him as if to confirm the surgeon's favorable prognosis. "You're going home, Lieutenant," someone said, very distinctly, at the moment he surrendered himself to the dark, peaceful abyss of unconsciousness.

Later, when he would recount these events to Katherine, and later still, to Agreen, he would concede that it could have been General Lincoln who said that. He had heard his words of deep concern as Lincoln came hurrying into the tent during the procedure. Or it could have been Captain Mercer, for that good man had been there throughout. Or even the kindly surgeon. But for the life of him, Richard would forever believe it was someone else who uttered those welcomed words of comfort, someone who was of his own blood and who Richard was convinced had never once left his side.

There could be no mistaking Will's voice.

A Preview of the Next Book in the Cutler Family Chronicles

For LOVE of COUNTRY

PROLOGUE

Off the Barbary Coast, August 1786

THE LOOKOUT stationed on the maintop was daydreaming. He was standing on the small oaken platform with arms folded, his back against the mainmast, his gaze half taking in the white billow of topsail and cloud above, his brain seduced by a soporific combination of a hot Mediterranean sun, the comforting sway of the brig as her cutwater sliced through the blood-warm turquoise sea, and, especially, Neapolitan women dancing provocatively in his mind. *Eagle*, out of Boston, was fast approaching her Italian port of call, having traversed the Atlantic and passed through the Straits of Gibraltar. Gladly would he exchange the chaste austerity of shipboard life, along with every bottle of Cutler rum in the hold, for the more wanton pleasures of physical abandonment with an untold number of ready, willing, and able accomplices, each endowed with the most beguiling of female adornments. Or so he fantasized.

Given the sailor's besotted state of mind, it is not surprising that he failed to detect the red triangular sails hovering over the distant horizon to starboard. There were nine of them, three to a vessel, and a sharp eye would have observed that the corsairs were sailing in a straight line on a northward course, perhaps two or three cable lengths apart from one another. And the one in the lead was already hauling her wind on a course of interception. But even from the height of the maintop, few could have discerned, at this distance, the seven open gunports on the larboard side of the vessels. Or the pistols and wide-bladed scimitars lashed to the hips of the renegade crews. It was the profile of the xebecs themselves that the sailor had been warned to look out for.

The angry shouting of John Dickerson, the ship's master, snapped the sailor out of his reveries. He stood befuddled and transfixed, staring down slack-jawed at those staring up at him, then ahead to where Captain Dickerson was furiously pointing. The corsairs were closing fast. They were now near enough for those on deck to clearly distinguish the foremast at the prow of each vessel and the huge lateen yard attached to it at a forty-five-degree angle. At any moment, the long, low, galleylike hulls would surge into view.

Before Dickerson had time to consider alternatives, the northernmost vessel veered slightly off the wind and opened fire with her forward battery, sending up two plumes of warning directly ahead of the merchant brig. Her companions did not hesitate and kept right on coming at *Eagle*. They would be alongside in a matter of minutes. Cursing with frustration and anguish, Captain Dickerson ordered his mate to heave to.

Eagle's weather deck was twice as high off the water as those of the xebecs bumping up against her starboard side. Nonetheless, the heavily armed boarding party had no trouble clawing its way up on ropes tossed over the brig's bulwarks to secure the two vessels together. On the corsairs' flush decks, pirates brandishing muskets covered them on the ascent while others stood by the six-pound guns.

There were eight in the boarding party, all but one bearing the physical attributes of Arabic pedigree. He appeared Germanic, Dutch perhaps, for he was blond and totally at ease with the ways of the sea. Their leader, distinguishable by the length of his jet-black beard, a menacing tone of authority, and the red sash he wore around the waist of his loose-fitting trousers, introduced himself to John Dickerson as Rais Ali bin Hassan. In broken English he announced that the Americans were now prisoners of Dey Baba Mohammad bin Osman, and would the captain please direct his crew to make sail for Algiers. *Allah Akbar min kulli shay!*

Among those reluctantly shuffling off to their stations to comply with their captain's order was a tall, sandy-haired, twenty-one-year-old foretopman from Hingham, Massachusetts, named Caleb Cutler.

I

ANTIGUA, BRITISH WEST INDIES

August 1786

*I*T HAD BEEN A memorable reunion. Richard Cutler had not seen Robin and Julia Cutler, his English cousins, since April 1782, when Richard and Katherine and baby Will had left Barbados to sail home to America. Upon his return, on his recent visit, he had found the family compound much as he had left it, tucked in among the rolling green fields northeast of Bridgetown, fully engaged in the production of sugar and its by-products. The only major addition to the compound had been a twenty-vat rum distillery, constructed in 1783 adjacent to the boiling house.

Though he considered himself a sailor, certainly not a planter or merchant, Richard had surprised even himself in the joy he took reviewing the entire process with Robin, from the slashing of the cane by Creole slaves wielding machetes, to the collection of juice under great horizontal rollers driven by the sails of two giant windmills, to the boiling in the coppers, to the glorious transformation of cane juice into molasses and sugar and, ultimately, rum. Just last month, after fermenting for almost three years in thick casks of New Hampshire white pine, the first shipments of dark Cutler rum had been dispatched aboard the Cutler brig *Eagle* from Long Wharf in Boston to the port of Naples.

With his usual flair for efficiency, Robin had redesigned and retooled the process until every ounce of juice was squeezed from the cane. Julia's connections to the local Mount Gay Rum families had played their role in generating tidy Cutler profits, today at their highest levels since before the Revolutionary War. The question was, could the Cutler family, with expenses and contractual obligations in England, America, and the West Indies to address, sustain such profitability now that Whitehall seemed determined to enforce the despised Navigation Acts. It was such concerns that had brought Richard to Bridgetown for a family conference.

During the week he was on the island that topic had received much attention but no clear resolution. The declaration that America and American ships were officially off-limits to both importers and exporters on the British-controlled islands of the West Indies brought with it a blessing as well as a curse. New business opportunities were there for the taking, and the Cutler family now had the clear incentive to exploit those opportunities. It had already extended its market reach to Europe, and Richard had much to relate to his cousin about Boston and Salem merchant captains who had ventured around the Cape of Good Hope, past the Isle of France, into Far Eastern waters in search of teas, calicoes, nankeens, and silks. Sugar and rum production would remain at the heart of Cutler commerce, Richard had maintained, but expediency dictated that untapped markets must also be considered. Total reliance on the old Atlantic trade routes no longer served. In Europe, demand for sugar products was far outpacing supply, forcing prices sharply upward; farther east, the opulence of Calcutta and Canton beckoned.

As lengthy and portentous as those discussions had been, there remained ample time during that week for Richard to become reacquainted with Robin and Julia, always favorites of his, as well as the island that evoked so many blissful memories for him. It was here, on Barbados, where he and his bride had spent the waning months of the war as guests of John Cutler, Robin's brother, who had returned to England with his wife, Cynthia, in 1784 to assist with family operations there. Despite his keen frustrations at having to withdraw from a conflict in which he had served as midshipman, then as an acting lieutenant under Capt. John Paul Jones, Richard would forever count those months as among his happiest. On this visit he had been up early every morning, before the demands of the day could intrude upon him, and he had strolled along the water's edge of the white sandy beach where he and Katherine had so often walked and laughed and loved. On those occasions he had talked to her as though she were there walking beside him, as if by doing so he could magically transport her from their home in Massachusetts and once again be soothed by her melodious English accent and be enraptured by her touch as gentle and inviting as the lush tropical breezes caressing his sunburned skin . . .

☆ ☆ ☆

"MR. CUTLER! Mr. Cutler, sir!"

The loud rap on the door of his stern cabin jolted him fully alert.

"Yes, Mr. Bryant," Richard replied, recognizing his mate's voice. Quickly he straightened himself in his chair, using both hands to coax back shoulder-length blond hair. "Come in. What is it?"

The broad-faced and muscular seaman ducked as he entered the small, snug space that defined a captain's privilege.

"Good morning, Captain. Cates reports a vessel three points on our starboard bow. Single mast, flying a royal," he added meaningfully. "It's a king's ship, sir, Cates is certain. A naval cutter, he believes."

Richard considered that. Jim Cates, the lookout on duty, was a man whose eyesight was normally as sharp as his observations—which was why, in these sensitive waters, Richard had ordered him sent up to the mainmast crosstrees at the first inklings of dawn. Like nearly everyone else aboard, Cates had served either in the Continental Navy or aboard a privateer during the war, and was thus well acquainted with British ship design and sail plans. If he believed this ship to be a naval cutter, she probably was.

"What's our course?"

"North by east. Nevis is off to larboard. Clear water lies ahead."

"We're still flying the Jack?"

"We are, sir."

"Very well. Thank you, Mr. Bryant. I shall be up presently. Please tell the helmsman to hold her course steady."

"Steady as she goes, aye, Captain."

With Bryant gone, Richard cursed himself under his breath. Every sailor worth his salt knew that what dawn might reveal should be of primary concern to a ship's master, especially when sailing in coastal waters patrolled by overly inquisitive foreigners and erstwhile enemies. It was why he had awoken so early, to update the ship's log at his writing desk and to be ready, in case. But he had allowed self-discipline to lapse into daydreaming, and the naval officer he once was would not easily forgive him.

As he tucked the hem of his loose-fitting cotton shirt into his white breeches and tightened the strings at the waist, Richard considered the possibilities. If this was a British warship, what was she doing bearing down on them from the north? The British naval base on Antigua lay to the east, and he had purposely steered clear of that island, on a wide arc around Guadeloupe and Montserrat. To the north lay the island of Saint-Barthélemy, recently acquired by the Swedes, and the Dutch island of Sint Maarten. Why was this Britisher patrolling those waters, at night, and why did she seem so intent on intercepting a vessel flying the Union Jack, the nationality of which her lookout should already have confirmed. It was as if she had been lying in wait for *Lavinia*, in full knowledge of her pedigree.

Richard picked up a long glass from its becket by the desk and stepped out of his cabin, up the short oaken ladder leading to the weather deck. There he was greeted by members of the twenty-two-man crew and steady northeasterly trades that ruffled his hair and shirt. He squinted northward. The hull of the approaching vessel was just now looming into view; she was thus about three miles away. He glanced up. *Lavinia* was still rigged for night sailing. She had her flying jib and jib furled at their tacks on the jibboom, and her single mainmast topsail was furled tight on its yard. Nevertheless, she was making fair speed close-hauled under fore topmast staysail and the large trapezoid-shaped fore-'n-aft sails on her foremast and mainmast.

Richard did his best to appear nonchalant as he walked toward the bow of the schooner, limping slightly, the result of taking a musket ball in his thigh at point-blank range five years earlier at Yorktown. At the starboard foremast chains he raised his glass and trained the lens on what was now unmistakably a Royal Navy cutter. She carried three square sails from mains'l up to t'gallant on a single mast, plus a large fore-'n-aft gaff-rigged spanker set out full on her larboard quarter in a following ten-knot breeze. Lunging out from her prow on a line parallel to the deck was a long, black bowsprit that appeared from this distance like an arrow pointing directly at *Lavinia*, above which a huge white jib billowed out, arced taut as a bow prepared to fire the arrow. She was a fast ship. Too fast for Richard to consider flight.

Suddenly a gun barked, the white patch of smoke shooting out to larboard whipped back in front of her by the brisk trades. In the distance a ball whined, growing louder to a screech as it shot past ahead of the schooner and slapped the sea, skipping twice before disappearing in a swirl of white water. A six-pounder, Richard mused. Oddly, despite the threat implicit in such a warning shot, he found himself wondering how so small a vessel could carry so great a press of sail. She could not be more than sixty or seventy feet in length, a good deal shorter than *Lavinia*. Must have a deep draft, Richard surmised, and be heavily laden with ballast.

"Shall I order the crew to heave to, sir?" Geoffrey Bryant asked, coming up beside him.

Richard nodded. "Yes, do, Mr. Bryant. Any other response would arouse suspicion. And we certainly wouldn't want to do that, would we?" The smile he gave his mate belied the dread that had begun creeping into his intestines with the firing of the gun.

The cutter swept past, shortened sail, and wore around under jib and spanker. As she feathered up in and off the wind to lie close astarboard to *Lavinia*, Richard walked slowly aft toward the helm. Lowering the tip of his tricorne hat to shield his eyes from the sun, he stood glowering at the cutter, his arms folded across his chest, his square jaw set, everything about him the image of a ship's master outraged at being forced to stop at sea.

For a brief span of time the two vessels drifted side by side, within pistol shot, each silently contemplating the other across a short, jewel-spattered stretch of water. Then, through a speaking trumpet, the crisp, confident tones of an English patrician shattered the early morning peace.

"What vessel is that?" he demanded to know.

"The schooner *Lavinia*," Richard promptly called back through his own speaking trumpet. "Out of Bridgetown."

"Bound for where?"

"St. Kitts."

"Your cargo?"

"None of your damn business," Richard wanted to shout out, realizing at once that such bravado would prove both futile and foolhardy. This British naval captain not only had license to challenge any merchant vessel under sail, he clearly had the wherewithal to enforce his will.

"Rum and molasses," he replied.

"Are you the ship's master?"

"I am."

"Your name, sir?"

"Richard Cutler."

There was a pause as this information was digested aboard the cutter. Then, in a voice rock hard with purpose: "Mr. Cutler, you will accompany this vessel forthwith to English Harbour. We are sending over a pilot to assist you. Please make ready to set sail."

Richard's tone in reply was equally insistent.

"Sir, this vessel has British registry. On whose authority do you act?"

The answer came back clear and concise and like a thunderbolt to Richard Cutler.

"On the authority of the senior naval officer of the Northern Division of the West Indies Station: Captain Horatio Nelson."

☆ ☆ ☆

SITUATED MIDWAY along the southern shore of Antigua's heavily indented coast-line, English Harbour was the epitome of a British naval base. At its heart was Freeman's Bay, a large circular area of water almost completely enclosed by promontories reaching out from the mainland like the claws of a mammoth crab. Once a vessel had gained entrance to the bay, she was thus protected from the wiles of nature by the natural geography of the island. Protection from man was provided by a ring of multilevel stone fortresses glistening with heavy black cannon perched high up in the steep-scarped hills rising above the harbor. From such a vantage point at the core of the Lesser Antilles, the Royal Navy had long held sway over the major sailing routes leading to and from the rich sugar colonies of the eastern Caribbean, making adjustments in naval strategy and tactics as appropriate, meting out punishments as necessary.

Getting into English Harbour, however, was tricky, and it took the skills of a native sea pilot to guide a vessel through the treacherous shallows and reefs that formed the first line of defense against would-be assailants. Once past the promontories and inside the often windless bay, a complex series of wooden bollards and huge iron rings ashore teamed up with an array of anchored buoys to secure the vessel with light hawsers and warp her in toward the quays or an anchorage.

As *Lavinia* was being hauled shoreward with her sails furled, Richard stood amidships, gripping a mainmast shroud. Despite the gravity of the moment, he could not resist taking in the scenery about him. Although he had read and heard much about Antigua, this was his first visit here. And he was as impressed by this British military installation as he was by others he had seen in England and the Caribbean. Above, in the Shirley Heights rising abruptly over the harbor, the austere-looking fortifications, observation posts, and army barracks kept watch over the southern approaches to the island and the goings-on in the harbor. Along the western reaches of the bay, at the naval dockyards, everything was abuzz with the bang of hammers, the rasp of saws, and the shouts, curses, and exhortations of foremen and laborers. In the town itself, across the bay, army and navy personnel, along with the administrators and tradesmen of empire, marched or scurried about amid thickets of co-conut palms, throngs of carriages and individuals ahorse wending their way along the main thoroughfare and between the clusters of yellowish brown limestone buildings typical of many West Indian ports.

His gaze swept back to the activity at the naval dockyards and lingered there. Clearly, the British government was investing serious money and man-power to renovate and enlarge these facilities. Not far from the quay to which *Lavinia* was being secured, Richard noted what appeared to be a dry dock under construction, the first, he presumed, outside of Kingston, Jamaica, the largest Royal Navy base in the West Indies. When that structure was com-pleted, it would save sheathers, caulkers, riggers, and carpenters the three weeks of backbreaking and often dangerous work required to careen a stripped-down vessel over on her side to clean or make repairs to her bottom.

At precisely three o'clock in the afternoon, a chorus of ships' bells clanged pleasantly from the seven warships anchored in the bay, six bells per ship. As if on cue, a chunky, officious officer of the Royal Navy in the glory of full dress uniform strode up the plank leading from the pier, boarded *Lavinia*, and, in a less-than-pleasant tone, bade the first seaman he came across to fetch the ship's master. His pomposity was curbed only slightly when that tall, young, fair-haired seaman with startling blue eyes indicated he *was* the ship's master.

"At your service, Lieutenant," Richard said, his sarcasm evident.

With a loud harrumph and a jiggle of his bulldog jowls, the officer indi-cated to Richard that he was to accompany him forthwith in a longboat, their destination the frigate anchored in midharbor, a ship Richard already had identified as HMS *Boreas*. He had noticed her immediately when *Lavinia* had entered Freeman's Bay, for he had admired her pale yellow varnish, her sails furled on their yards in Bristol fashion, her three masts stepped with just a hint of rake, and the unblemished black bands running along her gunport strakes. By all accounts she was a magnificent fighting machine, the pride of the Leeward Islands Station. *Nothing but the best for Capt. Horatio Nelson*, Richard thought bitterly. No sooner had that wave of hostility crashed over him, as it often did at the mere mention of Nelson's name, than Richard chided himself for harboring such sentiments in the first place. He realized they were groundless, pointless. It should be the other way around, common sense reminded him.

"Good luck, sir," Geoffrey Bryant said as Richard made ready to disembark.

"Thank you, Mr. Bryant," Richard replied. "You have command. Keep the men occupied. The tide turns within the hour, and I intend to be sailing with it."

The row over to the flagship was a short one. Richard sat in the sternsheets next to the lieutenant, watching intently as the frigate loomed ever larger into view. During the war he had been on one much like her, in Plymouth harbor when he was interrogated by British authorities after the Whitehaven raid by Captain Jones. So he assumed that *Boreas* was another Fourth Rate carrying fifty guns, not counting the swivel guns mounted on Y-brackets on her bulwarks and tops, or the murderous carronades affixed to iron-slide carriages along her weather deck and quarterdeck, their stubby barrels now becoming visible through gunports cut through the bulwarks. Richard had learned of these newly issued, lightweight weapons from brother-in-law Hugh Hardcastle, a flag lieutenant in the Royal Navy. First cast in the town of Carron, Scotland, they looked and loaded much like a mortar, and when fired at close range, Hugh had assured him, their thirty-two-pound shot could wreak bloody havoc upon enemy ships and crews. At the time, he was relating to Richard the glory he had witnessed from Adm. Sir George Rodney's flagship during the battle of the Saintes, and the high-pitched tones of excitement and defiance with which he had described the gore and mayhem inflicted by these "smashers," as he referred to the carronades, had seemed very much out of character for the normally staid British naval officer.

At the entry port of the frigate, Richard was turned over to a heavyset master-at-arms sporting a prominent red handlebar mustache. As he was escorted aft to a hatchway and ladder leading below, he glanced again at the black short-barreled iron guns bowsed up tight against the bulwarks. He longed for just a few moments to inspect them, to see for himself what all the excitement was about.

The scarlet-jacketed marine corporal standing guard belowdecks banged the butt of his musket on the deck in recognition of the master-at-arms' approaching the after cabin. Once the official had stated his business, the marine rapped gently on the oaken door.

"What is it?" queried a gentle voice from inside.

The corporal opened the door a crack and nodded at the master-at-arms to answer.

"Mr. Bowles, Captain. I have with me the ship's master of the American schooner, just arrived."

"Very good, Mr. Bowles. You may show him in."

The door opened wide and Richard was ushered into a spacious and well-appointed captain's cabin. Sunlight streamed in from open stern windows and reflected off the thick glass of the quarter-galley windows of the dining alcove on the starboard side aft and a sleeping cuddy to larboard. In the center of the space was a gilt-edged, freshly polished mahogany desk resting on a lush Persian rug laid over a deck painted dark red to mask the splatter of blood in battle. In front of the desk, their high wingbacks blocking much of Richard's view, were twin chairs of impeccable taste, their yellow-floral-on-blue upholstery matched by the thin padding on the settee running athwartship in front of the stern windows. Oil paintings of ships and seascapes graced the walls between rows of books clutched in tight by what must have been specially designed bookshelves. Completing the decor was a curved-front, ebony sideboard with gilt handles on the drawers. On top, among other items, sat a silver-sided tray containing cut-glass decanters of various wines and spirits.

"Shall I stay, sir?" the master-at-arms asked respectfully.

Horatio Nelson rose from the desk and shook his head.

"Thank you, no, Mr. Bowles. You may leave us. And kindly close the door on your way out."

With the door clicked shut, each man stood in silent contemplation of the other. They had not seen each other since 1774, twelve years ago on the quays at Bridgetown when Richard was seeking the whereabouts of Nelson's close friend and former shipmate, Hugh Hardcastle. At the time, Nelson was serving as a senior midshipman aboard HMS *Seahorse* in the Windward Squadron, his age just fifteen, a year older than Richard. His meteoric rise through the ranks had by now become the stuff of legend, and Richard was well aware it was not just "interest" in Whitehall that had propelled Nelson from a midshipman at the age of twelve to a post captain at the age of twenty. One did not achieve such prominent rank in the Royal Navy at so tender an age unless his superiors saw in him something extraordinarily unusual and promising.

"Well, Mr. Cutler," Nelson said. "It appears fate has played her hand in our lives once again."

"It would seem so," Richard replied cautiously. Nelson's cheerful greeting caught him off-guard.

Nelson motioned to the chairs in front of him.

"Please, sit down. Make yourself comfortable. The sun is most definitely over the yardarm, so may I offer you some sherry? A spot of claret, perhaps?"

"Thank you, no, Captain."

Richard did, however, accept the invitation to sit in the wingback chair. He set his tricorne hat on the desk in front of him, then leaned back, crossing his right leg over his left, all the while returning Nelson's steady gaze. To Richard's surprise, given all he had read about Nelson's illustrious career to date, Nelson hardly seemed the paragon of a British naval officer. He was a half foot shorter than Richard and appeared to be somewhat fragile of frame, though it was difficult to discern what might lie beneath the gilded finery of a naval captain's uniform. And finery it was, from the silk of his neckstock to the rich gold-edged and gold-embroidered indigo fabric of his dress jacket. His hair was a shade darker than Richard's and closer cropped, though still sweeping down over his ears, and the eyes making their own careful analysis of the situation were as pewter gray as a sea before a gathering storm. Despite yellow tinged, almost sickly looking skin—the result, Richard knew, of several near-fatal bouts with malaria—he was, nonetheless, a distinguished-looking individual who seemed entirely at ease with his rank and destiny—and with the span of silence that, for Richard, was becoming increasingly untenable.

"Well, where should we start?" Richard asked.

The question prompted Nelson back from wherever his thoughts had wandered. When he spoke, his tone was decidedly less inviting and more authoritative.

"A good place to start, I should think, is with an explanation. Tell me, I pray you, why you continue to smuggle cargo in and out of Barbados when you are perfectly aware that, by doing so, you are in violation of the Navigation Laws."

"With respect, Captain, I protest your accusation of smuggling."

Nelson's dark eyes flashed. "Come, come, Mr. Cutler. Let us not play games. You know damned well that's what you are doing. How can you claim otherwise?"

"I claim otherwise because *Lavinia* has British registry."

Nelson waved that away. "A tiresome ruse," he sighed, shaking his head. "Really, Mr. Cutler, I had expected better of you. These days, a British registry can be purchased for a song, especially by a family like yours with connections in England. Besides, it no longer has legal standing. You are aware of the recent order-in-council?"

"I'm afraid I'm not," Richard hedged.

Nelson's gaze took in Richard skeptically, as though he were not at all convinced of the American's claim of ignorance.

"The decree states, sir," Nelson said, in what was clearly a well-worn speech, "that American vessels are henceforth banned from trade in the West Indies. Shipments to and from these islands are reserved exclusively for British subjects sailing British-owned and British-built ships. That includes Canadians and Irishmen, but, alas, as a result of our recent squabbles, it most definitely does *not* include Americans. You are in clear violation of that decree, Mr. Cutler, since *Lavinia* is American-built and American-manned, even if I were to accept your registry claim, which I don't. And because you are in violation, I have the legal right to impound your cargo."

"Does having the legal right," Richard countered without hesitation, "give you the moral right? Your Navigation Laws are opposed by many English citizens on these islands. Including, I am told, your superior officer in Barbados, Admiral Hughes."

To Richard's surprise, Nelson actually smiled at that allegation. He leaned forward and beckoned Richard in toward him, looking every bit the school chum about to divulge a grand secret. "Admiral Hughes may be a decent sort," he said, his voice low, conspiratorial, "but I fear he's more a Jack Pudding than a fighting admiral. You have no doubt heard of his latest escapade? Poor fellow actually poked his own eye out with a fork whilst chasing a cockroach across his quarterdeck. Now tell me: does *this* seem like a man whose opinions matter?"

Richard was shocked to hear a Royal Navy officer speak of a superior in such an openly disparaging manner; nonetheless, he could not restrain a smile of his own. He had indeed read in a Boston newspaper about that unfortunate mishap. Try as the Admiralty might to suppress the story, it had leaked out from the fo'c'sle of HMS *Adamant* to the *Bridgetown Gazette*. From there it was picked up by London's *Morning Post and Daily Advertiser* and thus, inevitably, by most other English-language newspapers and magazines around the world.

It took a moment for Richard to suppress the chuckle bubbling up within him. When he composed himself, he said: "Nonetheless, it is an undisputed fact that your so-called Navigation Laws are strangling these islands. The governor of Antigua has called for their repeal. Governors and legislatures on other islands have joined him. Merchants everywhere are demanding redress. And it is widely acknowledged, Captain, that you are at serious odds with most of Antiguan society. Of course," he added, to drive home the point, "you must have already realized that. Which is why, I suspect, you seldom choose to go ashore."

Nelson winced slightly at the assertion. He clasped his hands together and lowered his head down close to them, as though a pilgrim sitting in supplication within his father's parish in Burnham Thorpe. For several intense moments the only sound to be heard was the ticking of a small pendulum clock on the sideboard. When Nelson did finally sit upright, he peered intently at Richard and spoke in a voice that was at once both weary and wary.

"Mr. Cutler," he said, "the reason I seldom go ashore is because there is not much there that appeals to me. Antigua I find to be a rather vile and sickly place. I greatly prefer Nevis and St. Christopher—or St. Kitts as we British now call it—but alas I am not able to spend much time on either island these days. Even if I were, my strong preference would still be to serve my country elsewhere, on some other station. However, I need not remind you that duty is the great business of a sea officer, and in my experience it has never involved a popularity contest. I was sent here, to the Leeward Islands Station, because my superiors in Whitehall have faith in my abilities. It is to them, and to them alone, that I owe my allegiance. Be assured I am prepared to grind whatever grist the mill requires to ensure I do not disappoint them."

That said, both men realized that further discussion on the topic would serve no purpose.

"Where, then, does that leave us?" Richard asked.

"Where . . . does . . . that . . . leave . . . us," Nelson intoned, repeating the words slowly, one by one, as if pondering the significance of the question. His answer apparently determined, he folded his arms across his chest and said, with conviction, "I don't know about *you*, Mr. Cutler, but where that leaves *me* is in a rather awkward position. It has always been my policy never to mix personal sentiments with the requirements of the service. But in this instance, for reasons I needn't explain to you, I am prepared to do just that. You are free to leave Antigua and sail home to . . . Hingham, is it not?"

"Yes sir."

Nelson studied Richard a moment. "You are free to leave Antigua with your cargo intact. But be forewarned," he added, his voice suddenly laced with menace, "you will never again receive such favorable treatment from me. Henceforth, the Royal Navy will keep a close eye on you and your family. We have spies everywhere, including Barbados, and those spies will be monitoring your every move. The next time a Cutler vessel is found in violation of the Navigation Acts, I shall have no choice but to order its cargo and crew impounded and the vessel seized as a prize. Do I make myself clear?"

"Perfectly," Richard replied, his lips tight. High on his forehead, an old wound began to pulse.

"Good. Then we understand each other."

"We do, Captain." Richard made to rise. "Will that be all? If I am free to leave, I'd best be sailing with the ebb tide."

That observation rattled Nelson.

"Yes . . . No," he quickly corrected himself, and as he did so his hard-set features dissolved as rapidly as sea mist at a summer sunrise. "A moment, if you please, Mr. Cutler." He fumbled, glancing this way and that before being drawn, unavoidably, into Richard's rigid stare. "I am compelled to ask . . . if I may . . . how is Katherine?"

"Well, thank you."

"Good. I am very pleased to hear it. You have a son, I understand."

"Two, actually."

"Two sons." He half whispered the words to himself, as if that fact had come as an astounding and profoundly sorrowful revelation to him. For a few moments he seemed lost, at sea. Then, as though emerging from a trance: "Well, I should think congratulations are in order. They are indeed fortunate young lads . . . to have such a mother."

"That, Captain, is one thing we can agree upon this afternoon." Richard arose from the chair, taken aback to see the man who had just threatened his family, who indeed could command the respect of nations, so obviously in distress. "Good day to you, sir," he managed civilly.

"Mr. Cutler . . . please . . . I have but one last request of you." It was a heartfelt plea that only a heart of granite could ignore. "I would be ever so much obliged if you would . . . see to . . . if you would send . . . dear Katherine . . . my warmest personal regards."

"I will do that, Captain," Richard promised. "And I am certain Mrs. Cutler would want me to send hers to you."

With that, he bowed slightly, turned around, and walked across the after cabin to the door, closing it gently behind him as he stepped out onto the gundeck.

GLOSSARY

aback: A sail is aback when it is pressed against the mast by a headwind.

abaft: Toward the stern of a ship. Used relatively, as in "abaft the beam" of a vessel.

able seaman: A general term for a sailor with considerable experience in performing the basic tasks of sailing a ship.

after cabin: The cabin in the after part of a ship used by the captain, commodore, or admiral.

aide-de-camp: An officer acting as a confidential assistant to a senior officer.

amidships: In or toward the middle of a vessel.

athwart: Across from side to side, transversely.

back: To turn a sail or a yard so that the wind blows directly on the front of a sail, thus slowing the ship's forward motion.

back and fill: to go backward and forward

backstay: A long rope that supports a mast and counters forward pull.

ballast: Any heavy material placed in a ship's hold to improve her stability, e.g., pig iron, gravel, stones, or lead.

before the mast: Term to describe common sailors who were berthed in the forecastle, fore of the foremast.

belay: To secure a running rope used to work the sails. Also, to disregard.

belaying pin: A fixed pin used aboard ship to secure a rope fastened around it.

binnacle: A box that houses the compass on the deck of a ship near the helm.

boatswain or bosun: A petty officer in charge of a ship's equipment and her crew.

bollard: A short post on a ship or quay for securing a rope.

bowsprit: A spar running out from the bow of a ship, to which the forestays are fastened.

brace: A rope attached to the end of a yard, used to swing or trim the sail. To "brace up" means to bring the yards closer to fore-and-aft by hauling on the lee braces.

brig: A two-masted square-rigged vessel having an additional fore-and-aft sail on the gaff and a boom on her mainmast.

Bristol-fashion: Shipshape

buntline: A line for restraining the loose center of a sail when it is furled.

burgoo: A thick porridge

by the wind: As close as possible to the direction from which the wind is blowing.

cable: A strong, thick rope to which the ship's anchor is fastened. Also a unit of measure equaling approximately one-tenth of a sea mile, or two hundred yards.

cable-tier: A place in a hold where cables are stored.

canister or case shot: Small iron balls packed in a cylindrical tin case and fired from a cannon.

capstan: A broad revolving cylinder with a vertical axis used for winding a rope or cable.

cartridge: A case made of paper, flannel, or metal that contains a powder charge for a firearm.

cathead or cat: A horizontal beam at each side of a ship's bow, used for raising and carrying an anchor.

catharpings: Small ropes that brace the shrouds of the lower masts.

chains or chain-wale or channel: A structure projecting horizontally from a ship's sides abreast of the masts, used to widen the basis for the shrouds.

clap on: To add on, as in more sail or more hands on a line.

close-hauled: Sailing with sails hauled in as tight as possible, which allows the vessel to lie as close to the wind as possible.

commodore: A captain appointed as commander in chief of a squadron or station.

companion: An opening in a ship's deck leading below to a cabin via a companion way.

cordage: Cords or ropes, especially those in the rigging of a ship.

corvette: A warship with a flush deck and a single tier of guns.

course: The sail that hangs on the lowest yard of a square-rigged vessel.

crosstrees: A pair of horizontal struts attached to a ship's mast to spread the rigging, especially at the head of a topmast.

cutwater: The forward edge of the stem or prow that divides the water before it reaches the bow.

deadlight: A protective cover fitted over a porthole or window on a ship.

dead reckoning: The process of calculating one's position at sea by estimating the direction and distance traveled.

dogwatch: Either of two short watches on a ship (1600–1800 hours and 1800–2000 hours).

East Indiaman: A large, heavily armed merchant ship built by the various East India companies. Considered the ultimate sea vessels of their day in comfort and ornamentation.

ensign: The flag carried by a ship to indicate her nationality.

fathom: Six feet in depth or length.

fiferail: A rail around the mainmast of a ship, holding belaying pins.

flag lieutenant: An officer acting as an aide-de-camp to an admiral.

fo'c'sle or forecastle: The forward part of a ship belowdecks, where the crew was traditionally quartered.

footrope: A rope beneath a yard for sailors to stand on while reefing or furling.

furl: To roll up and bind a sail neatly to a yard or boom.

gangway: On deep-waisted ships, a narrow platform from the quarterdeck to the forecastle. Also, a movable bridge linking a ship to the shore.

gig: A light, narrow ship's boat normally used by the commander.

grape or grapeshot: Small cast-iron balls bound together in a canvas bag that scatter like shotgun pellets when fired.

grappling hook: A device with iron claws attached to a rope and used for dragging or grasping, such as holding two ships together.

grating: The open woodwork cover for the hatchway.

half-seas over: Drunk

halyard: A rope or tackle used to raise or lower a sail.

hawser: A large rope used in warping and mooring

heave to: To halt a ship by setting the sails to counteract each other, a tactic often employed in heavy weather in order to ride out the storm.

hull-down: Another ship being so far away that only her masts and sails are visible.

impress: To force to serve in the navy.

jack: The small flag flown from the jackstaff on the bowsprit of a vessel, such as the British Union Jack and Dutch Jack.

jolly boat: A clinker-built ship's boat, smaller than a cutter, used for small work.

laudanum: An alcoholic solution of opium.

lee: The side of a ship, land mass, or rock that is sheltered from the wind.

leech: The free edges of a sail, e.g., the vertical edges of a square sail and the aft edge of a fore-and-aft sail.

lighter: A boat or barge used to ferry cargo to and from ships at anchor.

manger: A small triangular area in the bow of a warship in which animals are kept.

muster book: The official log of a ship's company.

ordnance: Mounted guns and mortars, munitions, and the like.

orlop: The lowest deck on a sailing ship having at least three decks

parole: Word of honor, especially the pledge made by a prisoner of war not to try to escape, or if released, to abide by certain conditions.

petty officer: A naval officer corresponding in rank to a noncommissioned officer in the army.

poop: A short, raised after deck found on only very large sailing ships.

privateer: An armed ship owned by private individuals with a government commission and authorized for use in war.

prize: An enemy vessel and its cargo captured at sea by a warship or a privateer.

purser: An officer responsible for keeping the ship's accounts and issuing food and clothing.

quadrant: An instrument to measure the angle of heavenly bodies for use in navigation.

quarterdeck: That part of a ship's upper deck near the stern, traditionally reserved for the ship's officers.

quay: A dock or landing place usually built of stone.

queue: A plait of hair that hangs down from the head; a pigtail.

quoin: A wooden wedge used to adjust the elevation of a gun.

ratlines: Small lines fastened horizontally to the shrouds of a vessels, used to climb up and down the rigging.

reef: A horizontal portion of a sail that can be rolled or folded up to reduce the amount of canvas exposed to the wind.

rig: The general way the masts and sails of a vessel are arranged. The two main categories are square-rigged and fore-and-aft rigged.

round shot: Balls of cast iron fired from smoothbore cannon.

royal: A small sail hoisted above the topgallant sail, used in light and favorable winds.

scupper: An opening in a ship's side that allows water to run from the deck into the sea.

sheet: A rope used to extend the sail or to alter its direction. To *sheet home* is to haul in a sheet until the foot of the sail is as straight and as taut as possible.

ship-rigged: Carrying square sails on all three masts.

shipwright: One employed in the construction of ships.

shrouds: Ropes forming part of the standing rigging and supporting the mast and topmast.

slow match: A fuse that burns very slowly, used to ignite the charge in a large gun.

stay: Part of the standing rigging, a rope that supports a mast.

staysail: A triangular fore-and-aft sail hoisted upon a stay.

stem: The curved upright bow timber of a vessel.

sternsheets: The rear of an open boat and the seats that are furnished there.

studdingsail or stunsail: An extra sail set outside the square sails during a fair wind.

swivel gun: A small cannon mounted on a swivel so that it can be fired in any direction.

tack: A sailing vessel's course relative: to the direction of the wind and the position of her sails, as in "starboard tack," meaning the wind is coming across the starboard side.
Also, the corner to which a rope is fastened to secure the sail.

taffrail: The rail at the upper end of a ship's stern.

thole pin or thole: One of a pair of pegs set in a gunwale of a boat to hold an oar in place.

tampion: A wooden stopper for the muzzle of a gun.

top: A platform constructed at the head of each of the lower masts of a ship to extend the topmast shrouds. Also used as a lookout and fighting platform.

topgallant: The third mast, sail, or yard above the deck.

top-hamper: A ship's masts, sails, and rigging.

topsail: The second sail above the deck, set above the course or mainsail.

touchhole: A vent in the breech of a firearm through which the charge is ignited.

tumble-home: The inward inclination of a ship's upper sides, causing the upper deck to be narrower than the lower decks.

waist: The middle part of a ship's upper deck, between the quarterdeck and the forecastle.

wardroom: The messroom for commissioned officers and senior warrant officers.

watch: A fixed period of duty on a ship, four hours in length, except for two two-hour dogwatches.

wherry: A rowboat used to carry passengers.

windward: Facing the wind or on the side facing the wind. Contrasted with leeward.

yard: A cylindrical spar slung across a ship's mast for a sail to hang from.

yardarm: The outer extremity of a yard.